CHAINS OF GWYNDORR

The Poison Tree Path Chronicles

BOOK 1

Joan Campbell

an imprint of
GILEAD PUBLISHING

Chains of Gwyndorr by Joan Campbell
Published by Enclave Publishing, an imprint of Gilead Publishing, Wheaton, IL 60187
www.enclavepublishing.com

ISBN: 978-1-68370-024-1

Chains of Gwyndorr
© 2016 by Joan Campbell

Published in the United States by Enclave Publishing, an imprint of Gilead Publishing
Wheaton, Illinois.

Cover designed by Charles Bernard
Edited by Ramona Richards
Interior designed by Larry Taylor

DEDICATION

To Nicole and Ashlyn

Now that you are
"old enough to start reading
fairy tales again."

(C.S. Lewis)

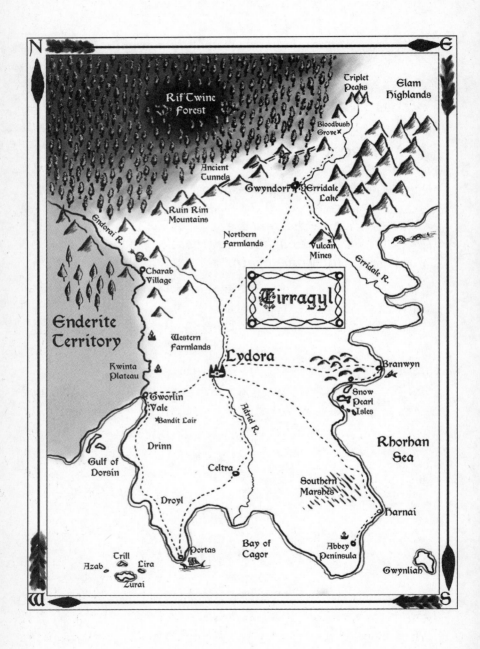

Acknowledgments

Writing might be a solitary pursuit, but the production of a book definitely isn't. Many people have been involved in transforming my lowly manuscript into an Enclave book. Thank you...

Steve Laube, for taking a chance on a first-time writer all the way from South Africa. I have so appreciated your competence, kindness, and wholehearted support through the publishing process.

Ramona Richards, for the immense experience you brought to the editing of *Chains of Gwyndorr.* I valued your honest and wise critique, encouragement, and in-depth explanations of what was required. You brought out the best in me.

Charles Bernard, for the remarkable cover, as well as the commitment and passion with which you produced it.

Ashlyn Campbell, for drawing a fabulous map to bring Tirragyl to life.

Without the following people's advice and guidance I doubt my manuscript would even have ended up on Steve's desk. Thank you...

Tony Collins, for taking the time to read twelve chapters of my manuscript at LittWorld Kenya. The note you wrote me started with "you are getting a lot of things right" and then proceeded to tell me everything I was getting wrong. Yet your words were the catalyst I needed to lift my manuscript to a new level.

Robin Jones Gunn, for your enthusiastic and selfless support that started at LittWorld and continues to this day. I cannot tell you how much courage it gave me to hear that rewrites send even you into a spin.

Alice Crider, for being one of the first people in the publishing industry to take me seriously. You helped me believe in the project.

MAI's wonderful John Maust, Lawrence Darmani, and Wambura Kimunyu, for your ongoing backing. And to all my LittWorld writer friends across the world, for adding such richness to my life.

The greatest gift I receive as a writer is encouragement. This comes from many sides, but I only have space to mention a few. Thank you...

Roy, for your faith in me and your steady love that even weathers intensive rewrites with a sense of humor.

Nicole, my first reader, for reading the book in a single weekend (which made me think you were fairly enthralled) and then for putting up with my endless insecure interrogation of what you thought. I promise I'll never put you through that again!

Adrie, for being my #1 fan and thinking every word I write is fabulous. You're not slightly biased because you're my Mom, right?

Denise Baisley, for going behind my back to get an early copy of the novel, and then raving about it to everyone we know. You never doubted I could find a publisher and that encouraged me when I needed it the most.

Finally, I want to acknowledge that God has been in every step of this journey—from the idea, to the writing, to the wonderful people he put on my path. I know without a shadow of a doubt that he opened the door for this book to be published and I pray that it brings him glory.

PROLOGUE

A figure slipped from the Rif'twine Forest in the predawn glow. One bony hand gripped a gnarled walking stick, the other a box wrapped in oilskin. His dark cloak camouflaged him as he hastened across the narrow stretch of land between the forest and the towering walls of Gwyndorr. But he knew first light was approaching.

The man slunk toward the Birch Grove, a stone's throw away from the town gate. Guards' voices and dogs' howls rang clearly through the crisp morning air and, as he glanced up, he could see the flicker of moving torches on the upper bailey.

The man reached the Grove and silently felt his way between the trees. Planted more than a hundred years ago, they were tall but did not grow as prolifically as the Rif'twine's plant life, and he soon found the perfect place to bury the box. He dropped to his knees, digging in the soft soil to the harder ground below. The smell of damp earth—so full of life—filled him with a pang of longing for his homeland.

His fingers ached by the time the hole was deep enough and he could lay the box in the hollow. Before he could cover it over, he heard the comfortingly familiar rustle of wings.

"Tabeal," he whispered in greeting as the red bird landed next to him, her breast glowing a warm gold. "This is the place."

Her call was soft but urgent, and he looked up to see the light patches of sky through the trees. He had taken too long.

"I know. Time is short."

He covered the box with soil, patting it down before scattering the spot with leaves to hide the evidence of his work. As he clambered back to his feet, the bird let out another low call and this time he understood more fully. The time grew short for all of them. The chains were tightening.

He retraced his steps through the Birch Grove, back to the open stretch of land between the wall and the forest.

The guards spotted the man when he was still a good distance from the forest and immediately let loose their dogs.

"He won't be able to outrun Brute!" one burly guard shouted to his companion as they ran in pursuit.

It did not take the dogs long to reach the man. They felled him, ripping first into his cloak and then deeper into the flesh of his hands, which were stretched out protectively in a plea for mercy.

The guards laughed as his cries reached them over the rocky ground. "They'll take a good chunk out of him before we get there."

Suddenly the growling frenzy changed to yelps of pain. The dogs jumped away from the man as if struck by lightning, just before a convulsive shaking overtook their bodies, driving them to the ground.

"What the ...?"

The guards, too, were knocked down. Later, they would be unable to explain the force that brought it about. A shattering sound pulsed deep into their heads, as waves of searing pain assaulted them. Eventually the agony overtook them, and they slipped into dark oblivion.

When they came around, they could not tell how much time had passed. Their heads ached as if they had drunk too much mead the previous night. The whimpering dogs slunk toward their masters, tails between their legs. There was no sign of the man. Only chunks of his woolen cloak and a few drops of blood showed where the dogs had taken him down.

CHAPTER 1

S hara startled awake. There was a commotion in the courtyard—shouting and hooves clattering on cobblestone. She threw her feet over the edge of her straw pallet onto the icy stone floor and sat for a moment before stumbling to the shuttered window.

Her sleep-numbed fingers struggled to release the latch on the wooden shutter, but finally it gave way. Cool air seeped into her room. A blanket of clouds was rolling in from the east and the air carried the smell of approaching rain. It was earlier than the household normally stirred awake. From her second story window, she could see the courtyard and stables below, and beyond that the rooftops of Gwyndorr.

An unfamiliar horse was tied to the tethering pole. Its rider was dressed in the uniform of a town guard and was speaking in a low, urgent tone to Randin. Shara's uncle snatched the reins of his own horse, mounted, and— together with the man—dashed toward the gate. The heavy gate swung open and for a moment Shara caught a tantalizing glimpse of the road and neighboring houses before it clanged shut again.

Shara turned away from the window and listened. All was quiet. Could this be the chance she had been waiting for? She crossed the room and creaked the door open a sliver, glancing at the two doors opposite her own. There was no sound from either of them. Olva, her aunt, seldom rose this early, but Ghris was usually gone before Shara awoke. Today her cousin's door was still closed.

It could open at any moment. If she was going to do what she had planned, she would have to do it quickly.

Shara padded down the steps on her bare feet, into the dining hall, the most beautiful room in the house. Warm rugs covered an intricately designed mosaic floor. A large hearth would normally welcome Olva and Randin's important visitors with a blazing fire, although today no flames warmed the air. Olva's expensive tastes were reflected in the jewel-bedecked vases, plates, and ornaments, displayed on the large mantel above the fireplace. Several had been bought from foreign merchants who arrived in Gwyndorr in the warmer months to peddle their wares, but Randin, who had his own methods of procuring valuable goods, had given most of them to her.

Moving past the long wooden table and benches, she reached her intended destination—the one room forbidden to her. A last glance to the stairs showed she was still alone. Her heart pounded, as she pulled the brass handle down. It creaked loudly. She stopped, holding her breath to listen for movement. After a long pause, she eased it down all the way and pushed. The door didn't budge. *Curse it!* Had Randin locked it? No—maybe it was just stuck. She heaved her shoulder against the door and felt it shift. Yes!

She slipped into the room and quickly closed the door behind her, standing dead still until her breathing returned to normal. It was only the third time that Shara had stood in Randin's chamber. The first had been as a child of eight when Randin told her that he and Olva were not her real parents. The second—a few weeks ago—when he had forbidden her from spending time in the kitchen with Marai.

The memory of this last encounter galvanized her into brazen action. Even if Randin returned right now and found her here, there was nothing left to lose, nothing more he could take from her. She paced past the large desk, to the shelves against the wall. Her eyes lingered on the leather-bound books. Would Randin even notice if one of them was gone? Unlikely—the only reason he owned them was because they were valuable.

Yet, she had no time to page through them now. It was the ivory box she was after. Her gaze had fallen on it the day Randin imposed the kitchen-ban, and she had known it was no ordinary box. Something that beautiful might contain secrets. Maybe even *hers.*

Cursing her short build, she stretched up to reach the box. Her fingers grazed it and she slowly edged it forward until she could grip it with her whole hand. When both hands had a steady hold on it, she lifted it from the shelf, and dropped down to the ground behind Randin's desk to examine it.

Again she was struck by just how beautiful the box was. The ivory lid was carved into a pattern of intricate flowers and swirls. She traced them with her finger, before feeling along the ridge where the lid and base met, looking for a catch. When this failed, she tried to prod a fingernail into the small crack, but the lid didn't open. She turned it upside down and shook it. Something rattled inside, but the lid held fast.

For a moment she considered finding one of Randin's daggers and forcing it open, but she discarded the idea. She had read once how bandits could break into locked rooms with a small, fine piece of wire, such as a hairpin. Instinctively, her fingers went to her own tangled mop of dark hair, but no hairpin held it together today. In fact, no hairpin held it together most days, for Shara seldom tried to tame it.

It was then that another idea crept into her mind. Randin's desk was made of a solid dark wood. Where would one hide something as important as a key in a solid desk like that? she wondered. A ridge of wood ran all the way around the desk, and Shara ran her fingers over its dusty, hidden interior until she reached the corner joint. It felt different. She dropped down and clambered under the desk to gain a better view of the joint. She glanced at the one opposite it and immediately saw that there was extra wood on this one, resting on two thin beams. Gently she pulled at the wood and as it slid toward her on the beams, her heart pounded with excitement. A secret compartment. Her fingers felt around for the box's key, but all she felt was a hard, oval object. Nothing more than a rock.

Yet, as she drew the object out, a small tremor passed through Shara. The rock was the most beautiful thing she had ever seen. Perfectly oval, its deep blue hue reminded her of an early evening sky and its gleaming surface, of moonlight. It felt comfortingly warm resting in her hand. This was no ordinary rock.

A loud whine drew her attention. Loar. The dog's timing couldn't have been worse, for Ghris—who slept through the loudest of storms—would wake at the smallest whimper from his beloved Loar. Already, Shara thought she heard movement upstairs.

Shara ran to the desk and lifted the box back onto the shelf before pounding out of the study. Only then did she realize that she was still gripping the rock. There was no time to put it back in the compartment for, above her, a door scraped open.

"I'm down here, Ghris. I'll let her in," Shara called, slipping the rock into her pocket.

Loar's wide smile and wagging tail showed her joy as Shara pulled the main door open. She pushed a wet snout into Shara's hand in her usual gesture of thanks. She wasn't particularly big—her back was the height of Shara's knee. Neither was she attractive, with her mottled coat of brown and black, and her one ear that perpetually folded forward even as the other stood upright. Yet her brown eyes were filled with intelligence, and she was a highly effective tracker dog, probably the only reason Randin allowed her to stay. For Shara, Loar's greatest quality was her loyalty.

"You realize quickly when the coast is clear, don't you?" Shara stroked Loar's head. Randin had expelled Ghris's dog from the house the moment he laid eyes on the little runt Ghris had rescued. However, it never took Loar long to realize Randin was gone.

The dog stood silently, tail wagging, although she glanced toward the stairs. Toward her Ghris. A surge of longing swept through Shara. If only *she* could be the object of such devotion and affection.

"Off you go then," she whispered and, with a grateful lick, the dog bounded across the dining hall and up the stairs.

Back in her own room, Shara laid aside the book her tutor, Brother Andreo, had given her to read and instead drew the rock out of her robe's deep pocket. She marveled at the object's loveliness. Fleetingly, she considered returning it to its hiding place, but something held her back. If the desk's dustiness was anything to go by, Randin wouldn't miss it soon. Surely it couldn't do any harm to keep it for just a little while?

• • •

Nicho pushed the door open a crack and looked out at the narrow, dirt road that wound through the Parashi Slum. Clouds billowed overhead, heavy with the coming storm. An old woman with a scarf-covered head edged along the road, and when she heard the door open, glanced back nervously. Nicho pulled deeper into the shadows and waited a few moments for her to disappear before he opened the door again. One had to be careful in the slums. There were many who would spy on their neighbors for a couple of coins from a town guard. Even this old woman could be a Whisperer.

His four young pupils, seated on the floor and speaking excitedly, were oblivious to the danger.

"The Parashi Warriors are the best swordsmen in all of Tirragyl. One warrior can kill a hundred king's men."

"Yes, and my papa says that one day they will march from the Guardian Grotto to Gwyndorr and fight all the Highborns so that they can't press us anymore."

Nicho turned around. "You mean *oppress*, Elrin. And nobody knows for sure if the Warriors still exist. Now finish forming your last letter, lads, and then put away your charcoal pieces. Almost dawn. The Guard patrol will be here soon. And there's a storm coming."

"My uncle Zeb says it's silly to learn letters," Elrin said, rubbing the charcoal stains from his hands. "He says letters are soft but swords are sharp. He says you should teach us to fight, Nicho."

"Letters are sharper than he thinks. Why would the Highborns forbid us from learning them otherwise? They fear what we Parashi can become with some learning."

"But can you still teach us to fight, Nicho?"

"I'm no warrior, Elrin. Just a groom." Nicho smiled at the boy's crestfallen expression. "Come now, lad. Time to go. The coast is clear."

The boy slipped out the door and ran down the street to the corner. He paused and looked back, giving Nicho a jaunty wave before disappearing from sight. *Curse the boy!* How many times had he told him not to do that? If anyone were watching, that wave could lead the Guards right to this house.

He signaled for the next boy to leave, and when he had disappeared from sight in the other direction, he opened the door wide enough to let out the oldest boy, Jabon.

"Bye, Nicho." Jabon smiled. "See you next Friday?"

"Right. Get going now. The patrol will be here soon."

No sooner had the boy dashed from the door, than Nicho heard the sound of hoofbeats. It was too late to call a warning to Jabon as two horsemen galloped from the direction of the main town.

Jabon had seen them and started to run to the alley between the closest houses. The horsemen reined in hard, and Nicho—watching through the slit of the open door—felt a surge of dread. He eased the door closed and cursed.

"What is it?" Rosa, the mother of the remaining boy, had just appeared from the sleeping area.

"It's Captain Randin." *His master. What in the abyss was he doing here this early in the morning?*

"Where? Is he outside?" Simhew ran to the window.

"Don't!" Rosa drew her son back.

Nicho pushed flat against the door. "If he finds me here …"

"Did the boys get out before he arrived?" Rosa asked.

"I think the first two were out of sight already, but he definitely saw Jabon."

"And the morning bell hasn't rung yet." Rosa bit her lip. "He'll know the lad is up to no good, out before the curfew lifts. They could drag his skinny rear end into a Rifter Gang faster than he recites his letters. He's the perfect size for them to make him a rooter."

"Jabon's a shrewd lad. He was heading for the slum alleys and few know them as well as he does," Nicho said. "The captain wouldn't be able to make it through them on a horse anyway."

"I hope you're right, Nicho."

They stood in anxious silence for a while.

"Shall I make us a nice hot cup of origo?" Rosa said eventually.

Nicho shook his head, somewhat regretfully. Although he was only seventeen and Rosa almost ten years older, he enjoyed talking to her. She was one of the few Parashi who agreed that the battle against the Highborns would be won through knowledge rather than the sword, and he admired her courage for letting them have lessons at her house. The other parents wanted their sons to learn, but were too afraid to put themselves at risk.

"I promised Yasmin I'd check in on Derry and Nana." He eased open the door to make sure the horsemen had left. "And I'll check that Jabon arrived home safely after that."

"Be careful, Nicho."

A sense of unease gnawed at Nicho as he left Rosa's house. *If you put your finger to a flame, expect to be burnt*, his mother always said. Today the flame had licked his hand.

CHAPTER 2

Derry's house was on the outskirts of the Parashi Slum—a decaying, overcrowded area of Gwyndorr allocated to the Lowborn. More than half of the city's Parashi population was packed into these few blocks of the town. The others—like Nicho and Yasmin—stayed on the properties of their Highborn masters.

As Nicho pushed Derry's door open, a child seated at a low table in the back leapt to his feet.

"Ko! Ko! Mama, Ko's here." He ran to Nicho with outstretched arms.

"Jed, you rascal," Nicho laughed as he lifted the boy up and spun him around. "When are you going to learn to say my name properly?"

"Look, Ko." The boy ran back to his seat. "Look what Papa made."

He came back carrying a little carved horse and pushed it proudly into Nicho's hand.

"It's beautiful, Jed." Nicho admired the careful handiwork. "What's his name?"

"Lian."

"Ah, of course. After the great Chief Troyin's horse. I think your Papa and I had a couple of carvings called Lian, is it not so, Derry?"

Derry had risen to his feet, the childlike smile on his round face as broad as always. "Nicho, you came to visit." He threw an arm around Nicho's shoulder, as enthusiastically as his son had done. Derry had been Nicho's friend from the time they were both two. Almost ten years later, the killing fever had ravaged the Parashi Slum. In this house, only Nana and Derry's sister, Yasmin, hadn't been touched by it, and ever since the plague's fever had held him in its grip, Derry had been more a boy than a man.

Derry's young wife, Hildah, rose from the table and greeted Nicho in a soft mumble, her face flushed crimson. It was still hard for Nicho to think of her as a mother. She had been only thirteen and Derry fourteen when she fell with child.

"Do you want some elder-beans and goat's milk, Nicho?" Hildah asked. It was the traditional Parashi breakfast, a cheap staple.

"Got some left?"

"The milk is rather watered down." She fetched a bowl, as Nicho greeted the last person seated at the table.

"Good morning, Nana," he said softly. Her watery eyes searched his face without recognition. It seemed almost impossible that she would not know him after all the years he had spent roughhousing with Derry and Yasmin. He could clearly recall her scolding them for walking mud into the room just after she had swept it. *You twins are double the trouble Pearce ever was, and with Nicho, you're downright impossible.*

"I just wanted to see how you were doing, Derry," Nicho said as Hildah filled his bowl. "The Captain of the Guard was in the slum a little earlier."

"I saw a soldier on a horse just now," Jed piped up.

"You did?" Nicho tried to keep his voice even. "Did he see you too, Jed?"

Jed nodded vigorously. "He waved at me."

"*Rat's breath,* Derry," Nicho said. "It's dangerous for the guards to know you have a child. Especially one Jed's age. You have to make sure he stays inside."

"Sorry, Nicho." His friend's gaze dropped to the floor. "Please don't be angry with me." The almost ever-present smile on his lips was gone. Nicho instantly regretted his quick words.

"Derry." Nicho pulled him into an embrace. "I'm not. Just worried about Jed." He ate without saying another word. Only Jed's imaginary horse battles broke the taut silence.

"I sold a few more shield tokens," Derry said, looking up hopefully at Nicho.

"Well done." Derry's smile was back instantly at his friend's approval. Nicho's fingers closed on the small wooden shield hung from a chain around his neck—a horse head carved onto it. It was the Parashi symbol of resistance. "Remember what I said though." Nicho tried to keep his voice as gentle as possible. "Don't sell them to the children, even if they beg you."

"I remember, Nicho. I'm not selling them to the children."

"You know that the town guards will look for any excuse to arrest them."

"I know. I promise. Not to the children."

As he left, Nicho signaled for Hildah to join him at the door.

"You still have the payoff money, Hildah?"

"Yes."

"How much is there?"

"Five bronze coins." It was a small fortune in a Parashi home, but one Nicho had insisted they have.

"Don't use that money, you hear, Hildah?"

"I'm trying not to, Nicho. But we'll need it soon for food. Derry hasn't sold many carvings lately."

"Don't use it! If the Guards come looking for rooters, they'll take Jed unless you have something to offer them."

"Jed's not even four. They won't take him yet."

"You never know."

"Money in a mouse hole doesn't fill Jed's tummy."

He wanted to say *at least you'll have a tummy to fill*, but he bit back the words. He had brought enough unrest here today.

"Don't touch the money. Please, Hildah. Promise me you won't."

"I promise I'll try."

• • •

Brother Andreo slipped out of the monastery gates in the cool of the early morning, his pony's hooves clopping softly on the dusty road. He looked back at the buildings and let the sense of his own smallness wrap around him. The Monastery of the Brethren of Taus was a large stone complex built against a curving sheer cliff. From a distance it was hardly visible. Hundreds of years ago the stones had been chiseled from the cliff itself, giving the monastery the appearance of being a natural extension of the rocks. To the northwest lay the Rif'twine Forest, but a vast sloping field of granite had arrested the forest's progress, protecting the monastery from invasion. Beyond the cliff lay the first foothills of the mountains that grew into the towering peaks of the Eastern Highlands.

Andreo was—once again—struck by the majesty of the monastery's location and the aura of tranquility, enhanced by the sound of Celebrants chanting mantras after the Morning Rites. All Brothers were expected to be present at the morning ceremony, but in these last few months Andreo had often been absent. With more than a hundred Brothers, all dressed in the same dark, cowled robes, Andreo had hoped he might get away with it at least a few months more. Yet, after this morning's encounter with Brother Angustus, he wasn't so sure he would. He didn't allow his thoughts to linger on what would happen if anyone discovered his disobedience, for what he did three times a week before his tutoring appointments in Gwyndorr was strictly prohibited by the Brethren of Taus.

In the monastery, everybody had his own task. Keepers saw to the maintenance of the monastery and clothed and fed the Brothers. Mentors trained the young acolytes and advised the Council of Six on their division placement. Celebrants led all the rituals and praise-chants. The most powerful Brothers of all were those in the Word Arts division. They knew words which, when uttered in the right tone and inflection and with just the right strength of mind-control, moved items or changed their form or caused them to shrivel up and die. These were powers that their founding father and deity, Taus, had imparted hundreds of years before.

Andreo, despite his quick intelligence, had not been among the handful chosen for training in this, the most revered gift of the monastery. Instead he had been chosen as a Brodon–those who imparted the monastery's teaching of Tirragylin history to the next generation of Highborns. It was a significant, but not a prestigious, calling, below even that of the Scribes, who meticulously copied and recopied history from the old scrolls.

Yet Andreo had discovered his own form of magic, one that could also cause things to change and possibly shrivel, even though his magic intended to bring life rather than death. Andreo had discovered the art of herbal alchemy.

Alchemy was spoken of in the oldest manuscripts, but it had fallen out of favor with the Great Purge, when all the ancient local practices had come into question. Unlike the Old Word Arts, which had been brought by Taus's Highborn invaders and was therefore acceptable, alchemy had been practiced by the Parashi healers of old and was therefore deemed undesirable. So the ancient art of mixing herbs and leaves and berries into healing potions and ointments had been eradicated over time. That art, which for generations had brought hope and life, was now all but forgotten.

But then Andreo picked some leaves of the frillbough bush that grew so prolifically at the foot of the Gray Cliffs and steeped them in hot water. After the concoction had brewed for several minutes, he took a few hesitant sips and that night found that sleep came easier than it ever had before. Andreo had just rediscovered what the old Parashi healers had known for centuries. The frillbough was an effective pain reliever and sleep inducer. From that moment on, Andreo's fascination with the ancient, forbidden art grew stronger and stronger.

Old scrolls that had survived the purge in the dark vaults of the monastery—hinting at seeds of rebellion amongst some in the brotherhood—taught Andreo several basic remedies. Yet most of his "discoveries" came by watching which berries and leaves the birds and animals ate, and which they left alone. Then it was a case of trial and error. Stomach cramps, diarrhea, rashes, blurred sight, and strange hallucinations were some of the milder side effects of Andreo's initial concoctions. But after fourteen years of experimenting and taking meticulous notes, Andreo had remedies for some of the most common complaints and maladies. Confident in his newfound knowledge, Andreo had—in the last few months—turned his scientific mind to the dangerous, but most fertile source of plant life in Tirragyl. Andreo had started to visit the Rif'twine Forest.

Today, however, there would be no time for Andreo to make the trip to the forest before his tutoring. Not only was a storm brewing, but he had been forced to attend Morning Rites when Brother Angustus, one of the Council of Six, waylaid him. Andreo couldn't shake the feeling that the Word Art Supreme had been watching him rather closely these last few days. Maybe even longer.

He shook off the thought and walked faster toward the town gate, hoping to get there before the rain set in.

• • •

On his way home from the incident with the guards, Randin again made his way through the narrow, dirty streets of the Parashi Slum that lay just to the west of the town gate. The houses were piled on top of each other—rough constructions of clay bricks and flat reed roofs. Often they lodged at least two or three families. Most of them were built in the traditional Parashi horseshoe shape, with doors opening from two rooms onto a small central courtyard, where a goat could be reared and elder beans grown.

The same young boy he had seen this morning stared at him from an open door, his grimy hand still clenching a small, carved horse. He had the tight curls and green eyes of a typical Parashi. Most parents kept their children out of sight and—as if she realized her mistake—the boy's young mother hurriedly pulled her son away from the door as Randin passed by.

The boy must have been about four, and Randin took note of his slight build with interest. A rooter's build. Lately rooters had been difficult to find. The Parashi were becoming adept at hiding their children.

His mind turned to the more urgent matter that faced him and the reason he had been called out to the gate so early this morning. An unknown figure had been seen near the town gate, running into the Rif'twine. Randin's men told a strange story of his escape. It worried him. As Captain of the Town Guard, he took the smallest breach of security as a personal insult.

At first, he had wondered if his men had been drinking at a tavern the night before, but he smelled no liquor on their breath. Both men involved had been dazed, but their stories concurred. Randin had to conclude that they were telling the truth, although there was no clear explanation for what had occurred. Was the strange man a Parashi trying to break free from a Rifter Gang? Then why had he been running *toward* the Rif'twine Forest? And what force had brought down the guards and their dogs?

Leaving the Parashi Slum behind, Randin now reached a wider, cobbled road that lead to the wealthier part of town. Suddenly a loud cry and the shriek of metal wheels jarred him from his thoughts. A fully laden cart bore down on him from the road to his right. The carthorse stopped with such force that the driver almost lost his seating.

"You fool! What are you doing in the middle of the road?" The driver bellowed. "I might have killed myself. Stupid maggot of a man! I have a good mind to ..."

The words died in the man's throat as recognition dawned on his face. Randin savored the brief pleasure of another's fear.

"You have a good mind to ... what?" he drawled, as he jumped off his stallion's back.

The driver clambered down from the cart and threw himself at Randin's feet.

"Forgive me, Captain, I didn't see it was you."

"Your name?"

"Langhaus, sir."

"Do you realize what happens to someone who assaults the Captain of the Guard?"

"Please forgive me, sir. It was an accident. I did not see you. The day is so dark and I ..."

"Your accent is from the north," Randin interrupted, "so you might not know how Gwyndorr deals with its criminals."

"I have lived here for more than ten years, sir. Ever since the Rif'twine crept through Hwelling."

"Ah, so you know about the Rifter Gangs?"

"Yes, Captain." The man swallowed and looked away. "I know."

"Going from driving a cart to fighting the Rif'twine. Would you consider that a promotion?" Randin laughed without humor.

"Captain, please, I beg you ..."

"Children, Langhaus?" The fear in the man's eyes betrayed him. "Ah! Any young ones? I'm always looking for good rooters for my Rifter Gangs. Only the small ones can crawl into the Darkzone to deal with the poison trees."

"Captain ..." Langhaus fell forward again, forehead in the dust. "Please, Captain. Take anything you want. Let me show you what I have in the cart. I hear you are a man of good tastes. I have some wonderful material, sir."

Randin felt a surge of contempt for this sniveling man. "Get up you ... what was it? Ah, yes ... maggot of a man. Show me."

The man scrambled to his feet, and Randin silently followed him to the back of his cart.

"Let's see what you have in there, Langhaus." He pulled off the taupe covering, smiling at the wealth of beautiful fabric buried underneath it.

"You are a cloth merchant?"

"I transport for the merchants, Captain. These are not mine."

"Not yours? And still you are willing to give them to me?" Randin laughed. "How very benevolent of you, Langhaus."

He deftly chose a bolt of rich maroon silk. He recognized it as Octora Spider Silk, spun from the egg casings of the Octora spider. It was rare and very valuable.

"This would make a lovely garment for my wife," he said, fingering the material. "Yes, with this in hand I might well forget the attempt on my life and the insults hurled at me."

Langhaus had paled. "Sir, could I ask you to choose something else?"

"Why's that, Langhaus? Didn't you say I could have *anything*?"

"Of course. Of course. But this ... well, this is rather exceptional."

"I know that."

"This is worth more than all the other material here. Sir, if I lose this ..."

"You're not losing it, Langhaus. You're *giving* it to me. Remember?"

The man stood stonily aside as Randin helped himself to the cloth, well aware of the level of punishment this inflicted. No trader would trust the man again for transport after this.

Fabric tucked under one arm, Randin mounted his stallion and made his way home to drop off the cloth. His house was an impressive stone structure, reflecting his wealth and prestige. The double-story living and sleeping quarters of the family backed directly against the city wall. Two separate single-story wings jutted out from this. The eastern wing housed the kitchen and the servants' quarters while the western wing consisted of stables and storerooms.

He was about fifty paces from the front side of this rectangle—a solid wall, with a large iron gate built into it—when he saw someone darting in through the gate. Randin hadn't seen his face, but by the plain dark robe, he knew the person was a Lowborn. The fact that the guards let him in must mean it was one of his servants. And the furtiveness with which it all happened meant that he had no good reason to be outside and had probably broken the curfew too.

As he rode through his gate, the two guards saluted him.

"A messenger came from Lord Lucian, Captain," the older of the two said.

"Really?" This was not good news. Could it mean that Gwyndorr's Lord had already heard about the gate incident? *Curse it!* Randin had planned to inform Lord Lucian about the gate incident as soon as he had made some sense of it himself. One thing Randin knew was that Gwyndorr's Lord *hated* being the last to know anything. If he thought Randin was keeping any information from him, Randin could wave farewell to his esteemed position. He'd better get over there *fast*.

"Right, take this fabric to Lady Olva right away." He dropped the bolt into the guard's arms. "I'm going to see Lord Lucian. Let's hope I can outride the worst of the storm."

CHAPTER 3

Shara watched the guard plod across the courtyard with a bolt of fabric, which looked expensive, even from her window. More embezzled goods, no doubt. Randin's house was full of them. Sometimes Shara imagined she could hear the voices of Gwyndorr's deprived and poor whispering through the shutters. At times, she pictured the animosity of the townspeople as a thick fog that crept through every crevice in the house, weighing it down with guilt. Was she complicit in Randin's corruption, she wondered, merely because she ate at his table?

One thing was certain, Randin and Olva never felt a twinge of guilt. Randin thought the goods were his just due for keeping Gwyndorr safe from outside attack, while Olva merely pretended that all the gains were legitimate. Ghris, always one to avoid conflict, said nothing. Only Shara spoke out, although lately she was learning to curb her tongue, for her outspokenness came at a cost. Not directly of course—Randin was too clever for that. Knowing Shara's deep feelings for their cook Marai, he had started to punish *her* instead. He would forbid Marai from helping the sick and needy who sought out her healing skills. Turning them away broke Marai's heart. Or her son, Nicho, would be given a lashing for some fictional offense.

Marai had stoically borne this undeserved punishment. Shara had not even known about it until Yasmin, the scullery maid, asked, *"Do you even know that Marai pays for every one of your loose words, Miss Shara?"* Marai had denied it. *"Who knows why Master Randin does what he does. Maybe Nicho or I deserved it, Shara. It has nothing to do with you. You keep speaking your heart, Petal."*

And speak she did. Five weeks ago Shara had announced at the dinner table that she would eat only bread. She would not—she declared—eat any more of Randin's rich fare, since so much of it was stolen.

Randin's face had turned scarlet, and Shara had watched with grim fascination, thinking he might be choking. Instead, he had called a servant and told her to bring a plate of the offcuts of meat innards and rotting vegetables, normally sold for a pittance to the pig farmers outside the town gate. He had stood over Shara and forced her to eat every scrap of the rubbish. Worse than the bellyache that lingered for three days was that Randin forbade Shara from ever setting foot in the kitchen again where, he said, *the Parashi scum were poisoning her mind.*

The fabric must have reached its intended destination, for Shara heard a screech of delight from downstairs. She might as well make good use of Olva's all-too-brief joy and make an appearance.

A few steps down the stairs, she could hear Olva calling for the seamstress to be sent. Sometimes Shara almost felt sorry for her aunt, for Olva's happiness seemed to leak away faster than water in a cracked jar. She wondered if Randin would have thought twice about marrying one of the few titled ladies of Gwyndorr, if he had known that keeping her content would be such all-consuming work.

Olva, standing by the dining room table fingering a deep red material, looked up as Shara reached the bottom step.

"Shara! Look at the beautiful Octora Spider Silk Randin gave me."

Shara went over to touch the fabric. It was the richest red she had ever seen, and it felt softly fluid and warm in her fingers.

"It's exquisite."

"It will make a magnificent gown, don't you think? For the spring feast? I think I will copy the design of my jade dress. This color will suit me perfectly, won't it?"

Olva was a particularly striking woman, and the fabric's color would, in fact, complement her light skin and fair hair.

"You will look lovely in it, Olva." What she really wanted to ask was how Olva could bear to be draped in stolen fabric. Still, her tone must have betrayed her.

"Oh, I almost forgot. The little foundling, who we have given food and shelter to for the last fourteen years, doesn't approve of our small indulgences."

"Only when they're stolen," Shara shot back. Instant regret filled her. *Would Marai pay for these words again?*

Olva's mouth puckered into a tight "o" and her eyes narrowed on Shara. "Well, well." Her voice dripped ice. "Don't you think you're something special, you ungrateful wench? Look at you with your obvious half-breed hair and eyes, calling *me*—a full-blooded lady—a thief."

"I'm sorry, Olva."

"You would have died in the gutters if we hadn't given you a home."

"I know, Olva. I am grateful," Shara said flatly.

"We had no obligation to take you in, you know? Why do you think we even cared?"

Shara had wondered this herself many times.

"But we did. Out of the goodness of our hearts we gave you everything." Olva's voice was at fever pitch now. "Everything!"

"You did, Olva. Thank you."

Olva stared at her with narrowed eyes. "Why aren't you holed up in your room with a book, instead of coming here to criticize me?"

"I just wanted a bit of fresh air."

"Outside?" Olva looked at her sharply. "You're not sneaking to the kitchen to visit that Parashi cook, are you?"

"No. I'm not going to visit Marai."

"Good. Randin made it very clear you were not to set foot in that kitchen again, didn't he?"

"Very clear, Olva. I'm just going into the courtyard."

"Don't go too far," Olva's lip curled into a smile.

"Not very far to go, is there?"

Shara could count on one hand the number of times she had been out of Randin's homestead. There had been walls hemming her in her entire life.

Shara used to stand outside the kitchen and look up at the clouds, imagining she was one of them, floating away, light and free. She had always believed that the walls around the homestead were there to keep Randin and Olva safe in the event of an uprising against the nobility and town guards, but lately she had started to wonder if the walls did not perhaps serve another function. Were they the fortifications of a prison?

Shara was determined to find out. If her instincts were right, it was the box—the ivory box—that held the key to her past, and maybe even the key to her freedom. A new thought pressed into her mind. Could the rock she found this morning lead her to the truth in some way? She sensed that there was more to the rock than its alluring beauty. She recalled the way it felt in her hand—warm, tingling, and alive. Mysterious. Was it possibly even one of Tirragyl's rare power rocks?

As she walked out into the courtyard, the cold wind brushed misty rain into her face. The end of winter always brought the moisture-laden east winds from the highlands, a welcome change from the harsh, dry western winds.

To her right was the kitchen wing. Shara imagined the usual flurry of activity taking place. How often she had been drawn there for the warmth and the comfortable banter of the cook and scullery maids. Marai, the large motherly cook, would let her sit by the fire and peel potatoes, and for a while at least, Shara could imagine herself to be in a real home with a mother of her own. The day after Randin had forbidden her from setting foot in the kitchen, Shara had slipped, unseen, into the kitchen larder, eavesdropping on the chatter.

"They don't do right by that young'un," Marai had said.

"What do you mean, Marai? Master Randin is known to never lay a hand on a woman. That girl has never had a beating in her life." Yasmin had said.

"There are worse ways to kill a soul than a beating, Yaz. Like telling us she is not to sit here anymore. That child got a comfort from us that she never gets back there." Marai pointed to the main house. "'Tis a cruel thing to take away small pleasures from someone who has so little."

The gathering strength of the rain brought Shara back to the present. She quickly moved to the western wing's stable entrance for shelter, breathing in the fresh, living smell of the rain and feeling the tightness in her throat loosen somewhat. There was still loveliness in the world that they could not shut away from her.

Suddenly she sensed movement on the stable roof. She heard a fast fluttering sound and then felt the coolness of moving air against her face. Something dropped onto the tethering pole to her right. A bird. And as she gazed at its ethereal beauty, Shara felt a strange stirring of joy and sorrow. Never had she seen anything so beautiful in her life. Its wings were a red—richer by far than Olva's fabric—and its breast a gold that, even on this dark day, shimmered with light. It seemed to be looking directly at her.

For a long while, the bird and Shara silently gazed at each other, until a clatter from inside the stable broke the spell. Shara whirled around to find Nicho, the groom, standing in the entrance, a bin of horse feed strewn across the floor. He was looking intently at the bird, which by now had taken to the air. They both watched its retreating red wings in reverent silence.

"Did you see it? Have you ever seen anything that beautiful?" Nicho's smile mirrored her own joy.

"I know. It was magnificent."

A sudden change came over Nicho. "Forgive me, Miss Shara. I forget my manners." His gaze slid down to the floor, the required posture of a Lowborn, speaking to a Highborn.

As quickly as Shara's joy had blossomed, it was gone. Standing here with Marai's son, Shara was once again in a place she had no purpose being. It had been almost five years since she had been this close to Nicho. He was no longer the gangly boy she used to play with in the courtyard. Now he had attained the full height of a man—well over a head taller than she was. However, there was still something boyish in the curve of his jaw and the tumble of his light brown curls. As his gaze had met her own, a jolt of familiarity had passed through her. How well she suddenly remembered those unusual eyes—startlingly green—and dimpled cheeks.

"It's fine, Nicho."

"Forgive me for frightening the bird away. I was trying to get a better view of it. It really was ... incredible."

"It was, wasn't it?"

"It seemed to be watching you," he said hesitantly, as if the very idea was ridiculous.

"Did you also think so? I thought that, but ..."

"... but it's only a bird," he finished.

She nodded silently. It was just a bird.

They stood a while longer in uncomfortable silence. She should probably go back to the house, but the thought of its walls pressing in on her kept her standing in the stable entrance.

"I'm just out for a bit of fresh air." She felt she should explain. "You can continue, Nicho."

"Yes, Miss Shara."

He turned around and started picking up the knocked-over horse feed.

She watched him, but quickly looked away as he glanced up. Truth be told, she used to watch him across the courtyard from the kitchen workbench too, as he went in and out of the stable. He had a way of calming down the most restless of horses that was fascinating to watch.

"He has the Parashi gift of horse-whispering, just like his grandfather before him," Marai would say proudly.

Marai was not the only one who spoke highly of him. Yasmin and Fortuni—Marai's two scullery maids—would wait for Marai to leave on an errand before they twittered on about Nicho's strength or beautiful eyes or smile.

Shara longed to be a part of their conspiratorial banter. She thought of telling them how Nicho used to play with her and Ghris when they were young, until that last day when everything had changed. Yet she always held her tongue. She was not one of them. Never had been and never would be.

"How is your mother, Nicho?"

"Fine, Miss Shara."

"It's been five weeks since I saw her."

"I know."

"Randin won't let me go there anymore."

"She told me."

"I ..." *miss her*, she wanted to say, but instead said, "... would like it if you sent her my greetings."

He hesitated and then nodded once.

"Will you?"

"If you command it, Miss Shara."

"Why should I command it? I just want you to pass on a message."

"I'm not sure it's what she needs to hear right now."

"Why?"

"Miss Shara." Nicho lifted his head, defiantly looking her in the face before dropping his eyes again. "My mother has suffered much hurt because of her interaction with you. I think it better for her to forget you now."

If the words had been a punch in her midriff, they would have doubled her over with pain. "Many bruises heal in one day, one word in many a year," Marai used to say but Shara had never fully understood the truth of this old Parashi saying. Until now.

The wind blew a sudden gust of cold rain into her face.

"You do not have a cloak, Miss Shara. You will catch a cold."

"Yes." She stood rooted to the spot, dazed by pain and guilt.

"Maybe you should go in before you are drenched to the bone."

"Yes. It is cold, suddenly. Very cold."

She turned and walked slowly through the downpour. Nicho's mother had suffered much hurt and she, Shara, had brought that on. And now Marai, the only one whose love had wrapped warmly around Shara's heart, was learning to forget her.

CHAPTER 4

Randin slowed his horse to a trot as he approached the gate of Lord Lucian's villa. More a castle than a villa, he thought wryly. There was no home in Gwyndorr that compared. Right at the center of the town, walls surrounded it as high as those around Gwyndorr. The villa was set apart not only by its size but also by its splendor. The great halls and most of the fifteen upstairs sleeping suites all had glass windows. Even Randin could afford no more than a few small panes of the rare and expensive luxury for his main bedroom.

The opulent gardens had been designed and laid out geometrically; hedges and flowerbeds radiated out from several marble statues. Many of these focal point statues were double the size of a man —warriors slaying mythical creatures, barely clad women, and fearful-looking monsters with multiple heads. Large blue and orange fish swam in a series of linked ponds fed by a manmade waterfall. Along the perimeter wall grew taller plants—all exotic specimens.

The guards opened the gate and Randin trotted through the heavy rain to the stables at the back. These stables were almost the same size as Randin's entire homestead, and he felt the usual stab of envy. He was sure that even the King of Tirragyl did not live in such luxury.

As he drew up to the stable, his eyes wandered to the upper rooms of the western wing, where–it was rumored–Lucian kept his concubines. Randin knew that Lucian was a man who enjoyed his pleasures. At the last banquet in this very villa, he had caught Lucian's eyes following Olva across the room, had seen the flirtatious smiles they shared. A groom dressed in the purple and black of Lucian's coat of arms ran to take his mount. Before Randin reached the villa's front door, it opened, and Lucian's steward appeared. Lyndis, a stately looking man with snow-white hair, bowed slightly.

"Welcome, sir." His voice sounded polished. "I wasn't aware that Lord Lucian was expecting you."

Randin always felt a twinge of irritation that Lucian insisted on the title of "Lord." Hadn't he married a lady too? Nobody called *him* "Lord Randin."

"He sent a messenger, and I have very urgent business to discuss with him," he said, handing Lyndis his wet cloak.

"Lord Lucian is unavailable at the moment, but should be able to give you an audience by midday."

Midday! Randin's anger surged at the insult.

"I am sure Lord Lucian wishes to know the information I have brought soon, as it impacts his personal security."

Randin felt a small measure of victory as he saw Lyndis's eyes widen. Lucian was obsessed with his personal security, even owning a small private army to protect his villa.

"Please wait in the parlor."

The crackling fire along the far wall of the parlor drew Randin. His outer garment had not prevented the rain from soaking through to his tunic, and he suddenly felt cold. The large fire did little to warm the vault-like room, but he pulled a stool closer to the fire, and after a while, felt some warmth seep back into his body.

Twice, a servant came in to replenish the fire with wood. By the time the fire had burnt low a third time, Randin's impatience had reached boiling point. He paced restlessly around the room. Several swords mounted against the wall drew his eye. The top one was a magnificent broad sword, which he judged would require a two-handed swing, even for a man of his own strength. Unusual stones decorated its hilt; ruby and topaz were the only two he recognized. On the blade, he could see some lettering, and he leaned forward to read it.

The writing was unusual—one he could not decipher. One of the Enderite scripts, maybe? Yet even those he would have recognized. It had a strangely ancient look—could it be Old Tongue? Surely not. Everything written in that script had been destroyed in the Great Purge almost four hundred years ago.

A soft rustle to his right warned him that he was no longer alone. Slowly, he turned to meet Lucian's cold stare.

Randin could never shake the edginess he felt staring into those brown eyes flecked with gold. There was something mesmerizing in Lucian's gaze that always left Randin feeling uncharacteristically feeble and inadequate.

Lucian's towering frame also added to the impression of power. The only advantage Randin held over Gwyndorr's Lord was his age. Lucian's greying hair and beard hinted that he was definitely not as young as he tried to appear.

He used all his willpower to break away from Lucian's hypnotic stare and inclined his head in a small bow. "Lord Lucian."

"What are you doing, Randin?"

That voice, soft and smooth, had the same compelling effect as the eyes. Randin always sensed that Lucian would be good as a drawer-of-secrets from men. Pity Lucian had married into such a high position; Randin could have used someone with strong interrogation skills on the Town Guard.

"I was just studying this … this magnificent sword, Lord Lucian."

"It is rather special to me." Lucian indicated for Randin to sit on the stool near the fire.

"The lettering is most unusual. I was wondering …" Randin knew instinctively that this was dangerous ground, "… what language is it written in?"

Lucian did not answer immediately, but his gaze seared deep into Randin, who shifted his own eyes to stare at the flames licking the wood in the fireplace.

"It has been in my family for generations. Its origins are of old and have been lost in the telling. Now tell me why you are here, Randin."

"There was … an incident. At the gate. This morning."

"Incident?"

"My men spotted a figure just before sunrise, running toward the forest."

Randin explained the story his men had told, and how the dogs and men had appeared bewildered and restless when he saw them. He was unduly pleased to see that he had Lucian's complete attention.

Lucian let Randin finish his account before he asked, "So they heard an ear-splitting sound?"

"Yes, Lord Lucian, they said the sound pierced into them, causing a pain in their heads. It even seems to have knocked them out for a while."

"There was no one else there, only the man the dogs took down?"

"That's what they said—only the man in the dark cloak."

"Did you go to the place to look for evidence?"

"I sent my second-in-command, Issor, while I was talking to them. He will report back to me."

"And just how do you think this will impact on my personal security?"

Randin suddenly remembered the rash statement he had made to Lyndis earlier, and felt the discomfort return. "If it affects the town's security, I fear it will impact you too, my Lord."

Lucian rose from his stool and paced to the fire and back. "I doubt it, Randin. It was probably just one of the rifters trying to escape."

"I thought that too, initially. But then why was he running *toward* the forest, and not away from it?"

"Who knows? The Rif'twine does strange things to the mind. "

Randin knew this all too well. The Rif'twine was not an ordinary forest. It had many names and often Randin thought the Parashi word *Zura*—crushing—was better at capturing its essence. For that was what the Rif'twine did. It ferociously crept, ever deeper, into Tirragyl, claiming farms, villages, and towns, and crushing all the life from them. In his own time, he had seen it lay claim to a string of villages, stretching all the way from Hwelling in the North to his own home village in the North West. Its roots crept under walls, and its vines and plants into buildings, steadily encroaching and poisoning the ground, forcing everything in its path to die or to flee.

Gwyndorr would have been its next victim. Until Lucian arrived.

It was Lucian who laid down the plans to fight the Rif'twine. At first, there had been opposition to his strategy. The forest was thick and impenetrable, filled with peculiar and dangerous plants that poisoned, strangled, ripped, or stuck to the skin. One bush, which flowered twice a year, even let off a scent that could send one into a dark delirium from which there was no return. Nobody was willing to set foot near the forest; most were happy merely to flee from its onslaught. Therefore, the remaining towns of Tirragyl were becoming more and more populated, the resources scarcer, and the people more desperate.

Lucian had insisted there was a way to defeat it, even to push it back, and his plan, to everyone's amazement, worked. For almost fifteen years, the Rif'twine had been held back from Gwyndorr's walls. For this, Lucian was a hero. In the streets, he was lauded as the Deliverer of Gwyndorr. Some even went as far as calling him the Deliverer of Tirragyl itself, because his Rifter Plan was now being used in other places and, finally, the Rif'twine's advance was slowing.

The cost was great; nobody knew this better than Randin. But it was measured in Parashi lives and Parashi lives were cheap and easy to come by.

"The girl. Is she still safe, Randin?"

"Girl? Which ... girl?"

"Shara. Is your house still secure enough to keep her?"

"Yes, Lord Lucian. You know yourself—there are walls and guards. She's not going anywhere. But what does this man have to do with her?"

"I'm not sure. One can never be too cautious. I always like to understand what I'm dealing with." Lucian absently stroked his top lip with his thumb and forefinger. "I think we need to move forward with the betrothal date. My house is safer than yours."

"But the girl is only in her sixteenth year. She is too young to be wed."

"In many cultures, girls marry at fourteen." Lucian made a sweeping motion, as if to dispel this minor inconvenience of age. "I don't think the town elders will object."

Probably not, Randin thought, if they wished to keep their esteemed positions. He felt a little bewildered at this sudden turn of events. True, the girl was troublesome; she had been from an early age. Always questioning, confronting, and arguing, mostly with Olva. Many days he would return home to find his wife in tears. There was little to take from the girl, though, and so it had been difficult to find a way to admonish her. Realizing how much she cared for that Parashi cook had been the turning point. It was always easy to control people when you understood what—or whom—they loved.

"The girl is fine where she is. Settled, in fact. I don't think we should make any hasty decisions."

"There's nothing hasty about this betrothal, Randin. We've been planning it for more than ten years. Your ward will marry my son. It's time to set that in motion."

"Didn't we agree that it would take place when she's eighteen and Maldor twenty?"

"Not quite ready to lose your handsome monthly stipend for taking her in?" Lucian smiled knowingly. "Tell you what—I'll carry on paying it for another six months. And the Bride Price will more than compensate for your loss."

"It's not just the money." Randin was unsure why giving Shara to Lucian's son filled him with a measure of discomfort. It wasn't as if she were his own flesh and blood, even though most people, including Shara, thought he and Olva were her aunt and uncle. A story to explain why they had taken her in.

No one needed to know they had done so only on Lucian's insistence. "The girl is young by Tirragyl standards. People will talk."

"Talk about *me*? Where have you been all this time, Randin? I can't do anything wrong in their eyes. I've saved their precious town."

"I still think you're being hasty. Let's just give this a while to ..."

"Enough! I have decided. We will set the marriage ceremony for a month's time. There is much to arrange. Lyndis will take care of it all. Just ensure the girl is safe until then."

"Of course, she will be safe. I'm the Captain of the Town Guard."

"True. That's why I chose you to take her in. Now, let's share some wine to celebrate the joining of our families. For this union is just the start of some very momentous events."

For the life of him, Randin could not explain the chill of trepidation that crept down his back.

CHAPTER 5

Lyndis had brought some mulled wine at Lucian's instruction and as the warmth of it spread through his body, Randin started to see the sense of what Lucian proposed. If he agreed to push the betrothal forward, Shara would no longer be his concern. That untamable tongue of hers could cause distress in Lucian's house instead. He smiled at the thought. In addition, Lucian would pay him a sizeable bride price, and Randin's family would be joined to the most powerful family in the area by the strong bond of marriage. It made perfect sense.

"Now," Lucian said. "I sent you a message because we need to talk about the rifters. By some accounts, we are short of numbers."

"Whose account?"

"Does it matter?"

"Well, sir, all the Rif'twine Guard units report to me. So if there is a shortage of rifters, I would be the first to hear about it."

"I have a few other ears to the ground. Can't always rely on your word for the truth. In fact, I hear that you never set foot near the forest."

"There's no need to, is there? That's what the Rif'twine Guard units are for."

"Might not do any harm though. Don't army generals go into the battle field to see the lay of the land?"

"I am a soldier, Lord Lucian. Trained to fight men. I have said it before and I will say it again. The Rif'twine is a forest, not an army. As such I do not feel that my men and I should be responsible to fight it. Our attention should be on military threats only."

"The Rif'twine is the greatest threat we have ever faced, Randin."

"But not a military one."

"I disagree. A human army would be out to breach the walls of Gwyndorr and capture everything within it. That is the intention of the Rif'twine too. It is a strong and fierce foe."

Randin knew the truth of his words. For as Lucian spoke, images had formed in his mind—images of a forest creeping and crushing through a western town called Cerulea. All had fled from its inevitable victory. All, except Randin's father. The owner of the only mine in Tirragyl where the Cerulean Dusk Dreamers were found, his father would not leave the precious, magic-imbued rocks behind. As the roots of the forest encroached on the mine, he was still chiseling the stones from the rock-bed, Randin by his side. The young Randin had begged him to leave his stones, but over the course of the week in which the mine entrance grew dark with forest undergrowth, he had refused. Randin had eventually fought his way back to the light, leaving his father behind. The Rif'twine was an evil killer, and it filled Randin with a deep and shameful fear.

Lucian was staring at him intently. "Well?"

"What did you say, my lord?"

"Unit Twenty-eight. On the monastery side. Completely wiped out, my sources tell me." He clicked his tongue impatiently. "You haven't heard?"

"No. I haven't heard anything. The whole unit wiped out in one day?"

"Yes."

"What killed them?"

"My sources didn't say. It matters little. What does matter is that we need fifteen new rifters to take their place. And at least two rooters."

One of Randin's roles was to supply Parashi for the Rifter Gangs. Generally, this wasn't too difficult. Criminals, simpletons, the old and useless—these were in constant supply in Gwyndorr. But it was the rooters who did the most important and dangerous job of all: tunneling into the forest undergrowth, boring into the Poison Trees and then filling the cavities with the oil of the gorgon berry, which over time would kill the tree. Adults, and even older children, were too large to reach the trees; only the small ones could do it. There was a constant shortage of rooters. Occasionally the children would grow too big to push through the forest wall, but more often than not, exposure to the milky sap of the trees and the toxins of the gorgon berries took its toll. Few rooters lived past the age of ten.

"You'll have to arrange a slum sweep soon," Lucian said.

"We just did one a week ago. If we do it again so soon, the people will get edgy."

"Oh, and we wouldn't want the Parashi to be edgy, would we?"

"Well. They seem to accept one every six weeks or so. It gives them a chance to —"

"— it gives them a chance to *hide* their children." Lucian's scorn was evident. "Just get a new unit together, Randin."

"Yes, sir."

A flick of Lucian's fingers, and Lyndis appeared at the parlor entrance. Randin wondered if he had overheard the entire conversation.

"Lyndis will see you out now."

"Thank you, Lord Lucian." Randin inclined his head in the smallest of bows and started to follow the steward. He was almost in the hallway when Lucian spoke.

"Wait." He came striding toward him. "Your men. Did they see any movement in the air?"

"My men?"

"This morning."

"You mean the incident with the dogs and —"

"Yes, Randin. What else could I possibly mean?"

"Movement, you ask?"

Lucian now spoke as if to a young child. "Did your men see anything in the air?"

Yes, Randin remembered now. One man had said that he saw a flash of red in the sky. Randin had dismissed it as irrelevant, part of the strange trauma they seemed to have undergone.

"A flash. One man saw a flash of red."

Over his years as captain, Randin had developed an uncanny ability to read a person's emotions from the smallest shift in their face. Now, for just an instant, he saw two overriding emotions on Lucian's normally controlled features. The first, in the subtle clenching of his jaw, was anger. The second, in the widening of his pupils, was unexpected. It was an emotion he had never seen in Lucian before —fear.

• • •

Tessor's hand on the stone wall guided her down the narrow passage. She liked the solid feeling of the uneven walls, a reminder that this house had stood for hundreds of years before her, and would stand for hundreds more. There was little light in this forgotten passage, which started in a small storage chamber before it wound around several of the larger rooms of the manor. Dust danced in narrow beams of light from the small peepholes into adjacent rooms. As children, Tessor and her younger sister, Yorina, had often snuck into this "eavesdrop aisle" when their grandfather—then Gwyndorr's Lord—entertained the town's nobility.

Tessor stopped at the place where she had stood so often as a child. These peepholes were barely visible, covered by a tapestry in the parlor. The wall-hanging blocked the light and muffled the sound. Yet over the years Tessor had become adept at standing in the shadows and listening to whispers.

Unlike Lucian, Fafa had always known his granddaughters were there. He would deliberately bring his guests over to the tapestry and say things like, *let me show you this lovely wall-hanging.* Then he would cough loudly to cover the girls' giggles.

Once he had even brought the King and Queen of Tirragyl over to study the tapestry. That day Tessor and Yorina had pinched themselves so they would not laugh. The Queen had been particularly interested in the tapestry that depicted a king and his children playing in a garden. Tessor still remembered her soft murmurs. *So lovely. What a skilled craftsman.* And Fafa's words: *If you think those princesses are beautiful, you haven't seen my granddaughters.*

But Fafa's voice had been silenced fifteen years ago.

Now it was the voice of his successor that Tessor listened to. Once that voice—smooth as Octora silk—had sounded beautiful to her. It had whispered endearments and promises of undying love. After all these years, Tessor no longer thought that the silky voice sounded beautiful. It was a dangerous voice, one that spun webs of deceit. A voice to trap and destroy. Nobody knew this better than she did, for it was the voice of her husband.

She strained to hear him speak. There was an unusual edginess in Lucian's tone as he asked about a girl called Shara. Tessor had not heard the name before. Was she another girl for him to bed? He used to have a little more discretion when it came to his conquests and concubines. Was he now discussing them openly with the Captain of the Town Guard?

No, there was talk of a betrothal. So not a concubine—a wife. For a moment, a flame of fear seared to life inside her. Was this the time when he would dispose of her and bring in a new wife, one more suited to his purposes? She had known such a time would come. Often she wondered why he hadn't done it already.

Her attention turned back to the voices. *Your ward will marry my son.* For a moment Tessor struggled to understand. Was this girl called Shara to marry Maldor? *Maldor?*

Her mind reeled with what this could mean. Why would Lucian marry his only son, Maldor, to some unknown girl? Tessor would have expected him to choose a daughter from Gwyndorr's gentry as a match for Maldor. It wouldn't even surprise her if he set his sights higher—beyond Gwyndorr—to a family with ties to Tirragyl's royal house.

This small match made no sense to Tessor.

She listened a little longer as Lucian called for Lyndis to bring them mulled wine. She imagined the haughty butler bringing in a tray, bowing to Lucian as if he deserved to be seated in this parlor as Gwyndorr's Lord.

She was the only one remaining who knew he wasn't. All Fafa's servants were gone now. Every one replaced by somebody who would bow to Lucian without question. Somebody who wouldn't compare him to Gwyndorr's last Lord and find him wanting.

Only she remained, standing in the shadows, listening to the whispers. Powerless, for that is what Lucian had made her. Before he came, she had been nurtured by Fafa to be strong. Fafa had not told the queen the whole truth when he said his granddaughters were more beautiful than the princesses of the wall hanging. Only Yorina was lovely. Tessor, with her long, angular face and close-set eyes was plain; some even said ugly. Yet it had never mattered much to Tessor. All that mattered was the pride and love she saw in Fafa's eyes when he looked at her. She was Tessor, his strong one, and—without a living male successor—the one he leaned on to manage his estate as she grew older.

Tessor laid her right cheek against the wall near the peepholes. The icy stone kiss drew her back from the memories, anchored her again to the present. More and more, the past tried to claim her. It called to her through the echoing voices of those long gone. At times Tessor yearned to give herself over to the past, to lose herself to those voices. At others, she feared she might drown in its deep lake of regrets and sorrows. One thing Tessor knew, however, was that she could not let the past claim her yet. She had to be strong one last time for Fafa and vindicate all that had been done.

Tessor had to find a way to bring down her husband.

Chapter 6

From the monastery, Andreo reached Gwyndorr's towering walls in just under an hour. Capital of the Northern Cantref, Gwyndorr's wealth and importance as a trading town—as well as its fortifications—matched those of the royal citadel, Lydora. Andreo glanced up at the archers as he moved between the turrets rising on either side of the gate. More archers were posted along the top of the bailey. If there was one thing to be said for the Captain of the Town Guard, it was that he was meticulous when it came to the defense of the town. Considering he reported to Lord Lucian, he would have to be.

There was already a crush in the gate passage as riders and pedestrians, tradesmen and travellers sought entrance into Gwyndorr. Some seemed to be using the gate merely as shelter from the rain, which had suddenly changed from a drizzle to a downpour. One of the guards recognized Andreo and waved him forward, under the portcullis, and into the sprawling town.

After the quiet of the monastery, Gwyndorr was always an assault to Andreo's senses. The area near the gate was overrun by the makeshift homes of people, many of whom had fled the encroaching Rif'twine Forest. Here a cacophony of bartering voices, screeching cart wheels, and bleating animals assaulted the ears. At least the rain breathed freshness into the air, disguising the usual smells of rotting food and sewage.

Andreo felt clammy from the rain seeping through his monk's cowl, and he quickened his pace, even though it meant his pony's hooves spattered mud onto his cloak. He consoled himself with the thought that there were only three tutoring sessions today, after which he would return to the small cave near the monastery and continue his work on the new potion he was brewing.

Fortunately, the first two sessions, with unusually well-behaved Highborn children, passed smoothly. The houses were nearby each other, and he barely got damp in the crossing. And by mid-afternoon, when Andreo arrived at his final tutoring session, the rain had mercifully stopped.

Randin's house lay on a quiet street near the main town gate. As he rode through the homestead's gate and across the courtyard to the stable, Nicho emerged to take his reins. Andreo was fond of the young groom, one of the few Parashi comfortable to engage him in conversation. Most Parashi were afraid of the Brethren's Word Art powers; in the past—while trying to repel the Highborn invasion—they had been the victims of the Brethren's magic skills.

"Afternoon, Nicho." He slid off the pony's back just inside the stable entrance.

"Afternoon, Brother."

"How is Krola doing?"

"Getting close." Nicho's serious eyes always lit up at mention of the pregnant mare.

"I hope to be here when she births. I've never seen a foaling."

"It's a remarkable sight."

"Is your master here today?"

"No, Brother. He was called out urgently to the town gate this morning and hasn't returned from seeing Lord Lucian."

"Something happen at the gate?"

Nicho shrugged and gave a wry smile. "He didn't exactly mention it over our companionable cup of origo."

"I see what you mean." Andreo chuckled. "Not the kind of information he shares with his Parashi groom?" This was the banter he enjoyed with Nicho. If this young man had been a Highborn, he would have made a remarkable Brodon. Intelligent. Quick-witted. Andreo even suspected the groom might be able to read, although he didn't know who had taught him. There was a heavy price to pay for teaching a Parashi letters.

"Mostly the master issues instructions regarding his horse. Although his whip on my back sometimes communicates a little more."

"Has it been bad again lately?"

"Not since Miss Shara learned to keep her opinions to herself." Nicho shrugged. "It seems I am the scapegoat for her sharp tongue. Or my mother."

"Randin whips you to hurt your mother, and thereby Shara."

"My master's actions aren't always fair."

As he made his way across to the house, Andreo considered that Randin's actions, although not fair, were cunning. He had found the one thing Shara cared for—Marai—and was using that to silence his outspoken ward.

Not many in Tirragyl considered blunt honesty an attractive quality in a young girl, but surprisingly, Andreo did. Every tutoring session with Shara was an interesting one. His only female student, Shara was the one he enjoyed the most. Interrogating everything he said, debating passionately and asking a multitude of questions, Shara's drive for answers far beyond the teachings of his Order had initially unsettled Andreo. Yet, more and more he found his own heart beating with the same questions. Questions no Brother of Taus should ask.

• • •

Shara normally enjoyed her tutoring sessions; Brother Andreo was the only person who welcomed her opinions and questions. Today, however, her thoughts kept drifting to those moments in the stable. The bird. Nicho. And the words he had spoken. *Marai was learning to forget her.* She could not loosen the sorrowful knot those words had wedged in her throat. Shara tried to draw her thoughts back to Brother Andreo's words.

"... and that is why the Highborns had to rule over the Parashi, ensuring the best lives for both our people, Highborn and Lowborn alike."

It sounded wrong to Shara. What did it benefit the Parashi to have Highborn overlords? Brother Andreo was looking at her expectantly, almost as if he anticipated—and welcomed—an argument. Yet Shara's mind was on all that had happened today, starting with the discovery of the rock.

The rock! Would Brother Andreo know about the rock? There was only one way to find out.

"Brother, can you tell us about Tirragyl's power rocks?"

Brother Andreo blinked several times at the sudden change of topic. He narrowed his eyes on Shara. "The power rocks, Shara?"

"Yes, Brother. I don't think you've ever told us about them. Has he, Ghris?"

Ghris shook his head, rather disinterestedly.

"Why do you ask?"

"Just curious."

"Well. It is a rather interesting topic, although not truly my specialty. Ghris, pass me that tablet, and I will draw a diagram."

Shara smiled. She liked the Brother with his thinning blonde hair and blue eyes. Most of the time he was a little distracted, as if his inner thoughts interested him far more than what was happening around him. Yet, in an instant, he could turn his eyes on you with searing intensity, as if he were studying a fascinating specimen. Their previous tutor, Brother Stefan, had been a dour, narrow-minded man who supported the commonly held view that women didn't need an education.

"Right," Brother Andreo said, scratching a triangle onto the tablet. "This is a very useful way of considering the power rocks. First, let's hear what you know about them. Ghris?"

"They're rocks imbued with some kind of magic."

"Indeed. Any ideas as to the source of the magic?"

"Yes," Shara interjected. "The rocks were infused with remnants of old magic when the world was created by the Ancient One."

"The Ancient One? The Parashi God?" Brother Andreo's eyebrows furrowed together, as if considering where Shara could have heard of a deity other than Taus.

Should she tell him that she had grown up with Marai's countless stories of Ab'El, the Ancient One who had ruled Tirragyl before the Highborn invasion? No, better not to distract him from the power rocks.

"What do you think causes the rock's powers, Brother?" she asked quickly.

"The theory disseminated by the Brethren of Taus is that thousands of years ago basic life forms lived and died in the rocks. It is their latent energy that gives the rocks power."

"Sounds like nonsense." Shara said. "How can anything live in a rock?"

"I think it requires more study, Shara," he smiled. "But let's move on." He drew several lines across the triangle. "There are seven known categories of power rocks. Some are very abundant." He pointed to the broad base of the triangle. "Others," now his finger lay on the topmost corner of the triangle, "are extremely rare. And there is an interesting correlation between quantity and power. The abundant stones at the bottom are not very powerful, whereas those at the top are exceptionally potent."

"What is the most potent one of all?" Ghris asked, stirred out of his dreamy stupor.

"Patience, Ghris. We are going to start at the bottom, where we have the common Light Changers. Some argue that this shouldn't even be classified as a power rock, for all it does is refract and channel light."

"So dreary!" Shara said. "We know all about the common rocks—Light Changers, Feather rocks, and Vulcans, Brother. Let's get to the interesting ones that everybody seems too scared to talk about."

Brother Andreo shook his head in an uncommon display of frustration. "Sometimes I can see why Brother Stefan refuses to teach in this household."

"My proudest accomplishment," Shara grinned. "But why is there so little written about the rocks on the higher levels of the triangle?"

"Well," he paused to consider her question. "Power is a fearful thing if used unwisely. These rocks are dangerous in inexperienced hands. We do not understand their forces well. It's not by chance that all these rocks on the upper level of the triangle are buried deep in the earth. Personally, I don't think they were ever meant to be found."

"But can't they also be used for good?"

"Maybe, Shara. But if there's one thing I know it's that using magic always comes at a cost. Either to the person using it, or to the one it is used on. It is wild, untamable, never to be used lightly."

Shara considered this briefly before jamming a finger onto the fourth level of the triangle. "So what are these?"

"Verity Gems. I have only ever seen one of these. In its natural state, it is opaque. When it is used correctly by a practitioner, it can identify lies being told."

"Practitioner?"

"Almost all these rocks are in the hands of a group of women known as 'The Verita Vestals.' Their beliefs are contrary to those of the Brethren, and they are, in fact, a forbidden sect. When the Verity Gem perceives a lie, it changes from its milky state to a dark grey. If the truth is told, it becomes completely clear."

Shara considered this. If this forbidden sect had Verity Gems, wouldn't they be a lot closer to knowing the truth than anybody else? Why would the Brethren of Taus outlaw truth? She almost spoke the thought aloud. No. The rock she had found was, after all, not opaque and she didn't want to draw Brother Andreo away from the topic.

"Then we have the Cerulean Dusk Dreamers," Brother Andreo continued. "Very rare since the Rif'twine crept through the only mine in the northwest."

"What do they look like?" Shara asked, and again the Brother's questioning eyes sought out her own.

"Deep blue. The color of the night sky just before all the light has seeped away. They say it is the most alluringly beautiful rock of all."

An invisible breath of cold crept over Shara's skin. *The color of the night sky*. Just like her rock. She had found a Cerulean Dusk Dreamer.

"What does it do?" She tried to keep her voice even. Nobody could know about the rock in her possession.

"They say that a person who sleeps with a Dusk Dreamer touching their body will have dreams that contain kernels of truth from the past or the future. It's a 'Seeing Rock' of sorts. Very powerful."

The past or future? Shara's heart fluttered. Perhaps all she needed, to discover who she was and why she was a captive in Randin's gilded cage, was the Cerulean Dusk Dreamer.

"The sixth rock is extraordinarily powerful," Brother Andreo continued, "but so rare that I have never come across one." He lowered his voice. "The Mind rock is said to be black, but, according to one writer I read on the subject—has small white flecks from which white light radiates.

"What makes it so powerful?" Ghris asked.

"It gives its possessor access to the thoughts of others. Just imagine."

Shara thought about it. "I don't know that I'd want to know your thoughts, Brother. Or Ghris's for that matter." She looked over at Ghris with a smile. "Loar, Loar, Loar probably."

"Better than what *you* think of all day," he threw back at her, like a real brother would. One of Shara's biggest sorrows when Randin had told her she wasn't their child was the thought that Ghris was not truly her brother.

"And the final rock, Brother?" Ghris asked.

"The Guardian rock. Only two of these exist. One is in the King' s Palace. The other's location is unknown, although legend tells it is hidden in the Guardian Grotto."

"The Guardian Grotto?" Ghris let out a derogatory laugh. "Parashi lore! There's no such place."

"What do the two rocks do?" Shara interjected.

"There is some uncertainty about that, Shara. They say the rocks are particularly powerful because of their rarity. But nobody has yet discovered what that power is because, like the Vulcans, the two rocks need to be placed together to release the power."

"Maybe they're nothing more than glorified Vulcan rocks then, with enough energy to light up all of Gwyndorr." Shara laughed.

"Perhaps, Shara," Brother Andreo said solemnly. "But I wouldn't want to be there when it happened."

CHAPTER 7

Nicho stepped over another puddle and cursed as his foot skated out on the slippery mud. In this neighborhood, it was difficult avoiding all the pitfalls and debris strewn across the road, even in daylight. At dusk on a rainy grey day, it was nearly impossible.

He also wasn't paying enough attention. His mind kept churning on the events of the day, always returning to that strange bird and his encounter with Shara. He was not sure which of the two had unsettled him more. There was something unusual about that bird, something that was difficult to put into words. Maybe it had to do with the way it had been staring at Shara—almost as if it *knew* her. Uncanny.

And Shara? Five years had passed since he had been allowed to play with her and Ghris. He remembered well the fiery little girl with the wild hair flying around her face, constantly telling him and Ghris what to do. Any deviations from her plan, and she would pull herself up to her full height, fold her arms and stare up at them with narrowed eyes, saying, "*I* am the captain of this game." If they didn't relent, she would run to Marai, who would always make sure the older boys gave in to her. He couldn't help smiling at the memory. She may not have had the looks of a Highborn, but she surely had the bossiness of one.

Yet there had been none of that fiery spark in her as she walked away from him that morning. If his words had hurt her, they had been necessary. She had brought enough pain into his mother's life; even into his own. How many lashings had he received in retaliation for something *she* had said to anger Randin? And, as important as it was for his mother to forget the Highborn girl, it was probably just as vital that *she* forget Marai.

He felt the water seep into his boots as his foot again sank into a deep slimy puddle. By the abyss! Why had he agreed to come out tonight? However, Yasmin had been insistent. Her brother wanted to see him. Tonight. It couldn't wait until tomorrow. She merely shook her head when he told her that he had seen Derry that very morning. "Much has happened since then," she had said cryptically, and refused to say another word.

All around him, he heard the familiar sounds of his childhood: young voices laughing, shouting, or crying; adult voices struggling to be heard over the clamor; pots clattering and doors slamming. He could hear the distant notes of a lute, accompanied by clapping. Already a few voices were singing a drunken tune. The Parashi Slum, as everyone outside called it, had been his home once and—despite the stench, the refuse, the rats, the flies—he still felt a strange sense of belonging when he returned to it.

He reached Derry's house and pushed open the door. A single flame now flickered on the table, around which Derry and Hildah sat with a visitor. Jed's voice was raised in excitement, but for once the boy didn't come running in welcome. His short legs stretched out across the lap of the stranger, who sat with his back to the door. As the door banged shut behind Nicho, the man turned. Nicho let out a short curse. "Is that you, Pearce?"

"Yes, indeed. Back from the dead." Derry's older brother rose, tall and muscled, and embraced Nicho. His face was thinner, more angular than Nicho remembered, but maybe it was only the shadows that made it appear so. A jagged line scarred his left eyebrow and forehead.

"Soup, Nicho?" Hildah asked quietly.

"No, thanks, Hildah. I've already eaten."

"Not quite up to your Mama's food?" The long absence had done nothing to soften Pearce's mocking tone.

"By the abyss, Pearce." Nicho sank to the ground between Derry and his brother. "Almost two years and not a word. We all thought ..."

"Yes, you all thought my flesh had rotted and been eaten by the maggots by now." Pearce laughed. "I'm not that easy to kill off. As some of my enemies have discovered to their detriment."

"He killed a man with his bare hands, Nicho," Derry said. "And the man even had a sword and a shield."

"Well, well. That's a tale and a half, isn't it?"

"You doubt its truth?" Pearce asked.

Nicho shrugged. "Anything's possible, of course."

"He found the Parashi Warriors, Nicho!" Derry shook him excitedly by the shoulders. "And he's come back to get men to train."

"Really? The mythical Parashi Warriors?"

"Not so mythical, as it turns out," Pearce said with a fleeting smile. "And I have a day or two to get a few brave men together, before I return. I'll train them there."

"Come on, Pearce. You'd have us believe that those legends we grew up with are true?"

"They're true, Nicho," Pearce said simply, without a hint of mockery. "I've spent two years training with them."

"The Parashi Warriors. The Guardian Grotto. All true?" Nicho had long cast aside the stories of his childhood. He felt a surge of anger that Pearce would suddenly appear with fantastical tales that stirred Derry—and even Jed—to believe in such illusions.

"I swear it on Nana's soul."

Nicho glanced at the old woman hunched in the corner. "You shouldn't do that, Pearce," he said in a low tone.

"Not if I'm lying. But I'm not. It's the truth."

"He's been telling us all about it!" Derry said. "There are over a thousand soldiers and hundreds of horses. And lit-up caves that stretch on and on, and go deeper and deeper into the earth. And they make swords there and —"

"Where is this amazing place?" Nicho interrupted. "How could they hide something that vast for all these hundreds of years of Highborn occupation?"

"It's hidden by Old Magic, Nicho," Derry answered, frowning at his friend's disbelief.

"Old Magic. But of course."

Pearce's eyes held his own and there was sadness in them as he asked, "When did you stop believing in magic, Nicho?"

That question looped through Nicho's mind during the evening, as he sat at the table listening to Pearce's alleged adventures. The candle burned low, and Jed finally succumbed to sleep on his uncle's lap. Pearce regaled them with countless stories. They were filled with a surprising amount of detail. All the facets of the harsh warrior training. Pearce's rapid rise through the ranks to become a commander of a two-hundred-man unit. His admiration for the High Commander, Mikel. Pearce even showed them a beautifully crafted knife as he spoke of the skill of the Parashi blade masters, and a headband woven from rough strands of the trofillia bush—a material used by the ancient Parashi. All warriors wore the headband, Pearce said, and it served a dual purpose as a sling.

Still skeptical, Pearce's stories had nevertheless stirred something in him, had reminded him of a time when he had actually believed that there could be hidden forces for good near at hand.

When did you stop believing in magic?

Nicho knew it wasn't true. He still believed. Only a fool denied that there was magic in this land. The fingers of dark magic crept through every vine of the Rif'twine, and nobody who had skirted the edges of that forest could deny the brooding sense of something malicious in its depths. Then there were the power rocks, imbued with magic—so the Parashi told—at the formation of the world, when Ab'El's words had shaped emptiness into form. Nicho had once held two of these together—Vulcan rocks—and seen the light and warmth they produced. What, too, of the dangerous magical abilities of the Brethren of Taus, who with a single word could move, change, wither, or kill any object of their choosing? No, it wasn't magic that Nicho had stopped believing in.

Nicho had cast aside his childish belief in the Parashi Warriors, or any other noble force that could ride into Gwyndorr and liberate the Parashi, on the day he found his father writhing on the ground, icy fingers still gripping a bunch of gorgon berries. More than six years had passed since then, but the image of his father's haunted eyes were branded into Nicho's soul as permanently as the number the Rif'twine Guards had branded into the old man's arm. His father had been one of the few to return from a Rifter Gang, but the forest had killed him long before the poisoned berries he swallowed did.

That was the day Nicho stopped believing. Not in magic. Not even in old tales. He'd stopped believing in hope.

CHAPTER 8

Sitting cross-legged on her sleeping pallet, Shara unwrapped the rock. It was encased in a square of green satin that Olva had given her as a child, a remnant of some gown. Her hand trembled as she carefully rolled back the material.

Two days had passed since she had discovered the mysterious blue rock and learned that it was a Cerulean Dusk Dreamer. She recalled that first flutter of excitement at the realization that she possessed one of Tirragyl's most powerful rocks. Still, Shara had not looked at, or touched, the rock since then. Her initial thrill was tempered by the fear Brother Andreo's words of warning instilled. *Wild, untamable, never to be used lightly.*

Although she hadn't uncovered the rock since that first day, Shara had been thinking about it. During the day her thoughts kept drifting to it. At night her dreams alluded to it. This is why she had decided to take one final look at the Dusk Dreamer before returning it to Randin's study. The last fold of fabric fell away from the rock.

Astounding. Pleasure coursed through her as she saw the rock again. She had wondered if it might disappoint a second time, but it didn't. If anything, it seemed even more beautiful than before.

Shara picked it up tentatively, Brother Andreo's words still ringing their clarion call of caution through her mind. Yet nothing happened. There was no shift of magic in the room, no pain jarring into her.

She sat, holding the rock lightly, enraptured by its beauty. Far from being untamable, it lay meekly in her hand, gentle and comforting. Shara felt herself relax. The hurt of Nicho's words about Marai learning to forget her, eased for the first time in two days. It mattered less while she held the Dusk Dreamer in her hands.

Shara lay back on her pallet and let the sense of peace wrap around her. She closed her eyes, lulled by the calm of the moment.

No! Her eyes sprang open. No! She mustn't let herself fall asleep holding the Dreamer. It was during sleep that the rock's powers were released. She returned it to the center of the fabric cloth spread across her lap. She would fold it back and wait for a chance to put it back in Randin's study, unseen.

But Shara hesitated. Surely something that beautiful couldn't be dangerous? The Dusk Dreamer was pleasurable to look at and hold. Wouldn't the dreams it induced be just as good?

She recalled Andreo's words. *A seeing rock. Kernels of truth from the past or the future.* Shara didn't much care to know what happened in the future, but she yearned to know more about her past. Her parents. How she had come to be here. Why she felt like a prisoner in Randin's house. Anger flared through her at the thought that Randin and Olva were withholding truth she deserved to know. Now, lying before her, was the key to defeat them at their own game. The rock would give her power over them.

Shara made up her mind. She picked up the Cerulean Dusk Dreamer again. She would use it just once to see exactly what it did. If the power was too fearful, she would simply put the rock back in Randin's study when she awoke, and never think of the Dreamer again. At least she might gain some knowledge of her past.

Shara lay back on her pallet and, this time, did not fight the encroaching sleep.

Shara strolled in a vast, rolling field of grass that stretched on as far as her eyes could see. She breathed in the sweet scent of flowers and marveled at the wide spaces around her. On and on she walked without seeing anybody and without any change in the scenery. Eventually she sat down on the grass and then stretched out, resting her head on the soft ground, marveling at the beauty of the cloud-flecked sky. She closed her eyes for just a moment and drifted off to the sound of distant laughter. When she opened her eyes again, it sounded louder and closer—children's laughter—and voices saying "again, again!" She looked intently around and finally her eyes spotted the small figures far in the distance—running, skipping, jumping, and rolling. Joyfully she ran to join them but the faster she ran, the farther they seemed to move away. She shouted, hoping to gain their attention, but nobody turned to look at her, although she could still clearly hear their happy voices. Eventually her throat ached from the effort of calling, and she stopped running and looked up again.

The sky had changed. Suddenly it wasn't a beautiful summer-blue anymore, but darker, more ominous. Lightning flashed far above her head, and she looked around for somewhere to shelter, but there was nowhere. The children were gone now; she was alone as the first angry drops of rain pelted down, stinging her with their intensity. And as they strafed the ground, something started to coil at her feet. She screamed and began to run, but as she looked behind her she could see that more and more of the small worm-like creatures were spiraling from the ground. Now they were around her and ahead of her, cutting off all hope of escape. She stopped running and felt the cold creeping up and around her legs. Leaves were unfurling from them and for a moment relief flooded through her—not worms or snakes, but plants. Yet, her relief was short lived as she tried to move her legs and found that the vines were as strong as ropes. She was trapped in their mesh and still they kept growing. Now they were up to her waist, now her chest and she could feel them pressing in on her, stealing her breath, so that even her last scream for help was little more than a whisper.

Shara's heart hammered a fast rhythm in her chest as her eyes flew open. It took her a moment to realize that she was back in her room and that no plants held her in a deathly grasp. Her right hand still gripped the Cerulean Dusk Dreamer, and as she became aware of how hot it felt in her hand, she started. Never had she had a dream as vivid or frightening as that one; it could only be because of the rock. She thrust it across the room and then lay quietly, willing her heart and breathing to slow down.

She tingled all the way from her scalp to her toes, as if parts of her body had just come alive for the very first time. Sounds were louder than before and, even though her eyes were closed, colors and light swam in and out of her vision.

Shara lay on her pallet a long time before the strange feelings began to subside. *Magic always comes at a cost*, Brother Andreo had said. How right he had been. She sat up and the world tilted slightly.

The rock had to go. Its power was too great—too frightening—for her.

Shara climbed from the pallet and stumbled to the far side of the room where the Cerulean Dusk Dreamer lay. She bent down and carefully picked it up. It was no longer hot, only as comfortably warm as is had been before, and just as beautiful.

She would take it back tomorrow and never think of the rock again.

Of all the places to eavesdrop in the forgotten passage, this was the best. The crack between two large stones near the mantelpiece gave Tessor a perfect view into Lucian's private dining chamber. His round table stood near the fireplace, so Tessor could listen to conversations with ease. When a large fire roared in the grate, the hiss and crackle of burning wood made it difficult to hear, but today only a small fire had been stoked—enough to warm the wall where Tessor stood, but not enough to obscure the voices of Lucian and Maldor.

Lucian still picked at the duck-leg Lyndis had brought in earlier. Maldor, long finished, stared sullenly at his father over the rim of his goblet. It struck Tessor anew how much he looked like the Lucian she had first laid eyes on. Tall, commanding, assured. How handsome she had thought Lucian to be. If that young Lucian had had hints of Maldor's arrogance and cruelty, she hadn't seen it when he first arrived at Fafa's manor, riding on a magnificent stallion and claiming to be a landowner from the South. Lucian had looked at her in a way no man ever had. Others had asked Fafa for her hand before, yet she had known they only wanted the lands and title. Lucian had seemed different—gentle and tender. He had made her laugh. When she spoke he had listened. She had seen her own longing reflected in his eyes. For the first time she had known how it felt to be Yorina. Beautiful. The object of someone's desire.

Tessor took a deep breath of the smoke-laced air and shook free of the memories. She must stay focused on the voices. One day she might hear something that could be a weapon in her hands.

"The captain's *ward*?" As always, Maldor's tone was belittling. "Why? When I can have my pick of Gwyndorr's finest daughters?" He smirked. "I have already plucked a few of those fine morsels, I might add."

Like his father in more than just looks, Tessor thought. Was this why she felt the fine string of her aversion tighten every time she looked at him? Would it have been different if he were her own son and not another woman's? Perhaps then she would have agreed with Gwyndorr's womenfolk that he was charming and suave.

"Because it was decided and agreed on many years ago," Lucian said.

"You are Lord of Gwyndorr and I am your heir." Clinks of goblets and bottles told Tessor that Maldor drank, as always, too much wine "It's a ridiculous match."

"Whether you think so or not, it's happening. I will represent you at the betrothal meeting in two week's time. The wedding takes place within two weeks after that."

"What does this girl even look like?"

"I last saw her as a child." Linens rustled as he finished. "In fact you were with me when we visited the captain's house."

Maldor scoffed. "By Taus! That scruffy-looking child playing in the dust with a Parashi servant?" The goblet hit the table so hard Tessor wondered if it snapped in half. "She's a half-breed, Father."

"She isn't." Lucian's chair scraped away from the table. "You don't have to think her attractive, Maldor. You just have to wed and bed her. Even just once if that's how you want things to be."

"Like you and Crazy Tessy, you mean?" Maldor too rose to his feet. "At least you got a title and lands for your one repulsive night. What do I get?"

Footsteps stalked to the door and the crash of it reverberated into Tessor, much like his parting sentence had done. *Crazy Tessy. Repulsive night.* Why did the words still hold the power to hurt her?

CHAPTER 9

"Are ya feelin' unwell, Nicho?" Marai frowned as she looked at her son's half-eaten plate of food.

"Just not so hungry, Ma." He pushed the plate away. "I'd best be off. Just going over to Derry's."

"You sure 'tis a good idea on the Highborn's sacred day, Nicho?"

"Don't worry Ma. I know a way into the slum that the Guards will never find."

"Yaz says Pearce is here?"

"That's right."

"Said something about him finding the Parashi Warriors?"

"So he claims." *Why couldn't Yasmin keep her mouth shut?*

"You won't go listenin' to all his talk of rebellion and uprisin', will you, Nic?"

"Now why would I do a thing like that, Ma?" He rose and brushed her forehead with a kiss.

"He's dangerous, that boy is. He'll go fillin' y'r mind with all that fightin' talk."

"Don't worry about me, Ma. Even if Pearce is telling the truth about the Grotto, they wouldn't want *me*."

His mother gave him a long, searching look. "Y'r a gentle soul, Nic. I recall ya cryin' at every little dead mouse in my pantry. But don't let anyone call ya a coward, son. Courage is more than being good with a sword. 'Tis carin' and protectin' and speakin' out for those who can't do any of that for themselves."

"Hard to do any of that under the Highborn's abuse." Nicho's fist clenched in anger. "The Rif'twine soon silences any voice that speaks out too loudly against them."

"Hush, Nicho." His mother looked anxiously at the door. "Don't ya be talkin' like that. See, Pearce's already got ya around to his way of thinkin'."

"He hasn't. I'm not sure the sword is the answer. But I've lived my whole life being mistreated by the Highborns, and I don't want Jed to grow up with it too."

Nicho considered telling his mother that he was fighting the Highborns in his own way by tutoring the boys, but he knew it would just cause her anxiety. Even now her hands fluttered to her mouth and her forehead creased with concern.

"Not all Highborns are bad, Nicho. They're jus' ordinary people who have continued what their fathers did and their forefathers started." Marai shifted her large weight. "They're the same as us. Blood and flesh and feelings."

Nicho shrugged. It was difficult for him to think of the Highborns that way. He didn't want to have this conversation with his mother—it confused him every time.

His mother wasn't ready to end it yet, however. "And ya know how I feel about Shara, don't ya? She's like a daughter to me, she is. I don't want my own son to be hurtin' her people now, do I?"

Shara again. His mother brought her into every conversation.

"Ma," he said as gently as he could. "Miss Shara's out of your life now. I really think you should try to forget her."

"Forget her?" His mother sputtered on the spoon of potatoes she had just lifted to her mouth. "How can I forget her? I *raised* her, Nicho. More than them Highborns in that house, that's for sure. Forgettin' Shara would be like forgettin' my own flesh and blood."

"She isn't flesh and blood, Ma. She's a Highborn."

"Does that girl act like a callous Highborn, Nicho?"

"Well ... sometimes. Remember how bossy she was when we were children and —"

"She was a mere child. Strong-willed, for sure, and that hasn't changed much." Marai laughed. "But she cares for me, Nicho. For our people. All those things that she says to Lady Olva and Master Randin —"

"You mean all those things I probably got a beating for?"

"That took courage Nicho. It takes courage to stand up against what's wrong. She's a special one, she is."

"Still, Ma. I really think you should let her go."

His mother merely shook her head sadly, and it reminded him of the pain he had seen in Shara's face two days earlier. What had he told her? Something about his mother learning to forget her? He felt a sudden wave of shame. Their love was far deeper than he had realized.

"You be careful with Yaz's brother," Marai said. "There's anger and hatred in his eyes."

"Of course, there's anger. What the Highborns are doing is wrong."

"I know, son, but that kind of hatred can be contagious."

"I'll be careful, Ma." He rose and was already at the door when he made a decision. He turned back to face her and said softly, "I saw Miss Shara on Friday."

"You did?" His mother's face brightened.

"At the stable. She told me to tell you she sends her greetings."

He slipped out of the house before he could see the full effect of his words. The day had been dry, and it made it a little easier to reach Derry's house. Again, there was no child throwing arms around his neck. Nicho made out Jed's sleeping form on the straw pallet that Derry and Hildah shared. Hildah sat next to him stroking his small back; her eyes looked red from crying. Nana was slumped near her. Sitting at the low table, Pearce and Derry were having a spirited conversation with three other men.

"Look, Nicho," Derry held out a narrow strip of green material. "It's the warrior headband."

"I know. Pearce showed it to me last time."

"But this one's mine," Derry said proudly.

"Yours?"

"A few of the lads from around here have agreed to come back with me tomorrow," Pearce interjected. "Madoc. Pwyll. Curtis." They nodded a greeting at Nicho as Pearce pointed to each one in turn. He paused before he said, "Derry is also coming."

"Derry?" Nicho looked up sharply at his friend. Jed had woken up and toddled over to his father. He curled up on Derry's lap, thumb in mouth. "You can't take Derry, Pearce. He has a wife and child to look after."

"The plan is to get the lads there to start their training and then smuggle their families over too." Pearce didn't meet Nicho's gaze. "We'll bring Hildah and Jed—and maybe even Nana—to the Guardian Grotto as soon as we have a safe way of moving between Gwyndorr and the Grotto. It's one of the things High Commander Mikel sent me to arrange."

"But what happens to them in the meantime, Pearce?"

"They've got Yasmin bringing them some food. They'll be fine."

"They are barely scraping by." Nicho's voice rose with anger. "You can't take Derry, Pearce!"

"It's his choice, not yours," Pearce said coldly, finally meeting Nicho's glare with one of his own.

"Derry, please don't do this." Nicho turned to his friend, but even as he said the words, he knew they were useless. "Derry. Jed and Hildah need you here," Nicho tried one last time.

"Nana and Yasmin will look after them," Derry said with a smile. "And Pearce says he'll come fetch them soon."

"It's too dangerous. Did Pearce tell you what they do to you if they find you on the roads? And what if the Town Guard arranges a slum sweep again and come for Jed? What then Derry?"

A flicker of doubt passed over Derry's face, but as he glanced at his brother, his smile returned. "If I'm with Pearce I'll be safe. Pearce said so. And there won't be a sweep for a few more weeks. They just did one. By then Hildah and Jed and Nana will be at the Grotto with me."

"Why don't you come too, Nicho?" Pearce asked softly. "That way you can keep an eye on Derry. And you can escape this cursed Highborn town."

"I can't Pearce. I ..." It was a cruel thing for Pearce to play on his concern for Derry.

"Are you scared?"

"No! I just can't do that to my mother." Or his pupils. He'd always told them letters were stronger than the sword. That one day their knowledge could be the weapon that freed their people. If that was true—and Nicho believed in his heart that it was—he knew he had to stay and teach them. There was nobody else who would.

"We'll bring Marai along too ... later. We could really use your skills with the horses."

Nicho shook his head. Pearce's stories had convinced him that there was a small resistance group, even though he found it difficult to believe that there could be a whole underground society that the Highborns hadn't found in all this time. Yet, Nicho knew that his place was not there. It was here with the boys and—when he was older—Jed. *They* were the ones who would one day change Gwyndorr and maybe even Tirragyl.

Pearce leaned across the table and gripped Nicho's wrist, his voice dropping. "You and I are more similar than you think, Nicho. You think I don't see that anger smoldering in your eyes? Soon you will hate the Highborns as much as I do. We were not made to bow and scrape, you and me. We were made for something greater."

Pearce broke the grip and straightened up again. "Think about it. We leave tomorrow at sunset."

In the silence that followed, the air was filled with all the unspoken pain, anger, and fear that had crept through this house—through this whole part of Gwyndorr—for longer than even the old ones could remember. It tore at friendships and families, stealing their once proud past and stunting any hope of a future. To be one of the Parashi—the Horse People—had once filled them with pride, but now it was a curse word, carrying only shame.

Nicho was about to rise when a voice crackled through the air. Nana spoke in a raspy, high voice and for just a moment her eyes were filled with a startling lucidity. She pointed a withered finger toward Nicho. "You warn them, Niki. Nothing good will come of this. Nothing good at all."

• • •

Randin rode beside Issor, his second-in-command, through the quiet streets of Gwyndorr. It was the first day of the week, when tavern doors remained closed and traders did not set out their wares. This was the day ordained by the Brethren of Taus to be a sacred day and those who violated it would find themselves before the Brethren's Council of Six, which imposed penalties and meted out punishments. For severe infringements, they might even use their Word Arts.

Occasionally Randin heard the chant of mantras from a home. He had learned the words to some of these himself as a child. *Taus is divine. Taus is great. To Taus be true.*

Yet most of Gwyndorr's inhabitants did not spend the day in meditation. Rather, they stayed indoors, drinking mead or cider and keeping a wary eye out for the Town Guard patrols. Drinking on the sacred day had its dangers. It was mainly wild, drunken behavior that grew the Brethren's coffers and gave their Word Art trainees practice in inflicting pain. Of course, Randin benefited on sacred days too. People were always willing to make a donation to stay out of the council's grasp.

Randin and Issor now rode toward the Parashi Slum. The Lowborns had to be the most careful of all on the sacred day. Even though they despised Taus as the one who had led the invasion into their land, for them a sacred day infringement meant only one thing—the Rif'twine.

The slum was quiet, the Parashi too careful to drink on this day. Rather they spent it in small groups, telling their children about their own god, Ab'El. The soft songs Randin often heard on passing a house were much more beautiful than his own people's mantras. If he was alone, he would sometimes stop and close his eyes to listen. Strangely, the haunting melodies stirred something in him.

Today, with Issor by his side, he did not stop. He was thinking instead of Lord Lucian's words two days before. *An entire rifter unit wiped out.* It was almost as if the forest grew more malicious as they became better at holding it back.

"Lord Lucian tells me Rifter Unit Twenty-eight was wiped out last week," Randin said. "Did the Rifter Guards not report this?"

"No, Captain."

"Probably thought they'd end up at the stake for a good lashing." Randin shook his head. "Never heard of a whole unit wiped out. You?"

"Never."

"We need to put a new unit together. Quickly too. I was hoping to pick up a few straying Parashi off the street today."

"They're too careful for that. Especially on sacred days."

"We'll have to do a slum sweep."

"Absolutely," Issor grinned. "Shall I arrange it for tomorrow, just after sunset, Captain?"

"Fine. We only need twelve adults and four children. No more."

"Of course."

"Keep the men reined in better this time, Issor. No unnecessary violence."

CHAPTER 10

Andreo's sturdy pony carried him over the rough, boulder-strewn ground with her usual ease. Today Andreo had managed to avoid Brother Angustus's watchful eyes and slip out of the monastery just before Morning Rites. He felt his usual surge of anticipation. The growth of the Rif'twine was so prolific that every time he visited it, Andreo found something new.

Andreo always went back to the same place. Halfway between the monastery and the town of Gwyndorr lay that part of the forest that was allotted to Rifter Unit Twenty-nine. It was a stretch of forest about five hundred paces long, and two hundred paces deep, until the Dimzone turned into the impenetrable Darkzone. Outside the forest, the borders of the unit's territory were marked by two triangular yellow flags; at each of these flags stood a guard from the Rif'twine Guard Unit.

"Morning, Brother," the guard said as Andreo dismounted and handed him the reins of his mount.

"Morning, Dorcan."

The guard held out his hand expectantly.

Andreo sighed and tugged at the small pouch slung across his back. Silence always came at a cost, but fortunately he had found the perfect currency. He dropped six dark green cylindrical shapes into Dorcan's hands. One of his discoveries had been that the roots of the yorak bush had a sedative effect. Ground and rolled into the leaves of the same bush, it gave a pleasant sensation for at least half an hour after being lit and inhaled. Andreo was rather proud of this, an invention he called a rollroot.

"Red needs some too," Dorcan indicated the guard at the other flag.

"That's for both of you."

"Not enough." Dorcan shook his head. "Do you know what kind of trouble we can get into for letting you go in there?"

"I only have another two," Andreo lied.

"It'll do. This time. Next time we want five each."

Andreo mumbled as he handed over another two rollroots. "Don't let my mount inhale any of that smoke," he said, pointing to his pony. "She ate a few from my pouch and was completely useless for half a day."

The guard laughed, already lighting the first of the rolled leaves.

"Are they in the Rif'twine already?"

"Yup. Except those three." The guard pointed behind him to where two rifter sleeping platforms stood. They were built on tall stilts to keep the forest animals away in the night. Andreo could see three forms curled up on one of the platforms.

"What happened to them?" Brother Andreo asked warily.

The guard shrugged indifferently.

"Can I go over and take a look?"

"Yes."

Brother Andreo walked to the base of the platforms and called out. After a few moments, a rope ladder was thrown down and, with some difficulty, Andreo clambered to the top.

A young woman with short hair met him. Her cheeks were sunk in and her eyes had the vacant look that was so common amongst the rifters. Andreo recognized her as the one who had shown him the dragon lily a few weeks ago.

"Frieya, isn't it?"

Something flared to life in her eyes for a moment. She laughed bitterly and pointed to the number branded in her arm. "Not anymore. Now just rifter 29-351."

"You're still Frieya to me," Andreo said softly, making his way over to the other two figures. "What's wrong with them?"

"The old one has been on the unit almost three years. I can't find anything wrong with him. He has the usual fire-larvae here"—she pointed to the dark objects wriggling under the skin on the man's legs—"but we all have them. Burns like the abyss, but it won't kill him."

Andreo felt the man's forehead. He was hot. The man mumbled something and his eyes fluttered open. But his eyes rolled back into his head until only the whites were visible. It was distressing to watch.

"He's been doing that since last night. I think he's near the end," Frieya said flatly. Andreo agreed. He didn't think there was much more he could do for the man.

"How about him?" He turned his attention to the small figure lying dead-still on the other side of the platform.

"A rooter," she said, as if no further explanation was necessary. Andreo heard the sorrow etched in her voice.

"Someone you care about?"

"It's Ethan, my brother. He's only eight."

Andreo knelt by the boy, whose dark green eyes opened and stared intently at the monk.

"It's only that strange plant monk, Ethan," Frieya whispered, stroking her brother's forehead. "You go back to sleep. I won't let anything else hurt you."

He closed his eyes again, until a cough wracked through his body. His sister pulled him up and held him against her chest until the attack ended, before gently laying him down again.

"I think it's spore illness," she said softly. "Most of us have a touch of it."

It was more than spore illness, Andreo thought. He had caught sight of the boy's almost-black fingers. He knew it was the first sign of gorgon poisoning. The sap of the berries crept under nails and through skin, eating away at the flesh and spreading its deadly touch throughout the entire body. It may not have been as fast as the toxin of the Poison Tree, but ultimately it was just as deadly.

"Does he eat or drink anything?"

"He has some sips of water," Frieya said. "I make him have them."

"Good girl. Soak these in some hot water and let him drink it when it's cooled." Andreo dropped some dried frillbough leaves in her hand.

The girl's eyes briefly lit up with something that resembled hope. "Will it make him better?"

"It will diminish his pain," Andreo said, not meeting her eyes again.

Sorrow weighed down his thoughts as he made his way down the rope ladder, past the guards and into the Rif'twine. He knew all the rhetoric: the forest was an enemy and the rifters the noble soldiers that fought it; the few would be sacrificed to save the many. It all made perfect sense ... until you looked into a dying boy's eyes.

He pushed the thought away as he took his first steps into the Dimzone. One thing he had learned was that walking through the Rif'twine required complete concentration. He walked slowly, as the rifters had taught him, watching intently where he put his feet. The air here was cooler, and he always felt strangely breathless on entering the Dimzone, as if every breath required an effort. He attributed this to the grainy spores that hung in the air and left a gritty sensation on your skin, in your mouth and even in your eyes if you were here too long. The forest itself was quiet, although Andreo knew that there was much life in the undergrowth. The rhythmic slicing of the rifters' scythes sounded like a heartbeat and only the occasional cough punctuated the pattern.

The smell of the air was unpleasant, reminding Andreo of a combination of cooking cabbage and rotting meat. Last time Frieya had shown him the plant responsible for the repulsive smell—the large Dragon Lily—whose odor attracted small rodent scavengers, which would then be caught in its twines and slowly ingested. Andreo had been fascinated; he had never seen a carnivorous plant before. Of all the dangers of the forest, it was the smell that Andreo found the most disconcerting. It clung to the back of his throat for a long time after he left the Rif'twine, and if he hadn't been so fixated on discovering new remedies, it was *this* that would have kept him away.

Rifter Units had a particular structure, one that had been set in place by Lord Lucian himself. They always consisted of fifteen rifters and two rooters, and the hierarchy was based solely on the length of time a person had been in the unit. Rifter 1 was therefore the person who had been there the longest, and he or she became the overseer of the group. If there were no escapees from his unit in a period of two years, the overseer was allowed to return to Gwyndorr, after spending a month in seclusion to ensure he carried no forest illnesses. The overseer assigned everybody their place and task in the forest: cutting away vines; weeding out the small poison tree shoots that sprung up almost overnight; eradicating the invasive thorn bushes or the Slinker liana, whose twines dug deep into the skin and caused infection if they were not pulled away quickly; or escorting the rooters deep into the Dimzone.

The overseer—a short man the others called Bristle—came over as he saw Andreo. His wild hair always stood upright, giving him an almost comical appearance.

"Morning Brother," he said with the usual wariness Andreo heard in Parashi voices. The Parashi had a deep fear of the Brethren's magic arts, and always treated them as carefully as one would treat anybody who could do you bodily harm with just one word.

"Morning, Bristle. Where is everyone?" It was difficult to look deep into the Dimzone, but Andreo had the impression that there were far fewer rifters at work than usual.

"We're having to work half of Unit Twenty-eight's area, until they bring in some new rifters."

"Why? What happened to the unit?"

"All dead. Overnight."

"By Taus! What happened?"

"No one is sure. Some say they must have all taken the gorgon berries, but the red-haired guard saw the bodies and says he doesn't think it was gorgon poison."

"What else could it be?"

"Have you heard of the deliria bloom?"

"Yes, but isn't it too early for it to flower? It's only dangerous twice a year, isn't it?"

"We're expecting it in the next two weeks or so. This might have just been an early flowering one."

"By Taus! The whole unit?" Death was an ever present reality in the Rifter Units, but Andreo had never heard of a whole unit dying in one night.

"It could be the Rif'iends." Most frightening of all Rif'twine creatures, were the so-called human shaped ones with magical powers. No rifters had lived to tell of an encounter with such a creature, but many claimed they had seen them lurking in the Darkzone. "Or it might even be something else we've never come across," Bristle said morosely.

There were constantly new dangers discovered in the forest. Whether these had always lurked in the Rif'twine's depths, or had evolved over time, was uncertain. It was one of the reasons Andreo brought parchment and a pen with him for each visit; he was cataloguing all the plant life of the Rif'twine.

"Right, Bristle." He handed the man two root rolls. "What have you got to show me today?"

CHAPTER 11

Shara had decided never to set foot in the stables again after her last conversation with Nicho, but on Monday morning Brother Andreo arrived in a rather disheveled state to tutor Ghris and her. "Ah, you are both here. Good. That large grey mare, Krola, is giving birth. We need to go quickly if we are to see it. Foaling can be a fast process."

Shara followed Ghris and Brother Andreo across the courtyard, shielding her eyes from the piercing light. Since using the Dusk Dreamer, bright lights, loud sounds, and even sudden movements jarred pain into her head.

It took a while for Shara's eyes to adjust to the darkness inside the stable, although she could hear the mare pawing the ground in a stall to her left. She followed Andreo and Ghris to its entrance, where Nicho and the stable master, Helvin, stood watching intently. Nicho looked up, his eyes lingering briefly on her face before turning back to study the mare.

Shara was soon engrossed in the drama of the birth, even forgetting her headache.

Krola lay on her side, her abdomen heaving with contractions. Shara could see one of the foal's legs, encased in a milky-colored membrane, starting to emerge. With successive pushes, the head and second foreleg appeared.

"The head and shoulders are the most difficult part," Nicho whispered, before he slowly stepped into the stall, speaking in a soothing voice to the mare.

Shara could see the tension etched on Helvin's face as time passed and the mare's exertions did not bring any further progress.

"Must be a big one," he muttered, and Shara imagined him pacing this nervously when his own wife was in labor, for Marai had told her once that the older man had a large brood of children, who now had children of their own.

The mare appeared to be tiring and Nicho knelt by her side, still speaking softly. "I'm going to make it easier, Kro. I'll give you a hand."

He took hold of the foal's legs above the knee joint and, as the next push trembled through Krola's body, pulled gently but firmly. Shara saw the foal start to move, until it slid out of its mother.

At that moment, it was as if everyone let out a deep sigh of relief, which resonated with Nicho's joyful outburst. "That's my girl, Kro. I knew you could do it."

"Well done, lad." Helvin slapped Nicho's back, as he returned to their side. "You have a touch with these horses, there's no doubt about it."

Brother Andreo nodded his appreciation. "It was remarkable. Thank you for letting us watch, Helvin." He smiled in Nicho's direction. "You did well, Nicho."

"Thank you, Brother."

Brother Andreo and Ghris left, but Shara stood a moment longer, watching the mare licking and nibbling the membrane off the foal. Nicho came to stand next to her.

"This is an important bonding time for them," he said. "Soon the foal will rise and begin to suck."

"It's beautiful."

"Miss Shara?" As she turned to look at him, his gaze dropped to the ground. "Helvin and I wondered if you would like to name the foal?"

"Me? Why would you want *me* to name her?" A flush of pleasure rose to her cheeks.

"It's a tradition that one of the gentlemen or ladies of the house names a foal. I could ask Master Ghris, but he named the last one." He motioned to the restless young stallion in the next stall. "Aventor. It means 'The Wild One' in the Enderite tongue. It suits him, I am afraid."

Shara laughed at Nicho's expression, a wistful tussle between pride and lament.

"Let's not allow Ghris to curse this poor little foal with any such name. I would be honored to name her, Nicho. Let me give it some thought."

His eyes sought out her own for a brief moment. "I gave my mother your message," he said as he looked down again. "It made her happy." As the dimples creased his cheeks, Shara felt a tingle high in her chest. "It seems you're not an easy one to forget, Miss Shara."

· · ·

When Shara had still been allowed to visit Marai, Andreo had often accompanied her to the kitchen after tutoring. Marai had always fussed over the two of them, making them cups of berry-tea and teasingly scolding them for stealing morsels of whatever she was preparing at the time.

Since Shara's banishment, Andreo had not returned to the kitchen. Yet, today—after the sadness of seeing the dying young rifter—he longed for Marai's warm, practical insights and wisdom. He sensed he would find comfort sitting with the cook for a little while.

As he crossed the courtyard, he glanced around. Randin couldn't very well banish *him* from the kitchen, but still Andreo preferred not to be seen. Also because he still had some frillbough leaves hidden in his robe, which he wanted to give to Marai.

The yeasty smell of baking bread welcomed him. Marai, pounding dough for the next loaves, didn't hear him come in.

"Morning, Marai."

Joy flashed on her face as she looked up, but her searching eyes didn't find the one she longed for. Andreo felt remorse for bringing her such false hope.

"Mornin', Brother." She recovered quickly and smiled. "'Tas been a while."

"How have you been?"

"Missin' my Shara. Ya heard the Master won't let her come here no more?"

"I'm sorry."

"Ya jus' saw her though." Marai's face lightened. "How's she lookin'?"

"Good. We watched the foaling together. She found it remarkable. We talked a lot about it afterward."

"Krola had her little 'un?"

"Not so little actually." Andreo laughed. "A difficult birth. Nicho was incredible."

Marai beamed. "He's got a gift, has my Nicho. Same as his grandfather." She wiped her hands on her apron. "But where are my manners? Cup of tea, Brother?"

"That would be lovely, thank you."

The wooden bench creaked a little as he sat down near the fire, which crackled and hissed as Marai hung the copper kettle above the flames.

"Where are Yasmin and Fortuni today?"

"Sent 'em to the market. Gives me some peace and quiet. Young 'uns always twitterin' on 'bout somethin'. Shara was different, mind ya. She thought before she spoke." Marai looked over at him searchingly. "But here I'm twitterin' myself. Ya look tired, Brother."

"I'm sad. A young boy I know is dying."

"No!" Her hand fluttered to her heart. "A pupil of yours?"

He hesitated. "A rooter."

"Really?" She tilted her head in question. "Now what would a good Brother of Taus be doin' settin' his sacred foot in the Rif'twine?"

"There's a unit I visit sometimes," he said evasively. "I bring them some leaves that grow near the monastery, to help them with pain. In fact," he pulled the frillbough leaves out of his robe and held the small pouch out to her, "perhaps you could use them too. You get called to births and illnesses, don't you?"

She sniffed at the pouch. "Bitter. What's it called?"

"Frillbough. Just steep it in hot water."

"Frillbough?" She looked at him curiously. "My grandmother spoke of havin' it as a child. Our healers used it, and you Highborns banned it, did ya not?'

"Do you want it, Marai?" Irritation stirred in him. Not many Parashi had the audacity to question him so closely.

"'Course I want it," she grinned. "Ya bring me some leaves every few weeks, and I'll make ya a marvelous fig pie every new moon."

He laughed. "Agreed."

"I'm sorry 'bout y'r young friend, Brother," she said as she placed his steaming tea next to him on the bench. "I'll be prayin' for the Ancient One to comfort ya and those who love him."

"Do you think your Ancient One listens to prayers for Highborn monks?" He asked playfully, but she was wise enough to sense its depth.

"No doubt. Ab'El is not just the Parashi God. He's the God of us all."

"How do you think Taus feels about that?"

She shrugged. "Sure he doesn't like it too much, but 'tis the truth. And when ya fight against truth, ya always lose."

• • •

That afternoon, Nicho pushed open the door to Derry's house with a heavy heart. The sorrow of having to say farewell to his friend drove away all the joy of the morning's foaling, and of Shara's smile when he told her he'd given his mother her message.

Derry leapt to his feet as he saw Nicho. "Nicho. You've decided to come! We're going to be the best Parashi Warriors ever."

"Derry ..." Nicho was aware of Pearce's intent gaze. "... I'm not coming with you. I just came to say goodbye."

"You're not coming?" Derry looked crestfallen. "But when we were boys, it's all we talked about. Remember?"

"I know, Derry. But we're not boys anymore." Nicho glanced at Hildah and Jed. "We have responsibilities."

"But the warriors need you! Pearce says they need you to help train the horses."

"Yes. Pearce says a lot of things, doesn't he?" Nicho met Pearce's gaze.

"But —"

"Let it go, Derry," Pearce interrupted his brother. "Every man must decide for himself. Not everyone has what it takes to be a warrior."

Nicho held Pearce's gaze a little longer before turning back to Derry. "Be careful, Derry." He pulled his friend into an embrace. "You have to come back for Hildah and Jed, you hear me?"

Tears stung his eyes as he stepped back from Derry. He had to fight the desire to turn and run from the house, but he had come for one more reason. "Pearce, could I speak with you outside for a moment?"

"Fine." Pearce rose and pushed past Nicho. "What is it?" he asked as the door slammed closed behind them. "We still have a lot of plans to make before we leave."

"You know taking Derry is a mistake, don't you, Pearce?"

"Derry has his strengths," Pearce said evasively. "They'll be able to use him in the armor workshops."

"He's more valuable here than there, and you know it."

"We've been over this already, Nicho. Derry wants to come, and I won't stand in the way of such courage and commitment."

"It's not courage, Pearce! He worships the ground you walk on and would follow you to the abyss and back. Only you can tell him to stay. He doesn't understand the dangers."

"He's going." Pearce turned back to the door, but Nicho grabbed him by the arm and pulled him back. There was only a handbreadth between them as they glared at each other.

"Just understand one thing, Pearce. If something happens to Derry, I will scour the highlands and hunt you down like a wild pig." Nicho shoved Pearce toward the door. Then he turned, desperate to be away from here.

He was halfway down the street when he heard running footsteps.

"Nicho! Wait!" He stopped to allow Derry a chance to reach him. "Nicho, now that you are staying ..." Derry struggled to catch his breath, "... will you look after Hildah and Jed while I am gone?"

"I can't look after them as well as you do, Derry," Nicho said softly, willing his friend to make the right choice.

"I know. I don't mean you have to come and stay with them. But just make sure they are safe. That they have food. You know? Just till I come back for them?"

It was no small thing Derry was asking of him, Nicho thought, even if Derry didn't realize it himself. Yet Nicho didn't hesitate as he said, "I will look after them, Derry. I promise."

CHAPTER 12

The news always spread surprisingly fast, even though the guards closed off all the streets leading into the slum. A few young boys usually managed to escape their net and put out the word, which carried through Gwyndorr's streets faster than the eastern wind.

This time it was Yasmin who flung open Marai's door with a wild expression. Startled, Nicho looked up from where he sat on his sleeping pallet as Marai lumbered to her feet. "What is it, Yaz?"

"Slum sweep." Yasmin's voice wavered.

"Oh no." Marai's hand flew to her mouth.

Yasmin's eyes sought out Nicho's. "Pearce and Derry left earlier this evening," she said unnecessarily, for it was the first thing he thought as he heard her words. He was already reaching for his boots.

"Nicho? What are you goin' to do?" Trepidation filled Marai's voice.

"To see if Hildah and Jed made it through."

"Now?"

"When else?"

"You'll be walkin' right into a Town Guard unit."

He shrugged. "I have to go, Ma. I promised Derry I'd look after them."

"But Nicho, there's nothin' you can do now. If Jed's been taken it's too late already. Rather stay safe. In all likelihood, they will be fine, but if you get taken now there won't be anybody to look after them."

He knew her words were true, but he could not stay here in the safety of Randin's homestead while Hildah, Nana, and Jed were in danger in the slum.

"I'm sorry, Ma." He kissed her on the forehead, and she touched her fingers to his cheek in a silent blessing.

"Go then and may the Ancient One go with you." She closed her eyes in a silent entreaty. When she opened them again, tears spilled from her cheek. "You are a worthy son, Nicho. A true Parashi."

Nicho knew the likely route the Town Guard would take back to the barracks with their prisoners, and so he skirted all the main roads on his way to the slum. Just at the outskirts of the Parashi area, he watched from the shadows as the last of the guards—or so he hoped—dragged two sobbing men down the street. As he slipped into the slum, the curfew bell rang out. His fate was sealed if a town guard saw him now.

He was thankful for the moonless sky as he pushed himself against the walls of the houses, creeping to that one house that he knew and loved so well. All around him he could hear the wailing of women and the cries of children. Normally their torment would have torn into him, but tonight all his thoughts were on that one small, vulnerable family entrusted to his care.

He was just about to dash to the wall of another house, when he heard the clatter of hooves. He thrust himself back against the wall as two horsemen appeared, walking less than five paces from where he stood.

"We did well, Captain. Got the full quotient. And five rooters, maybe six if that older boy we took is small enough."

Randin grunted. "I told you we didn't need more than four. Your men seem to find it pleasant to rip a child from his mother's arms and send him into that cursed forest. But I tell you, it's no place for a child to be."

"If we don't do it, you know as well as I do what would become of Gwyndorr." Their words grew softer as they moved away from Nicho.

He stood a while longer, allowing his rapid breathing to slow down before he carried on to Derry's house. He couldn't afford to make any mistakes now. There was nobody else out on the street—Randin and his companion must have been the last—and Nicho finally reached the familiar door.

He tried to push it open, but it was locked.

"Hildah?" he called, rattling the door. Only silence met his ears. "Hildah, it's me, Nicho." Still there was no response. Could Hildah and Jed both have been taken, leaving only Nana behind? Surely not. Nana wouldn't have thought to lock the door. Hildah had to be inside.

He knocked loudly on the window, throwing caution to the wind as desperation overcame him. "Hildah! Open up!"

Finally he heard a rustle of movement behind the door, and it opened a crack to reveal Hildah, wide-eyed with fear. "Nicho?" Her voice shook.

"Yes, it's me, Hildah," he said gently. "It's me. I've come to keep you safe."

She threw herself into his arms and clung to him so tightly that he suspected bruises would cover his arms the next day. Her body shivered like a leaf on a tree.

"What happened, Hildah?"

"They came Nicho. They came for Jed."

No! Please not Jed. Please, Ab'El. "They hammered on the door and said that if I didn't open it, they would break it down. So I did ..." She broke into a sob.

"I'm sorry, Hildah. I'm sorry I wasn't here. Oh no."

"I showed them the money. But they laughed. Said it wasn't enough. Said the going price was five coins."

"I thought you had five, Hildah? Didn't you say you had five?"

"There were five till this morning. But Pearce said they would need some for—"

"By the abyss!" Nicho exploded. "He took Derry *and* he took your ransom money? Jed's life is on his head. I will kill him for this, Hildah, that I promise you!"

"Mama?" A young voice spoke and as Hildah moved aside Nicho saw Jed, thumb in mouth and face streaked with tears, standing behind her.

Nicho let out a warped cry. "Jed? I thought you said ..."

"They came for him, yes, but they didn't end up taking him."

"But you said the money wasn't enough?"

"A man on a horse came past. I think it was the captain. They were just pulling Jed away from me. I was holding onto him and he was screaming and they were pulling." Hildah let out another shuddering sob. "But then the man on the horse said, 'For pity's sake, leave him be. He's too little anyway.' So they took the coins and left."

Relief washed over Nicho. Jed and Hildah were still here.

"Let me in, Hildah," he said softly. "This is no night to be on the street."

He sank to the floor as she bolted the door again, and Jed came over and curled on his lap. "Ko, they tried to take me away today," he said earnestly.

"I know, Jed. I know. But everything is going to be fine now." He rocked from side to side, whether to comfort the boy or himself he didn't know. Eventually, when sleep had overtaken the child, Nicho lifted him onto the sleeping pallet next to Nana.

He sat in silence with Hildah for another half an hour, both of them still stunned from the events of the night.

"I'd best be off, Hildah," he finally said. "You're safe now, but my mother will worry."

"But what of the curfew, Nicho?"

"I got here fine. I'm sure I can make it back."

He reluctantly slipped out of the door, making sure Hildah locked it behind him. Then he skirted between the houses, the same way he had came. Halfway through the slum, Nicho heard a low keening sound coming from the window of a house. Although he had heard the same sound before, mothers mourning for their children, this time it stopped him in his tracks. He crept forward toward the house and rapped lightly on the door. The sound hushed, and he heard shuffling feet before the door pushed open. Rosa stood there, anguish etched on every part of her face. Before she spoke, he *knew*.

"Simhew. They took Simhew, Nicho."

CHAPTER 13

"I will get him back, Rosa." It was the rashest thing he had ever said, and now, far past the curfew hour, Nicho felt powerless to keep his promise.

If it had been anybody other than Rosa—who had so courageously allowed him to use her house as a classroom—or Simhew—her studious son whose eyes were always so full of admiration when they looked into Nicho's—he would not have uttered such an impossible promise. When Rosa told him how the guards had found letters and numbers meticulously written by Simhew with a piece of charcoal, a deep sense of guilt had assailed him. Rosa had lost her son because of *him* and his lessons, and in that moment, he knew that he had to try something.

Now he stood at the juncture between Randin's homestead and the town gate. The new rifters would have been taken to the barracks for processing and would be transported to their rifter units at first light. Nicho's only plan was to go to the barracks and speak to Randin. The captain had the power to release the boy, but the dishonor of having his lowly Parashi groom ask it of him, would likely cause him to refuse. He might even be so offended as to throw Nicho into a rifter gang too. Simhew was lost to them. It was futile to believe otherwise.

Slowly he turned away from the road that lead to the barracks and started toward home. Yet, in that instant, he heard a fluttering sound and felt the movement of cool air on his face. He looked again in the direction of the barracks and saw a strange pulsing light hovering in the air. The Parashi were a superstitious people, but Nicho felt strangely unafraid. In fact, looking at the light filled him with a sense of calm and purpose. Resolve, even. Suddenly he knew he had to try, no matter what happened.

Nicho walked boldly down the main road to the gate, savoring the surprising sense of freedom that came from not hiding.

The guard stared at Nicho in disbelief as he strode up to him and announced, "I want to see the captain."

"You want to *what*?"

"I have a message for the captain from his household," Nicho said steadily.

"A message? And they sent you—a Parashi—after the curfew? You expect me to believe that?"

Nicho shrugged, as if to say *I'm just doing as I'm told.*

"Messages are always delivered by his gate guard. There is no way in the abyss that they would send you. What are you up to?"

"I'm not up to anything, sir." Nicho kept his eyes steadily on the ground. "The message is urgent, and I need to deliver it to Master Randin personally, those were Lady Olva's instructions."

"Hew!" The man called to a fellow guard, who came ambling over. "This Parashi says he has a message for the captain and refuses to tell me what it is. Says the Lady Olva told him to deliver it personally."

The older guard eyed Nicho suspiciously. "I've seen this lad before. Drives the cart from the captain's house to fetch hay sometimes."

Nicho nodded hastily. "Yes, sir. I am the captain's groom."

"Why would the lady entrust a message to a groom?" Hew asked.

"I think he's up to something," the first guard said. "If we let him in he'll bring out a knife and stab the captain in the back, or something."

"Search him then."

The guard patted down Nicho's entire body, but found no hidden weapon. Still, he remained unconvinced. "The lad has broken the curfew. That alone is punishable by rifter duty. I say we arrest him, and when the captain sees him for processing, he can tell him his urgent message then."

"But that will take too long. Lady Olva said I should —"

"It's a good idea," Hew laughed. "That way he will get his audience with the captain, and we will have done our duty. Take him to the others."

The first guard grabbed him roughly and shoved him through the gates, across the training field and through an arched doorway, where he handed Nicho over to another guard.

"Curfew breaker," he said.

"Well, well. We are having a good night," the guard laughed, revealing a gap where his two front teeth should have been.

"I have a message for the captain," Nicho cried, sensing the plan slipping out of his control.

"I'm sure you do." The toothless guard laughed. "Another hour or two and you can tell him your whole life story."

He pushed Nicho down some stone steps into a dimly lit passage lined with cells. Through the iron bars on the cells, Nicho could see people slumped against the far walls. In one of the last cells, a young girl clung to the bars, wailing.

The toothless guard hit the child's fingers with the stick he carried. "Shut that crying. Your mama's not coming to rescue you here, girl." There was movement in the dark interior of the cell, and Nicho heard a soft voice saying, "Come sit with me, Rahella." The speaker rose and drew protective arms around the girl. Simhew. For just a moment his eyes met Nicho's and his face showed surprise. But Simhew saw the quick shake of Nicho's head and said nothing.

Nicho was thrust into the cell two down from Simhew's. It contained the last two young men Nicho had seen the guards take from the slum. They were not much older than he and appeared to be brothers; they sat close and whispered to each other. A mother grieved two sons at that moment. Nicho's thoughts turned to his own mother and the heartbreak this would cause her. What had she said? *The Ancient One go with you.* Like most Parashi children, Nicho had grown up with stories of the Ancient King Ab'El who had created the world and then ruled over it with wisdom and power. Nicho found it hard to believe that a supposedly powerful King would be so ineffectual in this, the Parashi's greatest time of need. Yet a spark of childhood faith remained, for as Nicho sat in the dark cell, he echoed his mother's prayer.

Throughout the night, guards came and went, bringing the prisoners for processing. Nicho could hear the distant screams from another part of the building, where the branding must be happening. The two brothers were taken together. When they returned, they were whimpering softly and clinging to each other, as if in shock.

"You," the guard indicated for Nicho to follow him.

Fear gnawed inside Nicho, as he was led back up the stairs and across the vast space of the training courtyard, into a well-lit room where two men sat at a table cluttered with inkwells, pens, and parchment. Master Randin and the man he had been riding with through the slum.

"Right, just the rooters to deal with then, Issor?" Randin said, scratching something on the parchment. "And I can go home and catch a few hours of sleep."

"One more rifter, I'm afraid, sir. A curfew breaker."

Randin looked up. His bored expression changed to one of disbelief as he saw his groom. "*You*, lad?"

Issor looked up sharply. "You know this one, sir?"

"My groom," Randin said sourly.

"Sir, I didn't break the curfew, I merely —"

"You do not speak to the captain unless he asks you a question!" Issor barked out.

"I'm sorry, sir, but I have a message from —"

"What did I say, Parashi?" Issor had risen to his feet, and was striding toward Nicho.

"I have to —"

A blow smashed into Nicho's face. "I told you to ... stop ... talking," Issor hissed.

"Let the lad speak," Randin said from behind his second-in-command. "This is a story I'd like to hear."

"Could I speak with you alone, Master?" Nicho said softly, not looking up. His cheek stung with fire.

Randin nodded curtly, but Issor objected. "Sir, this is most irregular. Who knows what he has in mind?"

"I can handle my own groom, Issor," he said dryly. "You are dismissed."

"Yes, sir." Issor gave Nicho a searing look as he left.

"Right. Explain to me what my best groom is doing out after the curfew hour," Randin said when they were alone.

Nicho had run through his appeal the whole night. Not only did Simhew's life depend on it, but so did his own. Randin had little patience, and so Nicho decided a simple, direct approach would be the best.

"Master, a good friend of mine had her son taken tonight. She has no husband and the boy is her only child. I came to ask for your mercy on him."

Randin laughed in obvious disbelief. "Mercy? What makes you think I would grant mercy at the request of a Parashi groom?"

"He is a mere child. Ten years old. I sense that you don't like sending children to the Rif'twine." It was a risky statement to make; Randin might think Nicho was implying he was weak.

"Really?" Randin drawled. "You, who have spent so much time in my company and know me so well, think I have a soft spot for the children?" Nicho regretted his words, but Randin continued on a gentler note. "The point is, whether I like it or not, the Rif'twine is only halted by the work of the rooters. Somebody has to do the work, and today your friend's son was chosen."

"How many rooters did you need, Master?" It was an impertinent question, but surprisingly Randin answered.

"Four."

"But today you got six, so there are two not needed."

"We'll need one soon enough again," Randin said, scratching through his parchments. "What is the boy's name?"

"Simhew."

"Simhew? Here it is. Says the boy had written out charcoal letters. That is a severe offense. Worse than any of the other children here tonight."

Nicho had no reply. He knew the law as well as anybody else.

"Look at me, lad." Randin's words surprised him, but he obeyed. "Do you see any hint of mercy in my eyes?"

Nicho stared deeply into the steel-blue eyes of the hardened soldier. "I see no mercy," he finally admitted.

Randin nodded curtly. "Then you have your answer, don't you?"

"But neither do I see cruelty, sir."

"You see no cruelty?" Randin snorted with laughter. "You, who have received so many undeserved lashes at my hands?"

"The pain you inflict is for a purpose, Master, not for your own pleasure. Harsh—yes. Cruel—no."

"Who knew a Parashi could be this eloquent?" Randin laughed again. "Trent," he called, and the guard who had brought Nicho appeared. "Bring Issor and all the rooters. Let's get this processing over with."

"Shall I send this one for branding, Captain?"

"No." Randin turned his attention back to the documents as Nicho stood silently, head bowed to the ground. Issor appeared and sat down rather sullenly, also turning his attention to the parchments.

A few moments later, the guards brought in Simhew—holding Rahella's hand—and four other boys. Nicho and Simhew's eyes met again briefly, and Nicho gave him what he hoped was an encouraging smile.

Each of the four boys was questioned, sentenced, and taken off for branding with disturbing efficiency. How foolish he had been, Nicho thought, to expect any mercy in this system.

Only Simhew and Rahella remained. The young girl clung to the older boy's arm as if he were a life buoy.

"Rahella." Randin looked up, and Nicho imagined he heard a slight softening in the captain's voice. "You stand accused of barring entry to one of my guards. That is a criminal offense. I therefore sentence you to fifteen years on the Rifter Gang." He signed the parchment with a flurry, as one of the guards grabbed the girl's arm. She let out a wail and continued to cling to Simhew.

"Captain?" Simhew's voice spoke steadily over the crying. "Could we please go together? She trusts me." The guard who held Rahella froze, stunned that one of the prisoners dared to address the captain.

"You are Simhew?" Randin asked, appraising the boy with some interest.

"Yes, sir."

Nicho was surprised to see that Simhew did not drop his head. His gaze was steadily on Randin, and he showed little fear.

"Who taught you to write letters and numbers?"

"I am not willing to say, sir."

"What if I tell you that I will free both you and Rahella if you tell me the person's name?"

Simhew's eyes sought out Nicho's. Nicho nodded, willing the lad to save himself and the girl.

"I would still refuse, sir," Simhew said after only a moment's hesitation.

Nicho took a step forward. "Captain, let the boy and girl go. I —" The strong arms of a guard grabbed him from behind, cutting off his confession.

"The line between courage and foolishness is a very thin one, Simhew," Randin said. "But my groom risked his life to plead for yours. And so my decision is to let you go."

There was an outraged cry from Issor. "Captain, you can't do this. The law is clear ..."

"I am the judge here, Issor, and I have my purposes. Make sure the boy and my groom are returned to their homes. Take the girl for branding."

"Captain. Let Rahella go instead of me," Simhew said. "I will be a much better rooter than she could ever be."

"My decision is final."

"Then I don't want to be free, Captain. Please take us to the same unit," Simhew said.

Randin shrugged. "As you wish. Take them for branding. Unit Twenty-eight."

"Master!" Nicho cried. "You have the four rooters you need. Let them both go. I beg you."

Nobody moved for a long moment. Nicho hardly dared to breathe. Randin's eyes narrowed thoughtfully on the children.

Finally he nodded curtly. "Take both children back to the slum."

• • •

"Issor, I see the scorn in your eyes," Randin said. "You think I acted foolishly tonight, don't you?"

"I think," his second-in-command chose his words carefully, "that we should not allow rooters to slip out of our fingers the way we did tonight, Captain."

"How long have we worked together, Issor?"

"More than five years, sir."

"And in all that time, have you seen me pardon many prisoners?"

"No, sir."

"Then trust me when I say that there is a reason for letting them go. As somebody said recently, the things I do have a purpose."

"And what purpose does tonight's release serve, Captain?"

"The boy was being taught by a teacher. And if he was, then there is probably a whole group of them. Why settle for one rooter, when we could have five or six? Not to mention the teacher, of course."

Issor's face broke into a smile. "You are, as always, a great strategist, Captain."

"See to it that the Whisperers near the boy's house keep an eye on everyone who comes in and out."

"Yes, sir."

"Let's uncover this rebellion as soon as we can."

"Agreed, sir. And what of the girl?"

"Let the girl be, Issor."

. . .

Nicho thought Rosa might crush Simhew to death, and after Simhew, him.

"I can't believe you got him back, Nicho," she kept saying, not once taking her eyes off her son's face.

Dawn was already lighting up the horizon by the time Simhew saw Nicho off. "Thank you, Nicho," he whispered.

"Don't write any more letters, you hear?"

"Are you coming on Friday to teach?"

Nicho had discussed it briefly with Rosa. She had been adamant the classes should continue, but he was less sure.

"I'll think about it, Simhew. There are too many eyes in the slum, keeping watch for the Guards. Perhaps we should lay low for a while."

Nicho took a few paces and then turned back to the boy. "You were a fool, Simhew, to refuse the captain's terms."

"No more of a fool than you, Nicho," the boy smiled.

CHAPTER 14

S hara was pleased that Nicho had asked her to name the foal. No one in Randin's household ever asked her about her thoughts and opinions. This didn't exactly stop her from giving them, mind you, but here, finally, somebody thought one of her ideas would have value. What's more, Shara felt sure that imparting a name on the foal would give her a sense of connection to the horse, like Ghris had with Loar.

And Shara had the perfect name.

She waited for Randin and Ghris to leave that morning, and when Olva was nowhere in sight, crept downstairs and across the courtyard, slipping into the coolness of the stable. Anticipation fluttered through her as she saw Nicho. He had his back to her, mucking out the straw, but turned as Krola's snort alerted him to her presence. His smile was warm as he saw it was her, although he quickly dropped his head in the required Parashi way.

"Morning, Miss Shara." He nodded in the direction of the foal. "Our little one is doing well."

Shara moved closer and watched the long-legged foal nestle against her mother. She already seemed a little bigger.

"Did you think of a good calm name to give her, then?" Nicho asked.

"I did," she said a little shyly. "I'd like to name her Kharin. It means "gift" in the Old Parashi Tongue. In one of the ancient stories, it's the name of a heroine who gives her life to rescue her people."

His eyes briefly met her own. "I know the story well," he said. "My mother used to tell it when I was a child. Kharin leaves the man she loves and her Parashi people to wed the enemy so that he will not attack her people. It's a good name, Miss Shara. A strong name and worthy of this little one. But I do wonder how you came by it? Last I knew the Highborns were not in the habit of passing along our tales or names."

"*Your* tales?" She felt a stirring of anger. "Since when do the Parashi have the sole right to good stories?"

"I did not mean to imply —"

"— aren't stories for us all to enjoy? And if you must know, it was your mother who told it to me."

"I'm sorry, Miss Shara." His head dropped lower and Shara regretted her outburst. How she wished it could be easy between them again, as it had been when they were children. Yet always the rift of their different worlds loomed between them.

Next to her Nicho stretched out his arm toward the foal, like a king bestowing his favor on a subject. "Kharin, you are named." The foal suckled from her mother, oblivious to the noteworthy nature of the moment. "I really like the name you chose, Miss Shara. It's the first of our horses to have a Parashi name. Thank you."

She flushed with pleasure at his approval and then noticed the bruise on his cheek.

"What happened to your face, Nicho?" He flinched as she reached out to touch it, and she quickly withdrew her hand.

"I had a little run-in with a town guard last night."

"What happened?"

"It's a long story."

"I have a lot of time on my hands."

Again his eyes sought out her own briefly, and there was something questioning in them, as if he was judging her trustworthiness.

"I have a friend. Rosa. Her son was taken last night in the slum sweep."

Shara took in a sharp breath. "I'm sorry."

"I went down to the barracks for an audience with your uncle. It was past the curfew and they arrested me."

As he told her what had happened, fear and anger rushed through Shara. How could he endanger himself so? Wasn't he thinking of Marai?

"You're a fool, Nicho. A reckless fool!" she said at the end of the account, watching him take a step back at the ferocity of her words. "Imagine your mother's pain if you hadn't returned.

"I'm a fool?" His eyes flashed with surprised resentment. "I rescue two children from a death sentence imposed by you Highborns, and *I'm* the fool? I think not Miss Shara."

He returned to his work then as if she wasn't even there and Shara felt a blow similar to when he told her Marai was learning to forget her.

"Nicho?" she said softly. "Forgive me. I think what you did was remarkable and brave. I spoke out of fear. Fear for Marai, and even ..." *fear for herself?* "Anyway. I brought carrots for the foal. I'll just leave them here." She bent down and placed the vegetables on the floor. When she straightened, he was looking at her. Gently, the way she sometimes saw him look at the horses.

"The foal is a bit young for carrots, but if we give them to Krola, Kharin will benefit too. Why don't you give them to her?"

"Me?"

"Yes, just hold your hand flat, like this."

"I'm not sure. You'd better do it, Nicho. Those are big teeth."

He laughed. "No. It's easy." He took her small hand into his own, flattened out her fingers, placed one carrot in her palm, and guided it toward the horse. The short whiskers around Krola's mouth tickled Shara's hand as the horse gently took the treat. Shara laughed with delight.

"Let's do another one."

As he again reached for her hand, she became aware of his closeness. He smelled of smoke and work and the herbed soap Marai made. Their eyes locked, and warmth tingled through the spot where her fingers lay on his hand.

"By the abyss!" He dropped her hand and the carrot fell to the ground. He backed away and looked down. "Forgive me, Miss Shara."

"Forgive you for *what,* Nicho?"

"Looking at you. Touching your hand like that. I ... I don't know what came over me."

"We were just giving the horse a carrot, Nicho. Is that a crime?"

"In Gwyndorr it is. Something I could end up in a Rifter Gang for. I should have known better."

Anger rose up in Shara then. At Nicho, for being a Lowborn. At herself, for watching him from the kitchen all those years. Mostly at Tirragyl and its rules about who was High or Lowborn and who one could care for.

"I'm sorry too, Nicho. Sorry that I thought we could be friends again."

• • •

Nicho found little joy in his work that day. Normally the horses soothed him. As he spoke to them, they responded in little ways—a flick of the ear, a short neigh, a stomp of the foot—that told him far more than most people's words even did. He knew each horse better than a friend. Aventor, the wild one, who longed for open spaces. Krola, the gentle, protective one. Zaqwa, the moody one, who was afraid of the wind and rain, and lashed out at strangers. These were the ones he had a special bond with, but the others too knew—and responded to—his voice.

Today the horses were edgy, stomping around their stalls with flicking tails and flattened ears. Aventor kept throwing himself against the stall door and nothing Nicho said or did calmed him. Eventually, the tension grew too much for Nicho, and he slipped out of the stable and stood by the outside post.

It took him a while to realize that the sounds from the stable had subdued. Nicho shook his head and laughed. Didn't his mother say he had the ancient horse-whispering gifts of the Parashi? If that was true he would have sensed earlier that *he* was the one making the horses edgy. It had started with Shara's visit, of course. He thought he had pushed it from his mind, but the horses had known better.

Nicho looked up at Shara's darkened window and frowned. Why was he in turmoil about the Highborn girl? He thought again of their brief time together this morning. She had looked different from the girl who had been on the edges of his life for as long as he could remember. For once, her hair was not a mess of wild curls. It had been smoother, held back with small plaits, and it had framed her face in a way that made him notice her dark, expressive eyes. He remembered her small hand lying on his own—so soft and delicate—and her gleeful laughter as Krola took the carrot. The memory stirred something in him.

By the abyss! What was he doing thinking of a Highborn girl? Perhaps he was as big a fool as she had told him. It wasn't just his own life that was at stake now. So many people counted on him. His mother. Hildah and Jed. Nana. His pupils. The last thing he should be doing was letting his heart be captivated by a forbidden Highborn.

Nicho returned to the stable, determined to push all thoughts of Shara away. He sidled up to Aventor, who cast him an accusing look.

"I know boy, I've been miserable today. I'll make it up to you." He picked up the large brush and firmly stroked it over Aventor's long neck. "You enjoy that, don't you?" The horse flicked his tail nonchalantly and Nicho laughed. "You can't fool me, Av. Like I couldn't fool you today."

Yet it was difficult to keep his mind off the morning's encounter. Shara's parting words kept coming back to him. *Sorry that I thought we could be friends again.* Had they been friends before, he wondered? Ghris and him, yes. But Shara had always just been the annoying one who followed them around, copying what they did or trying to get them to do things her way.

Yet that had all ended on the last day of his childhood. He had tried to forget that day, but now it rushed back to Nicho as clearly as the one on which he found his father clutching gorgon berries.

It was a beautiful summer morning. Clouds cavorted through the air and a small breeze cooled his sunbaked skin. He, Ghris, and Shara were in their usual corner of the courtyard, outside his mother's quarters. Here they often pushed aside the loose stones and built trenches in the sand. That day his mother had given them a bowl of water, with which they turned the trenches into rivers. He and Shara were building houses from the stones, laughing if one of them placed a precarious pebble above the others that caused the structures to topple over.

Then Lord Lucian and Maldor rode through the gate. Ghris hurried across the courtyard and Master Randin came rushing to the important guests. A servant scurried over to where Shara still played and hastily steered her back to the house.

Nicho still remembered Lord Lucian's precise words to the captain. *She is playing in the mud, with a Parashi?* He felt again the rush of shame, the sense of his lowliness, his desire to shrink to the size of the pebbles he and Shara had played with.

The party went in to eat his mother's fig pie and Nicho helped Helvin rub down the Lord's horses—the most majestic stallions he had ever seen. When the guests returned to the courtyard, Nicho stood aside as Helvin untethered the mounts.

Maldor dug into his saddlebag. Even after five years, Nicho could remember the malice with which the boy spoke. "Father. I fear the five bronze coins you gave me earlier are no longer here. I put them in the saddlebag for safekeeping and now they are missing."

A strange quiet descended on the courtyard and then Maldor pointed at Nicho. "Did you brush my horse, Parashi?"

Nicho stepped forward, careful to keep his eyes to the ground. "I did, Master. But I did not go through your bag."

"I don't believe you. Give me back my coins." Nicho had understood then, in a deep part of himself, that he was nothing more than Maldor's plaything for the day.

"I don't have your coins." Nicho remembered looking the boy—only a little older than himself—straight in the eyes so that the Lord's son would know he understood his cruel game.

"See how this slum-rat looks at me, Father. I want my coins, and I want this thief punished."

Master Randin had nervously taken several coins from his own pocket and given them to Maldor, who smirked, "So what happens to the thief? Does he join the other thieving rooters?"

"I am not a thief." The words had come unbidden. He remembered everyone's eyes on him.

"Are you calling me a liar, you filthy dog?" Maldor lurched toward Nicho but Lucian pulled his son away.

"Let the captain deal with his own Lowborn. I think you need to quench this insolence quickly, Randin. This Parashi doesn't seem to realize his station in life."

Nicho remembered Randin coming back for him after he had seen the guests out. The beating was the first Randin gave him, and the worst; it had been given in rage at the shame Nicho had brought on the captain's family that day.

Only now did Nicho recall the wild-haired girl running into the stable as Master Randin whipped him, shouting: *Nicho's not a thief. That boy was lying.* Shara's cries only subsided when somebody—maybe even his mother—dragged her back to the house.

Even though he hadn't known it at the time, Nicho finally understood. Shara had always considered him her friend.

CHAPTER 15

T essor slipped into Fafa's library. This was the only room in the manor that retained the sense of her grandfather, the one room Lucian hadn't claimed as his own. Two walls were filled with book-laden shelves. Fafa's desk still stood against the third wall, at the same angle as always, one that had given him the perfect view of the gardens and his granddaughters playing below.

The room smelled of dust and old books. Of Fafa. Tessor walked to Fafa's old leather chair. It creaked as she sat down on it.

After Yorina married and moved south, Tessor and Fafa worked together here, sitting on opposite sides of the desk. He wrote letters to his tenant farmers. She kept records of payments and receipts. They had even been sitting here on the first day Lucian and two servants rode up to the house. Fafa had risen to go and welcome his guest, while Tessor had stood and watched Lucian dismount, admiring the way he moved with ease and fluidity. As he walked to the entrance, Lucian had sensed her there and glanced up; she had quickly stepped back into the shadows.

It was also here, a few weeks after Lucian first arrived, that Fafa told her of Lucian's proposal.

"He has asked for your hand in marriage, Tess." His tone solemn.

Tessor's heart had thudded against her chest. *He wanted her! Just as much as she wanted him.*

"I think we should wait." Fafa had known the depth of her feelings. "We need to know him better. Make sure his intentions are true."

"You don't think he could truly love me, Fafa? Am I too ugly for someone like him?" It was one of the few times she had been angry with her grandfather. "I know he loves me as deeply as I love him."

"There's just something about him, Tess. Beneath all that charm, I can't sense who he really is."

Tessor remembered now, with shame, that she had run from the room, slamming the door behind her.

She pushed herself up from Fafa's chair and walked to the shelves, letting her fingers trail across the books' dusty spines. Fafa had loved reading. Yorina had never sat long by his side as he read, but Tessor had always stayed, begging him to read just one more chapter. Fafa's deep voice had breathed life into the driest of words—history, battles, even farming and masonry techniques.

Fafa had been a wise and powerful man, but he'd had one weakness—Tessor. Gwyndorr's Lord had held off the betrothal for a few more weeks, but ultimately, swayed by Tessor's own wishes, had given her to Lucian as his wife.

The past swept her on to that single memory, so beautiful and sweet. Lying shyly in Lucian's arms for the first time as he looked at her, his eyes shining with love. Giving herself to him—body and heart—and knowing that life did not get more wonderful than this.

Maldor's words tore through the veil of memory. *At least you got a title and lands for your one repulsive night.*

One repulsive night?

No. It had been the single most perfect night of Tessor's life.

. . .

Shara lay on her sleeping pallet, sensing the indifferent walls pressing in to stifle her. Earlier, she had called Nicho a fool; now she knew that *she* was the biggest fool of all. She lived in the middle of opulence, yet was poorer than a destitute Lowborn. Ghris was Olva's son, Nicho was Marai's. They had belonging and love. Shara had neither. Even thinking Nicho could be her friend had been nothing more than an illusion.

A chasm of loneliness gaped in her heart. Shara had nothing.

No. She had the Cerulean Dusk Dreamer. Shara had an urge to hold the rock again. It had been so very warm to hold; perhaps that's what it felt like to have a mother wrap you in a blanket on a cold day. For a while the rock had taken away the grief of Nicho's words about Marai forgetting her. Perhaps it could also take away this gnawing emptiness inside her.

She slipped off her pallet and felt for the rock deep under the mattress, her heart beating a little faster as her hand closed on it. Today, she wouldn't let herself fall asleep. The dream the rock had imparted had made no sense to her anyway, although perhaps with more dreams, she would sense a pattern.

She lay back on the pallet, holding the Dusk Dreamer on her chest. Slowly, she felt her sorrow and loneliness ease. A sense of well-being enveloped her again. She wouldn't sleep now—the after-effects had been too unpleasant—but she would just close her eyes for a little while and enjoy the sense of harmony.

Shara sat on a blanket in a beautiful garden. The scents hit her, sweet and heavy, from flowers that stretched as far as she could see. She blinked at the riotous colors—red, orange, yellow, light blue—bursting from the base of leaves. Water splashed nearby, an alluring sound that called to her. But her legs wouldn't move. Trapped, buried beneath the vines.

Suddenly a man's arms reached down to her, lifting her up. Now the garden stretched out below her, and she could see—as if from a great height—the distant paths, leading to fountains, benches, and larger trees. The vast garden stretched far beyond her view. Higher and higher she went, and gradually she became aware that her own arms had changed to wings and her body had the sleek appearance of a bird. Tentatively, she dipped one of her wings and found herself lurching to the side. Wind rushed beneath her, lifting her, and around her, filling her ears with its rushing sound. She let out a whoop of joy at this new freedom. The whoop sounded more like the trill call of the Snowbarb falcon. Shara dipped and spun and glided for what might have been a day or an hour or a mere minute, completely alive in the joy of the moment.

Now she was falling from that giddy height, and she was falling fast. Her stomach reeled strangely, and her scream was pushed back into her throat by the force of the wind. She tried to flap her wings to break the fall, but when she looked down, her wings had changed back to arms and the flapping was nothing more than a useless waving. Down, down, down she fell, the earth looming ever closer as terror engulfed her. She grew aware of large dark shapes flying toward her. The creatures had the faces of humans, but they had thin, black-leathered wings that rustled to the rhythm of their beating approach. Shara called out to them to catch her but they merely turned impassive faces to look at her. Their eyes were frighteningly vacant. Then they were gone.

Before Shara could crash into the earth, she was caught by the same arms that had lifted her off the blanket, and she heard a man laughing. His voice was the most beautiful she had ever heard. Deep. Joyful. Alive. Although she couldn't see his face, she knew there was no safer place to be than in his arms.

He spun her around and around until the blue sky above and the green garden below were nothing more than a moving blur, and their joint laughter mingled into a jubilant chorus.

This time when Shara awoke, she thought her heart might pound her chest right open. The strange tingles in her body felt worse than before and her right leg jerked with every tremor. Yet Shara didn't throw the rock across the room, as she had before. She put it down carefully next to her pallet and lay down until her body stilled and the nausea, brought on by the patterns and colors swimming in her vision, passed.

Parts of this dream had been as frightening as the first, but Shara pushed that aside, and focused only on the memory of the man's arms lifting her and spinning her high, of his deep laughter mingled with her own. Today, the Cerulean Dusk Dreamer had given her what she yearned for the most. A sense that, at some time, she had belonged to somebody and had been loved. Deeply.

· · ·

As usual, only Olva spoke during dinner. The progress of her Octora silk dress. How different the new styles were this season. What she expected the other ladies to be wearing on the day. At times the mindless chatter made Randin wish he hadn't silenced Shara. In a way, the girl's opinions had enlivened the conversation, even if they had generally ended with Olva running upstairs in tears.

Randin glanced at Shara now. She looked different. For once her mop of hair had been arranged attractively, showing the curve of her cheeks. It struck him for the first time that she was no longer a child, but a woman, an attractive one if you discounted the color of her eyes and hair. Perhaps she *was* ready to be a wife. And what woman wouldn't be delighted, marrying into the family of Gwyndorr's Lord?

"Shara needs some new dresses." Randin cut through his wife's babble.

Three heads jerked up and three sets of eyes swiveled to him. Randin speared a piece of rabbit meat with his fork and chewed it nonchalantly.

"Why?" Olva asked.

"Because hers are worn and old-fashioned. Call your seamstress in the morning and arrange it."

"She never leaves the homestead. There's no reason for her to have anything pretty."

"Well, maybe that's about to change."

"What do you mean?" Shara lay down the fork with which she had been pushing her uneaten food around. "Where exactly am I going?"

"You're getting to an age where young men might take interest in you. You want to look your best, don't you?"

"No, I don't." Shara tucked a loose strand of hair behind her ear. "There's nothing wrong with my clothes. I'd rather not be decked out in your pilfered fabric like Olva is."

Olva let out a sharp, warbled cry. Randin knew the sound well. It was the precursor to the outburst of tears to follow. He sighed heavily and put down his own fork, wondering why—moments earlier—he had longed for a bit of Shara's forthrightness.

"Whether either of you thinks it necessary or not, I want the seamstress here soon. The dresses are to be ready in two weeks time."

"Two weeks!" Olva sputtered. "Impossible. She's working on *my* dresses."

"What's this all about?" Shara frowned. "What aren't you telling us?"

"By Taus!" The plates and goblets rattled as Randin punched his fist on the table. "You'd think I was trying to poison you instead of giving you a gift."

The scrape of his chair-legs against the tiled floor, grated his nerves. "Ghris. Come to my study when you're finished."

He strode to his study and pushed the heavy door closed with a sigh of relief. It would be good to have this wedding behind him. He couldn't quite shake his uneasy feeling about the union. As he sank into his chair, Randin considered the strange last few days. If he thought back now, everything had started to unravel with that mysterious man at the gate. Randin prided himself on his firm control of Gwyndorr. Yet this week, things had started to slip from his hand. First, the man had defied his men and best dogs. Then he learned that an entire Rifter Unit had died. Somebody was teaching Parashi in the slums to read and write. Lord Lucian seemed afraid, and it was that fear driving him to push forward Shara's wedding. Yes, Randin thought, it had all started with that cursed man at the gate.

The light knock on the door announced his son's presence.

"Enter."

Ghris struggled to push the heavy door open and then walked to the seat as quietly as if he were stalking a rabbit with Loar. Some days it still surprised Randin that Ghris was his son. He could never shake his disappointment in this soft, timid young man, so unlike himself. Where he was strong and decisive, Ghris was afraid and hesitant and no amount of sword-drill could turn him into the confident soldier Randin had hoped for in a son.

"Sit."

His son slipped into the seat without a word, fiddling with the ties of his jacket.

"Stop fidgeting! Sit up straight like a real man."

Ghris dropped his hands into his lap and straightened his shoulders without looking at his father. Far from making him look stronger, Randin thought he seemed even more defeated than before. Curse Olva for smothering the boy all his life.

"I have some news that affects our family," Randin drummed his fingers on the desk. "Lord Lucian has asked for Shara's hand in marriage to Maldor. The betrothal will take place next week and the wedding a week after that."

"Shara?" Ghris looked startled. "And Maldor?"

"Yes. It's a good union for Shara, as well as for our family."

"But why? Maldor is Lord Lucian's heir. Why Shara?"

"It was arranged when they were young." Randin waved his hand dismissively. He wanted to get to the real reason he'd asked Ghris here. "You know Maldor better than I do. What is he like? Will he be a good husband?"

Ghris shifted uncomfortably. "He's ... he's my friend, Father."

"That's why I ask."

"It's just that, I don't want to be disloyal to him. But I also ... well, it's Shara."

"You don't think he'll be good for her?"

"You must have heard the rumors." Ghris twisted the edge of his jacket. "If there's one thing Maldor is good at, it's causing people to talk."

"Are the rumors true? The women? The brawls?"

"I suspect so. When I see Maldor at hunts, he boasts aplenty of his conquests. From the lowest to the highest alike. He doesn't seem too picky."

"Much like his father." Randin shrugged. "It matters little as long as he treats Shara with respect." When Ghris said nothing, Randin asked, "Do you think he will?"

"He treats nobody with respect, Father."

"Perhaps respect is too much to ask. Will he lay a hand on her, though? Have you seen him hit a woman before?" If there was one thing Randin couldn't tolerate it was a man who took a fist to a woman.

Ghris shook his head. "There've been stories, but ..."

Neither of them filled the long silence that followed. Randin thought of self-centered Maldor with sharp-tongued Shara. Flint against flint, he thought. It would undoubtedly end in fire.

Yet, there was nothing he could do to stop this. From the time Lucian had brought the dark-haired baby to them, it had been ordained. To try and fight it now would only cause him to fall into disfavor with the lord.

"It will be a great honor for our family to be tied to Lord Lucian's," he said eventually.

Ghris nodded thoughtfully.

"It will allow us to make a much stronger match for you too."

"Yes?" Ghris looked up. "How strong?"

"Daughter of a minor nobleman. Perhaps even links to an elder's family." Randin smiled. "Why? Do you have someone in mind?"

"As a matter of fact, I do." Ghris returned his smile and for the first time Randin sensed a moment of kinship with his son. Perhaps this was just the stroke of luck they needed for Ghris to turn into someone Randin could be proud of.

"Good. It would be wise for you to get closer to Maldor. With that kind of influence, you could have the pick of Gwyndorr's young ladies. Why not go celebrate with him tonight, while I go tell your mother the news? I think she'll be pleased."

"When will you break it to Shara?" A frown creased Ghris's forehead. "She's not going to take it well."

"After the betrothal meeting."

As they both left the study, Randin felt an inkling of relief. This wedding was inevitable and, as a family, they might as well take advantage of it. Perhaps it would even be good for Shara to be with a strong man like Maldor.

CHAPTER 16

Andreo rode from the monastery at first light. As usual, the chanting of the monks filled him with a sense of ease. All were occupied—he could safely visit the Rif'twine for another day.

His visit to Unit Twenty-nine proved to be a sad one. Frieya's brother had passed away in the night, and the girl was inconsolable. Bristle had allowed one of the female rifters to stay with her on the platform, mainly, Andreo suspected, to prevent the girl from swallowing the gorgon berries or hurling herself to the ground. Andreo did what he could. He mixed a sleeping potion for the girl and forced her to drink it, then gave her companion some of the powder to use later. He doubted that the woman would keep it for Frieya, though. She would probably use it to dull her own darkness, and who could blame her?

The boy had been buried in a shallow grave a few hundred feet from the platform. Rifter units disposed of bodies in different ways. Several of the units merely left the body in the forest overnight, and by the next morning, little more than the bones remained. Even a grave wouldn't keep the body untouched. Already he could hear the shrieks of the fleshter birds. They had not dug to the body yet, but it was only a matter of time. Andreo could always tell the precise moment when they did, for their shrieks changed to something resembling high-pitched laughter.

Before today, Bristle had concentrated on showing Andreo the plants of the forest, but now he had something very different to show. The Dimzone was filled with strange and dangerous creatures that were forced outward to escape the press of the Darkzone. Snakes, scorpions, and spiders were some of the most dangerous, but none were more feared than the pale, worm-like creatures that the Parashi simply called "fingers."

Bristle and several of the rifters stood in a wide circle around such a thick, pale worm—the fear evident on their faces. Andreo had never seen one before and pushed through the circle, dropping to his knees. He reached out to touch the worm with a gloved hand, but Bristle spoke.

"Don't do that, Brother!"

"Is it poisonous?"

"No."

"Does it bite?"

Bristle shook his head.

"Sting?"

"No."

"What then, Bristle?" Andreo couldn't hide the impatience in his voice.

"It's dark magic, Brother."

"Magic?"

"Yes, if one of these touches you, the soul of this finger's dead person will attach itself to you."

"Are you saying that this is an actual finger, Bristle?"

"It is, Brother," Bristle said earnestly, and the other rifters nodded their confirmation. "It's the only living part of a person who died when the Rif'twine conquered their town."

"And what if I tell you that it is nothing more than a worm?"

"Look at it, Brother. It's a finger."

Andreo laughed. "No, you look at it Bristle. There is no nail. If you look closely, you can see the small pale legs at the bottom, and the mouth at the front. Come."

He tried to coax the rifters closer, but all of them refused. In the end, Andreo decided he could do little to change their superstitions and turned his attention to the plants.

Later, as he mounted his pony, he heard the first high-pitched laughter, which grew in intensity and volume as he spurred his horse forward. Andreo was thankful to leave the darkness of the Rif'twine behind him that day.

• • •

The clop-clop of hooves crossing the courtyard announced Brother Andreo's arrival. Stepping from the stable, Nicho again patted the pocket containing the note and wondered at the wisdom of his plan.

"Morning, Nicho." The monk slid from the pony's back. "How are you?"

"Well, Brother. You?" He took the reins.

"It's been a sad day so far." Brother Andreo hesitated before he said, "One of the Rifter Units I pass on the way to Gwyndorr just lost two people, one of them a young boy."

"A rooter."

"Yes. I ..." again Andreo paused and looked around, "... I sometimes visit them. The lad's sister is also on the unit. Her sorrow is heartbreaking."

Nicho said nothing, but he thought that if Brother Andreo was breaking rules visiting the Rif'twine, he might be more inclined to overlook Nicho's offense. His hand slipped to the note.

"Have you heard of the 'fingers' in the Rif'twine, Nicho?"

"Fingers?" The question surprised him. His father had spoken of them. "Yes, my people—rifters particularly—fear them greatly. I've always thought they're probably just large earthworms."

"Finally!" Brother Andreo threw back his head and laughed. "A Parashi with some sense." He slapped Nicho on the shoulder and smiled. "There is hope yet."

Nicho took a deep breath. "Brother?" He held out the note. "Could you give this to Miss Shara for me?"

Brother Andreo took it warily. "You wrote this, Nicho?"

"Yes." He could only hope now that Brother Andreo was the man he thought he was.

"Who taught you letters?"

Nicho ground his toes into the loose stones. "I'd rather not say."

"You should be careful."

Nicho felt relief as he heard the concern in the monk's voice.

"Somebody could report you."

"I am always careful, Brother, but this is important."

"Miss Shara, you say?"

"Yes, Brother."

"I'll give it to her. Just this once though. It's too much of a risk for you to be passing notes around."

"Thank you, Brother."

• • •

Shara was seated by the time Brother Andreo stepped into the small room that served as their classroom.

"Morning, Shara," he smiled. "I have something for you." He looked back at the door uneasily, before drawing a small note from the leather-bound book he carried. "Read it later. Put it away before Ghris comes."

"What must she put away before I come?" Ghris strode through the door. Shara had heard him come home early this morning after a late night of taverning. Unusual for her cousin, who preferred the company of his horse and Loar over the young men of Gwyndorr.

"Nothing. Just a book Andreo gave me to read." She had slipped the note into her own book as Ghris arrived. "Where were you last night?"

Ghris shifted uneasily in his seat. "Bidding well to the next bachelor about to be tied to a wife."

"Really? Who's the fortunate man?"

"No one you know, Shara," he snapped. "Let's start, Brother."

"Too much mead, Ghris? Should have slept in a bit longer?" Shara teased, expecting him to laugh. Instead, her cousin threw her a surprisingly dark look.

The lesson passed slowly. Andreo was talking about the finer points of Tirragylin property law and as he droned on, Shara's mind flittered between her flying dream and wondering what was written in the mystery note.

She didn't realize the lesson was over until Ghris sidled over to her and grabbed her book.

"Let's just see this illicit book Brother Andreo gave you."

"Ghris, give it back!" She lunged for it, but he was too quick, lifting it above her head.

"*A History of Tirragylin Vulcan Rock Mining through the Ages*," he read. His brow creased. "Riveting reading, I'm sure, so why can't I see it?" As he flipped through the book, it fell open to the place where Shara had tucked the note. His eyes narrowed on her. "I see. *This* is what you were trying to hide."

"Ghris. Give it back to her," Brother Andreo said softly.

"I think I'll just take a look at it first."

Shara jumped up to snatch the letter from his hands, but his one hand pinned down both her own in a painful grip as he held the note out of reach with the other.

"From Nicho?" His eyes narrowed on her before he read, "*Miss Shara. You were my friend once, and I'd like you to be my friend again. Bring more carrots, and we can give them to Krola.*"

He let go of her hands and Shara grabbed the note, her temples pounding with rage. "Satisfied, Ghris?"

"No. I'm not. What are you doing, Shara? Visiting the groom instead of his mother now?"

"The *groom*? Don't you mean our *friend* Nicho?"

"You might have been too young to remember what he did, Shara. He's a thieving Parashi through and through."

"Those coins of that boy, you mean?"

"Maldor's coins, yes."

"Nicho didn't take them. That was just a lie to get Nicho into trouble. You knew him, Ghris. He was better than both of us."

"He was—and is—a Parashi. And that note proves only one thing. He still hasn't learned his station in life."

Brother Andreo interjected. "Could both of you not mention the note to anybody? Nicho could be in grave danger if someone realizes he can write."

"If that's true, Ghris will be too." Shara glared at her cousin. "He's the one who taught him."

"*You* taught him, Ghris?"

"It was a mistake," Ghris said sullenly. "He convinced me, and I should have known better."

"Well, for you it would mean an uncomfortable morning with the Council of Six. For Nicho it's the Rif'twine. So let's not mention it again," Brother Andreo said.

"Maybe this *should* come out." Ghris glared at Shara. "Do you know the shame you could bring on this household if you're found cavorting with this Parashi?"

"I'm not cavorting. I'm feeding a horse. One of *our* horses." Yet Shara felt a flush rise to her face as she remembered. Her hand on his own. The closeness. The tingle that had run through her in that moment.

"No more feeding or passing notes. No more stable visits, in fact." Ghris leaned in close. "I don't trust this Parashi, and if I see just a hint of this *friend-ship* he speaks of, I'll make sure he's whispering to poison trees instead of horses."

CHAPTER 17

The haste with which Brother Andreo left should have warned Nicho of what was to come. Usually the Brother admired the horses, spoke of the weather or asked after his mother's health, but today the monk cast Nicho a quick, worried look before grabbing his pony's reins and bidding him farewell. Nicho didn't even have the chance to ask if he had passed on his note.

The answer to the unasked question came a little later as Ghris stormed from the house to the stable, his expression dark with rage.

"Morning, Master Ghris," Nicho said, eyes to the ground. "Shall I saddle up Zaqwa for you?"

"No." His old friend's voice was ice-brittle. "What I need is for you to leave Shara alone."

Nicho glanced up. "I ... I'm not sure what —"

"Don't act innocent, Parashi. I read the letter you sent her. *Friends!* You want to be *friends?*" Spittle flew from his mouth at the hiss of the forbidden word. "You're playing on her loneliness. Trying to win her to you. You! A Parashi."

Nicho silently cursed his own foolishness. His father had told him once of a man trapped in Rif'twine quicksand. At first, his father told, the man hardly knew the danger he was in, but then the sand slowly, stealthily, dragged him down, pulling him under even as he struggled to be free. Nicho suddenly knew how that would feel. He sensed that—from the moment he had held Shara's hand up to Krola and passed Brother Andreo the letter—he had stepped into perilous quicksand. Perhaps the danger had ensnared him much earlier, on the day he started teaching the boys their letters. Or the night he went to the barracks to beg for Simhew's life.

This perceived offense against Shara reached deep, into the heart of the captain's home and his family's pride and honor. It was the very thing that had been wounded by Maldor's accusations years earlier.

"I intended no shame on your family, Master Ghris."

"No? What *did* you intend, Parashi?"

How could he explain the muddle of his emotions? His sorrow that he had always looked past Shara—the only person brave enough to defend him all those years ago. His desire to pay back her debt of friendship and loyalty, even after all this time. And something else that he could not yet put into words, although if he could, it would probably send him to the Rif'twine even sooner.

"I thought Miss Shara would enjoy watching the foal."

"She has no business being here. With you."

"It's just, now that she no longer goes to the kitchen, she might —"

"She no longer goes to the kitchen for the same reason she will not set foot in this stable." Ghris kicked over a bucket of feed. "She is a Highborn and has spent far too much of her life steeped in Parashi lies."

Nicho met Ghris's gaze for just an instant. Was it enough to remind Ghris of the way they used to laugh and tease and rough-house together when Captain Randin was too busy and Lady Olva too distracted to care for their son?

From the time of that first beating, Nicho had been ripped from Ghris and Shara's life. There had been no more playing and no more forbidden learning of letters, for Nicho had been sent to the stable the next day. At first Ghris still gave Nicho furtive smiles behind his father's back, but over time he began to treat Nicho the same way the captain did. Nicho was no longer a friend. He was a servant. A Parashi. A nobody.

"Stay away from her, Nicho." Ghris grabbed the two ends of Nicho's cloak and pulled him closer. "Very soon she'll be out of your reach, but this game you're playing could hamper everything. I warn you, if I sense anything," — he pushed Nicho back into the door of Krola's stall— "anything at all— you'll be waking up in the Rif'twine."

. . .

Shara stood in the dark looking out to the stable, where a small lamp still burned. Was Nicho there? Was he perhaps looking across to her window, thinking of her? The words of his letter were seared into her memory. *You were my friend once, and I'd like you to be my friend again. Bring more carrots, and we can give them to Krola.* Had he mentioned that moment with the carrots because he had felt the same tingle of attraction as she had? Or was it just about the horse for him, and nothing more?

From that first day when they had seen the strange bird together, Shara's head had roiled with such confusing thoughts and unfamiliar feelings. Since then she had often thought how close he was and wondered what he was doing. She would imagine him whispering to a horse or—with a lick of jealousy—talking to Yasmin. She had even started sneaking into Olva's room to peer into the looking glass as she arranged her hair or pinched color into her cheeks.

I'd like you to be my friend again. He *wanted* her in his life. This single thought first pierced, then pulsed, pain deep into her chest. How surprising that such opposites as yearning and loss or delight and sorrow could distill into this strange ache that flared up every time she thought of him. Nicho wanted to be her friend.

But tonight her thoughts flittered bat-like, uneasy and dark. Ghris, the one who had always been her ally in Randin's house, had turned on her. Mild, gentle Ghris, who had played alongside her and Nicho, had threatened to send him to the Rif'twine. And Shara had seen in his eyes that it was no idle threat.

Shara felt her way back to her sleeping pallet and lay down, trying to still the frenzy of thoughts. When the soothing sleep refused to come, she drew out the Cerulean Dusk Dreamer. She had decided she wouldn't use the rock every night. Other than the strange dreams and side-effects, she felt more tired the day after a dream. Tonight, however, anything would be better than the turmoil Ghris's words had brought to her.

She was in a darkness so thick that when she lifted her hand to her face she saw no movement, but only felt her fingers touch her cheek. It filled her with a terror unlike any she had ever known before. She willed herself to wake up, but the rock's power would not release her. Gradually, she became aware of a chiseling-sound just to her right. Every few moments it would stop, replaced by low, raspy breathing. We need to get out of here, she thought, before the forest closes in on us completely. Although she had only thought it, a man's gruff voice spoke in answer.

"Just a few more, and we can leave."

Now she saw, far above her, a pinprick of light. She doubted that anything larger than a mouse could go through it, but still she dropped to her knees and started to crawl blindly toward it. She had to get away from this dark cave of terror. Behind her the scraping noise stopped for a moment, and the man spoke again.

"Deserter! Would you leave me here alone? Do you know the power in just one of these rocks? We can't leave them behind!"

Yet she carried on crawling over the ground, feeling the jagged rocks ripping at her hands and knees.

"Traitor!" The word echoed behind her, but she had reached the small hole and thrust her hand through it, desperately scratching at its edges, trying to enlarge it. It seemed to be working, for clumps of hard, stony soil came free in her hands and the light above her was growing. Just one more handful and the hole would be large enough to push through. Yet, as she loosened that last handful of soil, something cracked above her head, and a low rumble grew from somewhere deep in the cave. A cascade of soil and rocks was falling toward her, and now she was tumbling with them, head over heels, deeper and deeper into the cave, knowing that she would never see light again.

When the landslide finally subsided, she lay under a mound of Cerulean Dusk Dreamers. The darkness was gone; now the light was the beautiful blue of the night sky just before the last rays of sun have ebbed away. A short old man stood over her, his eyes sparkling with excitement.

"Look at them all. Aren't they beautiful? There is nothing hidden that they cannot reveal." He fell to his knees and started to fill his pockets with the stones, whispering, "Beautiful, so very beautiful," over and over again.

Shara awoke with three new insights. The first was that the rock could do more than show her truths about herself; it could also reveal truths about other people. In the old man's face, she had seen the likeness of Randin, and she had understood that the dream showed something of her uncle's past. Initially, this seemed rather useless, then, slowly she realized just what such secret knowledge would give her. With knowledge came power, and the sudden, intense thirst that gripped her—powerless prisoner that she was—for just such power, frightened her a little.

The final insight was that the Cerulean Dusk Dreamer was far more dangerous than she had ever imagined. The crazed expression of the old man lingered long in her mind as a reminder of the rock's alluring grip on those captured by its beauty and power.

CHAPTER 18

Andreo handed the reins of his pony to the acolyte who was on stable duty, and made his way to the somber grey building that served as the dining hall. He was tired today, despite having spent the morning collecting plant samples in the hills near the monastery. Perhaps his tiredness had something to do with the confrontation between Ghris and Shara the day before, and the sense that his actions had placed Nicho in danger. He sank down gratefully on the wooden bench and signaled for an acolyte to bring him a bowl of soup. He was later than normal and the dining hall was almost empty. He quickly glanced into the leather satchel slung across his body. It contained the leaves and roots he had picked earlier. The testing would have to wait until the hour of meditation-time, when the Brethren were released from their duties for a time of personal reflection.

Initially Brother Andreo had felt guilty using this time for his plants, but he had come to realize that finding something to alleviate someone's pain or sickness was the best way he could personally serve Taus. So, it had become his daily routine to follow the narrow trail into the hills that lay just to the east of the monastery. Here he had found a small cave, with creepers growing over the entrance, which he now used as his plant workroom. Well hidden, he felt free to leave the plants, powders and solutions in the cave—a much safer place than his own cell would be.

The young acolyte, a boy called Jufah, put the bowl of soup in front of Andreo.

"Thank you, Jufah." Andreo smiled at the boy, who had only been here a few months and couldn't be much older than twelve or thirteen. Andreo had come to the monastery at the same age and remembered well his homesickness. "If your duties are done, perhaps you wish to keep me company for a while, Jufah?"

The boy smiled and glanced back over the room. "I think that would be fine, Brother. Nobody else needs serving as far as I can tell." He sat down opposite Andreo.

"So how are you finding your training, Jufah?"

"Good, Brother, although rather tiring at times."

"Yes. I remember. The days are long between early morning and late night prayers, are they not?" The boy nodded with a sigh. "But you will adjust to it. We all did."

"I hope so, Brother. I don't want to be one who doesn't even make it through to the selection."

"Ah, yes, the selection. When does that happen?"

"In four weeks' time, Brother."

"And what is it that you are hoping to be selected for, Jufah?"

"Word Arts, Brother." The boy's face lit up as he said it.

Andreo chuckled. It was what all the acolytes hoped for, of course. He needn't even have asked. "Well, let's hope it comes to pass then."

"Why are you sitting around here shirking your duties, boy?" The words—from behind them—were spoken with clipped precision. Andreo instantly knew who the speaker was.

Jufah shot up, knocking over the bench in his haste. "S-s-s-sorry, Brother." He lifted the bench back into place and grabbed Andreo's empty bowl, making a hasty retreat.

"Good afternoon, Brother Angustus," Andreo rose to his feet. Angustus was second only to the Sacred Brother himself. Andreo had few dealings with him, for which he was glad. He felt uncomfortable around the tall, graying monk, whose mouth pinched constantly in disapproval.

Angustus lowered himself on the bench Jufah had so hurriedly vacated.

"I asked the boy to speak to me while I ate," Andreo said quietly.

Angustus's eyes narrowed on him. "You should know better, Brother. These acolytes need firm discipline, not revelry."

Andreo kept quiet and waited for Angustus to reveal the purpose behind this meeting, for purpose there had to be. Angustus was not one to mix unnecessarily with the lower ranks of the Brethren.

The senior brother cleared his throat. "It has come to my attention that you have not been attending dawn prayers regularly. Is this true?"

Anxiety clenched Andreo's stomach. He had known this question would come one day, and had already formulated his response.

"I have missed a few days, Brother."

"My sources tell me that it is more than a few days, Brother Andreo. What exactly is the purpose for these absences?"

"I have at times struggled with stomach cramps, and did not want to be near the others to pass on my illness." This was a half-truth, for some of Andreo's concoctions *had* made him rather ill in the past.

"You have not been riding out early, then?"

"No, Brother." This blatant lie could not be veiled. *Had someone seen him, or was Angustus just guessing at his absences?*

"How long have you been here?"

"About twenty minutes, Brother Angustus."

"No." That mouth pinched even tighter. "How long have you been at the monastery?"

"Twenty-nine years, Brother."

"Who was your endorsing Brother?"

"Brother Gladson." Andreo smiled at the memory of his gentle mentor. He had died eleven years earlier, and still Andreo missed him. Gladson, Andreo suspected, would have approved of his alchemy; would have seen the value of it to the people.

"Gladson?" The disapproval was evident in Angustus's voice. "Strange. I looked for your records today, but could not find them. Can you account for this?"

Andreo shook his head to hide his disquiet. "Maybe Brother Gladson misfiled it?"

"I will have to keep looking then." The rare smile on the senior brother's face did not comfort Andreo. "Anyway, Brother, I trust I will see you at Dawn Prayers tomorrow."

"I will be there, Brother Angustus."

A peculiar stillness settled on Andreo as he returned to his cell. For twenty-nine years, his past had remained a secret—one that he thought had been buried with Brother Gladson. Yet today had reminded him that something he had all but forgotten could be exposed in a single moment. Andreo knew that if Angustus found his records, the consequences would be severe.

· · ·

Tessor seldom went outside, but tonight the beautiful sunset sky, streaked with orange and red hues, drew her.

She used the servants' door and was forced to wait for a gaggle of young women—twittering loudly about Maldor and his flirtations—to leave. Then she slipped across the passage to the door.

As she stepped outside, Tessor breathed deeply of the fresh evening air, laced with cooking smoke and spices. The smell was a homey one, of families sitting around meals, telling stories of their day.

She turned left. In Fafa's day there had been a path here, a profusion of white flowers growing on either side of it, leading to a bench. The flowers, and their sweet heady smell, were gone now. A strange statue stood where the bench had been. Twice as tall as Tessor, the statue depicted a man wearing only a loin cloth. Where his arms should have been, two thick serpents twined, their heads turned toward him, as if whispering a dark secret. But the stone man's eyes were not on the snakes; rather they had the strange ability to follow Tessor as she snuck past him. Every time she walked here, she felt his icy stare on her back.

Tessor headed to the wall of the property, where none of Lucian's fearsome statues could keep watch over her. She sank down onto the tufts of moss that grew against the towering wall, her hands caressing the soft mounds as she breathed in the smell of earth and growing things. She and Yorina had played with the moss too, constructing hills out of it for the small fae-folk they imagined lived in Fafa's garden. If the fae had been real, they would have left long ago, Tessor thought. There were no more flowers to bed down in, no more seed pods to use for boats in little streams. And, of course, there were those monstrous statues with eyes that would not leave you be. She would have left with the fae herself, if she could.

That bench, where the statue now stood, had been the place where Fafa had wrapped his comforting arms around her the day after her wedding. That was the morning Tessor had woken to find her husband gone. The grooms told them that Lucian and his two servants had ridden out well before dawn. No, they had not told them where they were going. No, they had not said when they would be back.

Over the next four days, Tessor cried out all her questions onto Fafa's strong shoulders. *Why hadn't he told her he had urgent business? Didn't he know she would be worried? Should they send out a search-party? Where would they even begin to look?*

Fafa had been quiet, his eyes filled with unrest. He had hardly spoken, merely letting her cry and question and rage. Tessor had still believed her husband to be the man she had grown to love; she could not understand these actions. Fafa had never been that blind. He had known Lucian was not all he showed them. His leaving unannounced was merely a piece of the puzzle Fafa needed to understand the man.

Late on the fourth day Lucian returned, but he did not come alone.

Tessor could remember that first conversation after his return as if it had just happened a minute ago—every word, every nuance of expression in his eyes. She had rushed downstairs when she saw him arrive and met him in the entrance hall.

"Lucian, you are back!" She threw her arms around his shoulders and kissed his neck. He stood unresponsive as stone and when she pulled away and looked at his face, his eyes were dark and unfathomable.

"By Taus, I was so worried. Where did you go?"

He didn't answer. Instead he turned and gestured to the group of people behind him. As they moved closer, Tessor's attention shifted from Lucian's face to the boy, man, and woman. The child was dark-haired, and she knew instantly, from his eyes and chin, that he was Lucian's son. Despite his young age, his stare was hostile.

"You have a son?" The world felt as if it tilted suddenly. Why had he not told her?

"Yes, my son, Maldor." He offered no further explanation.

"And this is Nort, his tutor." The man stepped forward and nodded an acknowledgment. "You will have rooms readied for all of them, Tessor."

Lucian turned and spoke to the servants who were carrying in several trunks. "Just leave them there until the rooms are ready."

Tessor stood dead still, until Lucian glanced at her impatiently. "Well?"

"I don't believe," Tessor said, standing as tall as she could, "that the introductions are complete."

Something like a smile crept over Lucian's expression, except that it held no joy or humor. It was cold and cruel and the sudden realization that this was not the husband she knew punched the air from Tessor's body, making it hard to breathe.

"This," he pointed at the beautiful, dark woman, "is Jezrel. Jezrel, this is Tessor, of whom I have told you so much."

The woman laughed mirthlessly.

"Who, exactly, is she?" Tessor emphasized each word.

"Jezrel is my common-law wife. You might say concubine."

Fafa had tried to intervene. He spoke to Lucian, threatened to throw them all out. This was his home, he said. He gave Lucian an ultimatum. Three days and Jezrel must be gone. Only the boy and his tutor could stay.

Lucian had just laughed.

. . .

Shara had read once about a strange storm that occasionally lashed Southern Tirragyl. The book had called it a spiral storm, for the strong wind spun around and around, and, if it was particularly fierce, pulled everything that lay loose into itself. Milking buckets. Farm implements. Sometimes even fowl and piglets.

Tonight, Shara had such a storm blowing through her heart. Around and around it went, pulling thoughts and sentences, expressions and encounters into a large, spiraling jumble from which she could not break free. Words swimming on a page. *I'd really like you to be my friend again.* Other words spoken in anger. *Do you know the shame you could bring on this household if you're found cavorting with this Parashi?* The dark intent in Ghris's eyes. *I'll make sure he's whispering to poison trees instead of horses.* And other eyes, crazed with longing. *Do you know the power in just one of these rocks? We can't leave them behind.* The solemn warnings. *It is wild, untamable, never to be used lightly.* Arms catching and spinning her. Dark leather wings beating against her as she fell down, down, down. Fabric draped over her and Olva's expression at the fitting that afternoon—no longer resentful. Excited.

"Stop it! Stop it! Please stop." Shara pounded the side of her head with her palms. She wanted the storm to stop swirling its confusion into her mind. Perhaps this is another effect of the Dusk Dreamer, the thought mixed accusingly into the fray of her mind. *What have you begun?*

Then she noticed the soft golden light pulsing outside her window. Shara pushed the blanket aside and swung her legs off the pallet. The cold stone under her feet cooled her fevered thoughts. She moved slowly toward the light. So strange. It seemed to be hovering in mid-air. *Was this a dream? An illusion brought on by the Dusk Dreamer? Could she no longer tell reality from dreams?*

She pushed the window open and the light moved closer, until it was less than an arm's-length away. Only then did she realize what it was. The bird!

"It's *you*!" Joy flooded through her in that moment. "You came back."

Shara stood looking at the hovering bird. Time passed, although it felt of no consequence. Every part of her was enraptured by the beauty of the red creature with the pulsing gold breast, and her storm of thoughts was swept away in its brightness.

Momentarily the bird dropped onto the windowsill and let out a call, so pure and joyful that tears prickled Shara's eyes. Then it took to the air, dipping down over the courtyard, before flying away.

Lying on the windowsill was a single, bright red feather.

That night Shara did not fall asleep clutching the Cerulean Dusk Dreamer. Only the feather lay under her pillow, and her sleep was sound and peaceful.

CHAPTER 19

Nicho pushed open the door to Rosa's house. It was just before dawn on Friday morning, which meant that the boys should be here for their lessons. Yet the usual buzz of young voices was absent.

"Simhew? Rosa?"

Simhew darted from the next room, his face lighting up as he saw Nicho. "Morning, Nicho!"

"Where are the others, Sim?"

"I don't know. I saw Jabon yesterday, and he said his mother told him he can't come anymore. But Elrin told me *he* wasn't scared of no town guard—said he was still coming."

Nicho sighed. He had suspected this would happen once the news of Simhew's capture spread.

"Have you been all right, Sim?" He tousled the boy's hair. "That was quite an ordeal you went through earlier this week."

"Everybody wants to hear all about it, Nicho." Simhew smiled. "They think I was really brave. And they think you're a hero, you know."

"There's not too much value in that if you ask me."

"I know what you mean." Simhew rolled his eyes. "Rahella has been coming over and wants to go *everywhere* with me."

Nicho laughed heartily. "Girls," he said. "They're a difficult breed to understand."

"Are we now?" Rosa had slipped from the other room, a playful smile on her face.

"Hello, Rosa."

She came over and touched his cheekbone. "The bruise is gone," she said softly.

"That was nothing, Rosa."

"I'm not sure I really thanked you enough for what you did the other night." There were unspilled tears in her eyes. "Nobody has ever done anything that sacrificial for me or Simhew before."

"We have to take risks for our friends." Nicho said, awkward at the depth of devotion he saw in her eyes. "Besides, there's a time to stand up for what's right, even if it puts us in danger. That night was such a time." He turned toward Simhew. "Why don't you and I work on some letters?"

"And I'll make us all a cup of origo," Rosa said.

As Simhew meticulously copied the letters Nicho wrote, Nicho's mind wandered to the last words he had written in the letter for Shara. He had asked her to return to the stable, had told her he wanted to be friends. Was that still true after Master Ghris's threats? Nicho was both disappointed and relieved that she hadn't come. He was unsure how he would react if she suddenly appeared.

After the lesson was over, and just before the curfew bell was to ring, Nicho crept through the slum's streets to Derry's house. As Hildah opened the door, the strain was visible on her face. Her eyes were red, whether from tears or sleeplessness Nicho was not sure. Since the night of the slum sweep, Jed had been too terrified to sleep, she said, and when he eventually did, he would wake up screaming in the dark of the night. This last night had been a particularly bad one.

Nicho pulled the child onto his lap, humming an old Parashi tune, until Jed's eyes grew heavy and closed. Every now and then, a sob still shuddered through the boy's body. Nicho gently lifted him onto the sleeping pallet and stood back to look at him. Dirt and tears smudged his face and his small lips seemed pinched with disquiet, even in sleep. One hand obstinately grasped the horse that Derry had carved for him.

A fresh wave of anger assailed Nicho. Derry may not be good at many things the world considered important, yet if you gave him a piece of wood, he could carve it into something beautiful. This remarkable gift had brought in enough money to take care of Nana, Hildah, and Jed. Until Pearce took him away.

"Thank you, Nicho," Hildah said from behind him. "It's like this all the time. All he wants is Derry." Her voice broke as she said the name.

Nicho turned to the table, where Nana and Hildah were devouring the bread Marai had sent for them.

"He keeps asking when Derry is coming back. What should I say?" Her young eyes pleaded for him to give her hope, but he had none to offer.

"I don't know, Hildah. I'm sorry."

Nana's voice crackled to life. "The twins'll be here soon. I just sent 'em to run out for some water."

Hildah's eyes filled with tears, as she grasped the old woman's hand. "Yes, Nana, they'll all be here soon."

It had been only four days since Pearce and Derry left. How long, Nicho wondered, to reach this fabled Grotto—if it even existed—and send back a party for the families? There was so much that could go wrong along the way—patrols, injuries, Rifter Guards. He shook his head, as if to rid himself of the unwelcome images.

"You want some bread, Nicho?" Hildah asked shyly.

"No, thank you. There's plenty at home. Keep the rest for tomorrow. I'll be back again after the Sacred Day with a fresh loaf, and hopefully some cheese and fruit from the kitchen."

She nodded reluctantly. He realized that her offer was merely to keep him there a while longer. It must be lonely to be little more than a child, caring for two dependent souls.

He was probably the only visitor she'd had since Derry left. Yasmin had promised to visit Nana and Hildah of course, but lately her new lover had kept her a little preoccupied. That was Yasmin for you.

"I'll sit a bit with you though," he said, and her face brightened.

There was little to say, but he sat a while longer and sensed that she drew comfort from his presence.

• • •

Shara was conscious of Ghris sitting opposite her in the classroom. In the last tutoring session, he had grabbed her book and read the note, before threatening to expose Nicho. He hadn't been down for any meals since then. Perhaps he regretted his harsh words. Even now he didn't look up at her.

"Shara?"

She looked up with a start at Brother Andreo's expectant face.

"I'm sorry, Brother. I did not hear your question."

Brother Andreo turned his gaze on Shara in thoughtful appraisal. As usual, the smallest of smiles hinted at a private inner source of amusement. It always gave Shara the impression that he had answers to questions others hadn't even thought to ask yet.

"I asked what you thought of the fact that all the documents written in the Old Tongue were destroyed in the Great Purge."

"I think it is a great loss, Brother, that a large part of our history was devoured by fire."

"But what then of the argument that all of what was destroyed was lies, and harmful to the people?"

This was the kind of debate she loved having with Brother Andreo. He had an open, searching mind, as opposed to the closed-minded arrogance of their former tutor. She knew that Brother Andreo went beyond the narrow teachings of the Brotherhood in his search for answers. Once he had hinted to her, with his usual smile, that his constant investigations caused some difficulties for him with his brethren. Yet nobody could deny that he was an excellent teacher, and the one person Shara respected above any other.

"I would say that this was not something the Brotherhood should have decided. The old documents should have been kept, discussed, and cherished. We should be sitting here with them now, debating their truth or falsehood. Yet the purge robbed us of this ability."

"Well said, Shara. What do you think, Ghris?"

"I disagree, Brother." Finally Ghris looked up at her, his eyes narrowed and challenging. "I think the Brotherhood had our good in mind, and knew that most of what was written in the Old Tongue was Parashi propaganda, intended to make the Highborn look bad."

"It didn't have to make them *look* bad," Shara interjected. "They were invaders. They *were* bad—burning, pillaging, murdering. All the Parashi had to do was keep a record of their mistreatment."

"Of course. I forget your love for all things Parashi!"

"Enough," Brother Andreo said. "This is unlike the two of you. Haven't I taught you to respect another person's position, whether you agree with it or not? Now let's get back to talking about some of the great commanders of the war."

As Andreo's voice filled the study, Shara thought again of Ghris's betrayal. It twisted so deep because he was the only member of the family she had ever truly considered her kin.

"The two of you are impossible today." Andreo's voice broke through her thoughts. "I don't know who is more distracted. I think that's enough for today."

Ghris quickly packed away his quill and parchment, and with a hasty good-bye to Brother Andreo and a sideways glance at Shara, slipped from the room.

"Tell me, Shara. This thing between you and Ghris today. Is it still about Nicho's note?"

Shara shrugged. She didn't particularly want to dwell on it. There was something else she wanted to discuss with Brother Andreo. Her fingers stroked the object in her pocket. Soft. Comforting.

"You fear he will expose the groom?"

"He wants me to stay away from Nicho. If I do that, I think Ghris will keep it to himself."

"Yes. You are probably right." When she didn't make a move to leave, he asked, "Was there something else, Shara?"

Could she trust him? The bird felt too special to share with just anyone, but her desire to solve this mystery overrode her doubts.

"I found a feather, and wondered if you could tell me the bird it comes from."

Andreo's face lit up at this new challenge; ornithology was one of his interests. "Do you have it here, Shara?"

She pulled the feather out of her pocket and laid it on the desk in front of her. Andreo picked it up and slowly turned it over in his fingers, a puzzled look on his face.

After a long pause he spoke, as if to himself. "It's definitely a covert wing feather. Not a greater covert, I think, but a secondary. My first impression was that it might be from a black-ringed rover, but the feather seems too large. The rover's coloring is also lighter, almost more orange than red." He turned it over again slowly. "This is deep, rich, and absolutely beautiful. Where did you pick it up, Shara?"

"In the courtyard, Brother," Shara lied.

"It must be a migratory species. Although I thought I knew all of those, too." He sounded disappointed with himself. "I'm sorry to say I don't know, Shara."

Shara held out her hand for the feather, but Andreo was still studying it. "Maybe I could keep it, Shara? I could ask at the monastery if anybody can identify it. Brother Yorek is a keen birdwatcher."

"No, Brother." Shara wanted the feather back. Strange as it sounded, she felt as if it had been a gift. "I'll keep it. It doesn't matter if I don't know which bird it belongs to."

She held out her hand again. Andreo did not respond immediately, and she thought he might argue with her, but eventually he dropped it into her palm.

She hurriedly put away her parchment, ink and quill, suddenly keen to leave.

"There is one other bird with a red body," Andreo said with a chuckle, as he collected his books and map to follow her out. "But I can definitely rule out that one, since it is a mythical bird. Some old folklore tells of a bird of great beauty, called the Gold Breast. Not only was it beautiful, it was also powerful."

Waves of cold assailed Shara's body.

Brother Andreo hummed a tune as he gathered up his dark cloak. "Well, Shara, I will see you after the Sacred Day."

"Brother?" She tried to keep her tone casual. "Can you tell me some more of the Gold Breast myths?"

"Ah," he smiled. "Not only are you a great scholar, Shara, you also love a good story. Walk me to the courtyard, and I will tell you all I can remember."

Shara glanced around and, not seeing anyone, fell into step with him.

"Well, let me see. In the old legends, the Gold Breast was a bird whose beautiful coloring and melodic voice earned it a coveted place in the royal courts. It was more than a tame pet, however; but rather, it was a loyal friend and even a weapon of sorts, since it was known to attack anybody who tried to harm its loved ones. Its sharp beak could apparently inflict quite a bit of damage."

"That doesn't sound all that unusual," Shara said. "Couldn't other birds be taught to do that?"

"I was leaving the best until last, Shara, as a good story teller does. Apparently, the Gold Breast had extraordinary powers. In one of the tales I recall, a Gold Breast sang at the deathbed of a queen, and she woke up, completely healed from her death stupor, remembering only the bird's sweet melody."

He cleared his throat and continued. "But its song did not only bring life. Another story tells of a wicked ruler who fell to his knees screaming and grasping his ears at the sound of the Gold Breast's song. Even when the bird stopped singing, the ruler was never the same again. He always had a faraway look on his face and became so distracted that his son took over his throne simply by moving him off it."

They laughed together at the image Brother Andreo's words evoked.

"Rather a pity, is it not, that the mystery and magic in those old stories are all just fables to teach us lessons? I imagine sometimes what the world would be like if some of it were true. It would be remarkable, don't you think, Shara?"

"Yes, Brother," Shara said quietly, but her mind was filled with a strange new thought—the mythical bird was true and it had come to find her.

CHAPTER 20

"Three units have lost rooters in the last week, Captain," Issor said under his breath during Guard inspection.

Randin glared at the row of guards that he and his second-in-command walked past in the barracks courtyard.

"Straighten your sword belt, soldier," Randin growled to one young guard.

"We're going to have to do another sweep, sir," Issor continued.

"Three? Are we losing them faster and faster, Issor, or am I just imagining it?"

"It is an unusually high loss rate for one week."

"Let's see if we can do without a sweep. Maybe we can just pick up a few delinquents off the street?"

"That's not so easy lately, sir. Not many children roam the streets anymore."

"What of the Whisperers? You haven't had any reports we can follow up on?"

"It's been quiet. We picked up two adults earlier in the week. One was selling items on the black market, and the other—his brother—knew about it, so we seized him too, for failing to report it. But no children, sir."

"Is there any news from that boy we let go—the one who was caught writing letters?"

"The three Whisperers on his street have been watching the house closely, but they get few visitors, and never a group at once. Your groom has been seen there once or twice."

"Really?" Randin looked up with interest. "I wonder why?"

"The boy's mother is apparently quite good looking by Parashi standards, although a fair bit older than your groom. Still ..." Issor shrugged. "That young girl who we set free has also been seen there a few times. And the lad has many friends, who he visits."

"Not much to go on, is there?"

"We could just round up the whole lot of them and do a bit of an interrogation." Issor smiled. "It doesn't take too much to get children to talk. We could crack open that letters-ring in no time."

Randin's frown deepened. "Let's give it a bit more time, Issor. I'm sure something will come to light."

"Time is the one thing we don't have, sir."

• • •

"Nicho?" Tentative. A mere whisper.

He spun around at the sound of Shara's voice. She stood pressed against the inner wall of the stable, out of sight from the courtyard. Her hair was twisted up in the style Gwyndorr's gentry favored. It showed the noble curve of her cheekbones. It also reminded him that he, a Lowborn, had no right to be talking to her.

"Miss Shara."

She moved farther into the stable, casting a quick glance back to the entrance. "Ghris told me not to come see you." Undercurrents of emotion rippled in her dark eyes. "But I had to."

Nicho clenched his hands together, nervously. Ghris had ridden out more than an hour ago. He didn't expect him back soon, but there was too much at stake to take a chance.

"Master Ghris spoke to me too," he said, his eyes to the ground. "If he catches you here ..."

"Nicho. Please look at me." His throat tightened at the sorrow in her voice. He looked up to see a single tear running down her cheek. He almost reached out to wipe it away.

"I do not want to put you in danger. But please do just three things for me." Nicho nodded.

"I want things to be the way they were when we were children. You didn't look at the ground when you spoke to me then. Can you just look at me again? Like we're equals."

"We're not children, Miss Shara. And we're definitely not equals."

"Says who? Some ridiculous law that's hundreds of years old?" Her words held the indignant tone she had used so often as a child. Nicho smiled at the memory.

"What else do you want me to do, Miss Shara?" He looked her straight in the eyes as he spoke, and he saw by the slight upward curve of her lips, that she noticed.

"I want you to call me Shara again. Just Shara. No Miss anything."

He shook his head at that. "It will feel wrong. Disrespectful."

"No," she reached out her hand and laid it on his arm. "It will feel like we're friends again. Didn't you say you wanted that too? In your note?"

Nicho stepped away from her, shaking loose of her burning touch. He paced to Aventor's stall and stood looking as the wild one threw his head from side to side. He understood that kind of restlessness.

She came to stand next to him in silence.

"Do you remember the last day we played together?" he said eventually, his eyes on Aventor.

"The day the lord's son accused you of stealing the coins."

"I had forgotten that you came running to my defense." He looked over at her and she met his gaze. "I never got to thank you for that. I never got to give back that same friendship or loyalty." He made a decision then to give her what she asked of him; it was the least he could do. "Thank you ... Shara."

Speaking her name so simply echoed of long lost freedom. The joy he saw in her eyes pulsed into his own heart.

"See?" She grinned. "Not so difficult."

"What's the third?"

"Third what?"

"Third thing you want of me. I've given you one and two."

"Just a little of your time, Nicho." She glanced again at the stable entrance. "I've discovered something remarkable. Something I can only share with you."

"I want to give you that too, but ..."

"But you're afraid. Of Ghris and Randin."

"What they'll do if they find you here. Do you know much about the Rif'twine?"

"Only what Brother Andreo has told me. I think it sounds fairly interesting." The note of defiance also reminded him of their childhood.

"It's a death sentence, Miss Shara, I mean ... Shara. You do not return from the Rif'twine."

"So you're saying I shouldn't be here?" Her voice rose and quivered on the last word. "You want me to leave now and never come back?"

"It's not what I want, Shara." His tone might have given away too many of his feelings, for her eyes shimmered with surprise and expectation. "It's not what I *want*, but it's what we need to do." Pain stabbed through him as he saw his words eliminate the spark from her eyes.

"Yes. You're right." Her shoulders slumped. "I'll go now."

She turned and walked slowly to the stable exit. He had an urge to call her back. To take her in his arms and hold her. To pull her onto Aventor's back and ride with her as fast as the wind, break through Gwyndorr's walls and gates and rules.

If he let her walk away now, he would probably not see her again. Ghris's strange words came back to him. *Very soon she'll be out of your reach.* He did not know what they meant, but he knew that she had always been out of his reach. The rules of their society had made it so.

Shara stopped in the stable entrance and turned back to him.

"Goodbye, Nicho."

But before he could reply, there was a flash of red and gold, and a bird swooped over her shoulder.

. . .

Shara had planned to walk from the stable and not come back again. The risks were just too great with Ghris's threats looming over them both. For Nicho, it was death in the Rif'twine. For Shara, the unbearable guilt of knowing she had put him there. Yet, this was the last time she might see him and so she pushed aside a warning voice and turned back to look at him.

Which is when a soft rustle and a breath of air on her cheek made her look up, just as the Gold Breast swooped over her shoulder, and a now familiar joy swept right in with the bird. Every time she saw it, the red of its body looked richer and the gold of its chest, more dazzling. This was no ordinary bird. A bird of folklore and myth. How could it be perched right between her and Nicho, as real as Aventor and the foal? She drew her eyes away from the splendid bird to look at Nicho's expression of awe.

"Shara," he whispered. "It's that bird."

"I know." She pulled the feather from her pocket. "This is what I came to show you, Nicho. I know what kind of bird it is."

As she spoke, the Gold Breast took to the air again, flew toward Nicho and hovered by his chest. Then it dropped something and, by reflex, Nicho caught what looked like a twig. Together, they watched the bird fly from the stable, until it was a mere dot in the blue sky.

"What in the abyss was that about?" Nicho turned to Shara. He strode over to her and looked down at the feather. "Where did you get it?"

"Last night. The bird was at my window."

"Why is it coming to us? Is it hungry, you think? Perhaps it wants food?"

"No. This is no ordinary bird. I showed the feather to Brother Andreo this morning."

"You did?" He seemed surprised that she would trust the monk. Perhaps he was thinking that the last time one of them had done that, things had gone very wrong. "What did he say?"

"He didn't know what bird the feather comes from, and that's unusual because Brother Andreo is really good at identifying birds—it's one of his passions. Then, as I was leaving, he started to talk of a red bird with a gold chest, which he had read about, but never seen."

"Yes?"

"It's called a Gold Breast."

"A Gold Breast? That must be it then."

"It doesn't exist, Nicho."

He frowned. "What do you mean?"

"It's mythical. Some of the old legends and stories talk about a Gold Breast, and it's meant to have all sorts of powers."

"Powers?"

She repeated the stories that Brother Andreo had told her. Nicho didn't say anything for a very long time after she finished. Finally, he shook his head.

"This makes no sense, Shara. None whatsoever."

"I know."

"Are you sure Brother Andreo isn't wrong and it's not just a finch or something?"

"I'm sure. It has to be a Gold Breast."

"How can you be so sure?"

"Because ..." she struggled to find the right words, "... because I've *felt* its powers. Every time I see it ... it fills me with a kind of ... joy, I suppose. And when I picked up that feather last night, something stirred inside me that I've never experienced before. A sense of ... belonging."

"I felt its power too. When I look at it, I feel ... worth. And even—," after his father's death he had never expected to feel it again, "—hope."

"Do you believe me then? You think it's a Gold Breast?"

After a long pause he said, "I do. I believe. Even though I don't understand."

They stood side by side for a while until Shara noticed that Nicho was twirling something between his thumb and forefinger. As she grabbed his hand, he looked up, startled.

"Is that what the Gold Breast dropped?" She took it from him, disappointed to see that it was only a twig with silver-green leaves. "Just some leaves."

"No," Nicho said. "It's from a Silver Birch tree. There's only one place in Gwyndorr they grow."

"Where?"

"The Silver Birch Grove, near the main gate."

"Why would it bring you leaves?" Shara shook her head. "It makes no sense. Unless ..."

"Unless it's trying to tell us something."

"That's it!" Shara said with sudden insight. "It wants us to come to the Grove. We can go together."

"Impossible." Nicho shook his head emphatically. "I can't even leave Gwyndorr without a letter from a Highborn. And you?" He looked toward the guards at the gate. "You never even leave *those* gates, much less the heavily guarded ones of Gwyndorr."

"There has to be a way, Nicho." Shara rocked on the balls of her feet; she felt like taking Nicho's hands and dancing with delight. "We can do it. Why would the bird send us a message otherwise?"

"It's a bird. Mythical. Powerful. I don't know. But it's still just a bird." His solemn expression snuffed out every flicker of her excitement. "I can't imagine birds understand much about Gwyndorr's harsh laws and punishments."

"So it comes down to that again." Her voice was flat. Angry. "You're too scared of the Rif'twine to take a chance on me and the Gold Breast."

Anger stirred in his eyes too. "We'd just agreed that seeing each other was too much of a risk. Why does a bird with a twig change that? The danger is as real as ever. Those were not idle threats Master Ghris was making."

It was true. All of it. She had seen the intensity in Ghris's eyes. He had meant every word. And yet, while the Gold Breast was here, she had felt different—unafraid—and had hoped Nicho would feel it too.

"You're right. So I suppose this is really goodbye." This time as she walked from the stable, Shara did not look back.

CHAPTER 21

As Brother Andreo made his way to the monastery's record room late Saturday night, his thoughts returned to his encounter with Brother Angustus two days before. What could have alerted the Word Art Supreme to the fact that Andreo's past was not as it should be? The senior brother must have his suspicions. Why else would he be looking for Andreo's records? And where would Brother Gladson have hidden something as dangerous as Andreo's childhood history?

An important part of the enrollment process was the vetting of acolytes. Purity of thought and body were, after all, important principles for the monks. The young boys were questioned concerning their beliefs and education, and their parents and grandparents were investigated. All these finding were meticulously recorded in an entrant's record.

Should Brother Angustus find Andreo's records, he would discover a truth that made a mockery of the Brethren's purity laws. Andreo would be called to an immediate audience with the Council of Six. Just what would happen to him then, he did not know. But his biggest fear was that all his years of alchemy work might come to naught.

The same humidity that had Andreo struggling for breath, had wedged the record room door tightly into its frame. The room was built deep into the cliffs, where water seeped through the walls instead of fresh air. As his sharp shove dislodged the door, a sprinkling of moist dust fell down on him. Inside the room, his oil lamp cast its shadows on rows and rows of shelves and, as Andreo looked at the rolled parchments jammed haphazardly on top of each other, his heart sank. How was he meant to find his record in this three-hundred-year-old sea of history?

He picked out scrolls from various shelves, hoping to find some order. Alphabetical? Entrance year? Task Divisions? Yet, if there was a system, Andreo could not discern it. There was the option of asking the keeper in charge of records, old Brother Stopha, to find it for him. But it could harm him if news of his search reached the ears of Brother Angustus. Wouldn't it just prove his guilt even faster?

As he made his way back to the door, Andreo cast one last long look around him. Somewhere in the dusty recesses of this room lay his own story, the story of an illegitimate son. His father had been a wealthy and important trader, and by his fair features, the perfect Highborn. Yet few knew of the trader's one mark of disgrace—a son born out of wedlock, by a Parashi woman. Not many Highborn would have let themselves be burdened by such an inconvenience, but Andreo's father had been as intelligent and thoughtful as he was kind. He'd brought his son to live with him and allowed the boy's mother and grandmother to become servants in his household.

The record would not reflect whose coffers his father had lined to win his intelligent son a place amongst the Brethren. As a child entering monastery life, Andreo would have been unaware that his lineage excluded him from the privilege. It was only as the years passed that he thought back on these things and wondered. *Who amongst the Brethren knew that he had no right to be in the monastery?* His life here was as illegitimate as his birth had been.

Andreo slipped from the record room and froze. A soft sound echoed down the passage from which he had come. It sounded like retreating feet. No. His mind was playing tricks. Nobody would be here at this time of night. Andreo pulled the door to the record room closed and crept back through the stone passage to his own sleeping cell.

As he went, he thought of Brother Gladson, who must have known about Andreo's past. Andreo felt a renewed appreciation of his old mentor, that the knowledge had made no difference to Gladson. Yet, Gladson would have been astute enough to know that few of the Brethren would share his view.

Could it be that he had indeed hidden the records, or maybe even burnt them?

Perhaps Andreo's secret was still safe.

. . .

Shara sat on her sleeping pallet and ran a finger over the Cerulean Dusk Dreamer. What had happened to the power rock? Why wasn't it giving her dreams anymore? Before it had pulsed with warmth, but now it lay—cool and placid—in her hand, looking dull. It had lost its vitality.

Shara rubbed the rock on her cloak, regret coursing through her at the thought that she had used up the rock's magic. There was still so much she wanted to know, so many questions unanswered. And she wanted to escape, both the walls of her prison and her heart's deceptive games.

She may have walked out of the stable and out of Nicho's life three days earlier, but her heart was willfully defying her decision to forget him. It still beat with images of his smile, words spoken and unspoken, dreams of a future that could never be. The Cerulean Dusk Dreamer could help her forget him, of that she was sure.

Shara wrapped the power rock back into its satin covering and hid it under her sleeping pallet. Perhaps if she gave the rock a bit of a rest it would work again. Instinctively, her fingers found the feather tucked into a deep pocket. Her thoughts turned to the mystery of the Gold Breast and a sudden, startling insight filled her mind. The bird was powerful. What happened when two powers collided? Could the feather in her pocket be disrupting the powers of the Dusk Dreamer? It made sense, for since she had picked up the feather, her dreams had stopped. Maybe all she had to do to get the Dreamer to work was dispose of the feather.

It felt strangely like a betrayal as she made her way downstairs for dinner and, on the way, dropped the feather into one of Olva's expensive vases. She could come back for it later, she told herself.

That night she eagerly climbed onto her bed, closed her eyes, and willed the rock to transport her into its secret world. The dream came, but far from being the vivid experience of before, it felt to Shara as if she viewed it through a thick fog, and soft voices seemed to come from very far away, for she had to strain to hear them. The effort left her only half-asleep, and what she witnessed appeared to be more vision than sleep-laced dream.

Two riders, darkly clad, appeared to be arguing. One voice was deeper than the other was, and must have been raised in anger, for Shara could make out the words he spoke, "I know this area like the back of my hand."

Now a third voice spoke—a child's—and this too Shara could understand, for it came out as a high-pitched whine. "I am tired, Uncle Keros. I can't sit any longer. I want to stop."

The man snapped, "Shut up, boy. It's hard enough finding the pass without your whining."

Unconsciously, Shara gripped the stone ever tighter. There was something significant here, something related to her past—she sensed it in the deepest fiber of her being. The fog veiling the scene cleared a little and now Shara saw that the boy was seated on a large stallion, in front of the dark-haired man.

Their female companion said something that Shara could not understand. Tighter still Shara gripped the stone, and now the man's voice was clearer than before. "And have the Prince find us in the morning with our precious goods? Are you out of your mind, woman?"

A birdcall drowned out the next words, and—as if summoned—the fog returned, obscuring the scene in a thick blanket that muffled all sound and sight.

This time when Shara fully awoke, her heart pounded not only with the wild power of the rock, but also with anger. The strange magic that still coursed sickeningly through her body felt trifling compared to the rage that swept along with it. She was angry with the Gold Breast. Its feather was to blame for this, she knew. That feather was still far too close and would have to go once and for all.

CHAPTER 22

Nicho watched Hildah's notches grow in number. Last night he had counted eight. It was far too early to expect news that Pearce and Derry had reached their destination, but still he hoped for some news that they were safely on their way. If they had been caught or waylaid ...

Krola nickered as he brushed her down harder than usual.

"Sorry, girl."

Little Kharin pushed her nose against his side. He kept carrot shreds in his pocket for her, and the young foal was starting to learn where to look for them. He had a sudden longing for Shara to be here. She would have laughed at the foal. If only he could see her serious face break into a smile one more time.

"Stop it, Nicho," he berated himself.

"Stop what?" Helvin asked, carrying in a fresh pail of oats.

"Nothing much, Helvin."

"Didn't sound like nothin' ta me."

"Just thinking of a girl."

"Ah yes. 'Tis the age, isn't it? Young love—nothin' like it." Helvin grinned his toothless smile.

"No. It's not love, Helvin. This girl can never be a part of my life." He feared he was saying too much.

"Forbidden love," Helvin said knowingly. "'Tis a powerful force ... mighty powerful indeed."

Nicho wanted to say it was nothing like love—young or forbidden—but decided to change the subject instead.

"How's our supply of oats and hay then?"

"Pretty low. Think ya'd better make a trip to the farmlands in the next few days. I'll arrange a letter with Master Randin."

"Sure." Nicho always enjoyed the day away from Gwyndorr. "I'll go on Saturday."

"Ya do that, lad."

Helvin left, and Nicho was brushing down Ghris's mare, when Krola nickered her warning that he was not alone. He spun around, expecting to see Randin or Ghris, but instead it was the Gold Breast. It was perched on the bucket of oats, another silver-birch twig in its mouth.

The other two times Nicho had seen the bird had filled him with a sense of wonder, but today his annoyance overrode his awe.

"I know what you want me to do. It's impossible." It did not seem strange to speak to the bird. "If I get caught, I put more than my own life in danger. What about Jed and Hildah and Nana?"

The bird dropped the twig and let out a low note—so pure, it seemed to resonate right into Nicho. Then it let out two more notes, each one higher than the last. With each rising note, Nicho felt a surge of courage flowing through him.

"How do you do that?" Nicho whispered. *The bird has powers,* Shara had said.

"Fine. I'll come." He reached down to take the twig, but the bird picked it up first and flew to the stable entrance, where it sat looking back at Nicho, as if waiting for him. As he reached it, the Gold Breast took flight, not away from the house as it had done the other times, but rather toward it. It landed on the windowsill of Shara's window, where it dropped the twig before taking to the air again. It could not have been clearer. *Come to the Birch Grove. And bring Shara.*

It was a fool's risk to smuggle her out of Gwyndorr—one that could cost him his life. Why couldn't he just go find out what the bird wanted them there for? Then he could find a way of telling Shara whatever he discovered.

However, the uneasiness would not leave him alone that night, and eventually he knew that to gain any peace of mind he would have to do it the Gold Breast's way.

As Brother Andreo rode through the gates for his tutoring session the next day, Nicho finally made up his mind.

"Morning, Brother." He took the pony by the reins.

"Good morning, Nicho. How are you today?" The concern was evident on Brother Andreo's face. It had been there ever since Ghris had found the note.

"Good, thank you. Brother. I wonder if you could pass Miss Shara a message?" He saw the monk's frown, and added, "Not a note this time, just an invitation for her to come see the foal. It's been a while and I think she'll find Kharin has grown." The excuse sounded feeble, and Brother's Andreo's intense scrutiny made his lie feel even more transparent.

"I can tell her to visit, but are you sure it's wise? You know Ghris wants her to stay away. He threatened to send you to the Rif'twine if she visits you."

"I know. Please tell her when Master Ghris isn't there. She's sure to be careful." Again those blue eyes turned on him and he felt as if the monk could read his every thought. Yet Brother Andreo finally nodded.

"And I'll be careful too this time Nicho."

•   •   •

After the lesson, Brother Andreo waited until Ghris's footsteps creaked the floorboards above their heads before he passed on Nicho's message. Even then he spoke in a whisper.

"Are you sure it's a good idea to go though, Shara? Ghris was pretty serious about his threats."

"I know he was. And the last time I saw Nicho, he told me it was too much of a risk." She heard—and tasted—the bitterness on her tongue. "So I won't go, Brother. You don't have to worry."

"Good. I'm fond of that groom. Better for him if you stay away."

As he turned to leave, Shara remembered the feather. She caressed its softness one last time and felt a moment of uncertainty. Hadn't the feather been a gift to her? *No!* She had made up her mind.

"Brother. Would you like to keep the feather I showed you?" She held it out. "I have no use for it."

His gaze was searching as he took it. "Are you sure? You didn't seem to want to part with it last week."

"It'll be more useful to you. Perhaps you can use it to identify the bird." An image of the Gold Breast pulsed through her mind. *Would the bird know what she had done? Would it ever visit her again after this betrayal?*

She could tell Brother Andreo was pleased. As she walked him to the door, he kept looking at the feather. Shara deliberately averted her own eyes and overrode any sense of regret with the anticipation of what the Cerulean Dusk Dreamer would now be able to show her.

Shara had meant it when she told Brother Andreo that she wouldn't go to the stable. Yet her deceptive heart beat with excitement when she saw Ghris ride out the gate later that afternoon. Her palms felt sweaty and her fingers too impatient to do a decent hair style; she eventually settled for two simple twists that kept most of her curls away from her face. Then she snuck downstairs, across the courtyard and into the cool of the stable.

No one was in sight, but she followed the sound of humming to Aventor's stall. Nicho knelt down, examining the horse's shoe, and Shara stood for a moment admiring his broad back, the curve of his neck and the curls that grew at its nape. Then she put a deliberate coolness into her voice that was at odds with the warmth pulsing through her.

"You wanted to see me, Nicho?"

He started, knocking his head on the pail hanging on the wall. Shara had to suppress a smile at his unusual clumsiness.

"Miss ... I mean, Shara. You came." He clambered to his feet and wiped his hand on his trousers. "I wasn't sure you would. Brother Andreo said not to expect you."

"He said you wanted me to see Kharin? Sure it's not too much of a risk for you?"

"It's still a risk," he answered curtly before his tone softened. "But the Gold Breast isn't giving me any peace."

"About me seeing the foal?"

"About going to the Silver Birch Grove."

"Oh, that." She smiled slightly. "I think it left a twig on my windowsill yesterday too. I just can't think of a way to get there, though." And, now that she had chosen the Dusk Dreamer over the Gold Breast, she wasn't so sure she wanted to.

"I have a way we can go," Nicho said. "It's dangerous, but if you're willing to take the risk, so am I."

"What about the threat of the Rif'twine?" Her mind reeled. She'd never been outside Gwyndorr's walls before, had never walked in a glade of trees. And she would be with Nicho. Alone. Far from Ghris's prying eyes.

"I've decided to trust the bird," Nicho said simply and guilt stabbed through her. Nicho trusted the very bird she had betrayed earlier.

"What do you say?" His green eyes held her own so intently, that she again felt the fine tingle of pain and longing in her chest. "Shall we try, Shara?"

It was her heart that answered before her head could override its lovesick impulse. "Yes. Let's go to the Birch Grove."

Nicho smiled. "We go in three day's time. Here's what I want you to do."

Chapter 23

During the meditation hour, the Brethren were required to spend time in solitude, communing with Taus, the Divine. Instead, Andreo wound his way along the narrow path to his cave workroom.

The more he tried to commune with Taus, however, the farther Andreo felt from Tirragyl's god. He no longer sensed him in the musty, candle-lit chantry or the somber, repetitive mantras of his Brethren. He could not find peace in the hour of solitude, or meaning and purpose in teaching the Brethren's history and dogma. More and more the teaching felt at odds with the pain and sorrow he saw around him. The rigid structure of monastery life left Andreo with a disconcerting emptiness, which only his passion for plants and medicines alleviated.

Andreo had not risked riding out to the Rif'twine this week, for he sensed that he was being watched in the mornings—not only by Brother Angustus, but by the older monk's entire tight-knit circle of cohorts, mostly the Word Art practitioners. Yet Andreo found himself yearning for the Rif'twine. As dark and ominous as it might be, it still contained living, growing, breathing things. His longing was also for the rifters, who had come to depend on his small gifts of dried leaves and crushed roots to help them through their most difficult nights. It was only in serving them that he still sometimes sensed the soft breath of the Divine alight on him.

Coming to the cave was a risk too, but Andreo saw little purpose to monastery life without it. He now pushed the creeper curtain aside and slipped into his familiar den, breathing in the welcoming smells of earth and herbs. He lit several candles and then set to work at once, breaking off some new leaves he had gathered and placing them in the mortar dish. He ground the leaves fine with a pestle, and then carefully picked up a few of the leaf grains and transferred them to a shallow wooden bowl, before measuring out some water for his solution.

The work absorbed him and he found himself whistling a tune as he worked. Although he was not conscious of it, the tune was an old one, sung to him by his grandmother long before he ever entered the monastery. He did not know the words of the song, only the melody, for they had always been sung in an ancient, haunting, tongue.

Andreo turned his attention from the solution to some of the other bowls containing his older potions. He stirred the contents of one of the bowls, and then picked up another and held it to his nose—it let off a sharp, pungent whiff. *Interesting.* It reminded him a little of the smell of the frillbough leaf. In fact the leaves had a similar shape; possibly the plants were related and therefore also had similar properties. He was just reaching for a bag of dried frillbough leaves in order to make a more accurate comparison, when he froze.

He thought he had heard something. A footfall, perhaps ... and a fall of small rocks? He stood a while longer, listening, but all was quiet. It might have just been a hare or even a tsebee; the buck was a rare visitor, but was sometimes seen in these parts during the summer months.

Andreo turned back to the frillbough leaves and was soon completely absorbed in his work.

• • •

A single word echoed down the manor's busy passages and filtered through the cracks, even into the forgotten ones.

Betrothal.

From behind the tapestry, Tessor listened to the audiences that the merchants had with Lucian. Silver goblets, finely woven carpets, rings, blankets, Octora silk. The merchants talked confidently about their fine products. *How pleasing a lady of Gwyndorr would find them. How comforting they would be for a new bride leaving her home.* Their smooth voices complimented Lucian on his good taste. *How did he know this was their finest specimen? What a remarkable eye he had. He was a lord amongst lords.*

And then the haggling would start. *Surely he valued the new bride more than that? Of course he couldn't expect such fine quality for such a low price.* A few of the newer merchants were naïve enough to believe Gwyndorr's rules of bargaining applied under Lucian's roof, but they soon learnt that Lucian always got exactly what he wanted, at the price *he* was willing to pay.

They were fortunate to leave with several coins in their pocket and the lord's favor still intact.

From Fafa's library window, Tessor watched servants bring in flagons of wine and mead, and a large barrel of cider. In the passage outside the kitchen, she heard the cook berating the scullery maids for throwing away the bugloss flowers she had intended using in a pie for the betrothal in two days' time.

Standing behind the fireplace, Tessor heard a Town Elder counsel Lucian on all the Tirragylin traditions to follow at the betrothal ceremony and the acceptable price to pay for a Gwyndorr bride—ten to twelve gold coins was considered generous.

It was also here that she heard the escalating fights between Maldor and Lucian.

She's little more than a commoner. I don't mind bedding her, but why tie her to me as a wife?

And always Lucian's unshakeable response. *This is how it will be.*

The manor's walls hummed with anticipation at the new bride to come. So wanted by Lucian and so unwanted by Maldor. This was the contradiction that filled Tessor with a surprising mix of jealousy and pity for the girl. How did this Shara feel about becoming the bride of Gwyndorr's handsome heir? If every servant girl's reaction was something to go on, probably thrilled. Just as Tessor had been to become Lucian's wife. But Tessor could have told her that the joy would last no longer than a single night. Then the sorrow began.

She watched now from the crack of an open door as the last set of servants left the suite of rooms that had always been Yorina's. When she could no longer hear their footsteps down the passage, she slipped across to the door and creaked it open.

Tessor had known they would be there. The memories that sidled up to her, trying to draw her away from the present into the past. She saw Yorina running barefoot through the rooms, right on her own heels, squealing loudly as a blindfolded Fafa called in a deep giant's voice, *I hear little girls.* There sat Yorina on her bed, a little older and lovely as always, letting Tessor brush her sunlit hair and speaking about the latest boy who was vying for her attention.

But Tessor let the unfamiliar elements of the room jar the unwanted memories away. The dark fur rug on the floor had never been there before. A gift for the new bride. The portrait of Maldor hanging above the fireplace. The artist had captured a hint of the cruelty in his eyes. For a moment Tessor had the urge to take it down and smash it to pieces over her knee. What young bride wanted to look into eyes so dark, so menacing?

She sat down on the bed and let her hands glide over the soft Octora silk blanket. It was the finest she had ever seen. Again jealousy impaled her. Lucian had never bought *her* gifts that fine. *Who was this girl?*

But as night approached and Tessor sat in the steadily darkening room, another emotion slowly took root. It was one so long forgotten that she almost didn't recognize it. *Power.* If this girl meant as much to Lucian as Tessor was starting to suspect, how would he react if, in some way, she was taken from him?

Could Shara be the key to destroying Lucian?

CHAPTER 24

Saturday finally dawned and Shara was awake well before the sky lightened. She had tossed and turned most of the long night, gaining little sleep. This wasn't unusual for Shara lately. Since she had given Brother Andreo the Gold Breast feather, the Cerulean Dusk Dreamer had been ruling her nights again with strange, dark dreams filled with tantalizing insights.

Many of these dreams found her trapped in the forest, overhearing conversations of men—soldiers, she thought—or surrounded by the Dark creatures with vacant eyes. Occasionally the dreams were lighter—in gardens or courtyards filled with children's laughter. Her favorites were the ones where strong arms held her and spun her around and around; these filled her with joy, tinged with a longing for she knew not what.

Sometimes the dreams were of the people she knew: Randin in a mine with an old man; Olva as a girl, surrounded by servants, yet lonely and neglected. She even had a dream of Andreo as a baby in the arms of a beautiful, dark-haired woman who sang a haunting lullaby in an unknown tongue.

Yet last night, wishing to avoid the side effects of sleeping with the power rock, Shara had chosen not to sleep with the Dreamer. Without the rock's ability to draw her into sleep, and with the excitement and trepidation of her and Nicho's venture ahead of her, Shara lay awake well into the early morning hours.

Relieved when the light finally crept through her shutters, she dressed quickly and then sat and waited. Nicho had stressed that timing was important—everything had to go according to plan. When she heard movement downstairs, she pulled the small chalky stone that Nicho had given her three days before from her pocket and scraped it against a wall. She collected the falling white dust on a piece of cloth and carefully patted it on to her face. She wished she could check in Olva's small reflective glass to see if she had done it right. When they had tried it with Nicho, he had laughed and said she looked pale enough to have seen a Rif'iend.

Then she roughed her hair wildly and wet a few strands to make it look as if she had been perspiring. Again she longed for a reflective glass to see the whole effect, but she had done it just as Nicho had told her and would have to trust his judgment. It was time.

She went downstairs gripping her stomach. Randin and Olva were both at the table. Two servants hovered around them, serving a hot herb drink and freshly baked bread. They all looked up as Shara let out a groan and bent double, as if from pain.

"What's wrong with you?" Randin asked sharply.

"I don't know, sir. I feel so sick." Shara gave another groan.

"By Taus," Olva swore. "Look how pale the child is."

Randin eyed her suspiciously.

"Maybe we should fetch the doctor. We can't have her sick, or worse, before ..." Olva's sentence trailed off, and Shara saw her and Randin exchange a silent look.

Shara hadn't expected such concern. Maybe she had overdone it. "It might just be something I ate yesterday," she straightened slightly as she moved closer to the table.

The two servants moved away, as Nicho had predicted. There was a great fear of disease amongst the Parashi, who had been the hardest hit by the plague a few years before.

Randin and Olva were looking at her closely now, and she felt real perspiration on her brow. If she came too close they might realize she was acting.

"I didn't sleep well. I think the best thing would be to have a good long sleep. I'm sure I'll feel much better after that. We can send for the doctor this afternoon if I still feel ill."

Olva nodded and turned to carry on eating.

"Please tell the servants not to disturb me. If I need anything I will call for one of them."

Randin's eyes were still on her and she felt a drop of perspiration roll down her cheek. She had to get away from him now; the chalk would soon smudge and he would see through her performance.

She turned to go, but Randin barked out her name.

"I don't want my whole household sick with this. Stay in your room."

"Yes, sir."

Upstairs she let out a deep breath of pent up relief. The first part of Nicho's plan had succeeded. Now for the hard part—slipping into the stable.

There was usually someone downstairs, and the courtyard was seldom empty. She did not know how she could reach the stable unnoticed. But Nicho had given her a servant's shawl and cloak to wear and told her to wait till she heard the commotion in the courtyard. That was the time she was to walk—not run, he stressed—to the stable.

She put on the cloak and shawl and waited. It felt as if an eternity passed. Had she missed the sign? Or had he left without her? Nicho had refused to tell her exactly what the diversion would entail. She simply had to trust him, he said.

Suddenly there was shouting outside and footsteps running from all directions. She opened the door and stood quietly, listening. There was a hysterical scream, more shouting, calls for water, and the sound of many people in the courtyard. Ghris's door was open. He must have run downstairs already. She closed her door and quietly slipped down the stairs. There was no one left in the house. She could see one of the dining room chairs lying on the floor where it had been flung in haste.

She crossed to the front door, wondering how she would pass all the people in the courtyard unnoticed. When she reached the door she realized it would be fine. True, there were a lot of people, but nobody was paying her any attention. They were all focused on the kitchen, where smoke billowed from the door and windows. Had Nicho actually started a fire in there?

She walked calmly around the perimeter of the courtyard, away from the kitchen, until she reached the stable. The cart was standing just outside as Nicho had said it would. He had placed it at a perfect angle, for when she darted behind it she was out of sight of the kitchen. She made her way to the front, clambered up into the foot space and pulled the musty horse blankets over her. The next part of the plan had worked.

It was a long time before the cart bore down with the weight of Nicho climbing into the driver's seat. Neither of them spoke, Nicho only tongue-clicked for the horse to move forward and the cart jolted toward the gatehouse. She heard the gate swing open, and Nicho's muffled voice say something, and then she had to brace herself as the cart made a sharp turn into the town road. Under the heavy blanket, the stale air had become thin and she fought the urge to push it off her so she could gulp in fresh air. Just a little longer—she knew it wouldn't take long to get to the town gate.

Soon the cart slowed and came to a stop. She heard voices. For a while the cart would stop, jerk forward a few feet and then stop again. More voices. Were they at the gate? Then she heard footsteps move around the cart and a deep voice saying, "Where you off to today, lad?"

"Just fetching some hay for the stable, sir."

"You from the captain's household?"

"Yes, sir."

"You have a letter?"

"Yes, sir." There was a long pause as the man checked the note.

"Well, be off then."

As the cart moved forward again, relief flooded through her. Nicho had said it was unlikely they would search the cart, but just last week she had heard Randin telling Olva that they had increased the security at the town gate since the "incident," whatever that meant.

The cart turned again as they joined the main road and headed out toward the grove. The road around the town passed right next to the Birch Grove, but if they stopped there they would still be in sight of the gate. Nicho planned to pass the grove until they were well out of sight and then leave the road and weave around toward the back of the grove, where no one would see the horse and cart.

The Birch Grove was a small orchard planted well over a hundred years ago by a wealthy Highborn as a memorial for his two children. Nicho knew the story well, for the Parashi lore tellers told how the young girl had tragically drowned at Erridale Lake trying to save her brother. The father, consumed with grief, spent long days at the children's graves, and eventually planted the birch trees to shield the burial place. Nicho had told Shara the story three days earlier, adding that many Parashi feared the grove was haunted. When she had asked him if he felt the same way, he had waved her question away with a dismissive laugh.

Today, however, Nicho and Shara were more concerned with guards than with ghosts. There were no other people on this section of road, since most of the traffic out of the town headed east to join the main trade road that linked the Tirragylin towns. Nicho easily pulled off the road without being noticed by passersby.

The cart jolted wildly over the rough terrain and Shara hoped the wheel axles would withstand the abuse. She was thankful when the cart finally shuddered to a stop.

Nicho jumped off the cart and pulled the blankets away. Shara filled her lungs with the fresh, cold air.

"We did it!" they said in unison, and laughed.

"How did you set fire to the kitchen?"

"It was more smoke than anything else."

He grabbed her by the waist and lifted her down to the ground.

"Come. We mustn't be too long," he said with a smile.

His warm hand casually took her own. The grip was firm and sure and she was so aware of it, that it seemed to her as if she could feel the soft pulse of blood in his fingers. She was suddenly conscious of the clamminess of her own hands.

The first thing Shara noticed inside the Birch Grove was the stillness. The leaf-strewn earth muffled their steps and, as they moved further into the grove, the twittering of birds hushed, as if they were unaccustomed to intruders. She took deep breaths of the cool air, enjoying its sweet damp smell of life. They wound their way deeper into the grove—over fallen branches, roots, and creeping plants—and the beauty of the green, shadowed world captivated her. She wished she could stay here the whole day, soaking in the peace, the way the trees soaked up the rain.

Nicho's whisper felt out of place. "Eerie here, right? Feels sort of sad, don't you think?"

"Sad? No ... well maybe a little. Peaceful, I think."

She didn't think it was eerie, although maybe there was something a little sorrowful about the place.

As they came to a slight clearing, Nicho stopped and let go of her hand. She felt a fleeting regret that the closeness between them was broken.

"So what does your plan say we do now?" she asked. "Do we go looking for the bird?"

Nicho shook his head slightly, but didn't answer. All his planning had centered on reaching the grove. He hadn't given much thought to anything beyond that.

"It's too big and overgrown for us to find the bird." He shrugged. "I suppose she will have to find us."

They sat on a fallen log and talked of the morning's adventure. Nicho had brought some smoked ham and bread from his mother's kitchen and Shara savored the food and the time with him in this beautiful place. Yet she also kept scanning the surrounding trees for a hint of red and gold. They had risked much coming here to find the Gold Breast—what if it was all in vain?

Shara stood up and started pacing impatiently around the clearing.

"Maybe we should try to find her, Nicho." They had jokingly decided that something so beautiful must be a female and started talking about the bird as a "she." "What do you think?"

"I think we should stay here. I believe she will come." He nodded then, certainty on his face. "Yes. We just need to be still and wait patiently."

Shara had just sat down next to him again, when there was a flutter of wings and the Gold Breast landed on a low branch.

"You came," Shara murmured. She had started to wonder if the bird was staying away because she had betrayed it by giving up the feather.

The bird pushed out her breast and sang a song, full of elation, which felt strangely like a welcome. Joy surged through Shara, but also shame. How could she have chosen the Dusk Dreamer over this majestic creature? Would Andreo return the feather if she asked for it?

Nicho came over. "Where to now, Gold Breast?"

As if in answer, the bird flew higher up in the tree; then she flew and perched on a branch toward the eastern side of the clearing, turning to look at Shara and Nicho.

"She wants us to follow her," Shara said.

The Gold Breast led them to the eastern edge of the Grove, the opposite side to where they had hidden the cart. Through the trees they could now see the town walls and Shara tensed at the close proximity to the gate. The bird would fly a few feet—always within their sight—perch on a branch, and wait for them to reach her before taking to the air again. Finally she landed on the ground under a large tree. This time when they reached her, she didn't fly away.

"Is this it? Is this what you want us to see?" Nicho glanced around. There was nothing different about this tree or its location. He scanned the branches, looking for something—a nest maybe? Then he slowly circled the tree, feeling its rough bark with his hands.

Shara sat on the ground next to the Gold Breast. Suddenly she let out a small shout: "Nicho! Look—she's pecking at the ground with her beak."

"Birds are always scouring around for seeds." Nicho shrugged.

He seemed to be considering climbing the tree, for he tentatively pulled down on the lowest branch to see if it would bear his weight.

Shara went down on her knees and started to dig in the soft, damp soil where the bird was pecking. Nicho's baffled expression soon turned into a smile. "You think…?"

"Yes. Something is buried here!"

With both of them digging, it wasn't long before their fingers grazed against a hard object.

"Clear away the soil around it," Nicho said. "Then we should be able to get it loose."

They scooped the ground away until the object—a hard rectangular article wrapped in oilskin—was completely free of soil. Nicho reached down, grasping the base and tentatively pulling it up. The earth seemed reluctant to release its treasure. Eventually they shifted position so that Shara could also take hold of it. With them both pulling they managed to ease it up and out of the hole.

It felt like a solemn moment and neither of them reached out to pull the oilcloth cover away. Only when the Gold Breast landed on the object and broke into her joyful song again, did they feel as if they had permission to unwrap this treasure. Nicho pulled the material away.

Under his fingers lay a box of fine, reddish wood, polished to a high sheen. There was a beautiful symbol engraved on its lid, the likes of which neither of them had ever seen. It may have been a letter in another language.

The intricate clasp that held the box closed appeared to be made of gold. This time it was Shara who reached for the clasp, lifted it and pulled open the lid. Right on the top lay a small dagger. Shara had seen many daggers before—Randin had his fair share, all rough-hewn instruments of violence. But this one was beautiful. The sheath was attached to a belt and both were made of rich polished leather that felt smooth as she ran her fingers over it. The handle of the dagger was made of small green and red stones.

Nicho whistled. "Would you look at that?"

He reached out and picked up the dagger, carefully slipping it out of the sheaf. They could see their own reflections in the polished steel blade. To Shara's inexperienced eye the blade looked thin, but Nicho said, "It's sharp and strong, the best I've ever seen." He turned it around in his hand, feeling the weight of it. "Light and small. I think it is made for a woman."

Shara took it from him. It fitted perfectly into her hand.

They carefully laid it on the covering skin and reached back into the box. The other object was covered in more oilskin. It was a leather-bound book, engraved with the same symbol as that on the box.

Until then they had been kneeling over the box, but now they both sat flat on the ground and opened the book between them. The pages were heavy and thick, the edges yellowed. They gave off that musty book smell that Shara so loved. It was obvious that the handwritten script on the pages had been crafted with painstaking care, but as Shara leaned forward to decipher it, she felt a stab of disappointment. The letters were different—they looked nothing like the Tirragylin alphabet that she had learnt.

"Well, what does it say?" Nicho asked impatiently.

"It's not Tirragylin. I can't read it."

"Are you sure, Shara? Let me see."

Together they turned pages, both their eyes now scanning to see something they could recognize, but there was nothing. The beautiful script dancing across the pages was completely meaningless to them.

CHAPTER 25

Randin and Ghris rode in silence to the betrothal meeting. Randin, pre-occupied by Shara's pale face, wondered fleetingly what would become of the coins and gifts he was to receive today, if Shara died.

The guards at Lucian's gate bowed them through. Randin sensed a new-found respect amongst people, and it pleased him. For too long Gwyndorr's townsfolk had only feared him. With this marriage tie in place, they would realize his influence and treat him with the deference that was his due.

Even contemptuous Lyndis welcomed them with a deeper bow than usual and led them to Lord Lucian's private dining room. He swung the door open and stepped aside with another bow. Randin glanced around Lucian's inner sanctum—a small but richly furnished room.

"Our important guests arrive." For once Lucian's smile seemed sincere as he stepped forward to greet them. Perhaps this marriage would even cause the Lord of Gwyndorr to hold him in higher esteem. Lucian swept an arm toward the table. "We shall start with a meal, symbolic of the rich fare that will be provided for the daughter of your household."

The four town elders already seated at the table, rose in greeting. One of them was Lord Aknor, Randin's father-in-law. Little love passed between the two of them; both of them knew he had only given Olva to Randin because she was pregnant with Ghris. Still, Aknor greeted him cordially enough.

The table groaned with food. No expense had been spared. Three different kinds of meat, including boar, duck, and the river trout that Ghris was so fond of catching, were accompanied by breads, truffles, potatoes in a wine sauce, and vegetables. They finished off with unseasonal strawberries—Randin wondered at their source—and sweet pies. It was far too much food for the small party. The only thing missing was the usual mead. This was another custom, since betrothal discussions required all the parties to have a clear head. The alcohol would be served in celebration once the betrothal was concluded.

After the meal, the seven men made their way to the large parlor. Six stools had been placed in a circle around Lucian's seat. Randin and Ghris were placed in the seats of honor, to Lucian's right, while the four elders took their places to his left.

Dryndin, one of the elders, spoke, opening the betrothal discussions. "We are here today to solemnize the betrothal of Maldor—son of Lucian—and Shara, ward of Randin. This betrothal is binding, and once agreed on, cannot be broken by either party."

There was a murmur of assent, as he continued. "We start by asking the Four Questions. I ask, first, of you Lord Lucian, does your son, Maldor, agree to this betrothal?"

"He does." Lucian's voice was strong and steady.

"Next I ask of you, Randin, does your ward, Shara, agree to this betrothal?" Randin shot Ghris a quick warning glance as he replied. "She does, sir."

"My next question is, have both these parties kept themselves pure for marriage?"

Now it was Lucian who seemed to throw Ghris a cautionary glance, and Randin couldn't quite conceal his smile.

"They have, sir," Lucian and Randin said in unison.

"My third question is for both the male relatives of the bride. Do you wholeheartedly agree that this betrothal is beneficial to Shara?"

"I do," said Randin immediately.

"I do," Ghris said, after a moment's hesitation.

"My last question is for the groom's representatives. What then do you provide to this family for their gift of a daughter?"

Lucian had again followed tradition carefully in his selection of gifts. The first three were all symbolic.

"We offer the gift of a harmonious house." Here the fourth elder produced two beautiful silver goblets to symbolize that the couple would share meals in harmony.

"We offer the gift of a large family." Now a leather pouch was handed to Randin, which contained the seeds of the wild-fig tree, the Tirragylin symbol of fertility.

"We offer the gift of comfort." Lyndis appeared on cue, with a small carpet, which he unrolled for them all to see. Although small, it was a beautifully crafted wool carpet. Its design was unusual—not the bold, bright patterns that the Tirragylin craftsmen favored, but intricately detailed patterns in muted reds, browns, and creams. There was a mutual murmur of admiration at this obviously expensive, foreign gift.

"Finally we offer the gift of provision." This was sometimes where betrothal discussions broke down, as the parties could not agree on an amount for the bride. "We believe your ward to be of great value and therefore offer twenty pieces of gold to your family."

It was difficult to keep the surprise from showing on his face. The highest betrothal price that Randin had heard of was twelve pieces of gold. The Tirragylin custom was that the bride's party always reject the initial offer, to show that they valued their daughter more than the groom's family.

"I reject your offer. My ward is worth more," Randin said, slightly breathlessly.

"Twenty-five," said Lucian.

"Thirty," said Randin.

"You press a hard bargain, Randin. Thirty gold coins, it is." Lucian said dryly, but Randin caught the edge of a smile on his lips.

The elder again took over, although his own surprise had caused him, momentarily, to lose the thread of the proceedings. "Right," he said, clearing his throat. "That finalizes the betrothal of Maldor and Shara, for thirty pieces of gold. The betrothal is binding and the marriage may be consummated at any time in the next two years, when the couple will become man and wife."

The transaction was complete. Shara belonged to Maldor. Soon the mead was flowing freely. The drinking would go on well into the night.

• • •

Tessor watched from behind the fire as the men arrived. She recognized some of the elders, for they had been old friends of Fafa's. She remembered Aknor, father of Olva. Yorina had always been jealous of the pretty, younger girl. Tessor, however, had felt a little sorry for her. She remembered the beautifully dressed Olva coming to play with them. There had been hunger in the girl's eyes as she watched Fafa twirling Yorina around in the garden.

Olva's fine features—and a little of the same sadness—were visible in the face of her son, Ghris.

She watched the men as they gorged themselves on the food. How different to her own betrothal ceremony, solemnized between Lucian, Fafa, and two town elders in Fafa's study. There had been no meal, no gifts, not even a bride price paid because Fafa had declared that she was a treasure beyond value. Nothing Lucian gave him could compensate for his loss.

There was little to be learned, standing in the passage behind the fireplace, Tessor realized. The men spoke only about hunting, hounds, and horses. She slipped away from the warm wall and felt her way back to the other passage, from which she could listen to the voices in the parlor, the place the men would go to solemnize the betrothal. Tessor sat with her back to the cold wall, her fingers trailing through the dust until she heard the muffled voices. She rose and pressed her ear closer to the darkened peephole, straining to listen. It was difficult to follow all the proceedings. The elders spoke softly with age; the young man, Ghris, with nervousness. Only Lucian and Randin's voices rang out clearly enough for her to hear.

Still, there was only one thing Tessor wanted to know. *What would Lucian pay for this girl?* That price would confirm to Tessor what she was beginning to suspect.

Something trembled through her when she finally heard Lucian's smooth voice declare it. *Thirty gold coins.* And Tessor knew. This girl was far from ordinary. Thirty gold coins—an exorbitant, unheard of bride-price. Lucian had never wanted something so much in his life.

Tessor didn't know who the girl was or why Lucian desired her for Maldor, but of one thing she was now absolutely certain. In this girl—Shara—she had finally found a weapon to use against Lucian.

CHAPTER 26

Nicho carried the box, wrapped again in its oilcloth covering, back to the cart, where they concealed it in the foot space. They loosely pulled the horse blankets over it. Shara, in her servant's cloak, now sat next to Nicho as he coaxed the horse back over the rough terrain.

Nicho avoided the city gates by taking a long detour around the grove. The farther they drew away from the city, the more Shara enjoyed this, her very first outing. Initially they still passed the occasional merchant cart and Shara would quickly pull the shawl over her hair in an attempt to hide her face. However, as they moved along quieter roads where there were no other carts, she let the shawl fall on her shoulders. She enjoyed the bite of the wind on her face as she drank in the view of the forest and the distant mountains.

Nicho kept glancing over at her. "You will catch a cold, Shara. Why don't you cover your face a bit more?"

Shara, however, had never felt the exhilaration of wide-open spaces and fresh breezes, and wasn't going to lose a single moment of the short-lived freedom.

"It's worth it. I don't mind if I'm in bed for a month," she laughed.

Too soon they reached the farm and she again covered her hair and face as best she could. They had discussed whether she should hide again, but had decided against it. Besides the long period of discomfort, she would draw even more unwanted attention to herself if discovered.

The farmer's two adolescent sons emerged to help load the bales of hay and, seeing Shara, grinned and prodded Nicho with knowing smiles. Shara felt her face burn at some of the comments she overheard, but Nicho joked along with them and soon changed the subject to weather and crops.

It took a while for them to negotiate a price for the hay. The farmer himself arrived for this part of the sale. He glanced suspiciously at Shara, unlike his sons, making no comment.

When the cart was loaded and payment had been made, Nicho climbed back into the driver's seat. The farmer had walked around to the front, and before the horse could move, jerked back the reins. He was now within an arm's distance of Shara and she felt his eyes on her face, even though her own were looking down at her lap.

"I'm surprised Master Randin spares his servant girls for drives into the country," he said. "But now I see. Not a servant girl at all. The look of a noble-woman. Smooth skin. Hands that 'aven't scrubbed too many a pot."

Shara quickly moved her hands under her cloak and kept her eyes averted.

"Careful, Nicho. You are a good lad, but you be playin' with fire, frolicking with this young 'un."

He let go of the reins and, as he slapped the horse hard on the rump, the cart shot forward.

All Shara's carefree joy had evaporated at his words. *They had been discovered.*

Nicho seemed to sense her turmoil. "He won't tell, Shara."

"How do you know that?"

"He's a good man. He doesn't care much for Randin. He likes me, often offers me a share in their midday meal in fact."

"I should have hidden ... they saw right through me. I can't believe we were this careless."

"Shara." He stopped the cart, reaching for her shoulder and drawing her toward him. "He knows nothing. Only that I had a beautiful girl at my side. We have not been found out, I promise. We are still safe."

They sat like that for a while, Shara's fear easing away in the comfort of his embrace. Finally, reluctantly, she pulled away from him, a hint of a smile on her lips as she said: "Beautiful, Nicho? Really?"

He smiled, but when he spoke it was in earnest. "Very beautiful."

Shara looked away, embarrassed at the flush she felt on her cheeks. Nicho clicked at the horse and the cart rolled forward, toward Gwyndorr. Toward captivity. Yet it was difficult to concentrate on anything but the feelings Nicho had just revealed in those two simple words.

After a long ride, Nicho stopped the cart. "We are reaching the intersection of the road leading to Gwyndorr. After this point it will be more difficult to stop and let you hide without being seen."

They moved the wooden box containing the book and dagger to the back, hiding it between two bales of hay. Shara was soon wedged uncomfortably in the foot space again, under the cover of the horse blankets, which Nicho opened to a small slit to allow in some air.

It felt like an eternity before she heard Nicho warning that they were approaching Gwyndorr. Her numb legs demanded to be stretched. Relief that their journey was almost over mingled with the fear of discovery.

"We are almost there. I am going to close the slit now. Hush."

In the darkness, Shara's heart pounded so loudly that she wondered if the guards would be able to hear it. They hadn't discovered her on the way out, so they wouldn't discover her now. The cart slowed and stopped, bouncing forward every now and again. Finally the footsteps of the guards moved around the cart and she heard a muffled voice saying, "Got your hay then, lad?"

"Yes, sir."

"You took longer today, didn't you?" the voice now sounded closer to her.

"The farmer didn't have the bales ready yet, sir, so I had to wait."

"What's under these blankets then, Lad?"

"Nothing sir, just some horse blankets I bought from the farmer."

"In that case, you won't mind if I take a look, will you?"

Cool air and blinding light rushed over Shara as the blankets were ripped away. She looked straight into the close-set eyes of the guard. For an instant neither of them reacted and then he let out a sharp call. She heard other footsteps running and she turned to look at Nicho. He was bent over, face buried in his hands.

Shara had an overwhelming urge to fling her arms around him and tell him that she wouldn't let Randin punish him, but already hands were grasping at her, pulling her free of her hiding place. A commanding voice told Nicho to step down from the cart.

"I'm sorry, Nicho," she called, but her voice didn't carry well over the commotion.

Suddenly there was a piercing call that reverberated deep into her body. The hands that had started to pry her loose from the cart freed their grip and she watched in amazement as her captor—hands covering his ears—sank to the ground. All the guards that had run toward their cart were in various stages of dropping over, holding their heads and moaning as if an unseen arrow had shot each one of them down.

She turned to look at the cart-driver behind her. Although he hadn't fallen over, he too was holding his head, eyes closed, and face creased in pain.

Astonished, she saw the Gold Breast land on the seat between her and Nicho.

"What are you ...?" she started, before it dawned on her that the noise, which had now softened to a pulsating whoosh, was coming from the bird. In that moment, both she and Nicho grasped the significance of what had just happened. She clambered onto the front seat, just as he said, "Quick, Shara! Let's get out of here."

As Nicho pulled off, the Gold Breast took to the air and flew toward the line of carts. Shara glanced back to take a last look at the strange scene behind them. The guards were still lying on the ground, although one of the four now stirred, making an effort to roll onto his side. She heard the frenzied yelping of the guard dogs in their cages.

"Get under the blankets," Nicho hissed, as they tore around the bend toward the house.

Shara dove for cover again, still trying to make sense of all that had just happened. The one thought that crept into her mind and filled her with sickening dread, was that although they had made it through the town gate, the guard had seen her face as clearly as she had seen his.

· · ·

Randin watched Lucian's servants come in to the darkening parlor. One stoked the fire, while two others lit the tall silver candelabras lining the walls.

"More mead, sir?" Another servant stood by his side, flagon in hand.

Randin nodded and the light of the candles caught the golden liquid as it swilled into his goblet. He took a small sip, swallowing down the tooth-achingly sweet drink as quickly as he could. He had never liked mead.

The men around him did not seem to share his view. They had been quaffing it down since the end of the betrothal ceremony, and still were when Maldor sauntered in to the parlor followed by two friends.

"So, is my fate sealed then, Father?" So scornful. "I am to marry this trivial wench?"

The elders stiffened, and Lucian's eyes narrowed in anger on his son. Randin had felt the words like a blow.

"I suppose the only thing to do," the young man continued before anybody could react, "is to drown our sorrows. Lyndis. Send for the mead."

And drown his sorrows he had. Now Maldor and Ghris, arms around each others' shoulders, were doubled over with laughter as one of their friends poured mead down another's throat.

The elder speaking to Lucian by the fire was swaying slightly, two others were slumped over their chairs as if in sleep. Aknor was also sprawled in a chair, staring pensively into his goblet.

Only Lucian remained alert and sober.

Randin watched Lyndis cross the large parlor and whisper something in the lord's ear. Lucian looked up sharply and his eyes sought out Randin's. *Trouble*. Randin had been Town Captain too long not to sense it. He moved across the room and reached the parlor door just as Lucian and Lyndis did.

"What is it?" he whispered before his gaze fell on the man standing just outside the room. It was the last man Randin wanted to see—Issor.

His second-in-command jumped to attention. He had ridden hard and was out of breath. "Captain. It happened again. The same thing. At the gate."

"Not here, you fool," Lucian hissed, glancing back into the parlor. "We'll talk in my dining room."

Randin followed Lucian with mounting apprehension. This was not good. What had possessed Issor to come to the manor with this news, knowing how edgy Lucian was about security?

As soon as Lucian closed the door behind them, he spun around to Issor. "Tell me."

Issor looked nervously at Randin. "Well, I was inside the guardhouse when I suddenly heard the dogs howling and a noise unlike anything I've ever heard before," he said haltingly. "It was difficult for me to move. That sound was so,"— he clutched his head—"so consuming. But when I managed to get out, I saw four guards on the ground."

"Injured?" Lucian asked.

"No. Not really. They were … dazed."

"Dazed?"

"Yes, my lord. Confused. They couldn't remember anything. And their heads pounded with pain."

"They didn't know what had caused it?" Lucian asked.

"No, my lord. They couldn't remember anything except waking up on the ground."

"Were there other people at the gate?" Randin asked softly.

"Yes, sir. As you know, it's a busy time. There was a long row of carts and some riders and foot-travelers waiting to come in."

"Were they also knocked out?" Lucian asked.

"Not like the guards were. But the ones I spoke to said they also heard the shrill noise."

"Did they *see* anything, Issor?" Randin asked.

"The man closest to the gate remembers there was a cart ahead of him. Said it was loaded with hay. But there was no cart when I came out."

Lucian, who had paced across the small room to the fireplace, turned back to them. His voice was dangerously calm. "So your men let an enemy slip into the city, Randin."

"I don't think —" Randin began.

"It was a statement." Lucian's eyes flashed with menace. "*Not* a question."

"I am sure we can find out more when the guards have recovered, my lord."

"As you did the last time this happened?" Lucian scoffed.

It was true. The last time the guards were knocked out, they had remembered nothing when Randin questioned them the next day. He stiffened. "I will go right now to the barracks. We will increase the security at the gate and double the patrols inside Gwyndorr."

"Remember that you are not the only man for this job, Randin," Lucian said, looking over at Issor. "And there have been far too many mistakes lately. I suggest you rectify them soon."

Randin bowed. "Of course, Lord Lucian. I will ensure nothing like this happens again."

He turned, Issor on his heels. As he marched from the manor, Randin smarted at the unfairness of Lucian's accusations and threats. How was he supposed to fight a force that could not be seen, that wielded ear-splitting sounds instead of swords?

As he mounted his horse, the clink of coins reminded Randin of the pouch tucked deep inside his robe. He smiled. Despite the security breaches and Lucian's threats, it had still been a good day for him. Thirty gold coins for his dark-haired ward. *Trivial wench.* The memory of Maldor's words throbbed anger through him. Yet, today only Lucian's view counted, and *he* had considered Shara to be most valuable indeed.

Yes, it had still been a very good day for Randin.

CHAPTER 27

Shara was unsure how her shaky legs carried her from the stable to her room. After their discovery at the town gate, it seemed irrelevant if anyone also saw her at home, and she merely threw off the servant's clothes, crawled around the cart and ran through the courtyard to the house. As she opened the front door, a servant in the parlor let out a startled expression. "Weren't you in your room, Miss Shara?"

"I needed some fresh air." Shara hurtled up the steps.

For once her room felt like a sanctuary. She sank onto her bed, pulling the blanket over her and hiding in its quiet darkness. Slowly her breathing and heart stilled, but her thoughts were wilder in the silence than they had been in all the action. She lay like that for a long time, until darkness stole into her room.

Any minute now she thought she would hear the horses at the gate, the shouts as the town guards came for Nicho, Marai's desperate cries as her son was dragged away.

Yet all was silent.

She was straining so hard to hear any sound from the courtyard that the light knock on the door startled her.

"Miss Shara? Marai has sent some food up for you. She is worried that you have not eaten all day." Yasmin slipped inside and placed a tray of soup and bread on Shara's bed.

"'Tis so dark in here. Let me light some candles for you. Are you feeling better, Miss?"

"Yes, much." The mention of Marai's name brought on a wave of guilt. If anything became of Nicho, Marai would be devastated by grief. Why hadn't Shara thought of that before allowing Nicho to take her out of the town? Why had she risked so much on one little jaunt?

The vegetable soup smelled good and Shara ate a little, hoping to ease the gnawing pain in her stomach. Yasmin continued to flutter around, lighting candles and closing the shutters for the night.

Suddenly Shara heard it—hoofbeats and the jangle of stirrups. She leapt off the bed, spilling soup on the blanket, and ran to the window.

"How many are there?"

"Miss Shara. Do not concern yourself so." Yasmin laid a restraining arm on Shara in a way that showed that she was rather concerned herself. "I suspect 'tis merely Sir Randin and Master Ghris returning."

Shara pushed the blinds open again and could make out the shape of a single rider in the light of the rising moon. The cart no longer stood in the courtyard; Nicho must have emptied it and pulled it inside the stable. She watched his tall figure emerge now to take Ghris's horse, and marveled at his calm after all that had happened today. He should have run. He should be far from Gwyndorr by now. But, of course, Parashi could never leave, even if the noose was tightening around them.

Yasmin stood at her side, a worried look on her face. "Is there anything else you need, Miss?"

"No, thank you."

Could it be that the guards had not followed them? They had seen her face in clear daylight. They knew Nicho was from Randin's household. How was it possible that they had not come for him yet?

• • •

Shara finally found comfort in the warmth of the Dusk Dreamer. As she lay awake gripping it to her chest, the rock's powers wrapped her in its gentle embrace, convincing her that Nicho would not be arrested and Marai would not lose her son to the Rif'twine. All will be well, it seemed to whisper, all will be well. Then the rock lured her deeper. Into itself. Into sleep.

Shara walked down a dim passage and sensed the weight of the cold stone walls pressing down on her. No, she thought, more than just walls. History and memories and the heaviest of sorrows.

A woman—ear pushed to the wall—stood with her back to Shara. Her dress was made of dark brown velvet that might have been beautiful once. Now the sleeves were threadbare and the fabric stained. As the woman turned, Shara caught sight of her strangely elongated face and close-set eyes lined with dark shadows. Sadness clung to the woman like the frayed fabric of her dress. The one the house has forgotten, Shara thought as the woman dissolved into the shadows.

Voices whispered through the walls. Now Shara pressed her right ear to the small holes through which the light danced in beams. The first voice she heard sounded familiar. She's little more than a commoner. I don't mind bedding her, but why tie her to me as a wife? *Shara felt the chill of the words even more than the icy wall against which she leaned.* It has been decided. *That voice was different—smooth, warm, drawing her closer.*

The walls melted away, and now Shara stood in a large parlor lined with magnificent tapestries. Richly dressed people stood around her, their gazes as cool and appraising as those of buyers at a horse sale. They opened a path for her to walk down and her skin prickled with the intensity of their stares. Pain jarred through the soft flesh of her feet. When she looked down she was barefoot and walking on sharp gold coins.

She hobbled to the end of the aisle of people and looked up into the powerful face of a man with gold-flecked eyes. His cape of light gray fur looked so soft that Shara longed to reach out and touch it. When he spoke, she knew it had been his smooth voice that drew her from the passage. How I have longed for this day. *His words welcomed and warmed her.*

But from the shadows behind him crept the forgotten woman. She wore a sumptuous orange robe and her voice was a soft murmur that grew ever louder as it echoed through the room. I will vindicate you, Fafa. Whatever it takes.

In her hand she clutched an ancient, rusted dagger.

And her eyes were fixed on Shara.

Fear coursed through Shara's body with every pounding beat of her heart. What had she just seen? Something from her past or something still to come? Why did she still cling to the Dusk Dreamer when it took her to places so dark and people so ominous?

Not always. Shara tried to recall the joy she'd felt when deep laughter spun around her through the air, high above a garden.

It was only the memory of those light-filled dreams that finally soothed Shara back to sleep that night.

CHAPTER 28

The truth had been staring him in the face this whole time. How could he have missed something so obvious?

Randin had been riding through the Parashi slum on the morning of the Spring Feast, when the insight dawned on him, and since then his anger had been growing steadily, until it enveloped him in a taut net that allowed almost no room for other thoughts. To be made a fool of by *any* man was bad enough. To be made a fool of by his own Lowborn groom was completely intolerable. The lad would pay dearly—very dearly indeed.

Now, back at the barracks, Randin tried to rationalize his inattention to the matter. Of course, Randin reasoned, he had been dealing with far greater problems. Lucian had been sending messengers. He demanded news on the progress of the investigation into the latest incident at the gate. There had been nothing more to report. The mystery cart had vanished without a trace into the labyrinth of Gwyndorr's streets. One guard recalled that the driver was fairly young, another that there was something hidden under horse blankets in the footrest. Yet no amount of questioning or threatening could uncover any more details than those scant few. This did not satisfy Lord Lucian, however, who seemed to hold Randin personally accountable for this latest incident. Randin's argument that there was some magic at play fell on unsympathetic ears.

Yes, Randin had been too preoccupied, his instincts dulled by both gate dramas and the ensuing pressure from Lucian. Yet now—in one searing moment of clarity—he understood that the one teaching letters in the slum was none other than Nicho. Only Nicho visited the boy's house regularly, not, as Randin had initially thought, to be with the boy's mother. No, the last two Friday mornings Nicho had been at the boy's house, *teaching*. And, Issor informed him, there was another house that Nicho visited even more often. Probably there were other students to be uncovered there too.

A quiet rage simmered inside Randin as he thought about the night that Nicho had come to the barracks and convinced him to let the boy, Simhew, go free. Guilt had obviously driven the groom to it, knowing that the boy's arrest was due to his own teaching. How smoothly he had pleaded for the boy's life and he—Randin—had even felt a measure of pity. *Fool!* Once again Nicho had proved that a Parashi was totally untrustworthy.

Randin was astute enough to realize that he was also angry that he was about to lose a remarkable groom. There was no denying that the horses were calm and malleable in Nicho's hands. He would be difficult to replace. There was also his mother to consider—a rather good cook. She was unlikely to stay in Randin's household after he arrested her son and sent him off to the Rif'twine. He thought regretfully that he would truly miss her fig pie, the one that reminded him so much of his mother's.

Issor sauntered into the room.

"News, Issor?"

"Nothing, Captain. Still no eyewitnesses, and the more I try to talk to the guards, the less they have to say."

"It's magic. No doubt about it."

"Yes, sir. Wouldn't surprise me if there was a Mind rock involved."

"Mind rock?"

"Yes, Captain. It's one of the seven power rocks. Even more powerful than the Dusk Dreamer. The Dreamers are blue, while the Mind rocks are black. They—"

"By Taus! I know about power rocks. Do you think me a fool?"

"Of course not, Captain. You seemed a bit confused—"

"I am not confused. But *Mind rocks*? By Taus, Issor. They don't lie around on the street. In fact, I've never come across one at all."

"That's not to say that our enemies don't have one, sir."

"There are other forms of magic."

"True." Issor's eyes widened. "Do you think it could be the Brethren of Taus, sir? It's the kind of thing they could do with their Word Arts."

"I suppose they could." Randin sighed. This conversation was rather aimless, as far as he was concerned. "But they are not our enemies, Issor."

"No. Unless it is just one of them. Maybe they are seeking revenge for—"

"Enough, Issor. This conspiracy nonsense isn't getting us anywhere."

"Of course, Captain."

"Anyway, there is something else you need to take care of."

"Sir?"

Randin took a deep breath. "I know who is teaching the Parashi boys letters."

"You do?"

"Yes. It's obvious. It's my groom, Nicho."

"Your groom, Captain? I don't understand." Issor's forehead furrowed. "I thought we were looking for a Highborn or one of the Parashi elders. Surely a young groom doesn't know letters?"

Randin's mouth pinched with displeasure. He had considered this question already: who had taught Nicho letters? The answer didn't please him, for he had narrowed the possible suspects down to three—Brother Andreo, Shara, or Ghris. That there was such blatant disregard for the law in the household of the Captain of the Guard was shameful.

"It is of little consequence," he said dismissively.

"I will send out guards straightaway, Captain. To your house," —Issor looked down momentarily— "as well as to the young boy's house."

"No, not yet Issor."

"Captain?"

"You can't arrest my groom yet."

"May I ask why not, Captain?"

"His mother is my cook, and she has a bride feast to prepare in a we—time. I don't want anything upsetting that. You can be at the house to arres—Nicho the day after Sacred Day. And not a moment before the bridal party leaves."

• • •

"Miss Shara?" Yasmin's voice from behind her closed door sounded concerned. "Lady Olva is calling for you."

"Tell her I'm still sick." It's the excuse she had used the day before too as she waited—a hard stone of fear in her stomach—for the guards to come for Nicho. They hadn't come. Perhaps they did not make arrests on Tirragyl's Sacred Day.

"The seamstress is here with your dresses, Miss. She can't come back."

Shara swung the door open with a sigh. "I don't even want those cursed gowns." She was surprised to see that Yasmin was not dressed in her usual drab kitchen garb, but an attractive green dress and shawl. "You look different, Yasmin."

"Got the rest of the day off, Miss Shara," she grinned. "Spring Feast."

"Really?" Randin had never let her go to Gwyndorr's annual celebration, but she had heard Yasmin and Fortuni speak about it in the kitchen. The music and dancing and contests. Shara had imagined it all in her mind.

"So will you come, Miss Shara?"

"Randin never lets me." Yasmin frowned and Shara realized her mistake. "Oh, you mean will I come downstairs? Fine." She pulled the door closed behind her. "Might as well get it over with."

Downstairs, Olva was bedecked in the Octora-silk dress and a necklace of matching red stones. She beamed as she saw Shara. "Look. My dress was ready just in time for the Feast."

"How lovely for you." Shara's biting tone was lost on the excited Olva.

"Here are your outfits too, Shara. Try them on!"

Shara walked over to the three gowns and cloak that had been made for her. They were, she had to admit, exquisite. She fingered the smooth, cool fabric of the emerald green dress, admiring the gold lace woven in patterns over the bodice and draping sleeves.

"It's important you try them so that we can still make changes before ..."

Shara looked up as Olva's sentence trailed off. "Before what?" she asked sharply.

"Before the seamstress gets too busy," Olva said, waving her hand breezily. "Summer is a busy time for you, is it not, Hwyn?"

"Indeed, my lady." The seamstress bowed her head. "Let me help you with them, Miss."

Shara allowed the woman to help her into the emerald gown. She tightened ribbons and fastened loops and had Shara spin around in front of Olva's looking glass. Finally Hwyn and Olva declared it to be perfect.

Perfect for what? Shara wanted to ask. But she knew she would not receive an honest answer.

The second dress, made of a light blue fabric that made Shara think of a winter sky, was the loveliest of all. It was the one she was wearing when Randin came in.

His appraising look reminded her of the people in her last dream, but his gaze softened as he said, "You look lovely, Shara. Are you feeling better?"

"I'm fine, Randin."

He cast Olva a meaningful gaze. "Good. I need to ensure all the patrols are out during the Spring Feast, but the litter is ready to take you, my love."

"Can I go with Olva?" Shara asked impulsively. Yasmin's earlier excitement had been contagious. "I could even wear this gown."

"I think perhaps ..."

"Please. Everyone talks about it. I feel so left out."

"Lord Lucian won't like it," Olva murmured.

"What's he got to do with it?" Shara asked.

"He's concerned for your safety, that's all," Olva said.

"*My* safety? Why?"

"We'll take some of the extra guards Lucian sent over," Randin said. "It's time she stepped out a bit. Saw the world."

"We can't afford to make a mistake after all these years." Olva glowered at her husband. "Just when it's about to happen."

"When *what's* about to happen?" Shara said.

"I'm tired of Lord Lucian dictating what I can and can't do in my own household. Anyway, he never comes to the Spring Feast."

"You think he won't hear about it?" Olva snapped. "You're a fool. There's too much at stake."

"Why does he even care if I'm there?" Shara interjected.

"A fool, am I?" Randin's face reddened. "Well at least I'm a fool who still rules his own house."

CHAPTER 29

Nicho once again glanced up at Shara's room. The window was dark and he could hardly see into it at all, although he sometimes had the impression that there was movement inside. It had been two days since they had been outside the town and still Shara had not come to talk to him.

He had found it hard to concentrate on his work yesterday. Even though it was the Sacred Day, Nicho had still expected the town guards to come for him at any moment. His mind played out the scene of his arrest. Once, he had seen a few town guards drag a drunken man out of a tavern for some minor offense. He'd watched them beat and kick him, ripping his clothes in their abuse. Now his imagination created a similar scene for his own arrest—guards riding in through the gate, jumping from their horses, pulling him to the ground. He could feel the bite of the ropes as they bound him, see himself stumbling as they dragged him away. Worst of all, he imagined his mother's expression as she came running from the kitchen, begging them to show him leniency, and the guards laughing at the idea that somebody who opposed Randin should be shown mercy.

However, they had not come yesterday. When they still didn't appear this morning, some of Nicho's trepidation eased away. If they knew where to find him, wouldn't they have come for him by now? Could it be that they didn't know?

Only Ghris appeared suspicious. He had been in and out of the stable more than usual. The day before he had sauntered into the stable and asked Nicho what time he had been at the town gate on the day he fetched the supplies.

Another concern Nicho had—with Ghris's regular visits to the stable—was that the book and dagger would be discovered. He had hidden the box under a few broken floorboards, covered over with loose hay. It was not a good hiding place but it would have to do until he could give it to Shara.

As much as he fought it, thoughts of Shara also occupied him. One image, in particular, played over in his mind: Shara sitting on the cart, eyes dark with worry as the sun lit her black hair with hints of fire. He remembered how soft she had felt as he pulled her into his arms to comfort her, and a surge of shame filled him. How was it possible that he should have such strong feelings for a Highborn? Why had he allowed that to happen?

"Hey, stranger. Where you been hidin' out?" Yasmin's voice pulled him out of his reverie. She was wearing a tight green dress that drew attention to her curvaceous body and a sultry smile to accompany it. He guessed that meant she had grown bored with her latest lover and was once more turning her attention to him. "Don't you know Master Randin has given us all the rest of the day off? It's the Spring Feast today. Aren't you going?"

"Uh ... I wasn't planning to go. The foal hasn't been so well, I wanted to keep an eye on her." *And be here in case Shara came down to talk to him.*

"Come on, Nicho. We only get three days off in the whole year. It would be much more fun if you were there." She had moved closer to him, and now her eyes were silently communicating what her body and smile had suggested.

He couldn't help feeling slightly flattered. Yasmin was undeniably attractive and fun. Maybe this was just what he needed to take his mind off his worries.

"Well, you are persuasive, Yasmin. Who else is going then?"

She waved her hand in a dismissive way as she said, "Just a couple of the kitchen girls and the lads from the gate."

Nicho looked up in surprise at the guardhouse. "Master Randin gave them time off too?"

"Well, word is Lord Lucian has brought in some more highly trained guards to take over from them for a while. So the lads haven't had very much to do lately."

Nicho looked more carefully at the men at the exit. They weren't the usual three young men, but rather older, darker men, with an upright posture that suggested army training. He had been too distracted worrying about Shara and the hidden book to notice the switch, and the cold fear of discovery once again crept over him.

He tried to sound casual. "Lord Lucian? What does he have to do with Master Randin's household security?"

"No idea," Yasmin said in a bored voice. "So are you going to come, or not?"

It might be a good time to get away from this place, if the net was closing in on him.

"Yes, I'll come," he said.

Less than half an hour later he and Yasmin made their way across the courtyard to the gatehouse. She linked her arm through his own in an overly familiar grasp, but he didn't pull away; he was grateful for the support as he passed the guards. They appeared to pay him little heed.

He turned back to look over his shoulder a few times as they walked down the street, but as far as he could tell they were not being followed. As they turned the corner he and Shara had hurtled around two days earlier, they suddenly found themselves in the middle of the festive crowd.

The Spring Feast was Gwyndorr's most popular celebration, and the town folk, travelling merchants, farmers, and anybody near the town, came to join in the festivities. Most of them were clad in bright clothes. There were dancers and singers, musicians playing lyres, and bards standing on platforms reciting poetry. Children scampered through the crowd, playing chase or hide-and-seek as mothers called out warnings for them to stay near. The taverns had brought out large barrels of mead or cider and served them on the street, and the rich smell of roasting hog from the cooking pits built for the occasion filled the air.

Nicho and Yasmin were swept along toward the town center, where the contests would soon take place. As a child, this had been the best part of the festival for Nicho. He had always tried to push as far forward as he could to the large ring erected for the occasion, and watched in awe as the young men showed off their dueling, wrestling, or archery skills. There were contests that required less skill, like the mead drinking or sheep-stomach eating. Nicho had watched it all from beginning to end, laughing at the silly and marveling at the skilled.

Even now, the crowd's excitement and anticipation was contagious. Yasmin still had her arm linked in his, although now it was more out of necessity. It was easy to be separated in the jostling crowd, especially when a Highborn passed, for their servants wouldn't hesitate to shove you out the way to clear a path for their master or mistress. Some of the ladies were carried in curtained litters, which required an even wider berth.

Soon they could see the ring, encircled with flaming torches. Bales of hay had been placed around it as seating for the Highborns. Pressed in against these was the standing crowd. As usual, the children had slipped to the front.

Over the drone of the crowd a voice shouted: "Yaz! Over here."

Several other servants from Randin's household were seated on a large window ledge. Nicho and Yasmin struggled to cross through the current of people pushing toward the ring, but eventually their friends were pulling them up. The extra height gave them an excellent view of the ring, where two jugglers were throwing burning torches at each other.

Out of the pushing crowd, Nicho found himself enjoying the festival. As his mind edged away from the strain of discovery, he became absorbed in the excitement of the acts and contests, the cheers and jeers and the fun, joyful atmosphere.

Until he saw a face that had the same effect on him as washing with ice-cold water on a winter morning: Ghris. Instantly, the light feeling dissipated.

Ghris was pushing toward the ring and was now only a few paces away from them. Nicho hoped he wouldn't see them. He was so busy keeping an eye on Ghris that he didn't immediately notice Ghris's companion. Suddenly there was a loud commotion, as an older woman was shoved into a group of boys. Nicho looked at the source of the upheaval—a tall, muscled youth with Ghris that Nicho recognized as Lord Maldor. The old woman wailed, cradling her arm.

Over the crowd Nicho could hear Maldor say, "Shut your mouth, you old Parashi bag. Otherwise, I'll break the other arm too." Maldor had changed little in the four years since Nicho last saw him.

Suddenly he became aware that Maldor was gazing in his direction. No—not his—Yasmin's. Those eyes devoured Yasmin with intensity before Maldor turned and continued toward the ring, people now giving him and Ghris a wide berth. Nicho let out a ragged sigh as he looked over at Yasmin. From the flush on her cheeks, it seemed she had also been aware of Maldor's stare. And—far from being perturbed—her smile showed that she was particularly flattered by the young lord's attention.

. . .

Shara yearned to walk through Gwyndorr's streets, but it was Randin's one condition. She had to be carried by two of the new gate guards in a curtained box, with another of the guards walking beside her. It had taken some time to prepare another litter.

"Like an old rich lady," she grumbled under her breath as she climbed into the cushioned seat, and the gold curtain fell closed behind her. Still, she was going to the Spring Feast. It was almost too good to be true.

The box lurched to the right as they lifted it onto their shoulders and Shara braced herself with a soft curse. Yet, by the time they were on the street the two men had fallen into step with each other and the box swayed in a comfortable rhythm. Shara pulled one of the curtains aside and peered through the slit, but the tall guard walking next to her obscured most of her view. She still caught sight of patches of cobbled street milling with feet, the occasional flash of a passing face and the legs of children and dogs scampering in and out of view. As she opened the curtain a little wider, the guard scowled at her, and she quickly let it fall back into place. Still, she reveled in the crowd, bustling with excitement, laughter, and singing, and savored the smells of roasting meat wafting into the box. The Spring Feast was everything Yasmin had told her it would be.

It felt like they had travelled a long way when she heard the tall guard say, "We're here, Miss." The box listed again as they lowered it to the ground. As she stepped from the box, Shara's attention was immediately drawn to the ring, where several youths were trying to catch two squealing piglets, to great laughter and applause.

"This way, Miss," the guard said gruffly. He took her elbow and guided her through the crowd to the bale of hay on which Olva was already seated.

"So, Randin went through with his folly," Olva frowned as she looked at Shara and then moved over reluctantly. "You'd better sit here so you don't crush that new dress."

Shara sensed the gazes and whispers of the people around her. *Just like in her dream.* Unease prickled through her. Yet she forgot everything as she was drawn into the antics of the actors, the skill of the archers and the hilarity of the contests that unfolded before her.

The sound of a woman wailing finally broke the spell. Shara turned around. The woman's cries were drowned out by the voice of a man hurling insults. Around Shara the crowd grew silent, their eyes turned to take in the real drama happening off the stage. Shara couldn't see anything until the crowd pushed apart to let through two young men.

"It's Ghris," Olva said, but her face only lit up when she saw his companion. "And Maldor."

Maldor? The one who had falsely accused Nicho all those years ago?

Olva patted her dress nervously and cast a quick glance at Shara. "Stand up when you greet him and put on your best manners, Shara."

"For *him*? Why should I?"

"He's Lord Lucian's son, that's why."

As Ghris and Maldor reached them, Olva rose and curtsied. "How good to see you again, Lord Maldor."

"Lady Olva," he acknowledged, although his intense dark eyes were on Shara.

"What's she doing here?" Ghris hissed.

"Your father's idea."

Shara rose as Maldor stepped toward her.

"So this is Shara." Her name sounded flat and dull on his tongue. "Perhaps not quite as ordinary as I recall. Worth her weight in gold, I wonder?"

"Maldor. I see Bruna and Lyor." To Shara's relief, Ghris seemed keen to draw his friend away.

Maldor was still looking at her. "I look forward to the pleasure of our next meeting, Shara." His smile held no warmth, and Shara was relieved when he turned to follow Ghris to their group of friends.

"Handsome, isn't he?" Olva whispered.

Handsome? Maybe. But all Shara saw when she looked at him was the malice with which he had ruined Nicho's life.

The guard who had accompanied her here arrived just then with two goblets of cider and a copper platter piled high with roasted meat. The food tasted as good as it had smelled on the way here, although Shara didn't like the bitter taste of the cider.

As evening approached, the crowd grew more and more raucous. Only the guard behind her stood silent and sullen. All too soon he tapped her on the shoulder.

"Time to go, Miss."

"No. It's far from over. Right, Olva?" She turned, but she should have known better than to expect support. The tipsy Olva was deep in conversation with the man next to her.

"Master Randin said no later than twilight," the guard said.

Shara knew it was useless to argue, so she followed him back to the box, thinking that—after her day spent with Nicho outside Gwyndorr—this had surely been the happiest of her life.

And it would have stayed that way if she hadn't parted the curtain again as they carried her away from the ring. For as Shara glanced over the crowd, she saw them. Nicho and Yasmin. Yasmin was pressed in to Nicho, one arm draped possessively around his neck, Nicho laughing at something she whispered in his ear.

He looked up at the litter as it passed by, and Shara saw the moment of recognition in his eyes just before she dropped the curtain back into place.

You're a fool, Shara. Tears stung her eyes as the familiar ache pierced the center of her chest. *His heart was never yours.*

And all the joy of the afternoon washed away at the realization.

CHAPTER 30

Until he saw Shara, Nicho had been enjoying the Feast. As daylight dimmed, the cheap mead had flowed freely and the crowd had grown louder and more disorderly. Yasmin and the others were shouting loudly for their contest favorites and swaying to the rhythm of raunchy tavern tunes. Nicho, although he didn't touch the mead, was swept up in the festivities and found himself laughing and applauding wildly.

Until he looked up at the Highborn litter and saw Shara. For an instant—as their eyes locked—everything around him seemed to stand still. He no longer heard the music, only a steady droning in his ears. Then the curtain dropped, hiding her pain-filled eyes. Suddenly he saw what she must have seen. The closeness of Yasmin's body and the way her arm was flung around his neck. Nicho had an urge to leap off the window ledge and press through the crowd to that litter. He wanted to rip open the curtain and look into those expressive eyes again, to explain that it was nothing, just Yasmin's way. But instead he sat unmoving as the feast pulsed around him. He was no longer aware of what was happening on the stage or the voices calling and laughing. Now he thought only of how deeply Shara's pain had cut into him and wondered just what that could mean.

Toward the end of the feast, Yasmin tumbled off the ledge and clung to his legs, giggling like a young girl.

"Come, Yaz, let's get you home." He climbed down himself. "You're going to have an aching head tomorrow."

"Ah, Nic. Let's stay a bit longer," she slurred, but let herself be led back in the direction of the homestead.

Suddenly a solid body blocked Nicho's path. Before he even had time to make out the face in the dim light, he knew it was Lord Maldor. The authoritative voice confirmed it.

"Out of the way, lad. I'll take this one back to where she needs to be." Maldor reached forward and ran a finger down Yasmin's face. "Pretty for a Parashi, isn't she, Ghris? One of yours, you said?"

Only then did Nicho see Ghris standing behind Maldor. Nicho kept a tight hold on Yasmin's arm and hoped that Ghris would speak up. For a long moment he stood facing the lord, head down, unmoving. Ghris said nothing.

"I said move." Maldor gave Nicho a hard push. He stumbled backward, almost taking Yasmin down with him, but kept his footing.

"My lord, she is in no state to come with you. I will take her home myself."

"I disagree. I think she is in a perfect state." Maldor laughed, with a backward glance at Ghris.

"I will take her, my lord. She came with me."

"Well, now. Look at the brave ... what is it? Parashi groom?" Maldor's eyes suddenly widened in recognition and a smirk crept onto his lips. "Well, well. If it isn't the little thief. This *is* entertaining." He took a step closer to Nicho; there was alcohol on his breath. "I think, Ghris, this lad wants her all to himself. I *command* you to give her to me."

"I won't."

The crowd around them seemed to go strangely quiet.

"You *won't?*" Maldor couldn't keep the incredulity out of his voice. "I see this scum-worm still doesn't know his place in life. Didn't your father beat that out of him, Ghris?'

Finally Ghris spoke. "Come on, Maldor. She's not worth it."

"No, no. I disagree," his voice was dangerously soft now, "but even more importantly, I feel I need to help your father deal with this foul incursion in his household."

Ghris reached out for Maldor's shoulder, but Maldor shook it off. Even though he was looking at the ground, Nicho sensed the rage simmering in Maldor, and a small shudder of fear crept down his spine.

"Come, Yaz." Nicho tried to push past Maldor, but he merely shoved him backward.

"Where are you going scum-boy? Did I say you were dismissed?"

Nicho didn't respond.

"I asked you where you were going."

"Home, my lord."

"No, you're not. Not until you have learnt your lesson."

The first punch landed directly on his nose, and Nicho thought he heard crunching at the same time he felt the pain sear through his face and deep into his skull. He lifted his arms to shield his face, but the punches continued —driving, forceful, and angry. The kick to his groin drove him to the ground. After that the assault was relentless, although he had the impression that other hands were trying to pull Maldor away from him. He could taste blood in his mouth and his hands felt slippery with it, but the sights were hazing over and the sounds seemed to drift closer and then farther away again, until he heard nothing but a steady drone in his ears. He was grateful when the darkness and silence finally overtook the pain.

• • •

"Helvin says the groom was injured last night. Do you know anything more, Ghris?"

Shara looked up sharply at Randin's question. "Nicho?" The name quivered off her lips before she could stop it. She dropped her head to hide the flush rising to her face.

"Yes, him." Randin shoveled some food into his mouth. "Helvin says last night they struggled to rouse him. A particularly brutal beating, he said."

"Someone *beat* him?" Shara regretted speaking again, as she sensed Randin's appraisal.

"Apparently." He continued chewing. "You know how these Parashi get out of control if you give them just the smallest bit of freedom. Next year I'll think twice before allowing them to go to the Spring Feast."

"I couldn't agree more, my love," Olva spoke. "That Yasmin girl was completely hopeless this morning. She could hardly carry a dish. There should be a law against the Parashi touching mead and cider."

"Who beat him?" Shara struggled to keep her voice light, as if it was of little concern to her.

"Well, you were there, weren't you, Ghris?" Randin turned to his son.

"Yes, I saw the fight," he said slowly, not taking his eyes off Shara's face. "It was completely shameful, Father. Nicho refused to give way to Lord Maldor."

"No!" Olva's hand fluttered to her mouth.

"By Taus! That lad has been trouble since he first set foot here." Randin slapped the table with his hand. "It will be good to be rid of him."

"What do you mean, he wouldn't give way?" Shara asked.

"Just that. Maldor ordered him to move, and he blatantly refused."

"I can't believe it. Nicho wouldn't do that."

"Maybe you don't know him as well as you think, Shara." A smile tightened Ghris's lips. "Also, that girl Yasmin was draped all over him."

His words brought back the image of Nicho and Yasmin pressed together on a window ledge. Pain twisted deep inside her.

"Doesn't surprise me," Olva said. "They have absolutely no morals. I think it's good that Maldor put him in his place." Olva took a bite of her bread. "For their own good really—a beating every now and then. Reminds them of what they are."

"That's ridiculous." Shara had found her voice again. "A beating that leaves somebody half dead is definitely *not* for their benefit."

"Watch your tone, Shara," Randin said.

"I'm sure there's a bit more to this story, that's all. How is he? Nicho?"

"He'll live," Randin answered gruffly. "I'm leaving for a three-day trip today. When I get back on Thursday night I need to speak to you, Shara." He didn't meet her gaze, although she was aware that both Olva and Ghris glanced up sharply.

What was this about? Had Ghris told him about her and Nicho? Well, she thought bitterly, she could tell him not to worry anymore. It was blatantly clear who Nicho was in love with.

"Does this have something to do with Nicho? Because I haven't been to the stable lately. Not since the foal."

"The stable?" Randin frowned. "Why would you go there?"

"No reason. Just to see the foaling." She glanced up at Ghris; he had kept her secret after all.

"That reminds me," Randin continued. "I'll have to ask Helvin to hire a new groom."

Fear fluttered through her. "Nicho will get better won't he?" Why did she still care so much?

"I imagine he will." Now Randin's eyes narrowed speculatively on her. "But he's going to be moving on rather soon."

Even stranger than the words, was the small laugh he gave as he said them.

• • •

For a change it was the old groom, Helvin, who stepped from the stable to take Andreo's pony.

"Morning, Helvin. Nicho have the day off?"

"No, Brother." The old man didn't look him in the eye. The older generation was always more cautious around the Brethren. "The lad was in a fight two days ago. At the Spring Feast."

"A fight? Doesn't sound like him. What happened?"

The groom looked around uncomfortably. "'Twas Lord Lucian's son."

"He had a fight with a *Highborn*?" What was Nicho thinking? That kind of behavior could only lead to the Rif'twine.

"Not so much a fight. Just a beatin'. Nicho didn't throw a single punch." There was bitterness in the old man's voice.

"I'll just go take a quick look at him." Andreo felt for the pouch in his robe. It was filled with one of his latest discoveries—leaves which, steeped in water and tied into sack cloth, were particularly good at reducing swelling. He had hoped to drop them off with the Rifter Unit after Morning Rites, but again he had been waylaid by one of Brother Angustus's cohorts. The young Brother Druen had asked him all sorts of inane questions about his students, and Andreo couldn't shake the feeling that he had been delayed for a specific reason.

Now though, as he made his way to the small room that Nicho shared with his mother, Andreo was grateful that he had something that might alleviate the groom's discomfort.

The windowless room was dark, even though the door stood slightly ajar. Andreo could just make out Nicho through the small gap. He was curled in sleep on one of the pallets; Marai sat next to him on the other.

"Marai. It's me, Brother Andreo," he whispered as he pushed open the door. She swiped at her eyes and clambered to her feet.

The light from the fully open door now shone on Nicho's face. Dark bruises lined his eyes and cheeks. His nose was swollen and a deep gash ran across his puffy lips.

"By Taus!" Andreo whispered, sinking down onto his knees by Nicho's side. He looked up into Marai's reddened eyes. "It was brutal."

She nodded and a small sob shuddered through her body. "I thought I'd lost him. Monday night we couldn't wake him."

"I'm sorry, Marai."

"But today he ate some of my soup," she smiled weakly. "And y'r frillbough is keepin' the worst of the pain away."

"Good, good. Here is something else that will bring down the swelling." She took the pouch gratefully.

"Brother?" Nicho's eyes fluttered open. "Could you ask Shara to come see me?" It was difficult to make out the words; it sounded as if Nicho's mouth was full of small stones.

"He keeps askin' for her." Marai's face pinched with concern. "First words out of his mouth, in fact."

"Just get strong, lad," Andreo said, patting his arm.

"No. I got to tell her somethin'."

"You know that Ghris ..."

"Please." Nicho squeezed the top of his arm forcefully.

Andreo sighed and nodded, once more the reluctant messenger between these two young people.

But when he pulled Shara aside after the tutoring session, her response was cooler than he had expected.

"Nicho was in a beating. I went to see him this morning."

She shrugged. "I heard he was in a fight. How is he?"

"It was brutal. But Marai has done well to keep the swelling down, and she is giving him something for the pain. Also, he is young and strong. That should help him recover quickly."

"Marai is a good nurse."

"He asked about you." She looked up sharply.

"Why? Doesn't he have *Yasmin* to fuss over him?" Her cheeks seemed to flush slightly, whether from embarrassment or anger, Andreo couldn't be sure.

"He asked me if I could help you to visit him," Andreo continued after a while. "Maybe I can tell Olva I am showing you something in the courtyard and you could slip in to see him for a few minutes?"

"No." Shara shook her head. "Tell him I wish him well, but there is no reason for me to see him."

"Are you sure, Shara?"

"Yes. I do not want to visit Nicho."

CHAPTER 31

Tessor stepped out of the shadows and walked, head held high, to Lucian's dining room. The power she had discovered in Yorina's room still pulsed through her veins. She knew Lucian wanted something. Desperately. It gave her a weapon. And soon she would strike him with it.

She was vaguely aware of the startled glances of the servants she passed. Few had ever seen her. Only one or two servant girls silently slipped into her room with trays of food and washed robes. Usually Tessor pretended to be asleep so she wouldn't have to speak to them.

Lyndis was just closing the dining hall door behind him. He turned, tray in hand, and flinched at the sight of her.

"Good afternoon, Lyndis." She tried to sound haughty, but her voice cracked slightly from disuse. "I will be dining with my husband today. You can bring my food immediately."

The momentary confusion on the butler's face hardened into resolve. "Lord Lucian didn't inform me of your visit, madam."

Not *your husband*. Not *Lady Tessor*. Anger clawed inside her. Lucian had taught them to treat her this way.

"*I* am informing you." She pushed past him and thrust the door open. Lucian and Maldor both looked up, disbelief etched on their faces.

Lucian was the first to react. "Tessor. This is a surprise." For a brief, un-guarded moment his voice soothed her as it had before.

"I'm sorry, my lord," Lyndis said from behind her. "I tried to stop her."

"It's fine, Lyndis. She is, after all, lady of this manor." A smile she couldn't quite decipher.

"Crazy Tessy?" Maldor was looking at his father incredulously. "You still keep her around?"

"Where else would I keep her?" Lucian's gaze hadn't left her face and for a moment she felt like running back to the shadows. *No. She had to do this. For Fafa.*

"I have come to dine with you." She swept into the room and headed for the seat on Lucian's left.

"Dine with us? Like an honored guest?"

Hatred scorched through her as she looked at the young man. "No. Like your father's wife."

"Well, excuse me, if I don't stay for this moment of domestic bliss." Maldor started to rise.

She pulled the cushioned seat from under the table and sat down. "I hear we are attending a Bride Feast in six days' time."

That stopped Maldor in his tracks. "We? No. *You* are the last person I'd invite."

"That would be your father's decision. Not yours." Her voice sounded surprisingly calm.

"She's not coming." Maldor turned to his father. "We'll be the laughing stock of Gwyndorr if we bring Crazy Tessy out with us."

"I am Lady of Gwyndorr, Maldor." Still she sensed Lucian's appraising gaze. "I will be expected to be there. In fact, Lady Olva and I practically grew up together. She would wonder at my absence." It was a lie, of course. Nobody would think of her. Nobody would miss her.

"How do you even know about the wedding?" Lucian finally asked.

"I live in this house too." Her eyes roamed to the crack near the fireplace. Had she made a mistake? Would he discover her dark, hidden places—the only parts of the house that were still hers? "The servants are all speaking about the manor's next grand wedding."

"But you are not in the habit of speaking to servants, are you, Tessor?" She knew that tone all too well, the one that cajoled you into telling the truth.

"I *only* speak to servants." She met his gaze steadily. "You've seen to that."

"She's not coming, Father." A little more of that belligerent tone from Maldor, and Lucian might just agree to her request, she knew.

"Why would you even want to be there?"

This was important. He mustn't suspect she wanted to get close to the girl. Close enough to steal her from him forever.

"To see my old friend Olva. And to have a single day of celebrating." *Celebrating Fafa's vindication.*

"No. I will not have Crazy Tessy at my wedding. It's bad enough you have me marrying this ridiculous girl." *Good Maldor, good,* she thought. She sensed Lucian's rising irritation and saw the precise moment he gave in to it.

"Fine. You can come."

"This is ludicrous!" Maldor stormed out with a string of curses.

Lucian regarded her a little longer, then rose and flicked his fingers for Lyndis. "I have to go, but make sure Lady Tessor enjoys some of our choice food and wine."

Choice food and wine. The words churned through Tessor as she sat alone at the table and watched Lyndis place the steaming food in front of her. Her mouth watered as the rich flavors of roasted boar wafted from the plate. She watched the red wine swirl into the fluted silver goblet. One of Fafa's favorites. Her hand shook slightly as she lifted the goblet to her nose and twirled it around, just like Fafa had taught her. She detected hints of spice and citrus. Almond? No, she thought not.

Choice food and wine. Were those the words Lucian had used on the night he poisoned Fafa? Her mind reeled back to that darkest of nights, a mere week after her wedding. Edna came for her with the news that Fafa was ill. The smell of bile permeated his room. That, and something more bitter, something that reminded her of almonds. Servants were cleaning his face, mopping his sweaty brow. His face, in the glow of the candles, looked deathly pale, his cheeks sunk in. As he retched, his body shook and he moaned weakly. He noticed her by his side and beckoned her closer.

She leant over him. "Fafa, don't worry. We will make you well."

He shook his head. "Too late." The words were so soft that Tessor had to press in closer to hear them. "Careful, Tess ... careful ..."

After that, his eyes drifted closed and, though his body continued to shake, the moaning stopped as if he could no longer feel the pain. The doctor arrived a little later, but it was too late. Fafa had died before morning.

Only later did Tessor learn that hemlock, the most favored of assassin's poisons, smells like bitter almonds.

"Madam?" Lyndis's voice drew her back from the memories. She still had the goblet lifted to her nose. "Is there something wrong, madam?"

"Not at all." She put the goblet down with a trembling hand. "I'm just not very hungry anymore." She rose, conscious of his disapproving look.

After Tuesday it wouldn't matter anymore. Perhaps she would even tip the poison drops into her own drink. But she couldn't take any chances till then. Not until she had fulfilled her promise to the dying Fafa. *He will pay for this, Fafa. I promise. He will pay.*

• • •

Randin knew he couldn't delay telling Shara any longer. After all, it was only five days until the wedding, and the girl needed some time to prepare herself. Yet, now that the time was here to tell her, his initial sense of trepidation returned. Shara was so young and innocent, while Lord Lucian's son was brash and worldly. *Flint against flint.*

No. This was no time to grow soft. Shara should be grateful. And it was *Shara*, after all. With that tongue of hers, maybe it was Maldor that needed pitying.

"You wanted to see me?"

He looked up at her standing hesitantly in the doorway.

"Yes, Shara," he said brusquely. "Sit down."

She sat at the edge of the chair and scowled at him. "The tension in this house is like a knife's edge. Something is going on. So you might as well tell me what it is."

"I have news." He looked down; picked a ball of fluff from his cloak. He looked up again. "I have arranged a marriage for you."

"Marriage?" She looked at him blankly. "You mean like a ...?"

"I have betrothed you to a man."

"Oh." She sat back. "But shouldn't I get a say in that?"

"Not necessarily. Usually the fathers decide these matters."

"So ... are you saying that you promised me to some stranger without speaking to me?" There was something thunderous in her expression. "How dare you—"

"Enough!" He held up his hand, silencing her. "It's been arranged, whether you like it or not."

"But—"

"The main thing is that you prepare for Tuesday. That is when the Bride Feast will be held, and you will go to the groom's house."

She stared at him, shock etched into every feature. "Tuesday? You mean ... I am to ...?"

"Shara," he spoke gently. "You are about to become a wife. You will need to pack. Prepare."

"But how can ... I am only sixteen." She let out a long breath and then spoke slowly, reasonably. "Sir, when you said I was betrothed, I thought you meant I had been promised to someone for the future. But ... Tuesday?"

"Yes, Shara. Tuesday." He looked away.

She said nothing for a long time, and then, in the smallest voice, "Please, sir. I can't. Please don't make me."

One silent tear crept down her cheek. He couldn't remember when last he had seen her cry, and a wave of guilt assailed him. Yet, he hardened his heart and voice. "The wedding will happen, Shara. Whether you want it or not."

"I won't." She swiped away the tear. Her eyes were narrowed, her mouth pinched in a familiar stubborn pout. "I refuse."

"You *will*, Shara. Even if he has to carry you out of here. On Tuesday you leave here as Maldor's wife."

"Maldor? Lord Lucian's son?"

"Yes." Randin smiled. "You are moving up in society. He is a most eligible bachelor. Most young girls would be delighted at such a match."

"I hate him," Shara spat out. "How could you possibly think he would make me a good husband?"

"How can you hate him? You've hardly ever met him."

"He ruined everything for Nicho five years ago with his poisonous lies. And he beat him into a bloody pulp on Monday. How can you give me to someone like that?"

"Nicho? The groom?" Randin felt disorientated by this turn in the conversation. "What does he have to do with this?"

"He lied when he said Nicho stole his money." Shara was on her feet, and he recognized the rage on her face. "He's a liar! An arrogant sod of a liar!"

"He is Lord Lucian's son and soon to be your husband. You are not to speak of him like that," Randin said steadily. "One day he will be Lord of Gwyndorr, and you by his side, Lady Shara. When you are the most powerful woman in this town, you will thank me."

"Thank you?" Her voice wavered. "Thank you? For giving me to a deceiving, self-centered pig who thinks nothing of beating someone half to death?"

"Your opinion counts for little in this Shara." He waved his hand dismissively. "You may go now."

"No!" Shara shouted. "I will not go! I will stay here until you relent!"

"That won't happen."

"You rotten, thieving excuse of a father!" She lurched toward him, grabbed his shoulders, and dug nails into his skin. "I will not! I will not! I will not!"

Randin's strong fingers unfurled her own fine ones from his arms. He held her with bruising pressure until Ghris and a servant arrived and pulled her away, dragging her out of the room and up the stairs. Yet even when they had closed her into her room, Randin could still hear the screaming and thrashing. It was near midnight before quiet descended on his household.

• • •

Thanks to Shara's loud reaction, the news of the impending wedding was soon circulating among the servants. Nicho was in bed. He had returned to the stable that day and his body was tired and painful from the exertion. He looked up as his mother came in.

"How do you feel, Niki?" she said, tenderly pulling the hair away from his forehead to study the bruises.

"It was a hard day, but I feel a little stronger."

"Did you hear the ruckus up at the house just now?" she asked solemnly as she rearranged his blankets.

Nicho shook his head. He had been dozing.

"Seems they told Shara she is to be wed on Tuesday." Marai didn't notice his sharp intake of breath. "She didn't take well to the news, little Shara. Shoutin' and beggin' Master to change his mind." Marai wiped a tear away and then, with the air of a lifetime of resignation said, "They never do right by that little 'un. 'Tis always what I say, don't I, Niki?"

"Who?" Nicho's voice seemed to catch on that single word.

Marai shook her head, as if she still could not believe all she had just heard. "'Tis terrible that they would give my sweet young Shara to the likes of him. They don't do right by her. 'Tis absolutely terrible."

"Who is it?" Nicho had never feared an answer more.

"Lord Maldor. Can you believe it? The one who did this to you. 'Tis him."

Chapter 32

Brother Andreo was equally shocked to hear the news. Ghris had been the one to tell him, explaining that Shara was not at the lessons because she was packing her belongings.

This was not true. Shara was, in fact, refusing to get out of bed. Her eyes, red and swollen, had a faraway look to them which, Marai explained to the maid who had been sent—and failed—to fetch her that morning, was the reaction shock sometimes had on people.

The news had the opposite effect on Brother Andreo, who was galvanized into action. He immediately demanded to speak to Randin, but when he was informed that the captain had already left to inspect the western wall, he instead pushed past Olva's excuses and went to see Shara.

"My child," he said as he entered her room, his eyes struggling to make her out in the dim bedchamber.

She did not respond as he sat down and grasped her icy cold hand.

"Shara, I heard the news. I am so sorry."

Her eyes flickered onto him then, but she still said nothing. He too kept quiet, all the time holding her hand. After a long silence, he started to sing a well-known Tirragyl tune, a doleful song, which told the story of a lost love.

Finally, Shara's tears came. She sobbed out her sorrow and anger onto his shoulder, until he was surprised that she had any more tears to weep. When she eventually stilled, he said, "I am so sorry, Shara. This is a great injustice to one so young."

"It's not just my age, Brother. It's *him*. He's disgusting and cruel, and I already hate him. *I hate him*."

"I have heard some stories about him myself." Brother Andreo's forehead was deeply furrowed. "But he will treat you well. Your father and the elders will see to that." His voice wavered. *Would they?*

"I don't care how he treats me. He may as well beat me to death the first day, for then I will not need to go through a lifetime of hating him."

"My child. Do not speak such words. It is always possible for affection to grow between a husband and wife. You will see. Friendship takes time to develop."

"I will never—ever—care for him. Didn't *you* say it was the most brutal beating you had ever seen? He did that to Nicho!" Her eyes held an accusation as they met his. "I don't care what Nicho did to him, he had no right to ... to ..."

They sat in silence for some time before Brother Andreo spoke. "It was a brutal beating, Shara, and I know that Nicho could not have done anything to warrant it. But I do not want you to start this marriage believing the worst of your husband."

Shara turned away. "I don't want to speak anymore."

"My child. This may be one of the last times we speak at all. Let us not part in anger."

"I am not angry with you, Brother." Shara's voice sounded vacant. "Could you do just one thing for me, please?"

"Anything, Shara."

"Could you give this to Nicho?" She held out a rolled up sheet of parchment. "I wanted to say goodbye."

Nicho was nowhere in sight as Andreo entered the stable, but the scraping sounds coming from the back corner led Andreo to the groom. Nicho was on his haunches, lowering a floorboard into place. At the sound of Andreo's footsteps he rose and spun around. There was a book in his hand.

"Brother! You surprised me."

"What do you have there, lad?" Andreo held out his hand authoritatively.

"It's a book. Shara's book."

"May I have a look at it, Nicho? You know my fondness for reading."

Nicho didn't move. "I want to try and get it to her before she leaves."

"How do you plan to do that?"

The groom looked away, defeated, and shrugged.

"Why don't I take it to her, Nicho? You can trust me with it."

Nicho considered him carefully. Finally he held the book out to Andreo and said, "Please do not show it to anybody else. Especially Master Ghris. In fact ..." his expression lightened, "... maybe you will be able to read it. Shara and I did not recognize the script."

"You didn't?" Andreo's interest was piqued even more, and he sat down on a bench and studied the book. The leather binding looked old, and he slowly ran his finger over the strange symbol on its cover. He opened it and looked at the thick yellowing pages with fascination. The handwritten script was not Tirragylin, but he thought he might have seen it before.

"Hauntingly familiar," he muttered.

Nicho had turned back to the floorboard and now stood holding a box. "It came in this, Brother. Please give it to her as well. There is a dagger in it too."

"Beautiful wood." Andreo caressed the box. "One day you must tell me the history of this remarkable treasure. I will make sure it gets back to Shara. What time does Randin usually come home?"

"Just before sunset."

"I will return later to speak to him. Could I keep the book until then? Maybe I will be able to translate some of it."

Nicho hesitated, but finally nodded. "The book means a lot to us. Please take good care of it, Brother."

"I almost forgot." Andreo held out the small scroll. "It's from Shara."

• • •

As soon as Brother Andreo rode from the courtyard, Nicho hurried back into the stable, and dropped onto the hay where the light streamed in to light up a patch of ground. His fingers shook slightly as he unfurled the parchment and started to read.

Dear Nicho

I have asked Brother Andreo to give this to you. There is much I want to say, but I doubt that I will ever see you again to speak the words.

I am sorry about the beating. I have seen you at the stable, so you must be feeling better. I saw you with Yasmin at the Spring Feast. You both looked as if you were in love. I hope that you will be happy with her.

I am sure that you know I am to be married to Lord Lucian's son. I cannot tell you the despair I feel at the thought, but it has been decided, and I cannot think of a way to change the course of it.

Please tell your mother that all the time I spent with her meant everything to me. She was always so kind to me and I will never forget her. I love her as dearly as if she were my own flesh. I am glad that you and I were friends again for a short while too.

Goodbye, Nicho.

Shara

Until that moment, Nicho had refused to acknowledge the depths of his feelings for Shara. Yet, as he read her farewell letter, pain pierced through him sharper than any one of Maldor's blows. Finally he *knew*. He loved her. Maybe he had from that very first day when she'd sought shelter in the stable out of a winter storm. He loved her dark eyes and wild hair, her flaring temper, her courage to speak out, her gentleness with Kharin. He loved her for loving his mother, for choosing a Parashi name for the foal, for seeing him as a friend and not a Lowborn servant. He loved the softness in her eyes when he told her she was beautiful. Yes, he loved her, but he could never have her as his own. This he had always known, and maybe it was what had kept him from accepting with his head what his heart had been whispering: he loved Shara and he suspected that she loved him too.

In four day's time she would be gone. Forever. It was unlikely that he would ever see her again. She would leave thinking that he felt nothing for her, that it was Yasmin he loved. *I saw you with Yasmin at the Spring Feast. You both looked as if you were in love.* He remembered the pain he had seen in her eyes as she peered at them from behind the golden curtain.

Nicho knew then what he had to do. The thought of her with Maldor filled him with dread. He had looked into the young lord's eyes, had seen in them a cruelty unmatched by anybody he had ever encountered. He could not save her from her fate, but at least he would declare his love for her and pray that the thought of it would carry her through the darkest of nights.

• • •

Andreo rode into the monastery grounds. He could hear voices from the chantry and briefly considered joining his brothers in their midday mantras. Yet, he felt a gnawing restlessness to look more closely at the book Nicho had given him. Maybe he could make some sense of its contents before he gave it back to Shara. He headed for the library.

Of all the rooms of the monastery, the library had always been the most interesting to Andreo. Even as a young acolyte, he had been drawn here often to immerse himself in the old books. The library was one of several rooms that had been carved into the cliff itself and its cave-like interior held almost eight hundred books, most of which had been penned by the Brethren of previous generations.

Andreo was glad to find himself alone in the library. He went to sit at a desk against the outer wall, positioned under a window to receive maximum natural light. He pulled the book out of the wooden box and reverently opened it, letting his eyes trace the unfamiliar letters. He tried to recall where he had seen this font before. Most of the books in the library were written in Tirragylin, but there were some written in various other dialects and Brother Andreo found them on a high, dusty shelf. He studied the handful of books, but none of their scripts matched the one in Shara's book.

He mindlessly paged through Shara's book, trying to see something he might recognize, but every stroke and dot was unknown to his eyes. His mind went back to the period when he had spent the most time in the library— the days of his training. Brother Gladson and he had spent many wonderful afternoons here, poring over books as they discussed the history of the Brotherhood and Tirragyl. Andreo had a sudden longing for his old friend. Brother Gladson would have known the origin of this book, he thought, and maybe even how to interpret it. Nobody had known history and languages as well as he had.

At the sound of footsteps, he quickly slipped the book back into the box, threw his cape over it, and rose to leave. Prayer time was over, and the Scribes were returning to the library to work another hour before the mealtime. They murmured a greeting as they pushed past him in the entrance, and Andreo briefly considered asking one of them about the book. He decided against it; Nicho had been adamant that he should show it to nobody.

The rest of the afternoon settled into the slow, ordered routine of monastery life, from which Brother Andreo drew some strength and comfort. Work, prayer, lunch, study—these all had their known time and place, and finally soothed away most of the agitation that had grown in Andreo since the news of Shara's wedding.

The time soon came to return to Randin's house and, as Andreo rode back toward Gwyndorr, his thoughts revisited Shara's situation. It was as he recalled some of their recent conversations that he pulled his pony to a sudden halt.

The feather. There was something about that feather Shara had shown him—and then given him—something that tied in with the script in the book. He remembered the joke he had made about the mythical bird and her insistent pressing for more information. How did the feather relate to the book? A part of him felt that it did, but as he coaxed his pony forward, he struggled to uncover the key that he knew lay buried somewhere in his mind.

Again he replayed their conversation. He had told her about the Gold Breast, regaling her with the stories linked to the powerful bird—the king who went crazy and the queen who rose from her deathbed.

And suddenly Andreo *knew*.

The book that spoke of the Gold Breast, which he had devoured as an acolyte, was a translation of an ancient scroll kept at the monastery. He had seen the original scroll only once. Brother Gladson had shown it to him secretly, together with three other ancient scrolls.

All four were written in the same script as Shara's book. All were written in the forbidden Old Tongue. And, all should have been destroyed in the Great Purge.

CHAPTER 33

Nicho's jaw and head pounded with pain as he brushed down Krola. There was no reason for him to be at the stable this late. Still he lingered, hoping Brother Andreo would return with the book. The more he thought about it, the more Nicho regretted giving it to him. He *knew* that it had been the Gold Breast's gift to Shara. There was something as special about that book as there was about the bird, and didn't everyone know Taus's monks could not be trusted?

"Workin' late too, Nicho?" Yasmin sauntered into the stable. "Your mother has had me scrubbin' floors the whole day for this cursed Bride Feast."

"I was waiting for someone, but they didn't come." He put down the brush and touched the tender spot on the bridge of his nose. He needed to lay his head on a pillow. Soon.

"I saw Hildah and Nana last night," Yasmin said, stroking Krola's neck. "They asked me where you'd been. I told them about your beatin'."

"How are they?" Nicho's forehead creased with worry. "Have they heard anything from Derry?"

"Not a word. I took some food from your mam. I don't know how they'd manage if they didn't have it."

"I know." Nicho closed the stall door behind him.

"Pearce was wrong to take him, wasn't he? You said it all along, didn't you, Nicho? Pearce is so persuasive. Even I got caught up with the excitement. But you saw it from the start, didn't you?"

"They need Derry."

"You're a good man, Nicho. You've been in my life so long I haven't always seen just what a good man you are." She put her hand on his forearm. "The way you look after Nana and took over from Derry." She pushed her body against his, and her voice sounded husky as she said: "The way you took care of me the other night. I didn't even know you felt something for me till you took that beatin'."

"Yaz." Nicho took a step back. "You've got it wrong. I did that because you're my friend, nothing more."

Her face clouded momentarily. "You don't think I'm pretty?"

"I do ... I mean ... you're very pretty. But you're not the one I have those kind of ... feelings for." For a moment his eyes flickered to the windows of the main house.

Yasmin followed his gaze and then slowly turned back to him, an incredulous expression on her face.

"Her? Miss Shara? *She's* the one you have feelings for?" Her voice had risen, and Nicho quickly looked around.

"Hush, Yaz." He shook his head. "It's complicated."

"She's a *Highborn*, Nicho. By the abyss! You can't have feelings for a Highborn."

"Says who? The heart doesn't distinguish between High and Lowborn."

"You fool! She can never be yours, and you know it. I mean, she's getting married for pity's sake. What were you thinking, Nicho?"

"I didn't know she was betrothed, did I?" Nicho answered sullenly.

"Betrothed. Not betrothed. Who cares? Parashi and Highborn don't fall in love. It's a rule of Gwyndorr. And breaking it can be the end of you. You know that as well as anybody." She turned and spat into the hay. "And to think you would choose her over me."

Nicho said softly, "Like a river ..."

"... the heart sets its own course." Yasmin finished the well-known Parashi saying. "But, by the abyss, it's a dangerous course. Just as well you're not going to see that girl again after Tuesday."

Nicho looked down to where his toes were grinding a circle in the dust. Yasmin's tone softened. "You'll be all right, Nicho. Take it from one who's had her heart broken a few times."

"It's not me I'm worried about," he said, looking up at the main house again.

"Festering figs! You do have a bad case of it, don't you?" Yasmin shook her head. "If you're worrying about her, she'll be fine too. Imagine. The Lord of Gwyndorr's mansion. Every one of your whims met."

"But she'll be with *him*." Nicho spat out the last word as if it left a vile taste in his mouth.

"Yes. He's a dangerous one, that Lord Maldor. There's something in those eyes of his ..." Yasmin gave an involuntary shudder. "But they'll make sure Miss Shara is fine, won't they? Master Randin and Master Ghris, I mean?"

"If they wanted her to be fine, they wouldn't be giving her to him in the first place, would they?"

"You might be right. But best you get to bed now. You still need rest to recover from that beatin' and it's going to get busy around here, with all this feast nonsense in four day's time." She yawned. "If I don't get off these legs, they're going to buckle right under me."

"Thanks for trying to make me feel better." Nicho grabbed her hand and squeezed it. "Sometimes I think it would have been good if it was you ... who I had feelings for."

"But the heart sets its own course." She brightened. "Who knows? A river can change direction, right?"

• • •

Brother Andreo had turned his horse around when he realized that Shara's book was written in the same language as the ancient scrolls. Today, he would not go to see Randin or to return the book. One night was all he wanted. One night, to see if he could uncover something of what was written in the mystery book.

Now he sat in his small cell, with only an oil lamp casting a circle of light, and put the scrolls on the chest. The others were at their evening meal, but he had little time—only one night to uncover some of the words of the book. The day at the monastery was a long one, starting with prayers before dawn, so most of the Brothers chose to go to bed early. Brother Andreo was normally one of them, but tonight he could not. His heart pounded and his mind pulsed with excitement, as he picked up the scroll.

It had not been easy getting to the ancient scrolls. On his return to the monastery that afternoon, he had immediately gone to the library and located the four translated manuscripts. He had read through them briefly.

They were on a range of topics. The first was a diagram and explanation of the building of a bridge. The second appeared to be a legal document for the sale of land. The last two were the most interesting to Andreo. One contained drawings of animals and birds, with a description of each. Although there was no color on the manuscript, Andreo quickly found the ink drawing of the Gold Breast and read the brief description. Some of the other animals were familiar to Andreo, but several were–like the Gold Breast–mythical creatures: foghounds, firebreaths, and tusked lions. Andreo found it strange that the real and mythical were combined in one document.

The last scroll was written in childlike language and told three stories, each one about a Gold Breast. These were the stories that Andreo had told Shara, and he read through them again with interest.

These translated manuscripts were fascinating, but they would not help him understand any of Shara's book. To do *that* he needed the original scrolls. They were not kept in the main library, of that he was sure, but Brother Gladson had never told him where they were hidden. Not many in the monastery even knew of their existence, for they should have been burnt—together with all the old documents—in the Great Purge that had taken place hundreds of years earlier. The fact that they had not been destroyed showed that there were pockets of rebellion within the monastery.

Who would know where they were and who could he trust enough to ask?

He had settled on Brother Justus, the most senior Scribe, who he knew had been a friend of Brother Gladson's. He found him in a quiet corner of the library.

"Good afternoon, Brother. I wonder if you can help me."

Justus dragged his eyes away from the manuscript he was copying and squinted up at him.

Brother Andreo had decided that a quick, direct, and mostly truthful approach would work the best. He laid the translated copies that he had found in the library in front of the Scribe.

"Brother, I seem to recall that Brother Gladson showed me the ancient original scrolls of these documents, and I was wondering if you knew where they were kept."

Justus's eyes widened in surprise. "He did?" He quickly scanned the room, before speaking in a low whisper. "Did he tell you that we are not meant to have them at all?"

"Yes, Brother. They should have been destroyed in the Purge."

"Then do not put your hand in this hornet's nest, Andreo. You endanger us both even mentioning it."

"Does that mean you know where they are?" Andreo persisted.

"Yes, I know," Brother Justus snapped, "but this conversation is over."

"Don't you want to know why I want to see them?" Brother Andreo knew Brother Justus's greatest weakness was his curiosity—he was counting on it now.

"Why do you want to see them?" Brother Justus tried to sound disinterested.

"Because of this." With a flourish, Andreo took out a small piece of parchment with some ancient lettering on it. He too dropped his voice to a conspiratorial whisper. "It fell out of a book that I was reading this afternoon."

Justus looked like a hungry man who had just been offered a piece of bread. He held out his hand for the parchment. "May I?"

"Certainly." Brother Andreo handed it to him.

Justus held it close to his eyes. Most of the Scribes had poor eyesight. Brother Andreo held his breath. If he looked too closely, Brother Justus might realize that the ink on the parchment was fresh and the page yellowed and aged with the help of some tea-dye. Andreo had merely copied a few words from the third page of Shara's book.

Instead, Brother Justus let out a small sigh of appreciation. "Indeed. I believe it is the ancient script. How remarkable." He looked appraisingly at Brother Andreo. "What book did it fall out of?"

"A book on botany, I think. It looked as though it was being used as a bookmark." He tried to move the conversation away from his lies. "I thought I might be able to make some sense of the words if I could see the original scrolls alongside the translations."

Justus nodded. "It is possible. Difficult, but possible."

"Do you think you could let me have a little time with the ancient scrolls?" The fear was back on Justus's face, rapidly overcoming the inquisitiveness. "I will, of course, share my findings with you," Brother Andreo added hastily.

Justus was fingering the large bunch of keys that hung at his side. "If this is discovered, we could both be found guilty of rebellion against Taus and the Brotherhood."

"I will deny your involvement and take full responsibility myself. But no-one will discover it, I promise, Brother."

Just before dinner, when the library was once more empty of other monks, Justus had unlocked the vault that contained all the monastery's treasures. Here, in a dark corner, he had loosened several stones, and drawn the old scrolls from their hiding place. He had laid the scrolls in Brother Andreo's hands with a stern admonishment to guard them with his life.

Andreo skipped the evening meal and immediately set to work. With great care he now opened the first scroll, the one on animal and bird descriptions. He was amazed to see that the scroll, unlike the translation, was in color. The red and gold ink used in drawing the Gold Breast seemed to sparkle with life and he could not draw his eyes away from it.

Painstakingly he started trying to identify some words on the different scrolls, comparing sentences on the scrolls with the translated manuscripts. The headings were the easiest and, without too much effort he soon knew the script letters for the various animals and birds, the word for king and queen, bridge and land. This did not help him with Shara's book though. On the first page he only identified one mention of the word land and two mentions of the word king.

Andreo loved an intellectual challenge, however, and was soon totally absorbed in his work of trying to break what felt like a secret code. After a few more hours of work he had a list of approximately forty words and could now translate about ten words on the first page of Shara's book. His eyes were starting to feel the strain and he stood up to stretch his legs, taking stock of what he had discovered.

The heading on the first page consisted of three words and seemed to be "History of" and then a name, which he could not identify in Tirragylin. There was only one paragraph of writing and then what looked like a signature at the bottom. He could identify one or two words in each sentence, but not enough to understand what each sentence was about.

He decided he needed a new approach and for the next hour or so he looked at words on the first page of Shara's book and then tried to find them on one of the scrolls. In this way he managed to fill in the sentences with a few more words.

Exhaustion was starting to overtake him when he finally assessed the results of his night's work. He would get a few hours of sleep before the Dawn Prayer, he decided, as he rolled up the scrolls and closed the manuscripts.

He read over his scribbled translation of the first page one last time, trying to understand what it could possibly mean.

History of _____(*Place Name?*)

This.... history of (*Same Place Name*), ...Kingdom,....split into two......... (*Other Name?*). It......tells......deception......(*Other Name again*)......beautiful land. And.........great.........King of (*Same Place Name*). I, Signatory,......hand......*water?*.... Dark Forest....find.....day.

   Signature.

It made little sense, except that it appeared to be a historical account of some kingdom or other. The last sentence interested him, because it seemed to make mention of the Dark Forest. Was that another name for the Rif'twine, which lay so close to both the monastery and Gwyndorr?

As he finally climbed onto his sleeping pallet, his mind was still working on his night's project and his few hours of sleep were filled with dreams of scrolls and jumbled words.

Chapter 34

During the days leading up to the wedding, Shara's attachment to the Cerulean Dusk Dreamer grew ever stronger. Now, not only did she clutch the rock close to her at night, but she started to hide it in her clothes during the day too, often grasping its smoothness in her hand at meals or as she sat staring out into the courtyard. Occasionally, she would even drift into a light sleep as she did this, and strange scenes would flitter across her vision. These daydreams were not always as vivid as at night, but they were an escape nevertheless. She curled up on her bed now—the sun streaming in—and let the rock lead her away.

She was in a forest clearing at dawn. Somewhere near her, she heard the sound of gurgling water and she turned toward its source. Something caught her eye: a strange hovering light, which seemed to be rotating, for small trails of light spun around it. It was beautiful and Shara moved closer, but no matter how much she closed in on it, it was always just out of her reach. Then she heard a voice.

"Come, Shara. Let me show you something you've never seen before." An ethereal woman stood where the hovering light had been. "Come," she said again, I will show you your father's ring."

"Randin's ring?"

"No. Your real father."

"I don't even know who he is."

"But I do." The woman laughed and drew something from inside her cloak. It was a thick gold band with a large opaque stone inlay.

"Come with me, and I'll tell you all about him." The woman held out her hand, and Shara reached for it and let herself be guided by the mysterious woman, deeper and deeper into the forest.

Yet something started to change. Shara's grip on the woman's hand was loosening and the woman was now almost transparent. The forest sounds dulled; the trees grew hazy.

Shara fought to stay in the grip of the dream, but an insistent force was pulling her back.

"Shara! Shara!" Someone was shaking her, calling her name. She opened her eyes to see Brother Andreo peering anxiously into her face. "Shara. By the abyss, you gave me a fright. I've been trying to wake you for a good few minutes already."

"Brother?" She sat up. The familiar wave of nausea hit her as lights and patterns spun into her vision. "Where is the ring? And the woman?"

"You were dreaming, my child. Lie down a bit. It's not good to wake up so quickly."

"You fool!" Shara shouted. "She was about to tell me all about my father. You ruined everything!"

"Shara, hush." Concern lined Andreo's face. "It was just a dream."

"I've been waiting for weeks for this moment. How dare you?"

"Shara? What is wrong? You are trembling so. And your face is as pale as the moon."

Some of Shara's anger dissipated. The Dusk Dreamer was tucked deep into her robe, but still—if he saw the side-effects of the magic, Brother Andreo might suspect she had a power rock.

"Brother, would you open a shutter please? It's so hot in here."

As he turned away, she slipped the rock under her pillow.

"You look unwell." Andreo said turning back from the window. "Have you been eating?"

"I'm not hungry." She had absolutely no appetite at all, whether from the anxiety of the wedding or the effects of the Cerulean Dusk Dreamer, she didn't know.

He touched her forehead, pulling away a moist strand of hair. "You feel hot, you say?"

"Hot, cold. Sometimes both at once. I don't know. It doesn't matter."

"Have you been having many of these dreams? A fever can bring on hallucinations."

"I said it didn't matter." She pointed to the cloak-covered box in his hands. "So what's in there?"

"Ah, yes. Nicho asked me to give this to you." He pulled off the cloak and laid the box on her bed.

"The book." She lifted the lid and picked up the book, her finger tracing the pattern on the cover, as she remembered that day—that one glorious day—with Nicho.

"Where did you find this, Shara? It's of great worth, I believe. And written in the Old Tongue."

"The Old Tongue?" She opened the book and looked again at the strange script. "Rather useless if you ask me." Placing it back in the box, she picked up the dagger and felt its sharp edge with her forefinger, drawing a small drop of blood.

"Careful, Shara. It's very sharp."

"I will tell you how I found the book," she said, as if she had not heard his warning. She told him everything, starting from the first time Nicho and she had seen the bird in the rain, and ending with the stunned guards at the gate. All the time she studied the dagger, as if it was of much more interest than the words she spoke.

"And since then, I have not seen the bird again. It has left me," she ended. "Do you believe my story, Brother?" She looked up at him.

"I do. Strangely, I do. Yet it is all too remarkable for words. I don't understand what it means."

Shara nodded. "It all seemed to have some kind of purpose, leading us to the book, but now it's over. Too late."

Andreo had no words to contradict this, so instead he pulled out the translation he had worked on and explained the existence of the ancient scrolls. Shara read it with some of her old interest, before handing it back to him.

"You did well, Brother, for just one night's work."

"I think so too, although Nicho didn't think much of it."

"I don't suppose he understood the effort it took." She paused, before asking, "Did you give him the letter?"

"Yes. He gave me one for you." He held it out to her. "He told me you thought he and Yasmin were more than just friends. Apparently, the letter explains the truth."

Shara shrugged. "It doesn't matter, does it? Before I knew of my"—she swallowed hard—"marriage, I thought it important. But even so, I could never be with him."

"No you never could."

Silence enveloped them for a while, before Andreo cleared his throat.

"It's time for me to go." He broke every monastery rule by pulling her into an embrace. As they pulled apart, he said, "You are special—a clever mind and a good heart. I will not forget you, Shara. I will always care for you deeply."

The first stirrings of emotion broke through some of Shara's numbness. "I will miss you, Brother." Andreo was almost through the door, when she called out to him. "Brother, keep the book. It's useless to me, anyway."

"No, Shara. I believe it is intended for you."

"It's useless," Shara repeated flatly, holding out the book to him. As he took it from her, she picked up the dagger again. "But this I will keep. This may be very useful indeed."

• • •

Brother Andreo stared at the bird perched just above his head with a quiet awe. The picture in the ancient scroll had not come close to capturing its beauty. There it had looked merely like any bird, a pretty one, but just one of many species. Here, an arm's length away from him, its red and gold shimmered with light, radiating a quiet glory.

Shara had bequeathed him the book that morning and Andreo had stayed in his small cell for many hours, working on its translation, before coming out for some fresh air. This was his favorite part of the monastery gardens— the fruit orchard. He sat on a wooden bench, letting the heavy aroma of the plum and cherry blossoms wrap their sweetness around him.

Shara's book, his own translation, and one of the ancient scrolls lay on his knees. It was a risk, but all the brothers would be in the chantry for at least an hour longer. He would make sure he returned to his room before they finished.

He had just turned his attention away from the spring trees to the first page of the book, when he felt a slight rush of air and looked up to see the Gold Breast.

Time stood still. He did not know how long the bird and he looked at each other. It felt like a mere instant, but might as easily have been a slice of eternity. Finally, the Gold Breast moved. It did not fly away; instead, it came closer. So close that it perched on the edge of Shara's book, lying open on Andreo's lap.

Andreo hardly dared to breathe, but the bird did not seem frightened. It leaned forward and touched the page with its beak. When Andreo did not react, the Gold Breast repeated the action. Eventually, Andreo took his eyes off the bird and looked at the page. It was the one that he had spent so many hours poring over. By now, he knew every little squiggle and mark on it, even though he only knew what a few of them meant.

Every mark was exactly as he recalled it, but as he looked, something changed. It was as if the door of a dark room opened to allow in the daylight, for understanding filtered into his mind. With perfect clarity, he could now read the words that he had struggled to understand for the last few days.

This is the true story of Ajalon, the Great Kingdom, before it was split into two by the evil forces of Taus. It also tells of Tirragyl and the deception that Taus wove on this beautiful land. And of the great crimes committed against the King of Ajalon. I, Eliad, have written this in my own hand from the border pool in the Rif'twine Forest overlooking Gwyndorr, where you will find me on this day. Eliad

Andreo stared at the passage in amazement, reading it a few times to imprint it on his mind. The Border Pool in the Rif'twine Forest? How was it possible for someone to stay in the Rif'twine? The name Ajalon did not sound familiar, and he knew only of Taus, the one reverently referred to as "The Greater Light," the ancient—now deified—king of Tirragyl.

Keen to keep reading, he turned the page. But as he did so, the Gold Breast flew to perch next to him on the bench. Andreo's eyes scanned the words on the second page, but this time the understanding did not flow into his mind. All he saw was the unfamiliar script.

"You ... you let me understand the words?" It did not feel strange to speak to the bird. "But not the rest?"

Did the first page still make sense, though? Andreo turned back hastily. He need not have feared, for as soon as his eyes fell on the script, the meaning washed into his mind as it had done before.

"Thank you," he whispered.

He read the words again, slowly, trying to make sense of them in light of the Tirragylin history that he knew so well.

Taus had been the first king of Tirragyl, and, according to history, had brought great wealth and security to the country. He had also been the founder of the Brotherhood of Taus, the order to which Andreo belonged, and was revered by them as a god. This is what the monks had taught the people of Tirragyl and, over generations, Taus was worshiped as a divine king.

Andreo could not reconcile the words he now read with what he believed of Taus. The words in this book spoke of Taus's "evil forces" and the "deception" that he had woven on Tirragyl. How did this connect with the benevolent Taus that Andreo had been taught to venerate?

"I don't understand," he said, looking at the Gold Breast. "Is this another Taus? Or"—it was almost impossible to accept the blasphemous thought—"is Taus not what I believe him to be?"

Guilt seized him. How could he possibly think that Taus was anything less than perfect? "Forgive me for my offensive thought, Oh Greater Light," he whispered as he slammed the book closed. He glanced around nervously. If anybody heard his spoken doubt, who knew what would become of him. The Brotherhood did not allow any dissension and, to his knowledge, nobody had ever spoken a negative word against the Great Taus.

Still the bird sat silently looking at him.

"I'm sorry. I believe you were trying to help, but I ... I cannot." Could not *what*? he thought to himself. He could not entertain any negative thoughts about Taus, for it would mean his end.

But what if it is the truth? The thought came so fast, so unbidden, that it caught him off guard. The next one leapt into his mind before he even had time to contemplate the first one. *If Taus is truly divine and truly good, the truth will not hurt him.*

Andreo had a sudden overriding urge to get away from the Gold Breast. He picked up the book and scroll and looked at the bird, still perched on the bench. "I must go. Thank you for the understanding you brought."

He turned and, fighting against the impulse to take one last look at the magnificent bird, marched toward the monastery building. One more thought breezed through his mind. *Truth sets free, Andreo. Seek it with your whole heart.*

CHAPTER 35

The day after Andreo saw the Gold Breast, he returned to his cave. It was the Sacred Day, not a day he would normally use for his alchemy work, but Andreo had to escape the confines of his cell, his thoughts about the Gold Breast and book, and most of all, his doubts about Taus. Only here, surrounded by his life's work, did Andreo find the solace denied him since he laid eyes on the bird.

He was mixing two ingredients for a skin cream when the creepers at the entrance of the cave parted. Shock jarred through Andreo's body as he looked into the eyes of Brother Angustus. For one irrational moment, Andreo thought of gathering all the leaves, solutions, creams, and potions in his arms, and running. Worse than this discovery and the consequences to follow was the fact that fourteen years of work was about to be destroyed. No longer would the frillbough provide relief from pain or the bitter-bark diminish swelling. He would never again be able to help Frieya or Bristle and all their companions who, for a while, had benefited from his small gifts of healing. It was over.

"Well, well, well." There was a hard glint of pleasure on Angustus's features as he looked around. Two younger monks had slipped in behind him. "Brother Druen told me what you had hidden here, but I just had to see it with my own eyes." His disparaging gaze turned back to Andreo, who met it steadily; Andreo was not ashamed of all he had accomplished.

"So this is how you have been spending your meditation hour, Andreo? In forbidden Parashi practices? Creating banned potions against all the Brethren teaching?"

"Yes, Brother. I use the plants created for our benefit to bring healing to the people."

"What people?"

"Anybody I come across who is in need."

"No Highborn would demean himself so. Obviously you have been peddling this muck to the Parashi."

"Illness makes equals of us all, Brother. And I never sell anything."

"Well, I'm sure the council would like to see this." He snapped his fingers. "Druen, bring samples of everything you find. Destroy the rest."

Andreo watched as the two young monks set to work, throwing his carefully chronicled vials, dishes, leaves, berries, bark, and roots into a large sack. His notes, too, were stuffed in the bag, and everything that remained was swept into a second bag for burning. A quiet rage burned inside him at the injustice—the narrow-mindedness—of it all. How could their hearts be so full of hatred against the Old ways and teachings, that they did not appreciate the benefits of herbal alchemy? Did he really want to be part of a group so intolerant in its thinking? In that moment, Andreo knew that, if he could survive what was to come, he would do everything in his power to escape the walls and rules of the Brotherhood.

Truth sets free. Seek it with your whole heart. Yes, he would. He would seek and find. What's more, the knowledge of everything Angustus had ordered destroyed was deep inside him, more secure than ink on parchment could ever be.

Almost as if he sensed his hopeful thoughts, Angustus spoke. "You do realize what this means for you, don't you, Andreo? We can never trust you with such freedom again. No more tutoring. No more going outside the walls of the monastery."

"I think that is for the council to decide, Brother," Andreo answered mildly. "Perhaps they will even relieve me of my brethren ties."

Angustus let out a snort of laughter. "You would like that, wouldn't you? Then you can go and do your little illegal activities all by yourself. It's not that easy, Andreo. No, the promises you make to the Brotherhood are for life. There is no escape from their binding nature."

Andreo knew this. He had, after all, learnt the words by heart with all the other acolytes. *We bind ourselves to the Brotherhood and to Taus until death destroys the cords that tie us.*

"Don't fear. We may still make something useful of you yet."

The words sounded ominous. Andreo had heard that Word Art brothers often used their magic to twist people's unacceptable thoughts to follow the course set out by the Brotherhood. Yet, it was used on those *outside* the monastery, those such as the Verita Vestals, who were so clearly opposed to monastery teaching. Surely they wouldn't try it on one of their own. However, a cold dread crept into him as Angustus led him out of the cave. Hadn't he done just what generations of Vestals had been doing—opposed the mighty Brotherhood of Taus?

As they neared the monastery, a new concern wedged in Andreo's mind— Shara's book. He had left it in his cell, hidden under the straw pallet with the other scrolls. If Angustus had invaded the sanctity of Andreo's cave, he wouldn't think twice about ripping apart the cell too.

Yet Angustus seemed pleased that he had all the evidence he would need to convict Andreo, and he merely said, "Stay in your cell until you are summoned. I will call the council into an emergency session, and Brother Druen will fetch you when our decision has been made."

"I do not get to speak in my own defense?"

"There is nothing you can say. You are in blatant violation of the rules. All that remains to be decided is the form of your punishment."

"I insist on addressing the council before they pass judgment."

"I'm sure you do." Angustus smiled coldly. "But you threw away all your rights when you chose rebellion. Brother Druen will call you."

That night, no summons came. Andreo paced nervously into the night. He heard the dinner bell and the evening prayer bell. Should he go? He did not want to incur Angustus's wrath by disobeying him, so he stayed in his cell.

In the morning, however, hunger gnawed at him and at the second bell of the day, the break of fast, he slipped from his cell, and into the dining hall.

It was obvious to him that the news of his rebellion had not yet spread around the monastery, because his fellow brethren's greetings were still respectful and kind. All that would change soon, very soon indeed. Then, he imagined, their looks would be scornful, wary, accusing. No longer would he be one of their own. Instead, he would be the disgraced brother, the outsider of the monastery. A sadness stole into Andreo's heart. Twenty-nine years of fellowship with these men, his friends and brothers, was about to be torn apart.

He joined a table where several scribes, including Brother Justus, sat. Andreo thought there may have been a hint of anxiety on the old monk's face as he glanced up at Andreo.

"Morning, Brothers," Andreo smiled.

They ate in silence, as was the custom of the monastery. This was the time for reflection on all the goodness of Taus, and his provision for their physical needs. The Scribes, always keen to return to their inkpots and parchments, left as soon as their bowls were empty. Only Brother Justus remained.

"Where are the scrolls?" he whispered, glancing around nervously.

"In my cell, Brother."

"You must return them to me right away. Something is afoot."

"What do you mean?"

"The council met last night. They meet again this morning."

"For what reason?"

"There are rumors that one of our own has been caught in an act of rebellion."

"What kind of rebellion?"

"No one seems to know, but it must be significant for the council to meet so long." He looked stern as he said, "I want those scrolls back, Brother Andreo. You have had them too long already."

"I'll bring them now."

"Be careful no one sees you. Meet me at the vault in half an hour."

Brother Justus's concerns were unfounded. Andreo encountered nobody on his way to the library, and the scrolls were soon back in their hiding place. However, he had no sooner returned to his cell than Druen opened his door. Already there was a loss of respect, he realized. No Brother merely entered another's room without calling or knocking.

"It's time, Andreo," he announced in his high-pitched voice. No "Brother" either, Andreo noticed.

He silently followed the monk to the upper rooms of the monastery. He was aware of the stares of his fellow monks as he passed them; he didn't make eye contact with one of them. His fall from grace had begun.

• • •

As much as she tried, Shara could not return to the forest and the woman who would tell her everything about her father. If only Brother Andreo hadn't come in just when she had been so close to discovering the truth.

She reluctantly laid the rock aside and turned her attention to the note that Brother Andreo had brought on Saturday. She had read it many times in these last two days, had wept many tears over it. Finally she knew that Nicho loved her as much she loved him. He had explained that Yasmin and he were friends and that he had been protecting her from Maldor's advances, before he wrote the words now etched in her mind:

You are to me sunshine and sorrow, mountains and moors, a dark night filled with stars. You fill my thoughts, my dreams, my longings. You have captured my heart and mind. I am a city besieged, parched and hungry, dying because I lack the one thing I love and need—you. You may go to the farthest parts of Tirragyl, and even beyond the Rhorhan Sea, and still I will not forget you. I will not stop loving you.

She knew his words were true, for the same love he spoke of beat through her own heart. Yet, now she felt an even greater sense of dread at becoming Maldor's wife. It would have been better to never love, she thought, than to have loved and lost it so cruelly.

Shara tucked the note into one of her dresses, and laid it on top of her other belongings in her chest. She glanced at the Cerulean Dusk Dreamer. She had considered putting it back in the hidden compartment of Randin's desk. Surely, one day he would look for it, and on finding it gone, suspect that Shara had stolen it. Yet, she could not lose it; the rock had become a part of her that she would not give up. Even if Randin rode to Lucian's manor and demanded it back, she would deny everything. After all, a servant may have found the rock too. Or Ghris? Or Olva? The Dreamer was hers now. Randin would never find it.

One last item remained: a bracelet of shells that Ghris had given her three years ago. A southern trader from the port town of Portas had sold it to him, and as much as Shara liked it, she could still remember Marai's reaction the first time she saw it.

"Petal, that is just so beautiful," she had said, touching the fine shells. "The Creator's handiwork never ceases to amaze, does it?"

Shara had made a decision. She wanted to give the bracelet to Marai, as a keepsake of their cherished friendship. The night before, she had asked

Randin if she could go to the kitchen and say goodbye to the cook; he had agreed. However, when she asked if she could visit Nicho in the stables, he shook his head.

"No. Tell his mother to pass on your goodbyes."

Now Shara picked up the bracelet and made her way downstairs.

"Where are you going?" Olva asked as Shara headed for the door.

"To say goodbye to Marai." She turned, expecting a challenge from her aunt, but Olva merely shrugged.

As she entered the kitchen, a loud shriek split the air.

"Shara, my child!" Marai dropped the dough she was pounding. For such a large woman, she moved with surprising speed, enfolding Shara in her arms before Shara could even speak. This is real love, Shara thought, as the tears sprang to her eyes.

Marai drew back to look at her. She wiped a tear from Shara's face, although by now tears streaked her own face too. "Oh, my Petal." Again they held each other in silence, and Shara drew comfort from the soft, warm embrace of the woman she considered her mother.

"How long can you stay?" Marai said eventually, as they pulled apart. She drew a short wooden stool from next to the hearth and patted it. "Come, sit. Tell me what's on your heart."

"I can stay a while. Randin said I could come."

"You look so thin, my love. Here," Marai rustled in a dish and produced some dates. "Eat these. They're your favorites."

Shara ate, not because she was hungry, but because it gave Marai pleasure. The cook's eyes never left her face.

"I'm sure you have a lot of work for tomorrow, Marai. Can I help with something?"

"Absolutely not. You are the guest of honor after all," Marai answered with forced cheer. "Now tell me about this wedding gown of yours. Yasmin says 'tis exquisite.

Shara spoke of the gown with little enthusiasm; every word felt like drudgery. She wanted to pour out her heart, or fall once more into Marai's embrace and stay there for a lifetime, but she was aware of the scullery maids' eyes on her. What's more, the months of separation lay between her and Marai, a rift she had not expected, and did not know how to cross.

"I brought this for you, Marai." Shara dropped the bracelet into Marai's hand.

"Oh, my child!" Again tears sprang into Marai's eyes. "You know how much I loved this." She looked long and hard into Shara's eyes. "I have nothing to give you, Petal. Nothing for you to cherish."

"You've given me everything already, Marai." Shara looked away, as a flood of emotion threatened to overwhelm her. "You saved me."

"I wish I could save you from this," Marai said softly, and in that instant, the rift was gone. Marai understood. Shara knew that Marai felt all Shara's pain as if it was her own, and the realization wrapped around Shara, even warmer than Marai's embrace.

"I'll be all right, Marai. You know me."

"Yes. You are a strong 'un, no doubt about it."

There was little else to say, but Shara sat a while longer, just soaking in the place that had always filled her with a sense of home. How she had missed it these last few months, and how she would miss it in her new life.

Finally, they drew together into one last tear-filled hug.

"Tell Nicho Randin would not let me come say goodbye. But I read his letter. And his words meant the world to me," she said into Marai's ear.

Marai's eyes widened with surprise. "Letter?"

"Please just tell him, Marai. I won't be able to tell him myself."

"I will tell him, Petal." She planted a kiss on Shara's forehead. "Now you go and be as strong and beautiful as you've always been. And may the Ancient One keep your steps light and true."

Chapter 36

D ruen pushed open the door leading into the dark interior of the Decisions Hall. It was here that the Sacred Brother met with his Council of Six to make decisions concerning monastery life.

Andreo crossed the threshold into the room that few Brethren would ever enter; how he wished he had remained one of them. He hesitated, unsure of the protocol for approaching the High Council.

They were seated around a long table under the only source of light in the room—three tall windows. His eyes struggled to make out their individual faces against the light from the windows.

Druen paced forward confidently, and gave a slight bow to the man seated at the head of the table. "Here is the accused, Your Prominence."

"Thank you, Brother," the Sacred Brother said. "Bring him to the Verdict rug and then leave."

Druen pushed Andreo to the opposite end of the table, where a small red carpet lay on the floor. Andreo was again unsure what was required of him, but Brother Angustus rose and spoke in a loud voice.

"Kneel before your jury and await the verdict for your crime."

Andreo did as he was told, dropping onto his knees on the small red rug. All the way here, he had told himself that he was not ashamed of his actions, that he would defend himself with honor and show no shame for what he knew deep in his heart had been good and beneficial. Yet here, kneeling before the seven most powerful men in the monastery, listening to words such as "verdict" and "crime," he was suddenly less certain of his position. A wave of shame assaulted him.

"Andreo," Angustus continued. "You stand accused of rebelling against the Codes of the Brotherhood of Taus by your involvement in the forbidden ancient practice of alchemy. Twenty-nine years ago, you bound yourself to the Brotherhood and its Codes. You have therefore transgressed against yourself, every one of your brothers, and against the Great Light Giver, Taus.

"This council has considered all the evidence." He swept his arm toward the items on the table, and Andreo recognized his notes, solutions, and potions. "The Sacred Brother will now pronounce our judgment against you."

As Angustus sat, the Sacred Brother rose. His hair was white as snow and his eyes a blue so light that whenever Andreo looked into them, he had the sensation of looking into the depths of the sky itself. The Sacred Brother had a soft voice, yet every word he spoke carried authority.

"Before I pronounce judgment on you, Andreo, I would give you a chance to show contrition. I would suggest that you weigh your words carefully, for I will consider them in my sentence. You may rise to speak."

Andreo again did as he was told, pushing himself to his feet. His eyes had adjusted to the light, and he could now look into every face turned toward him. How strange to think that he had eaten meals with these men, had learned and debated and prayed with them. Yet here they were: his accusers and jury. How could he make them understand the motives that had driven him to disobey their Code? How could he show that what he had done had been done out of compassion and not to bring harm?

"Brothers," he started. "It is true that I have disobeyed the Code by investigating the properties of various plants, as the ancient Parashi were known to do. For this rebellion, I am truly sorry, for the Brotherhood is my life. Every man in this monastery is my brother, and I never intended to bring shame on any of you by my actions."

There was a slight murmur of approval from the men seated at the table.

"However," Andreo continued, "I believe that there is a wealth of goodness to be discovered in herbal alchemy, and our Code dates back to a time when everything the Parashi did or believed was considered evil. Yet, the plants are gifts of the Divine. They are there for our benefit. I have discovered ways to alleviate pain and sleeplessness. I have—"

"Enough!" Angustus bellowed across the table. "Sacred Brother, see how every word this man speaks condemns him. He shows no remorse whatsoever. I therefore argue for the course of action I proposed to this council earlier."

"I disagree," Brother Wrendil interjected. Andreo had had his share of disagreements with the monk who headed up the Brodon of the monastery and was surprised at the unexpected source of support. "It is true Andreo has gone astray and for that he should be disciplined." His eyes bored into Andreo's as he added, "Severely." He turned his gaze back to Angustus. "However, what you are proposing, Brother Angustus, goes against the very principles of the Brotherhood."

"Hear, hear!" Another voice—the Keeper Monk—added. "If we start allowing the Word Art brethren to use their power on fellow monks, where will it end? If you don't like the meal my brothers prepare, do you then cast a spell on them?"

"That's ridiculous," Angustus sputtered. "And it's not a spell. It's merely a thought-altering exercise that will ensure he sees things in the right light again. I mean, listen to the man speak. He is convinced that the Code—the sacred Code of Taus—is wrong!"

For a moment, uproar broke out as each of the council members voiced his thoughts and opinions.

"Silence!" The Sacred Brother was up on his feet. "Brothers, we have already discussed these points at great length, and we will not do so again. I agree with Brother Angustus that Andreo shows no remorse, that his thinking has been warped by the evil in this world, and therefore I believe Word Arts are the only course open to us."

"But Your Prominence—" Brother Wrendil started. The raised hand of the Sacred Brother silenced him.

"This does *not*, as you suggest, set a precedent for the Word Art brothers to use their skills on any other Brother in the monastery. This is an extreme case unlike any I have seen in my time here, and therefore requires extreme measures." He solemnly turned his attention back to Andreo. "Kneel as I pronounce my judgment."

Andreo sank to his knees, fear clawing at his throat. He had thought he could survive what was to come and still find a way to share his knowledge of healing. Yet, he knew now that his mind would not survive it. Every part of it would be stripped away, filled only with the meager thoughts Angustus allowed back into it.

"Andreo, this council finds you guilty of the practice of Alchemy Magic, and sentences you to a Disgracing. After that, you are to be remanded into the custody of the Word Art Brethren, who have permission to use any of their skills, other than those bringing death, to draw you back into the light-filled knowledge of the Brethren."

"Ko!" Jed's arms wrapped around his legs, as he pushed the door open. "Nana has a feefa."

"Hey there, Rascal." Nicho dropped to his knees and looked at the young boy, whose eyes had always been so alight with joy. Nicho had drawn strength from the innocent pleasure he saw in them. Yet, since Derry left, the joy had seeped away, replaced by a gravity unbefitting a child.

"Where's your Mama, Jed?"

"The market. Sometimes the traders give her the bad bits nobody likes."

"And she left you here by yourself?"

"Someone has to look after Nana." The boy sounded proud. "And the guards did a slum sweep already, so they won't come now to make me a rooter."

Nicho walked to the sleeping pallet in the back corner, and looked down at the curled-up shape of Nana. How small and thin she looked—like a fragile bird. He sank to his knees and reached for her hand. It was icy cold.

"Shh. Don't make her wake up. Mama will be cross," Jed whispered.

"I won't, Jed. Don't worry."

He turned back to the boy and smiled. "Why don't we play something?"

For a moment the childlike eagerness was back on Jed's face. "Like what?"

"Well, how about we do a battle between Troyin and the invaders. Where's that horse of yours, Erlian?"

"I don't know." The boy looked away quickly.

"You don't know? You always had him with you. He even slept with you, didn't he?"

"He got lost."

"Jed, I don't understand. You loved—"

"He's gone," the boy said. "Anyway, him and Troyin got killed. All the Parashi got killed because they were weak. It's a stupid game."

"Well, what do you want to play then?"

"Nothing."

"Come on! What was your favorite game to play with your father?"

"I can't remember."

"I remember you used to wrestle with him. That would always make you laugh. I bet you can't beat *me* in a wrestling match." He grabbed Jed's leg and pushed him down, tickling him in his side. A peal of laughter echoed around the room.

"I bet you I can," the boy said, pushing Nicho to the ground and clambering on top of him. They rolled, tussled, and laughed, until a high voice broke through their play.

"Jed! What did I tell you?" Hildah strode toward them—fury on her face—and grabbed him by his arm, almost lifting him off the ground. "I told you to take care of Nana, didn't I?" She shook him. "Didn't I?"

"I did, Mama. I did," he wailed.

"No, you've woken her up. Look!"

Indeed, Nana was stirring with all the commotion, moaning slightly as her eyes roamed around the room. Nicho reached for her. "It's okay, Nana. We're here."

"Where's Derry?" Her soft voice cracked. "Where are my boys?"

"They'll be back soon, Nana. It's me—Nicho—remember?"

"Nicho," she smiled, as her eyes found his face. "You came back. Make sure the boys come quickly too, will you?"

"Yes, Nana, they'll be here soon. You rest a bit more."

"Tell them to come soon. I'm so tired, Nicho ... must see them." The talking had tired her; she sank back into the bedding straw.

"She rambles all day like this," Hildah said. "The only rest we get is when she sleeps." She glared at her son and dropped some wilted leaves on the table.

"You get that at the market, Hildah?" Nicho said, trying to draw her attention away from Jed.

She nodded. "They give me less and less. Tell me they don't want beggars hanging around."

"I brought another bread. That should last a day or two."

She smiled weakly, then turned her attention back to Jed. "Go find some firewood." As the boy slunk out the door, she said, "He's useless at it. Brings nothing more than kindling."

"There's not much wood to be found in the slum, Hildah, and he's little. I didn't realize you were out. I'll try to bring some tomorrow."

She nodded again, her forehead furrowed.

"Hildah, shall I send my mother to take a look at Nana? She has some leaves for fever and pain that I'm sure will settle her a little."

Hildah shrugged. "All that will settle her is seeing Derry and Pearce. Jed and I are strangers to her."

"I'll send her tomorrow after the wedding." He stood a while longer in silence, as Hildah washed the leaves from the market.

"I'll be going now." She didn't look up. "Hildah?"

Finally, she turned dull eyes to him.

"What happened to the horse Derry made for Jed?"

"I got a bronze coin for it from an eastern trader," she said flatly. "It may just have been the last bread Derry ever put on our table."

CHAPTER 37

After the meditation hour, the Sacred Brother and Council of Six led Andreo through the monastery gate and down the road to where the rest of the monastery gathered to await his arrival; Andreo could hear their chanting as he drew nearer. The voices stopped and every face turned to look at him as he followed Brother Angustus. The few glances he met were filled with reproach or disappointment, and Andreo quickly dropped his gaze to the ground.

"Brethren," Angustus said, and Andreo had the sense that he was savoring every moment. "You are here to bear witness to the guilt of one of our own, Andreo, found guilty of breaking the Sacred Code by practicing Alchemy Magic." Angustus paused. "According to the council's sentence, the Disgracing will now begin."

Andreo, like most of the monks here, had never attended a Disgracing. Only a few of the very old ones could recall the last one at the monastery. Yet, every acolyte learnt the history and meaning of this, the most humiliating form of monastery discipline. The Disgracing was the symbolic stripping away of everything the monastery gave to its brethren.

Brother Wrendil was the first to step forward. "Andreo, your Brodon Sash, please." Andreo pulled the ceremonial crimson sash over his shoulders and laid it into the outstretched hand, as Brother Wrendil continued to speak. "You are hereby stripped of your position as a Brodon. Your rebellion makes you unfit to tutor young minds."

Brother Yugall was next. "Andreo, the scroll please." Andreo laid the scroll, given him on completion of his training, into the Scribe's hands. "You are hereby stripped of the knowledge gained in these walls."

Brother Sirin, the Celebrant, pushed forward. "Andreo, your ring please." It was the ring given to every acolyte on entering the monastery, the symbol of unity with the brothers. Andreo wrestled it from his finger. "You are hereby stripped of the right to communion with those present."

The Keeper was next. "Andreo, your robes please." Andreo felt shame wash over him as he disrobed of his outer garments, conscious of the stares of the brethren. "You are hereby stripped of all the comforts of food and clothes that this monastery has provided you."

Brother Fris, a compatriot of Brother Gladson, took his turn. His brief smile communicated a hidden message of sympathy, yet his words were possibly the harshest of them all. "You are hereby stripped of the name that the monastery granted you. From this point on you will answer to no name for, until you are restored to the Brotherhood, you are not."

Only Angustus remained, and his was a fearful stripping indeed. He stepped forward. "You have received—but by your actions denied—the great Light-Bringer Taus. Since you have rejected his light, you will now be cast into darkness." He reached out and touched Andreo's eyes, and spoke a single word that only Andreo heard. It was a sound like gristle grating between your teeth—harsh and gruff. In that moment, the light seeped from Andreo's eyes and blindness enfolded him. It was a frightening sensation and Andreo struggled not to cry out.

Now the Sacred Brother stepped forward. "You are nobody and have nothing but our scorn. Yet ours is not the judgment you need to fear. We will now lead you to face the wrath of Taus. Should you withstand his wrath tonight, your restoration will begin in the morning."

The Sacred Brother and council now led Andreo toward the Rock of Wrath, a high, narrow plateau that lay, ironically, just above his cave. It was here that the great King Taus had defeated the last of the Parashi chiefs, Troyin. And it was here that Andreo would spend the night—stripped and blinded.

The Mentors delighted in telling young acolytes tales of disgraced monks dying in blizzards or struck by lightning bolts on the Rock of Wrath. A few, they told, had even plummeted to their deaths on the rocks below. As they drew away from the monastery that had been his home for the last twenty-nine years, and the chanting grew softer, Andreo considered what lay ahead. If it had been mid-winter, spending a night exposed to the elements would have ended in death, but this summer evening promised to be fairly mild. As long as he didn't fumble around in his blind state, he should survive the night on the ledge. Then, tomorrow he would face Angustus's magic.

Andreo felt vulnerable as he stumbled toward Taus's judgment. Brother Angustus's crushing grip on his right arm contrasted with the softer hold of Brother Wrendil's on his left. He tripped often on the uneven ground and—especially where the path narrowed and they were forced into single file—his shins slammed into jutting rocks.

Eventually the ground leveled out.

"The Rock of Wrath," Brother Angustus announced sternly, letting go his hold of Andreo. "May Taus judge you according to his great sight." The other five Brothers echoed the words in soft murmurs.

Brother Wrendil squeezed his arm in a hidden message of encouragement, before he too released his grip. The small sign of kindness brought a lump to Andreo's throat.

He listened to their retreating footsteps, trying to gauge how many steps there were to the edge of the plateau. When he could no longer hear them, he sank down onto his haunches, the vast silence pressing down on him as heavily as his Brothers' judgment.

Did Taus judge him too for what he had done? He was not sure he could revere a god who ordained it wrong to heal people.

Andreo lay down on the ground then and sensed the soul-weariness that had crept over him today. He closed his eyes and drifted into an uncomfortable, restless sleep.

When he awoke, he lay tightly curled on the ground, not daring to move, for he could not tell how far away he lay from the cliff's edge. The midnight cold had slipped over him and his mouth felt parched from thirst. After the short respite of sleep, his mind again churned over the day.

The Disgracing had accomplished its purpose. Everything that Andreo had loved—his teaching, the fellowship, the sense of belonging—had been removed from him. Twenty-nine years of studying, working, praying and building had crumbled in one afternoon. Andreo was a mere husk—an empty shell of a man. Tomorrow he would be even less. Tomorrow his very essence would be altered. The thought of being in Angustus's clutches terrified him. If, with only one word, he could take Andreo's sight, what else could he take from him?

A strange new thought came to Andreo then. He still had one option open to him. He could end this torment here and now, denying Angustus the pleasure of tampering with his mind. All he had to do was find the edge of the cliff and keep on going. The Brethren would consider his death an act of Taus, proof of his guilt. The Mentors would have a new tale to tell the acolytes about the terrors of the Disgracing. It mattered little now.

He lifted himself to a crawling position and edged forward. His death would prove that the Code was infallible and that herbal alchemy was evil. This last realization stopped him momentarily. The Code was wrong about herbal alchemy; he did not want his death to prove otherwise. Yet, he would never be able to persuade the Brothers of his position. In fact, after Angustus had had his way, Andreo wouldn't even believe it himself.

Andreo started to move again. After a while, he didn't even move cautiously anymore. He was vaguely aware of sharp rocks slicing into his knees and hands, but he kept going, praying that the drop was near. Yet, as the solid ground continued, he considered changing direction. He clambered to his feet and turned to his right, taking large, deliberate steps. The thought that every step could be his last—could lead over the edge—filled him with a touch of dread, but he pushed it aside. The alternative awaiting him was far more frightening.

Stop.

The command resounded through his mind so forcefully, that he had no option but to obey it. He stood dead still, unsure what to do next. Now he felt warmth on his face, as when you draw near to a fire. He gradually became aware that the light was returning to his eyes, for stars pierced through the darkness again, and he could see a golden light pulsing ahead of him—the source of the heat he felt on his skin. As he looked more closely, he saw that it was the Gold Breast, its wings beating so fast that it gave off a slight humming sound. It stopped after a while, and settled on the ground, still casting light around it.

Now Andreo could see where he was. He stood right at the cliff's edge; another two paces and he would have plummeted to his death. A cold terror spread through his body at the insight. What had come over him? He didn't want to die.

He dropped to the ground next to the bird.

"You saved me," he whispered. "You found me here. You undid the blinding spell ... such power." Trepidation prickled through him. "What are you?"

A voice spoke from behind him. "Andreo?"

Andreo spun around to see an old man walking toward him. He was short, although this was partly due to his slightly age-curved back, and he was wrapped in a dark, rough cloak. Only one bony hand—gripping a gnarled walking stick—was visible beneath it. His silver hair was matted and wild and his face wrinkled with lines. Those around his eyes gave the impression of much laughter. It was a compelling face, even more so as it broke into a smile.

"Andreo. Finally we meet!" Another hand appeared from under the cloak, grasping Andreo's arm, and drawing him to his feet with surprising strength. "You are cold, my friend. Here." The old man pulled the cloak loose and laid it on Andreo's shoulders. It felt course and smelled of wood smoke; Andreo gratefully drew into its warmth.

"Come. I know a good cave in which to shelter the night." The man's voice was soft and husky—as if from disuse—and the words sounded slightly foreign as they rolled from his lips.

"Who are you?" Andreo asked.

"Oh, how remiss of me. I am Eliad, and this"—he pointed to the Gold Breast—"is Tabeal. I believe you have already met?"

"Eliad? The one who wrote the book?"

"Yes," the man smiled again. "I penned the book you have, it is true."

"I ... I don't have it anymore." Andreo looked away. "It was in my cell, but Brother Angustus is sure to have it by now. I'm so sorry."

"No, do not worry Andreo. Tabeal led me to it this afternoon. Luckily, the monastery was deserted; some commotion going on outside the gate."

"That would have been my Disgracing."

"The perfect diversion," Eliad said with a wry smile. "Now come."

They did not speak again as Eliad lead them off the plateau, even though Andreo's mind pulsed with a myriad of questions. Only when he realized that the old man was leading him to his own cave, did he speak again. "Eliad, will they not find us here in the morning?"

"A few hours remain till dawn. We will be gone before they return."

Inside the familiar cave, Eliad lit a small oil lamp. He must have been here earlier, Andreo realized as the cave lit up, for a makeshift bed of dry grass and leaves lay against one wall.

"Rest a while, my friend. You have been through an ordeal."

Andreo sank gratefully onto the bed.

"Are you hungry?"

"I should be I suppose, but ... no. Thirsty. Very thirsty."

"Drink." Eliad drew a large water skin from a sack on the ground, and passed it to Andreo, who drank like a parched desert wanderer.

"It's a peculiar practice, this Disgracing," Eliad commented as he watched him. "Take one of your own and leave him out to die of thirst or exposure. Does it happen often?"

"No. I'm the first in about fifty years. Nobody rebels in the Brotherhood."

"What was it you did?" The question held no judgment, but Andreo suddenly recalled the scornful looks of his brothers. He did not want Eliad to look at him in the same way.

"I infringed on a minor point of the Code," he mumbled, before quickly changing the subject. "So why did you come for me?"

"Tabeal," Eliad smiled as he looked at the bird. "She led me here."

"I don't understand. The *bird* decided to find me?"

Eliad shrugged. "When you get to know her better, you'll understand."

"Is she yours?"

"No. Her loyalty belongs to only one, and all he holds dear. She is the most wonderful companion." His face broke into a smile as he looked at the bird.

"She's a Gold Breast?"

"I believe that's how your books refer to her."

"You know they're meant to be mythical, right?"

"Myth-i-cal?" Eliad looked confused. "Forgive me, Andreo. I do not know that word. Your language is still young on my lips."

"It means they're not real. They only exist in stories."

"Ahh." Understanding dawned on the old man's face. "Yes. That would suit Taus's purposes. I'm sure much is declared myth-i-cal," he pronounced the word carefully, "in Tirragyl. Yet here she is. As real as you and me."

"Taus again." Andreo pursed his lips.

"Pardon?"

"The Gold Breast helped me understand a passage in the book."

"Yes," Eliad nodded vigorously. "One of her gifts."

"It said something about Taus's deception." Andreo faltered, before adding, "I have been taught to revere Taus."

"Yes, indeed," Eliad said somberly.

"I do not know anymore, Eliad. Even these last few days: the Code, the Disgracing. Nothing makes sense anymore. What is truth? What is false?"

"Such questioning is a good place to find oneself, my friend."

"What do you mean?"

"Your world has been—how do you say? Shaken?" Eliad smiled. "Now you have to seek the truth for yourself."

"Where do I seek it?" Andreo felt a surge of anger. "For twenty-nine years I sought it in the monastery. I thought I had found it. Now *you* tell me otherwise."

"I think, Andreo, your heart told you that long before I did. Think back. Sometimes you saw beyond the lies. But you did not *want* to believe what you saw, so you clung to the lies instead."

He spoke the truth—all those things that had felt "wrong" in the monastery and its history: the purge; the discrimination; a Code that would deny medicine to the people.

"That was just a few things." He heard the defensiveness in his voice. "Must I throw out a whole lifetime of teaching because of a few small things?"

"Just keep your eyes open, Andreo. The truth is much closer than you think."

Andreo felt a surge of annoyance at this man's riddles.

"We need some rest, my friend," Eliad said. "Tomorrow is Shara's wedding, and we must be prepared for whatever Tabeal would have us do."

His own concerns had so consumed him that Andreo had all but forgotten about Shara's. "By Taus! Tomorrow is Tuesday—her wedding day. But how do you know of my pupil?"

Eliad's deep, throaty laugh echoed around the cave. "You ask a lot of questions! Let's just say that Shara also has some truth to discover. She is the one who uncovered the book, and it holds many answers she seeks. In time they will all be revealed."

Andreo sensed that asking anything more was useless. Eliad wasted little time in blowing out the light and curling onto the bed of grass; soon he was snoring softly next to him. Despite his tiredness, Andreo's thoughts kept returning to all Eliad had said. One of his last thoughts before sleep finally overtook him was that—even if Tabeal led them there the next day—Shara would be completely beyond their reach in Lord Lucian's manor.

CHAPTER 38

Tessor had found the dress she had worn only once—on her wedding day—folded in a chest in a dusty storeroom. Over the years, Lucian's women had helped themselves to Tessor's beautiful garments. Yet, perhaps even they considered it bad fortune to wear the wedding dress of their lover's wife. The grief-filled memories threatened to drag her under as she lifted the burnished-orange silk gown from the chest. Hadn't she sworn never to touch this dress again? She had known the pain that would pulse through her at the smoothness of its fabric. That soft touch that had held the promise of lifelong love.

Yet she would wear it just one more time, to fulfill her own promise to Fafa.

Back in her room, only the power of that promise gave her the strength to pull on the gown. The covering over her looking glass was coated with fourteen years of dust; she thrust it aside and forced herself to confront what she had become. Staring back at her through dark-ringed eyes was a woman she didn't recognize, her sunken cheeks creased by time and grief. By Taus! How she had aged.

But this was no time for vanity. Tessor had a promise to fulfill. She plaited her long, listless hair and thrust her feet into the matching silk shoes that had been wrapped in the center of the gown. Then she marched down to the stables, moving through a parting sea of surprised faces.

She had almost expected Lucian and Maldor to have left without her, but they were just mounting their horses as she walked to the readied carriage. Maldor cast her a single, disparaging look and then spat down at her. Tessor lifted her head, pretending not to notice the wet mark of his contempt on the wide skirt of her dress. Briefly she met Lucian's gaze, but he turned away without saying a word.

She climbed into the covered carriage, which followed Lucian and Maldor through the gates of the manor house and out into the streets of Gwyndorr. For fourteen years she had not laid eyes on these streets, but she hardly noticed the sights and sounds rattling past. She thought only of what lay ahead.

Briefly she wondered if Lucian had recognized the dress and if, when this was all over, he would know the irony of it all. The dress she'd worn on the day her life ended was the same dress he would see on the day she took away what he wanted most.

. . .

The wedding day was finally here. Other than his mother, the servants seemed relieved; the intensity of their workload would soon diminish. Yet a cold dread gripped Nicho. Heavy grief constricted his chest so that even breathing felt difficult. Perhaps this was how a condemned man felt on the day of his execution. His resentment at Maldor's beating didn't compare to the anger and despair he felt that the young lord was taking Shara to be his wife.

He threw himself into his work long before it was light, hoping to soothe his inner turmoil, yet as the hours wore on and the time of the wedding feast drew near, the knot of dread expanded inside him. By the time the horsemen and carriage rode through the gate, it felt as solid and heavy as stone.

His feet carried him into the courtyard behind Helvin, although every part of him screamed to stay in the stable instead.

The two front horsemen, Lucian and Maldor, were in a heated discussion, but their conversation ended abruptly as they drew alongside Nicho and Helvin. Behind them the carriage and four additional horsemen, dressed in military uniform, drew to a halt.

Lucian was the first to dismount and didn't even cast a glance at the grooms. However, as Nicho grabbed the reins of Maldor's horse, he felt a crushing pressure on his wrist.

"Well, well. If it isn't the Parashi I beat to a pulp. Pity you're still able to stand, slum-boy. I should have punched a bit harder."

For just a second Nicho lifted his head in defiance, looking into light brown eyes filled with malice. How could Master Randin give Shara to this man?

"Maldor! Come greet your father-in-law," Lord Lucian called.

Maldor broke his hold on Nicho's wrist and strode toward the entrance, as the carriage's occupant alighted.

She was a tall woman, with a long face and dark rings under her eyes. The dress she wore, although made of beautiful fabric, did not improve her appearance; somehow its beauty only drew attention to her dullness. She appeared to be looking at him and he quickly diverted his glance. As she brushed past him, she said softly, "Maldor is ruthless to everyone who opposes him."

Nicho stared after her in surprise as she made her way to the entrance, where Olva was offering an effusive greeting, and Randin's voice boomed out a welcome.

"We present to you our daughter, Shara. May she be warmly welcomed into your eminent family."

Ghris had appeared in the entrance, supporting Shara on his arm. She wore an emerald green gown that shimmered in the light, and her hair was piled on her head, a few stray ringlets dropping around her face. Ghris pushed her slightly ahead of him, where she gave a small curtsy.

Nicho could not take his eyes off Shara. Never had he seen her look more beautiful or more vulnerable. Her face seemed paler than usual, enhancing the darkness of her eyes and hair.

As she rose from the curtsy, she looked up. Only then did Nicho realize how close he had moved to the guests, for he could clearly see Shara's eyes narrow on Maldor. As Randin invited the guests inside, her stare shifted from Maldor to him. For an instant, it felt as if only the two of them stood in that courtyard. He had never known that a single look could say so much. In her eyes, he saw sorrow, loss, and a tenderness that tore through his heart.

Then she turned and was gone.

• • •

It was a risk, but Shara had tucked the Cerulean Dusk Dreamer under the layers of her emerald green wedding gown. She did not want the rock out of her sight as the servants were loading her possessions; more importantly, the touch of it—warm against her body—filled her with the calm she needed to face the day ahead.

When Olva called "they are here" from the window, Ghris solemnly took Shara by the arm, and they followed his father and mother to the doorway.

Now even the Dreamer couldn't keep Shara's heart from fluttering or her palms from sweating. *She was leaving forever. As Maldor's wife.*

"Lord Lucian, what a joyful celebration this is." Olva was vivacious as Lucian bowed and kissed her hand.

"We present to you our daughter, Shara." Randin raised his arm toward her. "May she be warmly welcomed into your eminent family."

Shara sensed Lucian's gaze on her as she did the curtsy Olva had instructed, but it was Maldor—striding toward them—she looked at as she rose.

In that single look she hoped to communicate the depth of her loathing. Yet, the small surge of victory she felt as she saw him wince under the force of her hatred was obliterated by the smile that grew on his lips. *He found this amusing. She was a game to him.*

Just before she turned back into the house, she saw Nicho. He held the reins of two stallions, but had moved away from the stable and was standing only a few paces behind Maldor. *I will not forget you. I will not stop loving you.* If her gaze for Maldor had communicated the depth of her hatred, she hoped her last look at Nicho would echo with the same love he had expressed for her. It was the only thing left to give him.

Then Ghris drew her back inside to the dining room and led her to the seat at the long end of the table. Maldor sat to her left, and her skin bristled with the sense of his closeness. She caught a whiff of cloying musk on him. At the head of the table and to her right, sat Lord Lucian. Briefly, the smile he gave her soothed away some of her anxiety.

Only then did Shara notice the woman in orange, taking her place next to Ghris. It was the woman of the dream. The one the house had forgotten. A wave of cold surged down Shara's back. *Who was she? Why was she here?* Of all the dreams the rock had given her, the dream of the woman had been the most ominous. Perhaps the Dusk Dreamer had merely been warning her of her impending wedding, but Shara could not forget the rusted blade in the woman's hand and the words on her lips—*I will vindicate you, Fafa.*

Shara was relieved at the diversion Marai, Yasmin and Fortuni created as they bustled in with platters of food.

"Eat something, my petal," Marai whispered in her ear as she placed a tray of bread and fruit in front of her. Shara looked up into the face she loved so dearly and saw the unshed tears in Marai's eyes.

She gave what she hoped was a brave smile and filled her plate with food, taking a bite of bread as Marai turned away. Yet even this small morsel stuck in her throat.

For once Shara was relieved at Olva's chattiness, for she dominated Maldor's attention for much of the meal. Shara cast another look at the woman of the dream, sitting opposite her in silence. She was picking at the food on her plate, her head tilted slightly to the side as if listening to distant voices. She sensed Shara's gaze and looked up. Her fleeting smile was filled with sadness and a kind of knowing, as if she understood Shara's pain.

Suddenly Shara became aware that Maldor was leaning toward her. She stiffened as she heard soft words whispered into her ear.

"So, my fiery little bride, have you found your tongue yet?" She stared steadily ahead, pretending not to hear. "No? Well, I don't mind." He pulled away in a languid stretch, dropping his right arm around her shoulder and pulling her rigid body closer to him. "In fact, I prefer my girls quiet. That way I choose the way things are done." He laughed softly. "I didn't realize you had turned into the town beauty. The last time I saw you, you were just a snotty-faced brat playing in the dirt with Parashi dogs. Quite a pleasant surprise, you are. Taming you will be quite a game."

Shara hadn't intended to speak, but her answer came unbidden and—like the first stare—exposed all her loathing. "You will never tame me. I am not yours to tame."

"Such passion!" Again, the glint of amusement on his face. "I can't wait to begin. Soon, my scorching Shara, I will show you that you are *completely* mine to tame."

• • •

Tessor had not expected to feel compassion for the girl. She berated herself for it, knowing it would hamper her from fulfilling her promise.

Yet, from the time she saw Shara and the contemptuous way she looked at Maldor, she felt a strange kinship to the girl. Even the surprisingly tender way Shara looked at the Parashi groom filled Tessor with sympathy.

Now Tessor sat at the table, watching and listening. She noticed the moment of maternal care that passed between the cook and the girl, and she saw

Lucian's pleased gaze constantly returning to the young bride. She detected Maldor's boredom at Olva's stories and remembered how Olva's eyes had widened in surprise as Tessor strode across the courtyard. Her old friend had recovered well though. Her embrace was the first Tessor had had in fifteen years, and it had left her feeling a little shaky. She had missed the touch of another.

Tessor noticed something else. The alarm in Shara's eyes as she looked at her. Lucian's servants, Olva, and Randin had not looked at her that way. They were surprised, maybe even a little repulsed, but not afraid. Why did the girl fear her?

Now she watched as Maldor broke free of Olva and turned his attention to his bride. Shara stiffened as he whispered something and her sharp retort seemed to amuse Maldor. No matter how spirited the girl was, Tessor knew Maldor would not stop until he broke her. Breaking people was how he amused himself.

Perhaps it was a kindness to save the girl from years of his abuse, Tessor thought. It was a kindness she wished somebody had shown *her* fourteen years ago.

CHAPTER 39

All too soon, Lucian and Maldor pushed their chairs back and rose from the table, followed by the others. The time had come.

Only Shara remained seated and she felt all their eyes on her. She wanted to rise. She did not want to make a spectacle of herself now, here, in front of Maldor and his father. Yet, fear pinned her down, made her as weak as Kharin had been in those first moments after her birth.

Maldor's smile was mocking as he extended an arm to her. She had no choice but to take hold of it and allow herself to be lead outside. Every ounce of strength and resistance, even anger, had drained from her. She willed herself not to break down, not to give Maldor that pleasure. She just needed to make it to the carriage—*just the carriage.*

Her family bade her farewell in the courtyard before Maldor led her toward the carriage. She picked out Nicho's tall frame immediately, holding the reins of the carriage horse. As she came close to him, he lifted his head and looked at her. His eyes were pools reflecting all her own sorrow.

"Keep your head down, Parashi," Maldor spat at him, and Nicho dropped his head in subservience.

Shara felt like a traitor, holding on to the arm that had beaten Nicho unconscious. It was almost a relief when she was seated in the carriage, and Maldor had returned to his horse. But she stiffened again when the carriage swayed and the woman climbed in opposite her. As they rolled toward the gate, Shara swiveled her head around to look at Nicho. He was still staring at the ground.

"You care for him?"

Shara caught her last glance of Nicho before the carriage swung into the street. Only then did she turn back, warily, to the woman.

"Maldor? No. I hate him."

"I meant the groom." Her voice was deep for a woman's.

"Yes. He is my friend."

The woman nodded once, perhaps not convinced. "Why do you hate Maldor?"

Shara hesitated. "Are you his mother?"

The brief smile lifted something in the woman's countenance. "No. I'm just Tessor. Crazy Tessy to most." There was more sadness than bitterness in the words.

"Why do they call you that?" Shara instantly regretted the bold question. Hadn't the dream shown her the crazed look in the woman's eyes as, blade in hand, she came ever closer to Shara?

"I left their world," Tessor said after a long pause, gazing out over Gwyndorr's streets. "They could not understand. Grief and loneliness changes you."

Shara nodded. She had felt that too, in the dream. How solitude and sorrow clung to this woman.

After that neither of them spoke as the carriage bore Shara to her new home. She thought of all that still lay ahead and kept her eyes on Tessor's long pale fingers, folded mildly in her lap.

. . .

After setting off from the cave just before sunrise, Andreo and Eliad were finally within sight of Gwyndorr's gate. Andreo had found the walk long and tiring, particularly after the strain of his trial and Disgracing. They had only stopped once to rest, near Rifter Unit Twenty-nine, and as Andreo caught sight of the platform in the distance, an intense longing had risen up in him to see Bristle, Frieya and the others again. He had quelled it. Eliad was impatient to reach Gwyndorr. Also—a wave of sadness washed through him at the thought—he had nothing to give them; everything had been destroyed.

The guards at the gate gave them only a cursory glance. An old man and a monk posed little threat, Andreo assumed. When Eliad had presented him with a monk's cowl that morning, a wave of emotion had engulfed him. He had no right to wear it; that privilege had been stripped away the day before. Even if it hadn't been, Andreo was not sure he *wanted* to wear it. Yet, there had been little choice in the matter, and now he was glad for the anonymity it provided.

A group of six guards stood assembled just inside the gate and as they passed, Andreo could hear the voice of their commander.

"... the captain's instructions. We march to his house and arrest the Parashi groom who goes by the name of Nicho. Understood?"

"Yes, sir," the voices chorused.

"Jax and Yirla, position yourselves at the house gate, in case he tries to escape. The rest of you will come with me to arrest the traitor. Questions?"

"What is the charge, sir?"

"Teaching letters to Parashi boys. Treason. We are to bring him back here and Captain Randin will do the sentencing later this evening."

"Yes, sir."

Andreo did not hear the last of the instructions as they moved out of earshot, but he had heard enough. "Eliad!" he whispered. "I know the lad they speak of. We must warn him."

"I heard it too," Eliad said gravely. "We don't have much time."

• • •

As the carriage drove through the gates of her new home, Shara sat in stunned silence. She had heard that Lucian's house was a mansion, but could never have imagined the sheer grandeur that now met her eyes.

A long row of servants awaited their arrival and, as the carriage stopped, they went to work: putting a footstool in place for them; giving support to alight the carriage; gathering up her chest and disappearing into the house with it.

She was ushered into a large parlor with a fireplace at its far end, and told to wait for the lord. Maldor had sprung from his horse and stalked into the house before she had even alighted from the carriage, but she assumed he would come for her now.

Shara felt small in this room—small and insignificant. She was unsure what to do. Should she sit or merely stand by the doorway? Her palms were sweaty, yet she felt cold. Slowly she walked down the long room, toward the fireplace, disinterestedly studying the tapestries that adorned the walls, merely so she would appear busy when Maldor arrived. The tapestries were intricate and beautiful. They looked valuable. Each one depicted a different scene—armored men on horseback; women in elaborate gowns; a hunting party with hounds at their feet. A few of them portrayed kings and queens.

The very last tapestry before she reached the fireplace was different—its colors were brighter, as if less affected by light and the passing of time. Her gaze was drawn to the top right corner. Sitting on a delicately embroidered branch was a bird crafted from red and gold threads. It looked as regal as she knew it to be. A small, shocked breath escaped from Shara's lips. Silently she studied the rest of the tapestry. It was a garden scene, with children playing by a stream. She could not pull her gaze away from it.

She had not heard the large door opening, and jumped at the voice that came from a mere few paces away from her.

"One of my favorites. Do you like it?" Lord Lucian stood behind her.

"I do, my lord," she said as steadily as she could.

He moved closer, taking her by the arm and leading her toward the chairs at the fireplace. He indicated for her to sit as he sank down in the large manor chair. She lowered her eyes and studied the small flames licking behind the grate.

"Look at me, Shara."

With some reluctance, she met his gaze. His eyes were a light brown, flecked with gold. They were beautiful. As she looked into them some of her trepidation faded away; those strange eyes radiated assurance. If this man thought that Shara and Maldor would be good together, who was she to dispute it? Surely he was right. Surely she should trust him.

"I thought we might get to know each other a little," he said softly, and his voice, too, imparted the sense that all would be well, that she was where she should be.

"Were you treated well in Randin's household?" It was a strange question and she did not know how to answer it truthfully. Should she tell him of Randin and Olva's indifference? Would he even consider that mistreatment?

"Well enough, my lord," she said after a considerable pause.

"He never laid a hand on you?"

"No, my lord. Never." Although words left bruises too, she thought.

"And your tutor? I handpicked Brother Stefan for you—did he teach you well?"

Shara did not understand. Gwyndorr's lord had picked a tutor for *her*?

"Why?" The word slipped out, before she had time to censor it. Lucian laughed.

"A direct woman, I see. To be expected, really. I have always taken an interest in you, Shara, because I knew you were to marry my son."

She had the urge to ask why—if this had been common knowledge for so long—she had only discovered it four days ago, but kept the question to herself. A more pressing question needed asking, and she instinctively sensed that a man of his position would not tolerate a girl's questioning for long.

"Why was I considered appropriate to marry into your esteemed family?"

He laughed again. "Randin is an important man in his own right in this city. It seems like a good alliance to me, wouldn't you agree?"

The arrival of an older man with a pompous voice cut short their conversation. "My lord. The first guests have arrived."

"Thank you, Lyndis," Lucian said. "Please could you escort Lady Shara to her living quarters and introduce her to her handmaidens, who will help her prepare."

With that he rose, inclining his head slightly in her direction. "Shara, I trust that you will feel welcome in my family. You are a valuable addition to us and I believe your arrival heralds a time of great favor and success."

His voice held a note of fervency and, for an instant, Shara thought she saw a flash of fevered excitement in his eyes. Yet, a moment later, his soothing voice bade her farewell and she realized that what she had seen was merely a reflection of the firelight.

The living quarters to which Lyndis took Shara were light and spacious—a bedroom, dressing room, and sitting room. Curtains in a rich gold fabric draped the windows, and all the rooms were furnished with exquisite fixtures carved from a dark wood. Above the fireplace hung a portrait of Maldor. His eyes followed her threateningly through the room.

Her two allotted handmaidens were older than she was and, judging by their sullen reception, not particularly glad of their new assignment.

Shara had to fight back an entire day's tears when she realized that they had already unpacked her chest, containing two of her most precious possessions—the dagger and letter from Nicho. To her relief she found them lying under her cloak in the cupboard.

The two maids insisted on helping her dress into another outfit Olva's seamstress had sewn for her from a deep rose-colored fabric. They also brushed her hair, tying it into an elaborate arrangement with skill Yasmin could only dream of.

Their surly expressions dissipated only when Maldor flung open the door. They both smiled coyly in his direction and Brea, the younger and prettier of the two, said something flirtatious that elicited a playful slap from Maldor. As much as she detested her husband, Shara felt humiliated that he and this servant acted as if she was not there.

Yet when his attention finally turned on her, she instantly wished that he would keep flirting with Brea.

"You look even lovelier than this morning, my fiery bride." He strode over to her, extending his arm in her direction. "Fiery dress, fiery lips, all to match that fiery tongue. Come."

She stood stonily, arms crossed over her body like a shield, cursing the heat rising to her face.

He had seen it too. "Look, Brea, even a fiery face to match the dress."

Both maids giggled. "Well, you know where to find a *real* woman, my lord," Brea said, casting Shara one last disparaging look as they slipped out the door, leaving Maldor alone with her.

His eyes were suddenly darker—more dangerous. As he took the last step toward her, Shara was aware of just how tall he was. His face moved closer and closer to hers and she found herself holding her breath, bracing herself for the expected kiss. Instead, his fingers curled around the loose strands of hair that hung on the side of her face. She cried as he wrenched her head down by the hair.

"Never," he said softly, "make a fool of me in front of anyone again." He let go of her hair. "Do you understand?" She fought down the tears, nodding mutely.

"Pleasure is better than pain, wouldn't you agree, my flame?" His fingers touched her cheek in a soft caress. "Make sure you don't give me a reason to hurt you again. Now," he held his arm out in her direction, "let's try that again."

This time Shara complied, slipping her hand onto his arm.

"You see how easy it is to be tamed, Shara?"

Silently, he led her toward the sound of music and raised voices, toward the place where he would introduce her as his new wife. As the noise increased, a strange dullness crept over Shara, as if she was entering a deep, dark tomb.

CHAPTER 40

A strange tension prickled through the air of the stable. Some of the horses whinnied; others bucked.

"Hush, hush," Nicho whispered, looking toward the entrance. There was no one there. Maybe the animals were responding to his own fretfulness, which had only increased since Shara left.

He turned back to Krola, who was pawing the ground. "There's nothing there, girl. Mere phantoms." Yet her eyes were wide with fear, and apprehension prickled through Nicho's body.

Leave now. The thought ricocheted into his mind from nowhere, more forceful than any Highborn command. He turned again. The Gold Breast now hovered—as he had sometimes seen the Drone birds do—in the entrance of the stable. *Leave!* The hovering sent an even louder message to Nicho than the strange thought—there was no time to tarry. Whatever danger he was in, was real and imminent. Nicho dropped the pitchfork and started for the entrance.

"Let me just go tell my mother that ..."

No!

No time for goodbye? This was serious.

He was halfway across the courtyard, toward the gate, when two disheveled figures suddenly appeared. One was Brother Andreo; the other a stranger. By the time Nicho had reached the gate, he could hear the Brother speaking in urgent tones.

"... just came to give our respects to the captain and Lady Olva," he gulped for air, "on the wedding of their daughter."

The guard shook his head and said warily, "The captain has gone to the wedding feast. Lady Olva is resting, I believe. You can return on the day you tutor and pay your respects then, Brother."

The stranger had caught sight of Nicho, and a brief smile tugged at his lips. "We will do that. Thank you." He pulled Brother Andreo away from the gate.

"But ... no ... we have to ..." Brother Andreo sputtered, before he, too, saw Nicho. His relief was evident. "I suppose you are right. I will see them tomorrow."

The guard again shook his head, before noticing Nicho. "Where are *you* off to then, lad? Aren't you on stable duty for the rest of the day?"

"I'm just ... umm. Well, we're all out of ..."

"Well?" The guard frowned. "What on earth is going on here?"

"Helvin asked me to fetch some nails from the market. One of the horse shoes is coming loose, and we're all out."

"Oh. Well, don't be long." The guard said brusquely. "If the captain comes back and you're not here, there will be hell to pay."

"I'll be quick." Nicho turned in the direction of the town gate.

Brother Andreo and the other man had headed in the opposite direction, and his instincts told him to do the same, but he was conscious of the gate guard's gaze on his back.

He was near the corner of the main road, when he saw the town guards. There were seven of them. They had just turned into the road on which he walked. In less than fifteen paces, their paths would cross. Shock jarred through him as he recognized the man in the front. He was the one called Issor, the captain's second-in-command, who had been so scornful when the captain let him and Simhew go free.

Ten paces.

Nicho turned his head and dropped to his knees, fidgeting with his shoe, as if trying to loosen a stone.

Five paces.

He wiggled the shoe off and shook it.

A boot kicked him in the back. "Keep moving, Parashi," a low voice growled. "These are not your streets to loiter on."

"Yes, sir," he mumbled, not looking up, as he replaced his shoe and struggled to his feet.

The urge to run was great, but he fought it down and continued to walk calmly to the corner. When he reached it, he took one last look back. The town guards had stopped outside the captain's gate.

As he turned the corner, Nicho started to run.

Tessor slunk around the edges of the hall, watching, listening and waiting for just the right time to fulfill her promise. She saw Maldor's smug expression as he entered the Main Hall. Shara, at his side, had a look of resigned desperation that reminded Tessor of a hare surrounded by hunting dogs.

Maldor led her from one group to the next, introducing her to all the important men and women of Tirragyl society, and Tessor noticed, with some surprise, that Shara exuded a natural grace, quite in contrast to Maldor's arrogant brusqueness. She might just have made a better Lady of Gwyndorr than Tessor ever had.

Tessor listened to the whispers of the people around her. They spoke of Shara's dark beauty and youthfulness. They speculated as to why she had been chosen for Lord Lucian's son. They regaled tales of Maldor's wild exploits and pondered at the excessive bride price that Lucian had paid for Shara.

Tessor watched Lucian too. He was in uncommonly high spirits. He laughed louder, joked wilder, drank, and spoke more freely than she had ever seen him do before. He looked and acted like one who had just won a great victory on the battlefield. His eyes kept finding Shara in the crowd, as if to convince himself that she was truly here.

Tessor ate little of the rich fare that continued to be served and drank none of the mead or wine. She wanted to be alert when the time was right. She felt a twinge of pity for Shara as she saw her standing alone, studying one of the tapestries. Maldor was on the opposite side of the hall, in the center of a loud crowd of young men. It had not taken Maldor long to discard his new wife.

Tessor reluctantly moved over to her. It served no purpose to befriend this child, but she needed to stay close to her. She sensed that the moment of vengeance was near.

"It's a lovely tapestry, isn't it?"

The girl spun around and again there was a hint of fear in her eyes. "Tessor!"

"Come, walk with me." Tessor headed toward the fireplace, the girl at her side. "How did you find your quarters?"

"Beautiful, thank you." There was little enthusiasm in her words.

"They used to be my sister's." Tessor quickly thought of another question, before the child could ask about Yorina. "And your maids—were they kind to you?"

Shara nodded.

Tessor tried to think how she could fill the silence. She had forgotten the art of conversation.

"That color is beautiful on you. Everyone is saying how lovely you look."

A small smile crept onto Shara's face and Tessor felt a surprising surge of compassion. How very young this girl was. It still pleased her to have others tell her she looked pretty. As Tessor looked up and caught Lucian's gaze on them, something protective—almost motherly—rose up in her. Quietly, she slipped her arm around Shara's shoulder.

They walked through the large hall between the throng of people, who paid them little heed. As they neared Maldor and his friends, Shara's body stiffened. Tessor looked at the group of loud, obviously drunk, young men and saw what Shara had seen. Two of Maldor's friends were holding a young serving girl and Maldor was caressing her face. Then he whispered something in her ear and, though she tried to squirm away, kissed her on the mouth.

She heard Shara's sharp intake of breath, and quickly started to draw her in the other direction. It was too late, however. One of Maldor's friends had seen them and shouted something lewd. As they hurried away, she heard Maldor's laugh. "Don't worry, my fiery bride will have her turn later."

Tessor could feel Shara's body shaking.

"Shara, do you want to go back to your quarters? I think you have met everybody now."

Shara shook her head violently.

"Nobody would object if you retired," Tessor gently pressed.

"I don't want to go to my room," Shara's voice was barely audible, "because he'll find me there."

Tessor knew no words of comfort to soothe Shara's fear. The old practical Tessor would have said, *well, you can't hide from him forever,* but Tessor was no longer that woman. She understood terror, for it had held her captive for many years.

JOAN CAMPBELL

"Come." She drew Shara through the door. "I know a place where he won't find you for a while." And perhaps it was there that she could finally fulfill her promise to Fafa.

• • •

From the top of the road, Andreo and Eliad anxiously watched the close encounter Nicho had with the town guards. Fortunately Nicho had slipped out of sight by the time the guards realized he had eluded capture. Pressed against the neighboring wall, the two men heard the commotion from the house, and a voice shouting commands.

"You three, after him! Jax and Thorn, with me to the Slum. That's where he'll head. Yirla, to the gate. Warn them not to let *any* Parashi out. We don't want to face the captain's wrath. Move it!"

They watched the men tear down the road.

"By Taus, that was close," Andreo whispered. "But how did he know to come to the gate?"

"Tabeal warned him." Eliad said.

"For a bird, she is very good at communicating." He remembered his own encounter with her near the cliff edge. "What now, Eliad?"

"We find Nicho," Eliad answered, as if it was as easy as returning to your horse in its stable stall.

"In Gwyndorr? The town guards have a better chance of finding him than we do. At least there are many of them."

Eliad laughed. "I doubt it. Besides, somebody knows exactly where he is."

"Who knows?"

Eliad regarded him intently, and shook his head. "When are you going to start seeing with new eyes, Andreo?"

"Seeing what?"

"The wonders all around you."

"You mean the Gold Breast? Are you saying she knows where he is?"

"Of course, Tabeal knows." He pointed to the bird perched on a wall to their east. "All we have to do is follow her. Come."

It had taken close to an hour to find Nicho. The commander had been right—Nicho *had* headed to the Slum's winding alleyways. Yet, the groom's knowledge of the area gave him an innate advantage over the guards. Eliad and Andreo found him pressed into a dark shaft that connected two of the filthiest Slum zones. It was the common escape route for boys on Slum sweep nights; the guards had always avoided its dank, reeking interior.

"Nicho," Andreo whispered into the tunnel. "Come out."

Nicho emerged warily, his face and hair wet from exertion, and his breathing labored. He cast an anxious look at Eliad. "Who's this, Brother?"

"Eliad. He's with the Gold Breast. You can trust him. The guards are in the Slum, Nicho. We saw them," Andreo continued. "We need to get away from here."

"Where to? Nowhere is safe, Brother."

"We must leave Gwyndorr," Eliad said quietly.

"Get out of Gwyndorr?" Nicho said. "You are a stranger, sir, and do not understand. There will be guards crawling all over this town, looking for me. The gates will be more secure than the king's fortress. I have about as much chance of getting out of here as the Parashi warlord Troyin had of single-handedly fighting Taus and his men." He bit his lip. "It's hopeless. The best thing is to hand myself over right now."

"We have the greater power, Nicho," Eliad said.

"You are deceived or blinded, sir," Nicho said. "Power? You have not seen power until you have seen all of Gwyndorr's forces arrayed against you."

"Possibly," Eliad said. "But they will be looking for a Parashi groom and you, my friend, will be a Prince of Tirragyl."

CHAPTER 41

The girl looked around the darkened room. Tessor spent hours in her quarters every day, but suddenly she saw it as Shara must. Dark, dusty, and neglected. For the first time, she realized how stale the air smelled in here.

"Let me open the curtain." She moved to the window and pulled the heavy drape aside. "It's dark in here."

"I don't mind." Shara folded her arms and leaned against the wall. "As long as he doesn't find me."

They would find her in this room eventually, of course. And Tessor would be here to see the look on Lucian's face when he realized what she had done.

Now. She should do it now. The longer she waited, the more difficult it would be. Tessor slid open the top drawer and looked at the dagger lying there. It had been Fafa's once; the wide handle was made for a man's hand. Tessor had sharpened the blade just this morning, but there were patches of rust on it from years of neglect. It would do, though. As she picked it up, her hand trembled slightly.

She cast a quick look at Shara, who had moved to the window and was staring out at the garden. It was ideal. This way she wouldn't have to look into the girl's eyes and see the questions or pain hanging there before it was over. How could she explain to the child that this had to be done? For Fafa. Even for her. Tessor was saving her from a lifetime of sorrow. Would she understand that?

Tessor took a step closer to her, gripping the handle tightly to stop the shaking. She studied the girl's back. Between the shoulder blades, that was the right place. She mustn't suffer.

"It's a large garden, isn't it?" The girl turned to face her as she spoke, and Tessor quickly hid the blade behind her back.

"Yes. In Fafa's time it was beautiful and colorful," she said lightly. "Lots of flowers."

"Fafa?" Fear flashed in the girl's eyes.

"My grandfather. The last Lord of Gwyndorr."

"Oh." The girl's gaze moved slowly down, studying Tessor's hands. As she noticed Tessor's hidden hand, she began to back away toward the door. Almost as if she knew. "I think I'll go back to Maldor now."

"Why? Stay a while. He won't find you here for some time."

The girl shook her head. "I must go."

"You can't go, Shara. There's something I must —"

Just then the girl gave a startled shout and ran, not toward the door, but back to the window. "The Gold Breast!"

Tessor turned to see a bird hovering by the window. It looked like the one in the tapestry, but instantly she knew that it was no ordinary bird. Not only was it the most magnificent creature she had ever seen, but—as she gazed at it—she was filled with a sense of shame at what she had almost done to Shara. Suddenly she understood that vengeance was not hers to take. With the realization came a sense of peace so deep, it brought tears to Tessor's eyes.

Tessor released the dagger and it clattered to the floor.

"She's got something in her beak," Shara was saying. "Can we open this window?"

"No. It is a solid pane of glass."

"How do you get fresh air in here?" Shara asked.

"There's a gap between the stones up there." Tessor pointed high above the window to where a tapestry hung. "I covered it. It was too cold in winter."

The Gold Breast had already flown upward and was now out of sight. Had it seen the crack?

"Can we move the tapestry?"

Tessor pulled a lower tapestry off the wall and hooked its pole under the high tapestry's support. She gave a hard tug and it fell to the floor with a dusty *thunk*.

They stared at the deep crack in the wall. After a few moments, a small parchment appeared and dropped at their feet. Shara's hand shook as she picked it up.

"It's written in Brother Andreo's hand," she said, passing it to Tessor.

Tessor read the words. *Meet us behind the stable in half an hour. Be brave, all will be well, A.* She looked up at Shara. "Who's Andreo?"

"My tutor."

"You think he's come to rescue you?"

"No." Shara smiled. "The Gold Breast has come to rescue me."

To Tessor the idea didn't seem strange at all, and suddenly she knew. *This* was the time she had been waiting for all these years. She could still be an instrument in denying Lucian what he wanted most.

"There's no time to waste." She grabbed Shara by the hand and pulled her toward the door. "I will take you to the stable through passages Lucian knows nothing of. Is there anything you need from your room?"

"Yes, but do you think we should risk it?"

"Nobody will see us," Tessor smiled. "They haven't seen me for years."

. . .

"There are two ways to do this," Eliad said. "The fair way, or the unfair way."

Andreo and Nicho looked at him doubtfully. They were huddled together outside Lucian's impressive walls, trying to catch their breath after running most of the way here from the Slum. On their way, they had caught sight of several guards, but Tabeal had somehow managed to lead them to safety. Still, Nicho thought, it was just a matter of time before a town guard spotted him.

Now this crazed old man wanted to penetrate Lord Lucian's mansion and save Shara. It was completely insane. He had made Andreo write a note saying that Shara was to meet them in half an hour, and sent the Gold Breast off with it, although whether the bird would even find her was doubtful. *Tabeal can find anybody in the darkest of places*, Eliad had said when Nicho pointed out this obvious shortcoming. Yet, even if the bird found her, how would she escape from Maldor long enough to reach their meeting place? Then there was the small problem of the walls, the gates and the guards. If they managed to pass all these obstacles to get inside, what was the chance that they would manage to get out again, this time with Shara by their side?

It was a doomed mission. All they would do was draw attention to themselves and bring the town guards swooping down on them. Then it was a Rifter Gang and certain death, at least for Nicho. Futile. Completely, completely futile, Nicho thought.

"What do you think, Nicho? Fair or unfair?" Eliad's voice broke through his despondency. The old man showed none of Nicho's own misgivings. In fact, his expression was more like that of a young boy whose father has just promised to take him on his first hunting trip.

"What do you mean, Eliad?" Andreo asked.

"To get into the grounds, my friends." He turned lively eyes on them. "We can use some of Tabeal's powers, something a little unfair to our opponents. Nicho, I believe you have experienced her stun call?"

At the town gate! Of course, how could he have forgotten? He and Shara had made it past the gate and guards, thanks to the Gold Breast. Could they do it again?

Eliad's next words quelled the first spark of optimism Nicho had felt the entire day. "But she is not here right now, so I think we will have to play fair today. It will be our own ingenuity that gets us in." He rubbed his hands gleefully. "Any ideas?"

Nicho merely shook his head and Andreo glumly studied the high walls. "Nothing comes to mind, Eliad."

Eliad's grin grew even wider. "Well, fortunately I *do* have an idea, friends. We'll have to make a bit of magic of our own. And all we need is ... a carriage."

Nicho almost laughed. A carriage! This man *was* crazy. Where would they find a carriage?

Eliad was digging in his large blanket-sack, and mumbling to himself. "Yes, we'll definitely need that. And that, of course. Glad I brought it." He took something out of his bag. The afternoon was growing darker and Nicho struggled to see what it was.

"Andreo will be better in character, I think. Yes, yes. Ah, I've always liked this one. Look rather dashing in it, if I say so myself."

More mysterious objects were unpacked from the bag. One last dig around in it produced another small item and finally he set the bag aside, with a measure of satisfaction.

"I think we may just pull this off, friends," he said. "Let's get to work. In my youth, one of my greatest accomplishments at the king's court was as a jester. I have a real knack for it. You have heard of jesters?" He looked at Nicho, who nodded, although he couldn't hide his confusion. He had seen a jester at the Spring Festival before, but he hadn't known that the king liked that sort of entertainment at court.

Andreo seemed equally confused. "I have never heard of jesters at Tirragyl's court. They say King Altaus is rather somber."

"No, no! Not that sour old so-called king. But you miss the point, friends. What I'm trying to say is that I am a great pretender." There was a hint of pride in his voice. "How about you, Nicho? Do you think you can play the part of a prince with some flair?"

He threw a bundle at Nicho. It was a cloak made of a rich, soft material. Nicho could not tell if it was purple or a very dark blue. As he opened it, a small gold crown fell from its folds.

"Me? I am a groom, Eliad. Not a pretender, and definitely not a prince," he said. "In fact, I'm starting to think this is a particularly bad idea. The town guards will be on us in no time if we pursue this craziness."

Eliad waved the objection aside like an irritating fly. "All you need to act the part of a Tirragyl prince is a bit of arrogance. You have watched the gentry all your life. It won't be difficult for you."

"Right." His attention shifted to Andreo. "You will play the role of a Brother in the monastery, something you do quite successfully already. And I will be the young Prince's escort. At your service, Sire."

His mock bow brought an involuntary grin to Nicho's face. "Where did you find this man?" he whispered to Andreo.

"I think he's been in the Rif'twine Forest too long," Andreo said.

"He was in the *Rif'twine*?"

"It is a long story, one I don't think we have time for now." Andreo pointed at Eliad, who was pulling on a cloak. "I think he probably wants you in your costume, Nicho."

"I can't believe I'm doing this." Nicho fumbled to find the front of the cloak.

"For Shara, my friend. We'll do it for her," Andreo said.

When they were dressed, Eliad gave them an outline of his plan. Nicho didn't think that anybody would believe the implausible story Eliad had concocted, but since he didn't have a better plan, he kept silent. He drew little comfort from Eliad's seemingly unshakeable confidence. Shara's future was at stake here, as was his own life, something the old man seemed to have forgotten in his enthusiasm for their roleplaying.

"Right, the next carriage that comes along," Eliad said. "But first we need to light this oil lamp."

One of the items he had taken from his bag, it cast a surprisingly bright glow in the early evening gloom.

It took some time before a carriage turned in their direction. Presumably, it had just pulled away from Lucian's gate, which was not visible from their position.

"This is the one," Eliad whispered and boldly strode out into the center of the road, waving the oil lamp above his head. The horses, just starting to pick up speed, saw him first and pulled slightly to the left, just as the driver called "whoa" and jerked hard on the reins. The carriage shuddered to a halt just in front of Eliad.

The driver leapt off his seat in obvious anger. "What in Taus's name are you doing in the middle of the road?"

"Forgive me, sir. It is a desperate act on behalf of my ward, Prince Alexor." Before the stunned driver could speak, Eliad continued. "I am Lord Elida, Visor of King Tausorlin of the Tirragyl court, and charged to bring the crown prince, Alexor," here he beckoned Nicho into the circle of light, "to send the King's well wishes to Lord Lucian and his son on this significant day."

As Eliad spoke, a well-dressed man emerged from inside the carriage. His and the driver's eyes were now on Nicho, who stood self-consciously under their perusal, wondering if a real prince would say something at this point. Instead, he inclined his head ever so slightly in their direction, glad when Eliad continued to speak.

"Regrettably, misfortune befell us, just a few blocks south of here. Our carriage horse stepped into a deep hole and twisted her leg so severely that we were forced to stop. The prince, against my wishes, insisted that he would be willing to reach Lord Lucian's homestead on foot, to comply with his father's wishes in bringing a royal gift."

To Nicho the story sounded ridiculous, so he was amazed when both men dropped to their knees and bowed deeply in his direction. Maybe Eliad *was* an exceptional pretender, with a bit of magic of his own. The men were still on their knees and Eliad was coughing ever so slightly and indicating something with his hands. Nicho realized what was expected of him.

"You may rise," he mumbled.

As the men lurched to their feet, Eliad continued to speak. "The prince may have convinced me to come this far on foot, but I insist that he enters

Lord Lucian's homestead in a manner befitting royalty. This is why we would ask the use of your carriage for a short while."

The men hesitated as they glanced at each other.

"The prince will, of course, be willing to reward you amply for this gracious act." Eliad pulled a small pouch out of his pocket and stepped toward the man who had been inside the carriage. The man let out a startled cry as a silver coin dropped into his hand.

"We are anxious to return this evening, so we will not take much of your precious time," Eliad said hastily, possibly afraid that the story would not hold up under much scrutiny.

He walked toward the entrance of the carriage, and now beckoned Nicho toward him. "Your Highness, let us make haste."

Nicho passed the two astonished men and climbed into the carriage. Eliad clambered onto the driver's seat.

"This good monk was so kind as to assist us when our horse injured herself. Brother, would you be so kind as to care for our two friends till our return?" Eliad said, already turning the carriage around.

As they headed toward the corner leading to the gate, Nicho stole one last glance back at the startled men.

"You are right, Eliad. You are quite the pretender. You created a whirlwind of confusion there," he said softly.

"One that I'm afraid won't last very long. We must make haste. Oh, and Nicho, act a bit more princely at the gate.

CHAPTER 42

The candle in Tessor's hand did not give much light in the dark passage, and Shara pressed in close to the older woman, struggling to keep her footing on the irregular stones.

Earlier, Tessor had hidden Shara in a room off the passage leading to her quarters, while she went to retrieve some of her belongings. Shara had felt her heart beating wildly in her chest as she waited. As the moments stretched on and on, the fear grew in Shara. Had Tessor been discovered? Yet just as she was trying to work out in which direction the stables lay, Tessor had returned with a small bag containing some clothes and the dagger. She had led Shara to a dusty storeroom and slipped behind a wardrobe, to reveal the entrance to a dark, forgotten passage. They had followed this around the main rooms of the house and sometimes Shara could hear the sound of muffled laughter or talking through small holes in the wall.

Tessor steadied Shara as her foot caught on a raised stone. They had left the forgotten passage a while ago and were now in a rear passage, sometimes used by the servants.

"Are we almost there?" Shara whispered, tasting the dust in her mouth.

"We are close."

There was a scurrying sound ahead of them. Just rats, Shara thought once the jolt of fright had passed. It was becoming more and more difficult to put one foot in front of the next. More than once she had felt herself falter, wanting nothing more than to sink to the ground and rest a while. Yet Brother Andreo was risking a great deal, and she would be brave. What lay ahead was unknown, but what lay behind was a lifetime of bondage. Shara would rather choose the unknown.

The light illuminated something solid ahead of them. For an instant her tired mind thought that the passage must have been blocked off since Tessor was last here, but at Tessor's pleased exclamation she realized that they had reached the outside door.

Tessor placed the candle on the ground while she tried to turn the large brass key. Years of dirt and rust wedged the key into place. If the situation had not been this desperate, they may have given up. However, with great strain, Tessor eventually managed to turn it. Now they both threw their weight against the heavy door; Shara almost cried when it would not budge.

"Again." Tessor said firmly.

Over and over they ran against it with all their desperate strength, until finally a small creaking sound indicated that there was some movement. They continued throwing themselves at the door, oblivious to the pain. The small shaft of light grew a little wider each time.

"Just one more. With everything we've got," Tessor said.

Shara put all her loss, fear, and hope into that last lurch. The door gave way, swinging almost fully open and causing them both to fall to the ground. They were outside!

Tessor was the first to recover. "We are here. But we need to hide. Blow out the candle, someone might see us."

She pulled Shara to her feet and ran into the darkness, heading for a building at the back of the stable.

The laughter and talking Shara could hear grew louder as they approached the outside building. It seemed wrong to be running *toward* the people, yet she had little choice but to follow Tessor. Shara almost bumped into her when she stopped abruptly. Right ahead of them hovered the Gold Breast.

• • •

Nicho didn't need to do much more than wave in as royal a way as he could manage, for even at the gate Eliad's convincing authority had effect. One of the guards swung the gate open, while another, despite Eliad's protests, ran to the house to announce the "Prince's" arrival.

As they drove toward the stable, Nicho sensed the first note of concern in Eliad's voice. "Let's hope she has made it out. Once Lucian hears of our arrival, he will suspect something is amiss."

Eliad stopped the carriage just in front of the stable. Many torches lit the area, and the crowd of servants milling around all stared at the well-dressed arrivals. A groom grabbed the horse's reins. Nicho was unsure what to do next, but he followed Eliad's lead and climbed from the carriage. There was no sign of Shara and his stomach clenched with anxiety. Still, he tried to play his part, waving and nodding in a stately way as he followed Eliad around the stable.

"Excuse me, sir. The entrance of the house is that way." Eliad ignored the groom and continued walking, whistling as he went. Nicho suddenly understood. He was calling the Gold Breast.

In the next moment, a few things happened simultaneously. The Gold Breast suddenly appeared, as if from thin air, and landed on Eliad's shoulder. An older woman, who Nicho recognized as Lord Lucian's wife, came running around the building. Right behind her was Shara. Nicho would have called to her, but another shout from the house distracted him. As he spun toward the sound, he saw men running toward them. They had been discovered!

"Quick. To the carriage," Eliad commanded. He grabbed Lucian's wife by the hand while Nicho rushed toward Shara, who gave a small startled cry as she saw him. She reached for his arm and together they ran for the carriage.

The people around them had stood frozen by all the sudden, unexpected activity but, as the shouting from the house grew in intensity, several of them sluggishly responded. Nicho now felt someone grasping his cloak. He pressed Shara ahead of him to shield her from the hands and pushed her onto the carriage.

Lucian's wife must have stumbled because as Nicho clambered in behind Shara, he turned to see Eliad pulling her to her feet. A group of men surrounded Eliad and the woman, making it impossible for them to reach the carriage. They had come so close; Nicho had almost dared believe they might get away.

Just then a sharp sound vibrated through the air.

Shara's eyes locked on his own. "The Gold Breast!"

The effect was immediate. The men surrounding Eliad fell to the ground, clasping their ears; all the horses, except their own, were shaking their heads, whinnying or even buckling to the ground. Lucian's wife stood transfixed, a look of amazement on her face, as Eliad tried to coax her forward.

Out of the corner of his eye, Nicho saw movement from the direction of the house. Amongst all the writhing figures on the ground, strode a man: Lord Lucian. The expression on his face was one that Nicho would never forget—a combination of pain and intense rage. Although he was covering his ears, he still managed to move toward them.

Eliad had seen him too. He grabbed the woman and pulled her over the men on the ground. At the foot of the carriage, she turned toward Eliad, and even over the pulsing sound of Tabeal's call Nicho could hear her words.

"I'm not coming."

"Come, my lady! It's the only way to safety." Eliad glanced at Lucian's fast approaching figure.

"I'm staying. I want to see his face when you get away."

"Do not let your hatred and bitterness influence this decision," Eliad pleaded.

"Quick, get up. I will untie you." She stood aside so that Eliad could step onto the front of the carriage and quickly undid the reins, handing them to Eliad.

"Tessor, come!" Shara pleaded.

But Tessor merely shook her head and cuffed the horse on its rump.

"Go far and go fast," she shouted as they drew away. "I don't know why, but I know he will stop at nothing to find you."

* * *

By the time Lucian reached Tessor's side, the carriage was through the gates. He continued shouting for somebody—anybody—to stop them, but every one of his men lay incapacitated on the ground. Only she and he still stood to witness the girl's escape.

She should have been afraid as he slowly turned toward her, but she wasn't. His mouth was clenched in a taut line and his eyes filled with a rage so hot, it could have burned right through her if there had been anything left to burn.

"You did this." The familiar warm allure in his words was gone. It was a voice of ice, hard and hateful. *His true voice.*

"No. The Gold Breast did this," she said, and wondered at the momentary fear in his eyes. "But I helped."

"You will die for this, Tessor." His hand went to the dagger at his side.

"I died a long time ago. The day you poisoned Fafa was the day I stopped living."

"Fafa!" He spat the word out. "I would make your death as unpleasant as his, but I have a girl to chase down." He took one last step toward her and thrust his dagger deep into her abdomen. Pain sliced through her. Such a searing, white-hot pain that it stole away the breath she needed to scream out her anguish. She looked down to the hilt of the dagger and the small patch of red blossoming around it. As Lucian pulled it free, more pain ripped through her, and this time a long cry warbled from her lips. Her knees buckled and she fell to the ground.

Tessor stared at the blue sky overhead, trying to breath through the agony. She was aware of Lucian moving away from her, and the small part of her that had never stopped loving him wanted to call him back, wanted to beg him to take her in his arms and comfort her. Just this once.

Her hand found the wound, slick with blood. Too late now to apply pressure and stop the bleeding. Too late. Her blood was draining out onto the cobbled stones, and her life with it. Terror coursed through her at that moment, filling her with one last spurt of energy. She tried to lift herself up and call for help, but the word was a mere whisper and there was nobody to hear it.

She lay back again. The pain was starting to dull and everything around her was fading.

As the darkness closed in, Tessor heard a rustle of wings.

CHAPTER 43

Randin awoke, as if from a deep, drunken sleep, vaguely aware that someone was whimpering next to him. He stared around in confusion. All
around him, men were lying on the ground, writhing and groaning. Randin's
head pounded and pain shot behind his eyes every time he moved. Had he
drunk so much mead? Never in his life had he felt like this, even after a whole
night of feasting. His thoughts felt as thick as the mud that clogged up the
banks of Erridale Lake. He recognized that he was at Lucian's house, but what
was he doing here? And how had he ended up with all these other people,
lying under the stars, feeling this close to death?

Slowly some memories surfaced. There had been a wedding feast ... Maldor
and ... Shara. Yes, they had been drinking. That would explain the pain in the
head. He seemed to recall a carriage, and shouting.

There was shouting now—the same voice—jarring more pain into his
head. He flinched and put his hands to his ears, trying to shut out the clamor.

"Did you hear me? Get up! We need to follow them!"

Randin slowly turned in the direction of the voice. Was it directed at him?
He saw Lucian, shaking and kicking anybody in his path. A few people were
trying to clamber to their feet; one or two actually fell straight over again. He
might have laughed at this unreal scene, but then he realized that Lucian was
heading toward *him*. Groggily, he pushed himself up. Next to him, Maldor
and Ghris were doing the same. Lucian grabbed the two young men in a
strong grasp and began pulling them to their feet.

"Come!" His gaze bore into Randin, as he shoved Maldor and Ghris toward
the stables. Randin stumbled after them, holding his head as pain jarred
through it with every step.

"They've got Shara, you fools. She is gone!" Lucian said. "They are probably
halfway to the town gate by now. I will hold you accountable for this, Randin.
If she gets away, I will—"

"Who has her?" Randin asked, still trying to make sense of the strange
scene all around him.

Lucian didn't reply as he burst into the stable. The horses inside looked shaky and kept buckling at the knees. They wouldn't go far. Lucian must have come to the same conclusion, for he swore loudly. What in Taus's name had happened here?

Lucian's stallion stood upright in the corner, restlessly swaying his head from side to side. As Lucian went over to him and spoke soothingly, the horse quieted a little. Still, he looked difficult enough to ride on a good day; Randin wouldn't want to be on his back when he was this spooked.

Lucian—either fearless or desperate—beckoned Maldor to bend down so that he could vault himself from his shoulders onto the horse's high back. There was no saddle or bridle; only a rope tethered him to his post. Maldor undid this and passed it to Lucian, who guided the stallion to the gate, still speaking quietly to him.

"I'll bring some horses from the stables next door. Rouse the men. Now!"

Randin's overwhelming desire was to find a quiet, dark place and lie down in the hope that the pounding of his head would die down. Maldor, however, had caught some of his father's urgency.

"You go wake the men in the courtyard. I'll do these ones here. Tell them my father will punish them severely if they are still lying around when he gets back."

Randin had no doubt about that. He stumbled back to the place where he had been lying and started shaking every man he came across, calling loudly for them to rouse themselves.

Then he saw her. Lord Lucian's wife, crumpled on the ground. Initially, he thought she was suffering from the same stupor as the men, but then he noticed that her bodice was covered in blood.

"By Taus!" He dropped to his knees by her side, trying to dab the blood away with his sleeve, but there was too much of it. He tore off his shirt, and pushed it over the wound, trying to stall the blood flow.

A small crowd of men had gathered around him and Maldor pushed his way through them. He looked down at his stepmother with as much interest as he might study an injured duck.

"It's fatal." Maldor shrugged. "Not much we can do."

"Was it those men? The ones who came for Shara?"

"Must have been. Come we'd better hurry. My father will be back soon."

"But what of ...?"

"Leave her. There's nothing to be done." When Randin didn't move, he hissed, "Listen. My father will hardly notice if Crazy Tessy is around or not. But I'll tell you what he *will* notice. If we're not all waiting by the gate when he comes back."

The men reacted to these last words and followed Maldor to the gate, leaving Randin alone with the woman. He picked up her ice-cold hand and felt for a pulse. There wasn't any. She had already slipped away.

Randin gently placed her hand back at her side and leaned forward, closing her eyes with his thumb and forefinger.

He rose unsteadily to his feet and headed for the gate. One did not just steal into the manor of Gwyndorr's lord and steal away a bride. Whatever magic was afoot it was a powerful force indeed. As Town Guard Captain, this insight filled Randin with dread.

• • •

Once he was out of Lucian's gate, Eliad had slowed briefly to allow Brother Andreo to make a running jump onto the front of the carriage. The angry cries of the carriage owner carried to Nicho as they sped away.

Eliad had driven them through the narrow, mostly empty streets of Gwyndorr, at a swift pace. Only the sounds of pounding hooves and clanging wheels broke the terse silence. Nicho pulled Shara close to him and held her tightly, feeling the small tremors in her body.

Now, near the town gate, Eliad slowed the horse to a gentle trot. There was a long line of men, horses, and carriages, and the guards appeared to be doing a particularly thorough search.

"I think they're looking for *me*," Nicho whispered.

"Why?" Shara's eyes filled with worry.

"For teaching the boys, I suspect. Master Randin sent some of his townies to arrest me, just after the bridal feast."

"Maybe they're looking for *me*," Andreo winked back at them from the front of the carriage. "Who knows, the Brethren might have told them to keep an eye out for a balding monk on the run."

Shara smiled. "What in the abyss have you been doing, Brother?"

His voice was sorrowful as he said, "Mixing forbidden potions."

"So, it appears each one of us is a fugitive," Nicho glanced behind them. "But if they don't clear this logjam quickly, we could be in Lord Lucian's grip faster than it takes to fall off a horse."

"Be at peace, lad. Tabeal's stun power takes a while to wear off," Eliad said under his breath, just as a guard appeared at his side.

"What's the wait here, guard? Eliad's voice changed, taking on a pompous note. "My lord and lady have a long way to go after the wedding feast and see no need to wait at the gate of this backwater town."

He was indeed quite the pretender, Nicho thought.

"Our apologies," the guard said without a trace of sincerity, swinging a lantern close to them to study their faces. "But a dangerous rebel is on the run, and we have instructions to search every carriage that passes."

Dangerous rebel. Those two words were Nicho's undoing, for, combined with the strain of the day, they broke something loose inside him that rose to the surface as a bellow of laughter. Once released, it could not be contained. It continued—a body-shaking, side-aching mirth—and spread to Shara, whose peals of laughter combined with his own.

"What's so funny?" the guard growled.

"Young people," Eliad said with a conspiratorial shrug. "Heady with Lord Lucian's spirits."

By the time they reached the front of the queue, Nicho and Shara had managed to contain their laughter, although it felt far too close to the surface. Nicho was sure that if he just looked at Shara, it would start all over again, so he pinched himself as hard as he could and looked steadily ahead.

As a guard investigated the undercarriage, another stepped up to look in the footrest.

"Are you the drunk lot?" he sneered. "I have a good mind to dry you all out in the cell tonight."

A loud guffaw broke from Shara at his words.

"You think that's funny?" The man drew so close to Shara that their faces were almost touching. "Well, it might be funny for a few of the guards, but I can tell you it wouldn't be much fun for you."

All the mirth was suddenly gone. A cold rage crept over Nicho at the man's insinuation. His hand balled into a fist.

"Are we free to go, sir?" Eliad cast Nicho a warning look.

The man nodded and jumped from their carriage. His feet had hardly touched the ground before Eliad urged the horse forward.

They were on the eastern road when he hissed, "By the Abyss! You almost got us all locked up, Nicho. You and Shara laughing as if you were at a bright Spring Feast, instead of facing a rebel's execution."

"I'm sorry. I don't know what came over me," Nicho said.

"You've both been through an ordeal," Andreo said. "We all have. Let us focus on what lies ahead now."

"What *does* lie ahead?" Shara asked. "Tessor said Lord Lucian would stop at nothing to find me. Go far and go fast. That's what she said."

"She is right," Eliad replied. "It won't be long before they'll be trawling through every cantref of Tirragyl in search of you."

"So where do I hide, Eliad?"

"There is only one place I know where you will be safe for a while," Eliad said, "and the way is not an easy one."

"Where?" Shara asked.

Eliad turned back to look at them, but it was Nicho's eyes he met. "It's called the Guardian Grotto."

In the silence that followed, Nicho suddenly recalled another night, not so very long ago. He could almost hear Pearce's voice spinning his tales of the Grotto and the Warriors. He remembered Derry's face in the candlelight, alive with wonder, and his own heart, bruised and parched, yearning for a few drops of hope to seep through. *When did you stop believing in magic?* Pearce's words resonated through his mind. Nicho thought he *had* stopped believing that something good might still come to his people. At the time, he'd thought he no longer believed in the Parashi Resistance or their caves guarded by Old Magic. Despair had long replaced his hope. But that was *before*. Before the Gold Breast, whose very presence infused him with courage. Before Shara, whose hand now lay softly in his own. Before opening the ancient book, whose hidden secrets whispered to him in a forbidden tongue. Before meeting this old man, Eliad, with eyes so full of wisdom and laughter ... and confidence.

"What is the Guardian Grotto?" Shara asked.

"A place hidden by Old Magic," Nicho said. "A place of hope."

CHAPTER 44

By the time Lucian returned, all the men had assembled at his gate. He rode a chestnut stallion, and five men accompanied him, each leading several horses.

"Randin, ride to the barracks as fast as you can," Lucian shouted as he reined in the horse. "Call every one of your men to arms and send them off immediately to search for the girl."

"But my lord, what of Gwyndorr's defenses?" Randin objected.

"Gwyndorr has already been breached, you fool! Your guards let those men into the town, and if they do not find Shara, I will see to it that their rotting corpses litter Gwyndorr's roads."

Randin shook his head, but mounted one of the larger horses in silence. He heard Lucian instructing others to gather the men of Gwyndorr and meet him with food supplies at the town gate within the hour. It struck Randin then that this would not be over soon. Lucian would leave no stone unturned in his hunt for Shara and those who had come for her.

Despite his pounding head, he made it to the town gate in record time. There was a commotion as Randin arrived. His guards were out in full force, searching carriages, lining up those on foot for questioning and, following his own example, confiscating goods. If the loud grumbling and occasional insult was anything to go by, the travelers did not appreciate the delay.

Yet it filled Randin with a sudden surge of hope. Could Shara and the men still be here, caught in this melee?

"Close the gates!" he bellowed.

His men reacted immediately, pushing people back and dropping the heavy portcullis into place. Its deep groaning drowned out the protests of the travelers.

"Surround them! Don't let anyone leave. We're looking for my ward and ... some others."

Randin tried to recall the faces of Shara's captors, but his memories of those moments were strangely dulled. He remembered running out of Lucian's house and seeing people milling around a carriage. He now dimly remembered that Shara was holding the hand of a young man in fine clothing, whose bearing had seemed strangely familiar. There had been others too. And Lucian's wife. But after that Randin remembered nothing but a high-pitched screech and a throbbing pain in his ears and head.

"My ward has been captured," he shouted. "She has dark hair and was wearing a rose-colored gown. There was a well-dressed young man with her. Search every carriage."

"Dark-haired, you said, Captain?" one of his men spoke up. "There was a dark noble lady a while ago. Unusual, that color hair on a Highborn. She might have been wearing a red dress. Yes—thinking about it now—it was definitely red, and she was as drunk as a deckhand.

"Drunk?"

"Yes, she and the young lord were hysterical with spirits. And there was an old man and a monk too."

"Where are they now?"

"They left. Probably twenty minutes ago. I was rather glad to wave them through, I was. All that merriment makes your head ache when you're trying to do a job."

"By the abyss! Did you see which way they turned?"

"East, I think. They almost knocked me off my feet too."

"To me! Guards, to me!" Randin shouted. "Yirla! Groyl. Search the rest of the carriages, just to make sure my ward isn't in one of them. Open the gates. Now!"

The men, spurred on by his anxious tone, ran to open the gate.

"Issor, take some men, bring all the horses that are saddled, and set off on the eastern road. Jax, call all the men out of the barracks and tell them to saddle up. The Morning Guards can all go west, but the rest east. If we don't find the girl, bodies will swing at the lord's command. This is life and death, guards!"

"Sir, you want us to leave our posts?" Issor said. "To leave Gwyndorr unguarded?"

"Yirla and Groyl can stay."

"Two men to guard a whole city, sir? I strongly obj —"

"I have given my commands, Issor. Make sure they are obeyed. Now open the gates!"

Before the portcullis was even fully raised, Randin ducked down and galloped under it, swinging onto the eastern road. With the last daylight seeped from the sky and the moon not yet risen, he dared not push the horse too fast on the potholed road. The men who had abducted Shara would have the same limitation, he thought. In fact, the carriage's weight would slow them down even more. It was only a matter of time before he and his men caught up with them.

Issor and nine of his guards soon joined Randin. They had brought torches, which improved visibility and allowed them to set a faster pace. They rode in silence for half an hour, before reaching a split in the road. The eastern fork led to the small hamlet of Frieyn, while the southern fork joined up with the main road leading to the large town of Achla. If he was a fugitive, Randin knew he would head south, to large roads and towns where one could melt into the crowd. To head east was to be hemmed in by the towering walls of the highlands.

Randin split the group, sending Issor and two men east, while he led the other six guards south. Another hour of riding brought them to the main road, and again he split the group, taking three men with him in the direction of Achla. The road here was smoother and he picked up the pace, fighting his fatigue.

Before they reached Achla—just as discouragement was starting to set in—Randin thought he heard the rattle of wheels and called his men to a halt. In the silence, they could clearly hear the squeak of wheels and the jangle of halters ahead of them.

"We've got them," Randin whispered, a surge of relief washing through him. He had tried not to think of Lucian's threat and whether *his* corpse would be amongst those of his men.

He could now make out the dark outline of a carriage, tearing down the distant road at a surprisingly fast pace. No wonder it had taken them so long to catch up.

"Douse the torches," Randin whispered. "We might still be able to take them by surprise. They are armed"—his thoughts returned to the body of

Lady Tessor—"but they won't be a match for us. Eron and Cran, you ride to the left of the carriage and kill the driver. See if you can gain control of the carriage. Vin and I will go right. Only the girl is not to be harmed." The men nodded. "We'll catch up with them first, and when I give the sign, we'll split around the carriage. Let's go!"

He spurred on the horse, no longer thinking of the obstacles on the road. His men were right behind him. As the carriage grew nearer, a sense of excitement filled Randin. He couldn't recall the last time he had chased down an enemy; it made him feel young again. About ten strides from the carriage, Randin lifted his hand to direct the men to split. He pushed his horse to the right and drove forward, until they were almost parallel to the carriage.

He had expected to hear shouting from the carriage, or a sudden veering to the side as they realized they were under attack. But all was quiet. In fact, he hadn't even caught sight of one of the men yet—they were keeping their heads down.

It was Eron's shout that he heard first. He could hear the young guard shouting, "Whoa," to the horse, and sensed the carriage slowing down. It surprised him that his men had taken control of the carriage without the sounds of a skirmish, and it was then that he suspected something was wrong. By the time Eron had brought the horse and carriage to a complete halt, Randin *knew* it.

The carriage was empty.

"By Taus!" Randin bellowed. "We've been taken for fools. Back, back to Gwyndorr!" He didn't know how they had done it, but somehow Shara and her captors had slipped away into the darkness, leaving only a horse and carriage behind them.

Now Randin had to return to Gwyndorr and face Lord Lucian's wrath.

• • •

The night had taken on an almost dream-like quality for Shara. More than once she wondered if she might wake up soon to discover it was all a dream woven by the rock.

In a few brief hours, everything in her life had changed.

That very morning she'd woken up with her impending marriage to Maldor casting an even longer shadow over her than the towering walls of Gwyndorr.

Now, she walked free in a vast open space. The night's starlit dome stretched from horizon to horizon, and only the solid mass of a distant towering mountain blocked out the infinite sky. A sliver of moon slashed the darkness, its lopsided smile a silent conspirator to her escape. Instead of Maldor, Nicho's warm fingers entwined with her own.

Before, her fate had rested on the decisions of Randin and Lord Lucian, but here she was following the soft glow emanating from the breast of Tabeal, a bird of ancient legend. Leaving behind the riches of her Highborn home, they now sought out the rough caves of the Parashi Warriors.

Freedom. How she had longed for it. Dreamed of it. Prayed for it. She walked free now, and it filled her with a giddy sense of wonder.

Yet she could not forget Tessor's words. *Go far and go fast. He will stop at nothing to find you.* Shara had seen that fervor in Lucian's eyes, had even tried to tell herself it was merely a reflection of the firelight. But it wasn't. *She* was the object of Lucian's obsession, and this knowledge filled her with fear.

Ahead of her, Andreo stopped, shifting the weight of the rucksack to his left shoulder. His bag was much heavier than her own, for he carried the book to which the Gold Breast had led them. Nobody had agreed with Shara's suggestion to leave the heavy book in the carriage. As far as she was concerned, the book, with its strange old script, had proven to be useless.

Yet even Nicho had sided with Eliad and Andreo. "The Gold Breast wouldn't have led us to it, if it wasn't important, Shara."

Fine—let them carry it, Shara thought, and if they unlocked its secrets, she would be glad to listen. After all, secrets were the rickety foundation of her life, and she wanted to *know*. Who she was. Where she came from. Why Lucian wanted her joined to his son. Why he would tear apart Tirragyl to find her. Yet Shara doubted the book would lead her to the truth.

No, there was something else that would do that. She slid her fingers into the deep pocket of her gown and wrapped her hand around the comforting warmth of the rock. If there was anything that could answer the questions of her heart, it was this—the most beautiful of all rocks, blue as the night sky just before all the light seeped away—the Cerulean Dusk Dreamer.

EPILOGUE

Lucian turned the smooth black rock over and over in his hand, watching the patterns of white light dancing across the mosaic floor. The rock was hot in his hand—almost too hot—but still he held it, trying to understand the thoughts flittering through his mind.

They were jumbled, broken snippets that made little sense. A strange array of emotions—fear, intermingled with hope; longing, shadowed by confusion. He caught glimpses of high mountains and deep ravines, of a man with a scar over his left eye and hatred in his gaze.

Eventually, the rock seared his skin and he dropped it. Instantly the images were gone.

Lucian sat for a long time in the gathering gloom of the evening, and tried to make sense of what he had seen.

He had been in the mind of the girl. *But how?* Lucian knew the Mind rock's powers were great. Yet the girl was—he had assumed—very far away by now, and the Mind rock had its limits. He had seldom managed to reach a mind beyond Gwyndorr.

And why was there a distortion of thoughts, almost as if something was causing interference? Could it be the distance? No. There was something else at work.

Two months had passed since the girl had slipped from his clutches. Lucian knew who had come to rescue her, and he knew why. He even thought he knew where they were taking her, the very reason he had watchers on alert at every place where the Rif'twine might be penetrated.

If they hadn't taken her into the Rif'twine, there was only one other place where she could be safe for a while: the Guardian Grotto. The Gold Breast knew the way, of course. Yet surely the Old Magic that guarded the Grotto would have kept him from reaching Shara's mind?

Except ...

The idea was startling.

... Except if Shara possessed a power rock. Was it even possible? How in the name of Taus would the girl have laid her hands on one?

Yet, the more he thought about it, the more it made sense to Lucian. The power rocks were all connected, and if Shara had acquired one, it would explain how he could reach her mind over such a long distance. The Grotto's magic was strong, but not strong enough.

He smiled for the first time in two months. With access to the girl's mind, it was just a matter of time before he would breach its defenses.

• • •